KATE'S PROGRESS

Kate's latest failure on the London dating scene leads her to escape to an idyllic Exmoor, West Country village where she finds her 'Cinderella Project' – a run-down cottage on the edge of the moors. Her attempt to lead a quiet life there is thwarted, however, by a community seething with passion and intrigue.

Recent Titles by Cynthia Harrod-Eagles available from Severn House

THE COLONEL'S DAUGHTER
A CORNISH AFFAIR
COUNTRY PLOT
DANGEROUS LOVE
DIVIDED LOVE
EVEN CHANCE
HARTE'S DESIRE
THE HORSEMASTERS
JULIA
KATE'S PROGRESS
LAST RUN
THE LONGEST DANCE
NOBODY'S FOOL
ON WINGS OF LOVE
PLAY FOR LOVE
A RAINBOW SUMMER
REAL LIFE (*Short Stories*)

The Bill Slider Mysteries
GAME OVER
FELL PURPOSE
BODY LINE
KILL MY DARLING
BLOOD NEVER DIES

KATE'S PROGRESS

Cynthia Harrod-Eagles

Severn House Large Print
London & New York

This first large print edition published 2014
in Great Britain and the USA by
SEVERN HOUSE PUBLISHERS LTD of
19 Cedar Road, Sutton, Surrey, England, SM2 5DA.
First world regular print edition published 2013 by
Severn House Publishers Ltd., London and New York.

British Library Cataloguing in Publication Data

Harrod-Eagles, Cynthia author.
Kate's progress. -- Large print edition.~
1. Triangles (Interpersonal relations)--Fiction.
2. Gentry--Fiction. 3. Country life--England--Exmoor--
Fiction. 4. Cottages--Remodeling--Fiction. 5. Large type
books.
I. Title
823.9'2-dc23

ISBN-13: 9780727896704

Severn House Publishers support the Forest Stewardship Council™ [FSC™], the leading international forest certification organisation. All our titles that are printed on FSC certified paper carry the FSC logo.

Printed and bound in Great Britain by
TJ International, Padstow, Cornwall.

One

The May sunshine was warm in the sheltered spot between the cottage and the garden wall. Kate was peacefully rubbing down a window frame with sandpaper and enjoying the warmth on her back when she was interrupted by a stern male voice behind her.

'Hey, you! You boy! What the hell d'you think you're doing?'

It's perhaps not the worst thing in the world to be taken for a boy, especially from the back. It suggests you have the slim boyish figure models aspire to; and to be fair, she was wearing androgynous jeans-and-sweatshirt, and had her hair tucked up in a beanie to keep the dust out of it. Kate, however, had often felt chagrined by her small size and lack of distinguishing frontal furniture (32B, hardly enough to make a cleavage), so it was with a scowl that she turned to see who was shouting at her.

She could only see the top half of the intruder over the garden wall as he stood in the road beyond. It was a tall man, in his thirties, well-built about the shoulders, with wavy dark hair. He was wearing the local uniform of a battered wax jacket, and held one of those tall walking-sticks that serious yompers carry, which Kate thought just plain pretentious.

Instead of answering, she walked towards him, flourishing the sandpaper. She saw the exact moment when he realized she was female, because his mouth made a soundless, 'Oh!' and he blushed a little under his all-weather tan.

'I thought you were trying to break in,' he said. 'We've had a lot of trouble with empty properties round here being vandalized.'

As an explanation it was pretty good – neighbourliness and good citizenship combined. Nothing one could object to. And beyond him, across the road, a black lab and an Italian greyhound were sniffing around on the grass verge, while two other dogs she couldn't see properly were running about in the bracken. Kate loved dogs and was always ready to give dog-owners the benefit of the doubt.

On the other hand, as an apology it lacked a certain tone. He didn't sound a bit sorry, actually, for having bellowed at her. In fact, he sounded almost indignant, as though she had deliberately tricked him, tried to make a fool of him. And his scowl hadn't abated.

He went on impatiently, as if he had the right to know, 'So what *are* you doing?'

None of your business, she thought. Instead of thanking him for his public-spirited concern, she said, somewhat snarkily, 'I own the place. Good enough for you, or must I break out some ID?'

'You most certainly do not own it,' he snapped. 'And I can tell you we don't tolerate squatters in these parts.'

'Squatters!' she exclaimed. 'You've got a

cheek. I bought the place. Bought it, paid for it, got the deeds. *If* it's any of your business.'

He was staring at her as if he had never seen a girl before. Well, who knew, out here in the wilds of the country? These days she was pretty much a townie, used to a shortage of men: perhaps in the boonies there was the opposite problem. She stared back. His eyes, she noticed, were very blue. He wouldn't be bad looking, if he ever ran to any expression warmer than a frown.

He broke the eye-hold almost with a jerk, looking away over her shoulder at the cottage, and said, 'I don't believe you.'

'Are you calling me a liar?' she said indignantly.

'You obviously don't realize who I am,' he said.

'Why should I?' she snapped. 'What difference would that make?'

His eyes returned to her, and he gave her a grim, ironic quirk of the lips. 'Everyone knows everyone else in a country community like this. And I know you don't own this cottage.'

Why would I be rubbing down the windows if I didn't own the place? she thought. But she didn't say it. It was such a stupid argument that she tired of it suddenly. 'Well, much as I enjoy being insulted by complete strangers in my own garden,' she said, 'I have work to do. I suggest you continue this conversation with Stinner and Huxtable in Taunton.'

That got him. The mention of the estate agents evidently gave him pause. His glare became less certain. 'I *shall* check up, you know,' he said.

'Be my guest,' she said. She turned away and headed for her window again.

'Wait!' he said. And then, a little less imperiously, 'Look here—'

She turned and looked at him. He seemed puzzled now, rather than angry, which was a distinct improvement, and – just by the way – she noticed that he was, indeed, very handsome. From his posh accent, he was probably some local squirelet, used to the yokels tugging their forelocks, and county girls chasing him for his fortune.

'What?' she said impatiently.

'We seem to have got off on the wrong foot,' he began.

'*You* did,' she said.

He flushed a little. 'You must admit it looks fishy. I've heard nothing about Little's Cottage being for sale. And suddenly here you are, with a London accent—'

Oh, that was it, was it? The old 'incomer' phobia rearing its horrid head. 'So you conclude I'm a squatter,' she finished for him. 'Of course, all Londoners are criminals, it's a well-known fact. Or, just possibly, everyone in Somerset does not tell you everything. You haven't considered that possibility, have you?'

The slight softening hardened again. 'I shall find out what's going on, and then, I warn you, I *shall* be back.'

'I can't wait,' she muttered.

He called to the dogs and walked on. She watched him out of sight, and then went back to her window, feeling unsettled. She wasn't entirely satisfied with herself. Probably he *had* been motivated by the best of intentions, and she hadn't exactly been helpful or friendly.

But then, why did he have to go in so hard? He was hostile from the beginning. And he *had* said to her face that he didn't believe her, which was plain rude.

Yes, but it was important to get on with her neighbours in a place like this. Creating bad blood in a closed community was not the best idea.

But his whole attitude, putting her in her place, the lord looking down on the peasant ... Not to be tolerated!

Nice dogs, though. She'd always wanted a dog.

At this stage of her internal dialogue she addressed her window frame again, but found she'd lost the urge. She had so much to do she oughtn't to skive off, but sanding down is pretty boring work, and it was a fine day – how many of those do you get to the pound in England? Anyway, it was nearly lunchtime. She could walk down to the village and have a pint and a ploughman's at one of the two pubs, and have a chat to whoever was there. In a small community like this, she told herself wisely, it was important that she got to know the locals – in both senses of the word.

It wasn't exactly a mid-life crisis – Kate would hate to think she was halfway through her life already, when she was only twenty-eight. But it *had* been a turning-point. She just had to get away from the whole awful dating business before it destroyed her sunny personality completely. She and her friends/flatmates Lauren and Jess had been going through it together for years, ever since Kate first arrived wide-eyed in London at the age of twenty-one, and it didn't look like getting any better.

Where had all the good men gone? Her sister Sheila had found one, was married with the standard two children, and seemed to be blissfully happy with Ken – so happy Kate had taken to calling her 'Barbie'. Sheila was eight years older than her, the second eldest of the family (Denise, the eldest, was a nun), and it was tempting to think she had got the last marriageable man before the stocks ran out.

Ursula, the next after her, had dedicated herself to her career in the beauty industry, moved with it to California, and lived a life of high-powered singleness where work took the place of marriage, friends took the place of lovers, sex took the place of relationships, and the only men in her life were Rick, her GBF – Gay Best Friend – and her two male cockerpoos.

Aileen, who came between Kate and Ursula, had been seeing, and intermittently living with, the same man for ten years, since uni days, which Kate found infinitely depressing. Denny was good-looking in a sulky, James Dean sort of way, and amusing company when he was in the mood, but he was unreliable and commitment-phobic. Their relationship was up and down and on and off. They'd move in together and then he'd say he needed space and demand a sabbatical. They would have a period of happiness and then he would do something awful, like getting caught with another woman. Aileen kept taking him back, but Kate could not believe anything would ever come of it. Denny used her; and she let him, so why would he ever marry her? And would she really want to be married to a waster like him anyway?

Aileen apparently answered yes to that question; Kate said no. As soon as she finished university she had upped sticks, fled to London, shortened Kathleen to Kate, got a job and a flat, and breathed a sigh of relief at having escaped. She had thrown herself into the London scene and the dating world, and along with her new friends had experienced the inexplicable vagaries of the men out there.

Gradually she had lowered her expectations, ceased to look for Mr Right and trawled instead for Mr OK-he'd-do. Gradually her wide eyes had narrowed. She and Lauren and Jess had tried, they really had. In between the multiplicity of dates that never got past the first or second meeting, and the endless-seeming fallow patches, and the 'man diets' when the three of them had sworn to give up altogether, she had had three long relationships.

The first had been Oliver, or Mean, Moody and Magnificent as Lauren had dubbed him. He came under the heading of emotionally unavailable: they dated, but he never told her how he felt about her, was sparing of embraces, would never talk about their relationship, could never be brought to make any future plan. If she pressed him for response he grew more distant, punished her by not seeing her or answering her calls for days. She'd be tearful and believe it was all over, and then he'd ring up with a perfectly viable excuse for his silence (usually work-related) and ask her out again.

It went on for the best part of two years, until one day he calmly told her that he was getting married to a girl he had known all his life, the daughter of friends of his parents, whose father, coincidentally, was a partner in the accountancy firm he was hoping to join.

He hadn't even been two-timing her, so she had no excuse for face-saving fury. He had met this woman again by chance, and it had all happened very quickly. He had told Kate as soon as there was anything to tell. There was no deception.

And after all, he and Kate had never discussed marriage or any long-term plans, had they? It had been fun, that was all. He hoped they could remain friends.

It must have been a sort of rebound from Oliver that had led her to Andy. He was as emotionally available as a large, friendly puppy. He told her all the time that she was gorgeous, that he couldn't believe his luck, was free with his hugs and kisses and compliments, wanted to see her as often as possible and, though he was not a great conversationalist, never minded her phoning him up at work for a chat – a frivolity definitely *verboten* by Oliver.

The trouble with Andy was that he came in a package with his large, exuberant friends, chief among whom were Steve, Mick, and Scrogger.

He was a sports correspondent for a newspaper, and sport was his whole life, particularly football, which he played on Wednesday nights and Sunday mornings with the aforesaid trio of mates. When he wasn't playing it, he was attending football matches, or watching it on television or discussing it with his friends at the pub or on the sofa of her flat or his.

She tried to be interested in football, particularly at the beginning, and would stand on touchlines on freezing winter mud or with rain dripping from her nose, cheering as her breath formed clouds in front of her. Afterwards, in the pub, she learned to enjoy pints, and did her best to join in the conversation, comforted by Andy's big, warm arm around her shoulders and his evident pride in having captured her. But it was hard work to sustain an interest in the exclusively male subjects (when it wasn't sport, it was engines of one sort or another) and even harder work to get any comment she might make heard. They were all much taller than her (Andy called her 'Pixie', which she almost managed to like), and even if they did hear her, all the way down there, they would listen with a sort of embarrassed respectfulness, and then carry on as if she hadn't spoken.

It was even harder work when there were four or five of them sprawled around the sitting room, beer cans in hand, watching the footy on the television. They took up so much space. They made so much noise. They were so complete unto themselves. They would say thank you nicely when she brought them snacks or more cans, but otherwise they would hardly have noticed the Second Coming while the match was on, and for a goodish time afterwards as they dissected it.

And the more she saw of it, the more Kate was convinced that soccer was the most boring game ever invented. Every match followed the same pattern as every other one. If it weren't for the different strips, she reckoned the TV companies could have screened the same match over and over and saved themselves money – no-one would notice.

It was the approach of the World Cup that finally defeated her. She knew she could never survive it. And big, lovable, cuddly Andy – did he really distinguish all that much between her and his mates? He quite often said he loved her, but then he would say, 'Love ya, ya big poof,' to Steve and give him a bone-cracking one-armed hug, which was not dissimilar to his gestures of affection to her. He was a happy, friendly, simple soul, and he behaved much the same towards everyone.

And they rarely went out alone together. If they went to the pictures he would fall asleep, waking when the credits rolled to say, 'Fancy a pint? Mick and Scrogger will be down the Red Lion.' He didn't like eating out: restaurant tables and chairs had not been designed for people his size, and he seemed almost ill at ease with cutlery. He was like a trapped bear. They sometimes went for a nice walk, but it always ended at a pub which seemed miraculously to be showing a match on the big screen. Clubbing was sheer cruelty to animals – he was too self-conscious to dance, and hated the noise, standing hunched and miserable by the bar with a beer in his hand saying, 'No, you go on and dance. Don't mind me. I want you to have fun,' until she gave in and took him away. And then he'd say, 'Fancy a pint? Steve'll be down the Three Kings...'

When she broke it off, he looked puzzled and unhappy, like a puppy or a toddler that doesn't know why it's being scolded, and she'd felt like Cruella de Vil. She even heard herself say, 'I hope we can still be friends.' But she remembered the World Cup, and knew it had to be done.

Which led to Mark, her most recent relationship, and the one that really hurt. Mark was in the same business as her, PR, and she met him at a press conference for a movie in which they both had actors. The attraction had been instant. He was only moderately good-looking – the fact that he was not mega-handsome was somehow reassuring – but he made up for it in charm. He was smartly dressed, intelligent and funny. When he first caught her eye during a particularly dire speech and winked and gave her a great urchin grin, she felt as though they were the only two people in the world who knew what was what. She had taken her eye off him for a moment, and when she looked again he was easing his way through the crowd to get to her side. They watched the rest of the speeches together, and when they had to part, to attend to their own celebs, he had made a date with her with flattering urgency.

He was everything her previous boyfriends were not. He was great company; he made her laugh; more than that, he really listened when she talked to him, and seemed to like as much as she did those long telephone chats that go anywhere and nowhere. He'd send her funny and sometimes mildly obscene emails and texts when she was at work, which made her snort inelegantly, so she'd have to pretend she'd been sneezing.

He told her all the time how great she was, and made her feel that she was the only person in the world who mattered. He was generous: the best restaurants, taxis, good seats at the theatre, and flowers sent for no reason except 'I was thinking 'bout you!'

He liked her friends – how rare was that? – and was interested in everything, always up for any outing or activity, whatever it was, from hang-gliding to a picnic in the park. He was a good dancer; he liked the same books and movies as she did. The sex was amazing, but he also loved to cuddle – how many men could you say that about?

Kate was deep in love. She hadn't stood a chance, really, against such a pattern of a man. She was convinced he was The One. He was so perfect that Jess sighed and asked how Kate could be so lucky and where she could find one like him. Lauren called him Darcy – she always had sharp names for everyone. 'He's too good to be true,' she said, and, 'Handsome is as handsome does. We'll see.' But he made her laugh, and she liked him too, albeit grudgingly.

It was Lauren who pointed out one day that he and Kate always met at the girls' flat, or went out – Kate had never been to his place.

'So what?' she said defiantly.

'So nothing,' Lauren said. 'I just wondered, that's all.'

It was some days before Kate asked him – she hated herself for allowing Lauren to make her suspicious. She dropped it into the conversation casually one evening. 'Why don't we go back to your place tonight?'

He was not at all fazed. 'We're nearer to yours.' They always were – he lived way down in South London.

'But I've never even seen it,' she said.

'Nothing to see.' He shrugged. 'It's a bit of a tip. My flatmate's a slob. We'll be more comfortable at your place. But if you're so curious...'

'Oh, I'm not really,' she said, feeling foolish. And when the time came they went back to the girls' flat as always, and she didn't press the point. If there had been anything wrong, he would have looked uneasy or acted guilty, and he hadn't. And he'd said they could go to his place if she wanted. That proved it, didn't it?

But Lauren had planted the seed, and as months passed it grew and festered in the back of her mind, spoiling her serenity. One day, hating herself for it, she went round to his address. He was away, gone to Amsterdam for a shoot, and she was missing him. She told herself it couldn't hurt just to walk past, see what sort of a place it was. Why shouldn't she? He knew everything about her, they were in love, he could have no secrets to keep. Just looking at his door would keep her going until he got back.

It wasn't a flat; it was a narrow, modern townhouse. She hadn't known that area of London before, but it was obviously quite smart – the sort of place young professionals were buying into, pushing it up the social ladder. She stood on the other side of the street staring at it, frowning, wondering. Maybe she'd made a mistake, written the address down wrong? But she was sure she hadn't. She debated going across and ringing the bell, seeing if his 'flatmate' was in. But what would she say? She didn't want to make a fool of herself. She was torn, in two minds, one half hating this 'checking up on him', the other half arguing that as his girlfriend she had every right to call at his address if she happened to be in the area.

And as she stood wrestling with internal debate, the door opened and out came a very smart, pretty Japanese woman, her make-up perfect, her short dark hair shining in the sun as though lacquered. She was leading two little half-Japanese boys, cute as buttons, immaculately dressed in what looked like Tommy Hilfiger for Kids. The elder one definitely had Mark's nose.

The blood rushed from her head so fast she almost fell down, and had to clutch on to a car roof for support. Her mind gabbled with possible reasons and explanations, but her heart knew the truth from that moment.

He didn't try to deny it, and she could never decide if that made it worse or not. That was Mariko. And his boys. Yes, he was married. He'd never said he wasn't. What was the problem? He and Kate had fun, didn't they?

'You said you loved me.'

'I do. You're a gorgeous, gorgeous girl and I love you to bits.'

'But I thought—'

That was the trouble. When she went over it in her mind, *what she thought* had been made up of assumptions, which were entirely reasonable in the circumstances but were not based on anything he had said, only on the way he had *seemed*. The only lie he had told her was that his flatmate was messy. The house was not a flat and she could not believe from that glimpse that Mariko was anything but obsessively tidy. But when she taxed him with it, he said he *had* lived in a flat once, and his flatmate there *had* been a complete slob, so it wasn't really a lie.

'But it was a deception,' she said.

'Well, maybe a little. But you wouldn't have liked to know the truth, so I was saving you from it. Haven't we had nice times together?'

He must have known it was all over, because he became alarmingly frank. She wasn't the only one: there was a Swedish woman, a pilot with Lufthansa, whom he saw when she had a layover in London. Or, on that particular occasion, Amsterdam. He didn't see anything wrong with it. He kept them all happy, didn't he? Hadn't Kate been happy? As long as none of them knew about the others...

That was the trouble. She knew *now*. Her house of cards had come tumbling down. Not only was her heart broken, but she felt a fool – a trusting fool. If you were to be punished for believing in people, what point was there in any of it? She could not, would not see him again;

but she missed him, and hated herself for missing him when he was such a swine, a creep, a hateful lying philandering bastard.

Lauren and Jess were brilliant, of course, rallied round, plied her with tissues and hugs and ever more savage epithets to describe the deceiver. Kate went from a state of shock into mourning, and when she was over the first acute pain of it, she knew she had to get out. She hated London, men, the dating scene, even her job, which reminded her of Mark (of course, how perfect a niche for him, to be a PR man!).

'Don't throw everything away,' Lauren begged her. 'Don't let him ruin your whole life. Take a break, sure, but don't cut off your nose to spite his face. I always thought it was a silly face,' she added parenthetically. 'Weak. Soft. Self-indulgent. I told you so at the time.'

'Did you?' Kate said, face swollen with tears. She didn't remember. She only knew her twenty-eighth birthday was approaching and her lovely romance had turned to dust and ashes. Two years of Oliver, six months of Andy and just over a year of Mark. Three and a half of the best years of her prime given away for nothing. There had to be something better to do with your life than that.

It was at that low point, like a miracle, that Gaga, her darling grandmother in Ireland, had sent her the money.

The letter came as a complete surprise, the enclosure even more so.

You know I always meant to leave my fortune to you girls, Gaga wrote, *at least the four of you, because if I left Denise anything she'd only give it to the convent, and you know how I feel about the nuns. But I was talking to the solicitor the other day and I suddenly thought, why wait till I'm dead? I'd get no joy out of that. I'm a selfish old woman and I want the pleasure of being thanked and hearing about all the fun you have with it. So here's what I'm doing, Katie my pet. I've got the house, and Daddo's pension is enough to live on, and all that cash he left me is doing nothing good in the bank. So I'm dividing it between you girls, and sending you each a cheque right now, on condition that you tell me all about what you spend it on. I want all the details, mind!*

And whatever it is, I hope it gives you pleasure, and makes you think often of

your loving,

Gaga.

There followed a flurry of intra-family phone calls.

'It's true, she's sent the same to me, God love her.'

'Has she gone crackers, do you think?'

'Denise thinks she's having a spiritual house-cleaning.'

'I think she means just what she says.'

Kate's mother said, 'I've spoken to her, and she's determined. No, there's nothing wrong with her, as far as I know – she's not at her last knockings, or anything. I told her it was folly to give away all her money when she doesn't know how much longer she'll live, but you know how stubborn she is, once she gets an idea. She wants to give you all the money while she can still have the fun of seeing you spend it, and that's that.'

Kate's father said, 'She's got enough to live on, and there's always us. We wouldn't let her starve. Enjoy it, pet. It's what she wants. I don't see why she shouldn't do what she likes with her own money. She owes nobody anything.'

And Denise – aka Sister Luke – said, 'You can't take it with you. Gaga knows that all right.'

When she had got over the first shock, Kate showed the cheque to Lauren and Jess.

Jess whistled. 'You are *kidding* me! A hundred and twenty-five thousand? It's a bloody fortune!' Then she laughed. 'I know what I'd do with it!'

Lauren said, 'It's a serious amount of money. You need to think about this. There's no point in investing it with the stock market the way it is, and deposit accounts pay nothing these days.'

'Sensible cow,' Jess said. 'I was thinking of a fabulous car or a fabulous holiday. Even better, both.'

'Bricks and mortar's the only way to go,' Lauren insisted.

'Of course I thought of that first. But it isn't enough to buy a house or a flat,' Kate said.

'Not unless it was in the back of beyond,' Jess agreed.

'It'd make a hefty deposit, though,' Lauren said. 'Which would bring the mortgage for the rest within reach.'

They rented the flat together: buying had never been an option for any of them. Property in

London – and most other places they'd want to live – was just too expensive.

'Still, that wouldn't be much fun for her grandma,' Jess pointed out. 'Just putting it down on a flat.'

'She could tell her all about the hunt for the right place,' Lauren said. 'String it out into a story. Anyway, it's Kate's money now, and she has to use it wisely, whatever her granny says. She'll never get another windfall like this in her life. Take your time and think about it carefully, Kate.'

'I'll certainly do that,' Kate promised. 'Though I agree with Jess, I'm not sure using it wisely is what Gaga has in mind. I fancy she wants me to have wild adventures.'

'You can't just blow it!' Lauren said, shocked.

'No, of course not. But I'm going to take a couple of hundred out of it to take you two out for a slap-up celebration. That'll be something to tell her, at least.'

But the thought had already come to her that she could use the money to get away. She had wanted a complete change, to escape from the scene of her shame, from Mark, and from London, where, because of her job, she was always likely to bump into him or hear his name mentioned. Yes, escape! She just had to think how best to achieve it. It was true, as Lauren said, that she'd never get a sum like this again, and she didn't want to fritter it away: she wanted something to show for it at the end, and it was also true that bricks and mortar were the best investment. It could be her only chance to get on the property ladder.

Gradually an idea began to form, nebulously at first, around Jess's words, 'the back of beyond'. How to get away, but not blow the money? How to have a complete break, but be able to come back?

And then she saw the advert.

Two

Exmoor's River Burr wound its way through probably the most beautiful valley in England. Brawling in winter, burbling in summer, it tumbled over rocks between steep valley sides draped with hanging woods that rose up to the open moors, Burford Hill on one side and Lar Common on the other. At the end of the valley, the contours softened to a gentler, more open country, and here, where the Burr met the Elder Brook, there was a complex junction: a cross-roads of two main roads (or as main as they got in that part of the world) and a minor one, all of which also bridged both waters. Here the village of Bursford had grown up. With the two arched stone bridges and the backdrop of the woods it was extremely picturesque, and only its remoteness kept it from being a hot tourist attraction and consequently getting spoilt.

The other side of Kate's family, her father's side, came from Exmoor – Jennings was an old Exmoor name. She had spent happy childhood holidays there, but Granny and Grandpa were much older than the Irish grandparents – her father had been the youngest of a long family – and they had died when she was about ten or eleven, so the holidays had stopped and she had hardly been there since. But she treasured memories of the wonderful greenness, the rolling hills and wooded folds, the little stone villages, the wide open moors and the wandering ponies.

And she remembered stopping in Bursford for an ice cream from the Post Office stores, always a highlight of any day out. So when, while idly looking through the property section of the newspaper, she had seen the name, her attention was caught and she homed in on the advert.

Exmoor National Park: Little's Cottage, School Lane, Bursford. Period two bedroom cottage in need of renovation. Mains services. £119,950.

It wasn't much to go on, but there was the coincidence of the place, which she knew, and the price, which was within her grasp. She felt a shiver on the back of her neck as though Fate was directing her towards it. Anyway, it would cost nothing to find out. She hadn't thought about Exmoor and her childhood holidays for a long time, but now she did, the images came tumbling back into her mind, fresh and alluring. What could be more different from her present life, more completely the change she craved?

All the same, it was probably a crazy idea, so she wouldn't say anything to Lauren or Jess yet. She would just ring up the estate agents, Stinner and Huxtable, first thing the next morning, and see what happened.

John, a young man with an indoor pallor and a rather shiny suit, met her at Taunton station and drove her to the place.

'You do understand,' he asked, giving her an anxious glance, 'that you wouldn't be able to develop the site at all? There's absolutely no chance of getting planning permission in the National Park.'

'Yes, it was explained to me,' she said.

'Because I was afraid a lot of people might get a bit excited about the five acres,' he went on.

'I promise I'm not excited by the five acres,' she told him. But she sort of was. The more extensive details that had been sent to her said that the cottage came with five acres of adjacent land, described as 'rough grazing'. She had always wanted to own land. The thought of standing on a stretch of England and being able to say 'this is mine' seemed a bit like a fairy tale. She was sure Gaga would approve. Hadn't 'land hunger' sent the Irish wandering to every corner of the globe?

'It's not even really grazing now,' John went on. 'You see, the Browns, who last lived there, kept chickens on it and sold the eggs. After he died his wife stayed on but she didn't do any of that. She got rid of the chickens and just lived on her pension and let everything go. Well, up there, if you leave grazing, the heather and bracken come back in no time. It's all gone back to the wild. It'd be a stiff job clearing the scrub, and even if you did, it's not a big enough area to do anything much with, unless you wanted to keep a pony.'

He looked at her questioningly.

'I hadn't thought about that,' she said. 'It's the house that's my main concern at the moment.'

'I see. Well, I don't want to put you off or

anything, but it's not a very pretty cottage, and when Mrs Brown died, she'd been on her own in there a long time. It needs modernizing. And it's a bit grotty. Well, a lot grotty, really.'

'You want me to turn around and go back without seeing it?' Kate suggested humorously.

He looked embarrassed. 'No, of course not. I'm only saying that I hope you haven't got your hopes up too much, because coming from London and everything, you might think...'

'My father's family was from round here,' she interrupted quickly. 'My grandparents lived in Exford. I used to visit them when I was a kid.'

It was amazing how his face cleared. She wasn't a townie, so she was all right. 'Oh, then I 'spect you know Bursford.'

'Yes, I remember it well,' she said, and he relaxed almost exaggeratedly, like someone in a drama class.

The journey was only about thirty miles, as she had established from a study of a map before she left home (it was only ten miles from Minehead but there was no railway to Minehead any more). Still, it took more than an hour, partly because of the narrow winding roads of the latter part of it, and partly because of John's nervous driving, which made him view even the clearest bend like a dangerous animal poised to spring.

But at last they drove over the first bridge ('That's the Elder Bridge,' John said helpfully), turned sharp right, and reached the crossroads and the second bridge ('The Burr Bridge'), and there they were, in the heart of the village. There were the handsome stone-built houses, clustered around the scrap of green she remembered so well, with the red telephone box and the bench where you could sit and look at the burling river while you ate your ice-cream.

Next to the green was the same old tin-roofed garage with its single petrol pump outside – did they still sell petrol? The square tower of the church poked up beyond the houses down the left arm of the crossroads, backed by the woods that rose up to the skyline. The two pubs, the Blue Ball and the Royal Oak, faced each other across the wider of the two roads which, having sprung over the Burr Bridge, curved round the flank of the hill and wandered off, up over the high moors towards Exford.

Kate ran down her window and stuck her head out. She could smell the damp woods and the green freshness. She could hear wood pigeons and jackdaws, and the muted roar of the weir that held back the Elder waters for the mill, which was down the right arm of the crossroads, and even in her day had been converted to a private dwelling. As they stopped at the crossroads while John consulted the map, they were not holding up the traffic because there wasn't any: they were the only car in sight that was not parked. A girl on a bay horse clattered past them, giving them a curious look, and turned left. Kate stared at the pretty jumble of houses and knew she had lost her heart. It seemed unchanged since her childhood, and how many places could you say that about?

'Right,' said John, and he put the map aside, and drove on. They went along the Exford road and turned left at the first turning past the Royal Oak, called School Lane. The school was still there, a Victorian, red-brick, ecclesiastical kind of building which was now obviously a private house. Beyond that the road sloped steeply up, with small houses and cottages on either side, and at the top, John stopped alongside the three-foot-high stone wall on their left. Behind it was the cottage.

Here the road ended in a T-junction with a track, on the other side of which were the open moors. Kate got out of the car, drew in a deep lungful of the air, clean and sharp and with a brown hint of peat in it. She stared across the track at the expanse of heather and bracken rollicking away for miles and miles, all the way to the sky, heard the profound silence under the small nearby sounds, and felt she would never be able to tear herself away from this place.

'But why didn't you tell us where you were going?' Jess complained from the kitchen where she was making cheese on toast. 'We could have come with you.'

'I didn't want to tell you about my plan in case you thought I was crazy.'

'We *do* think you're crazy,' Laura assured her kindly. 'We won't think it any less for not having seen the place. Don't you see, as it is our imaginations have been left to run wild.'

'Yes, we really need to inspect the place,' Jess agreed.

'To make sure you're not being rooked,' Laura concluded.

Kate laughed. 'I may take that from you – but from Jess, who thought the really cheap Prada bag on that market stall might be genuine?'

'You never let go of that one,' Jess complained, coming in with the tray. 'I didn't buy it, did I?'

'Only because we wouldn't let you.'

'But it was pretty. It would have gone so well with my new coat.'

'Not at that price.'

'You just said it was cheap.'

'Not cheap enough.'

Jess plonked the tray down on the coffee table. Three plates of toasted cheese and three mugs of hot chocolate threaded their smells into the warm air, a bulwark against the cold wet evening outside. 'So tell us,' she said, 'all the details. I hope you took photos?'

'I did, but they'll only depress you. It isn't very pretty – not cute and picturesque.'

The large garden was overgrown – well, that was probably an understatement. It was a horribleness of brambles and nettles, ivy and convolvulus, through which the occasional plant thrust forlornly, begging for rescue. The cottage was square and plain, with the maroon paint peeling from the filthy, cobwebbed windows, and grass sprouting from the gutters. But it was at least stone-built.

'And the roof is sound,' Kate said quickly at this point in her exposition. That had been a major relief to her. 'In fact, all the fabric is sound, though the chimney probably wants re-pointing. But that's not a big job, just painstaking. I can do that.'

'*You* can? How come?' Jess said, sinking her teeth into the first slice.

'My dad's a builder. I thought I'd told you that.'

Jess waved a hand. 'It doesn't follow,' she said indistinctly.

'Well, it was pretty tough for him, having five daughters and no son, and I was the tomboy of the family, so he took me with him and taught me stuff. I used to help him on Saturdays and school holidays. I can do it all, pretty much.'

'She did manage to put those flat-pack bookshelves from Ikea together,' Jess remarked to Lauren.

'Piece of cake,' Kate said. 'I can lay bricks, point, hang wallpaper, glaze a window if it's not too big. I'm a fair hand at carpentry. I'm not brilliant at plastering, but these days there's plasterboard. And I don't do plumbing. Dad always said, don't mess about with water if you don't know what you're doing. He'll do everything but that. He says if you get the electrics wrong, the worst thing you can do is kill yourself, but get the plumbing wrong and you can ruin the whole house.'

Lauren looked amused. 'So you can do the electrics as well?'

'Well, I *could*,' Kate said, 'but I probably wouldn't.'

'So how bad is this house?' Lauren went on. 'How much is there to do?'

'It looks pretty bad when you step in, but mostly it's just grottiness.' She remembered the horrible patterned wallpaper, marked with use and scuffed right through here and there, where the old lady had scraped her Zimmer frame in later days; the paintwork clogged with lumpy old layers, the last of which was a depressing maroon; the cracked panes in the cobwebbed windows; the chipped and warped architraves; the doors which had been clumsily hard-boarded over in the days when that was the fashion, with cheap'n'nasty chrome handles with the chrome peeling off. The ceilings were so stained with age and smoke that they were practically mahogany. Two of the floorboards needed replacing. The kitchen was furnished with horrible old melamine units from early eighties, and the bathroom suite dated from the same period, and was in the shade known then as avocado, though what with stains and limescale the colour didn't exactly shine through.

'So it has *got* a bathroom,' Lauren said, the relief evident in her voice. 'I was imagining you having to fill a tin bath with a kettle, and going down the garden for the whatnot.'

'Actually, there *is* a whatnot down the garden,' Kate said. 'I suppose it saved old Mr Brown coming indoors in his muddy boots when he was working. It's a little, narrow wooden hut like the guards' huts outside Buckingham Palace. Only with a door, of course.'

Jess made a sympathetic face. 'Did it smell terrible?'

'Actually, it didn't smell at all. No-one's used it for years. And there's a rambling rose growing over it – I expect it'll look quite pretty in the summer. I'm looking forward to using it, with the door open – there's a fine view of the moors from there.'

'*Kate*!'

'Why not? Don't be such a townie! There were still squares of newspaper threaded on a string hanging in there,' she added. 'The *Daily Mail*. April 2000. Rather poignant, really. Mrs B obviously preferred to go indoors.'

Doggedly, Lauren got back to the point. 'But there *is* a bathroom, with mains drainage?'

'Yes, and mains water and electricity. No gas, of course, but you can't have everything.'

Downstairs, the front door opened directly into the living room, with the stairs in it, directly opposite the door on the left – an arrangement quite common in the area. Behind that was the kitchen, and at the back there was an open-fronted lean-to with a corrugated roof, in which was stored the remains of a log-pile and some old junk and a few tools.

Upstairs there was a bedroom on the mezzanine floor over the kitchen, which had been converted into the bathroom, and up a further half flight of stairs were two more bedrooms, a decent-sized one over the sitting room and a tiny one in between.

Kate said, 'My plan is to knock out two-thirds of the wall between the sitting room and the kitchen, and make the downstairs semi-open plan, so as to get some more light in, and more of a feeling of space.'

'Can you do that?' Jess asked.

'Oh, yes, it isn't load-bearing,' Kate answered.

'I think she means, do you know how to?'

Lauren said.

'Nothing to it. It's only lath and plaster. You can cut through that with a kitchen knife.'

'Why only two-thirds?' Jess asked.

'Because you need some wall in the kitchen to put units against. And I think it'll look better than completely open plan – cosier. I'm imagining a nice dresser on the sitting room side, with pretty plates on it.'

'What else? I mean, what else will you do?' Jess said.

'Well, other than that, it's pretty much just decorating. Stripping everything out, making good, repainting. Take the hardboard off the doors – if they're panelled underneath, they'll look brilliant. I'll rub them down and wax them, new handles. Replace a couple of floorboards, and some bits of architrave. New kitchen and bathroom. *Et voila*!'

'Oh, that's all, is it?' Lauren said drily. 'You'll fit the kitchen and bathroom yourself, of course.'

'No, I'll get someone in for that. I *could* fit the kitchen units, but there's the electrics and plumbing to think of, and—'

'—your dad said never mess around with water.'

'And then what?' Lauren asked. 'When you've done it all up?'

'Sell it,' Kate said blithely. 'At a profit. And come back to London having purged my soul of misery with honest hard work and a sense of achievement. What do you think?'

'It's certainly a *plan*,' Lauren said, in the tone of voice that doubted what *sort* of a plan it was, whether lunatic or merely half-baked. 'But, Kate, you've only got a hundred and twenty-five thou.'

'I never thought to hear anyone call that "only",' Jess murmured.

Lauren waved the interruption away. 'How long will all this take? And what will you live on while you're doing it?'

'I've got it all worked out,' Kate said. 'Do you think I'd dare to face *you* without having thought it through? You'd chop me into little bits.'

'*Someone*'s got to have sense in this house. The two of you are about as level-headed as a pair of puppies with a carpet slipper.'

'I've always wondered why it was called a carpet slipper,' Kate said. 'It's not made of carpet.'

'Stop being evasive. Answer the question.'

'I will,' said Kate. 'The place is pretty grotty-looking, and John from the estate agent says the owners want a quick sale and will drop the price, especially as I've got no chain. He thinks they'll go for one-oh-two-nine-fifty. If I allow five thousand each for a bathroom and kitchen, couple of thou for materials, couple more for contingencies, that leaves me eight thousand to live on. I reckon I can do it easily in six months.'

'Can you live for six months on eight thousand?' Jess said doubtfully. 'It doesn't sound like much. It isn't half of your present salary.'

'But you have to remember that's deduction-free. Eight thousand take-home pay. And I don't suppose there'll be much to spend it on down there.'

'Except the cottage. I think you'll find all sorts

of extras coming up once you start,' Lauren said.

'Well, if I find myself running out, I can always get myself an evening job as a barmaid or a waitress. There'll be lots of jobs like that once the season starts. But at the end of it, I'll have had my adventure, got the restlessness out of my system, had time to think about what I want to do with my life – and best of all, I'll have something to tell Gaga, an adventure. Oh, and I'll end up with a profit. John says once it's done up it ought to sell as a holiday cottage for a hundred and thirty-nine thousand, easily. More, if the market's picked up by then.'

They all thought about it, in a silence punctuated only by the crunching of toast and the sipping of chocolate. Kate was pretending insouciance, but she was worried about what Lauren would say. Not that she would be prevented from doing what she wanted by her opinion, but Lauren *was* the level-headed one, and if she thought the whole thing was nuts, it would plant an uneasy seed of doubt in Kate's mind. And she didn't want to doubt herself. She *wanted* to do this. Bursford called to her from the recesses of her mind like a siren song. She wanted the peace, a complete break in lovely surroundings, and the satisfaction of saving that ugly little cottage: the Cinderella project – wasn't that always irresistible? She knew she could do it: she had the skills – disasters excepted. And she knew Gaga would approve, not because it was a sound investment, but because it would be fun.

Lauren spoke. 'Well, I can't see that it will be much fun,' she said, uncannily picking up Kate's thought, 'living in a dirty old cottage, surrounded by rubbish, dust everywhere, nowhere clean to relax after the day's work, grinding away day after day at the same old job – and all alone. And I think, as I said, you'll find all sorts of extras you haven't budgeted for.'

'We've all watched those restoration programmes on the telly,' Kate said. 'But you haven't seen it – it's so small, there's really nothing *to* uncover. Everything's in plain view. And you can't not do something because of what might happen. That way you'd never do anything.'

'It seems to me,' Lauren said, 'that at worst, all you can do is lose everything. And since you believe you've lost everything already...'

Kate grinned. 'You approve!'

'I wouldn't go that far. But if it worked out the way you hope, you'd have gained valuable life experience—'

'And a few valuable thousand on the way,' Jess finished for her. 'Hooray for Kate, the Sarah Beeny of Crouch Hill!'

They were both smiling at her. 'You guys!' she said gratefully. 'That's the worst thing, really, having to leave you two.'

'Only for six months,' said Jess. 'And we'll come down and visit you. Maybe not stay in the cottage,' she added hastily, 'but there must be B&Bs in the area.'

'Bound to be,' Kate said. 'But it'll be more than a six-month separation, because I'll have to give up my share of the flat.'

'Oh,' said Jess, suddenly realizing.

'I couldn't afford the rent here as well,' Kate

said sadly, 'and you couldn't manage with just the two of you, so you'll have to replace me.'

'And then there's your job!' Jess cried. 'Your lovely job! You'll have to give it up.'

Kate had thought about that. 'I know,' she said. 'It's a shame. But I expect I can get another when I come back. PR's about the one sector that's always expanding.'

Lauren had been thoughtful. 'I can't answer for your job,' she said, 'but I may be able to ease the pain a bit over the flat.'

'What do you mean?'

'Well, do you remember Marta, the Dutch woman I found a place for last year?' Lauren worked as a freelance relocation agent.

'Of course,' Kate said. 'She was a blast.'

'I always said it was a waste finding her a flat,' Jess said, 'because she seemed to spend more of her spare time here than at home.'

'Exactly,' said Lauren, 'and I had a message from her last week that she's coming over again in April for six months, asking me to keep an eye out for a place for her. I'd be willing to bet she'd be just as happy taking over your share of the flat as being in one on her own. Anyway, I can but ask her.'

'But that would be brilliant!' Kate exclaimed. 'Then I could come back here afterwards.'

'It's as though it's *meant*,' breathed Jess, who could be a bit fey at times.

'You'd have to clear everything out of your room,' Lauren warned. 'And we'd have to have a grand clean and tidy up of everything. Hotel standards, you know.' She looked at Kate thoughtfully. 'And who knows how you'll feel at the end of six months? You might not want to come back.'

'I shall,' Kate said firmly.

'But at least it gives you the option,' Lauren finished, as if she hadn't spoken.

After that, things seemed to move really fast. Kate telephoned the estate agents, and the next day they came back to say the owner had accepted the offer. 'It helps that it was cash,' John said. 'They're keen on a quick sale, so the sooner we can complete the better – assuming that's what you want.'

'Oh yes,' Kate said. 'I want to get on with it as quickly as possible.'

Lauren contacted Marta, who was delighted with the idea of sharing the flat. It meant that Kate now had a firm date for moving out, which would be awkward if she couldn't get into the house in time: it looked like being a close shave, one way or the other, and she might find herself looking for a sofa to sleep on, and a garage to store her stuff.

But there was good news on the job front. She explained the situation to her boss, Ben, when she handed in her notice, and he was flatteringly dismayed that she was going. 'I know you've had a bad love affair,' he said. The office was very chummy and everyone knew everyone else's business. And besides, the PR world was a small one. 'And I *have* offered to go and punch that bastard's lights out for you.'

'I know, and I'm grateful,' Kate said. Ben was

in his late forties, still squeezing himself into tight jeans, driving a souped-up sports car, twice-divorced and dating girls half his age. He called himself a walking cliché, but he was genuinely kind-hearted and all the staff were fond of him. He got good work out of them and commanded loyalty in a notoriously shifting sector of the business world.

'One thing, he'll never be able to pull that trick again,' Ben went on. 'Everybody knows about him now.'

'Too late for me,' Kate said.

'I know, lovely,' he said, rubbing her arm comfortingly, 'but write it down to experience. The right guy will come along soon. And as far as your job goes, I'm pretty sure I can keep it open for you. If we get someone in – an intern, maybe – to do the mechanical stuff, the envelope stuffing and ringing round and so on, the rest of us can manage your clients for six months.'

'Do you mean it?' Kate cried in delight.

'Listen, it would take six months to recruit and train a new person anyway. As long as it's no longer than that, your job's here for you.'

She flung her arms round him and kissed him. 'God, you're marvellous, do you know that?'

'Yes,' he said solemnly. 'Yes, I do.'

It certainly looked, as she said to Jess that evening, as though Fate was directing her. Everything was falling into place.

'It's meant to be,' Jess agreed. Kate's scheme was getting the big Go Ahead from the celestial powers.

Three

There wasn't much to moving in. All Kate's belongings – mostly books and clothes – were put in boxes, and she'd taken the opportunity to have a bit of a clear-out and thin the stuff down a bit anyway. The charity shops had a happy day. The flat she shared with the girls was furnished, so she had to buy a few bits to tide her over. She and Jess had a nice time going round Ikea and picking out what she would need. She bought a flat-pack bed, chest of drawers, bedside lamp, kitchen table and two wooden chairs, a cane sofa for relaxing on, crockery and cutlery, cooking implements, a couple of saucepans, electric kettle, frying pan and a casserole dish.

'It adds up, doesn't it?' Kate said, slightly dismayed to realize that even the minimum one needed to survive on made quite a large heap. Jess thought she hadn't got nearly enough, and kept urging her to further purchases. Kate was easily able to resist the parlour palm in a pot, the 'gorgeous' light fittings, the 'cute' candelabrum, the glass-topped coffee table; but she did see the point of the bale of three cheerfully-coloured woven cotton rugs. 'You can't walk about on bare floorboards for six months!' Jess cried. 'You must have *something*, even if just by your bedside.'

Kate was too excited about the adventure to feel more than a brief pang as she said good-bye to the girls and climbed into her overloaded car at the crack of dawn to drive down to her new home. The weather was springlike, the sky changeable, with large, watery-looking clouds bowling across the pale blue, gleams of sunshine between them, and one or two brief showers on the way down. There were lambs in the fields, mostly too busy eating to frisk, but charming none the less, and the trees were all in new leaf. A new start, she thought, a new life, and no more of the old mistakes: I'm going to be strong, independent, and happy from now on.

She had to stop in Taunton to collect the keys, and that was the first hitch in the smoothness of the day, because she couldn't find her way around the town, the traffic was diabolical, and she couldn't see anywhere to park. In the end was obliged to park at the station, which she *could* find, and take a taxi to the estate agent's – an annoying expense when she was committed to saving every penny. But she took the opportunity to do a shop at Morrison's, which was conveniently close to the station, and told herself that the groceries would be cheaper there and probably make up for the taxi fare.

She passed through several heavy showers on the way from Taunton to Bursford, but as she turned at last into School Lane the rain stopped, though the clouds were still gathered frowningly. By rights, she thought, there should have been a Cecil B. DeMille column of sunlight poking through them to spotlight the cottage as she drew up. But, no, it sat there, looking dreary in its tangle of neglected garden, and somehow smaller than she remembered. The door had swollen with the recent damp, and was stuck, so she had to wrestle it open; and inside everything looked dingy, bare and decidedly unwelcoming.

Stupid, she told herself. Of course it was bare. And dingy was what she was here to change. She dismissed the image of the sitting room back at the flat, with the big saggy sofa and the gas fire roaring and the girls chatting over mugs of hot chocolate. It was the depths of feebleness to feel daunted in the first minute of the first day! She started carting in her boxes and the bags of groceries. Ikea would be delivering most of her stuff that afternoon, and she would have a busy time making up the flat packs.

Her stomach grumbling told her it was past time for lunch, so she got out the sandwich and apple she had bought at Morrison's, found the electric kettle and a mug, and ate sitting on a box of books, for want of anywhere else. Until her furniture arrived there wasn't much she could do by way of unpacking, so while she waited she amused herself by going round the house and renewing her plans in her head.

The four-hour delivery slot crawled past, and the van didn't arrive. She went out into the garden and hung over the gate, wondering what on earth she would do if it didn't come, leaving her with no bed to sleep on. She supposed she'd have to go and find a hotel room – more extra expense!

It was almost dark when at last she saw the top of a white van labouring up the hill, and she waved to it vigorously and beckoned it on.

'We're a bit late,' the driver's mate said, jumping down and looking around him with an air of astonishment that anyone could want to live in a place like this. 'Got lost. Couldn't find the place.'

'But it's easy,' Kate protested. 'Just one turning off the main road. Didn't you have a map?'

The driver had got down too and came over. 'Map?' he said derisively. 'We don't do maps.'

'Satnav,' said the non-driver. 'Had us going the wrong way to start with. Burford instead of Bursford. And there's no School Lane.'

'There is. You're in it,' Kate said.

'Not on satnav,' the driver said firmly. It was clear that when reality and satnav clashed, it was all reality's fault. 'Had to stop and ask someone,' he concluded with an air of outrage. A man should never have to ask directions. That was in the Constitution.

'Well, you're here now,' Kate said soothingly. 'Better late than never.'

'Going back in the dark, round all them lanes,' the driver sniffed. 'Back o' beyond, this.'

'Better get this stuff out,' the non-driver said.

'Make us a cuppa tea, eh?' the driver urged. 'Two sugars.'

It was late by the time Kate had the bed put together and made up: the rest would have to wait until the next day. She was hungry, extremely dirty (everything she touched seemed to have a layer of grime over it) and somewhat depressed. The cottage, far from looking like home, seemed cold and comfortless, and the black night outside, unbroken by any artificial lights, seemed to press against the windows in a hostile and threatening way. It was utterly silent, too, and she felt as if she was all alone in the world. *What have I done*? she asked herself bleakly.

Burned your boats, that's what, she answered herself.

She was stuck here, in this horrible place, far from her friends and the comforts of civilization. She could have spent Gaga's money on a world cruise, the bright lights, generally having a fabulous time; but no, she had to be a sensible cow and *invest* it in property – and such a property!

Well, one thing was sure, she couldn't crawl back with her tail between her legs. Pride wouldn't allow. And besides, she told herself briskly, it's just the first night, for goodness sake! Don't be so feeble. You're bound to feel disorientated the first night. And you're hungry. She really didn't feel like cooking, and not in that kitchen, until she had scrubbed it from end to end – *and* in daylight, so she could see what she was doing. So she opened a tin of soup and heated that up, and had it with some bread and cheese.

And what a good job that she had thought to put a couple of bottles of wine in when she did the Morrison's shop! She had a glass or two, sitting cross-legged on her new sofa and watching something mindless on her little portable television, and felt a lot more normal. But when she fell into bed at last, it took her a long time to get off to sleep, because of the silence outside.

Things seemed a bit better in daylight. Not that the cottage looked less grim, but at least it felt more familiar the second day, and as she walked about with a mug of tea in her hand, she began to feel the pleasure of ownership, and visualized what it would look like when she had finished it. Outside the sun was shining fitfully between the clouds, and sunshine always gave everything a more cheerful aspect. She went out into the garden to look out across the moors, and the first thing she saw was a group of ponies walking along the track behind her cottage. Wild ponies, like zebra, lived in maternal groups, a dominant mare with a couple of sisters or daughters and any of their foals. This was a group of five, two of them looking very pregnant. You could tell the boss mare because she had the biggest bottom, and she gave Kate a stern look from under her bushy forelock as they passed. They turned off the track further along on to a sheep-trod, and plodded away through the heather, leaving Kate feeling it was a good omen. *I'm going to like it here*, she told herself.

While eating breakfast she phoned the girls to say she was safely arrived and settling in; then telephoned to order a skip; and then washed up her plate and mug and made a start. First she had to put together the rest of the furniture, and unpack her things. She put in a solid morning's work, then, with a sense of achievement, stepped outside to get a breath of air.

A woman was in the garden of the next house along. She was plumpish, with short blonde hair growing out at the roots, and was dressed in pink leggings and a mauve top. She was hanging washing on the line: a large number of blue and checked shirts, and pairs of jeans, from which Kate deduced she had a husband – a tall one, from the size of them.

Kate watched the shirts waving their arms in the breeze a moment, and called out, 'Good drying day!'

The woman started and looked round, and her face instantly creased into a friendly smile.

'Oooh, I didn't see you there. You gave me a start.' She came over to the dividing wall with an air of being ever ready to exchange housework for a chat. 'I heard Little's was let, but I never saw a moving van. When did you come?'

'Yesterday. The van got lost, so it was after dark when it got here. I'm Kate, by the way – Kate Jennings.'

'Karen Tonkin,' she said, and they shook hands.

'But it's not let,' Kate added. 'I bought it.'

'Bought it? Well, I never! Doing it up, are you?'

'That's right. I'm doing most of the work myself. Luckily my father's a builder and he taught me everything.'

'What, decorating and that?'

'And pulling down walls, and carpentry, and repointing.'

'Well, you must be a useful person to know,'

Karen said with a grin. 'My Darren's not much of a handyman, which is queer, given he's an engineer by trade. My husband,' she amplified. 'Karen and Darren – we didn't half get the piss taken when we first started going out. He calls me Kay, though. Most people call me Kay. There, I'm Kay and you're Kate – we could be sisters! So you're doing up the old cottage? Terrible state it must be in, never been touched in donkey's years, and poor old Margie Brown all on her own in there all that time, after her old man died.' She wrinkled her nose, and then frowned as she worked something out. 'But you're never living there? Not while you're doing it?'

Kate nodded. 'I have to. Can't afford any other way.'

'Oh my lor!' She seemed quite struck with the idea. 'And pulling down walls? The dust! However will you keep anything clean?'

'Well, for the moment I've got all my stuff upstairs, sleeping in one bedroom and using the other for a sitting room, while I work downstairs. When I've finished that, I'll swap over, live downstairs and work up.'

'Still, it'll be that dirty! And it don't sound very comfortable. You poor toad! Listen, any time you want to come over ours and sit with us, you just do.'

'You're very kind,' Kate said, really touched. The woman hadn't known her two minutes.

'Never. I'd have it on my conscience, thinking of you up there all alone,' she said warmly. 'Got to look out for each other in this world, haven't

you? You had your lunch?'
'I was just stopping for it.'
'Well, come and have something with me. No, go on, you're all right! I like a bit of company.'
'Well, thank you,' Kate said. 'And perhaps you can tell me something about the place.'
'Glad to. You don't need to encourage me to talk. Darren says my tongue runs on wheels. I love a bit of gossip, me.'

In the kitchen, which was warm and bright and smelled of washing powder, they sat at the table and ate baked beans on toast and, as promised, Kay talked with Olympic fluency.
'I was surprised when you said you'd bought Little's, because that's part of the estate. The Blackmore estate. Most of the land round here's Blackmore's – owned most of the village, too, at one time, back in history. Very old family round these parts, the Blackmores. I never thought they'd sell, especially with it so hard to find rented places these days.'
'Why is the cottage called Little's?' Kate asked.
'Cos the Littles lived in it. Generations of 'em. Worked for the estate, lived in that cottage. Even Margie – Mrs Brown, the old lady that lived there last – she was a Little before she married.' She took a mouthful of tea. 'When my mum was a kid, the Littles that lived there then, they had six kids.'
'Six!' Kate exclaimed. 'How on earth did they all fit in?'
'Fact!' Kay nodded. ''Course, that was before

Sir George put the bathroom in – Sir George Blackmore – so they had three bedrooms then. Still...'

Yes, still ... Kate thought, and imagined washing six kids in a tin bath in the kitchen. 'So you're a local girl?'

'Born and bred in Bursford. My dad worked for the estate, and my mum's dad ran the Royal Oak – you know, the pub in the village? Darren's not from round here, though. He's a foreigner. He's from Watchet.' She smiled as she said it, but Kate knew that it both was and wasn't a joke. Watchet was over on the coast, a good fifteen or sixteen miles away – another world. 'He works at the paper mill there.'

'How did you come to meet him?'

'It was the shooting,' Kay said. 'There's always big parties come down here in the autumn and winter for the shooting. I was working in the Blue Ball, waitress and chambermaid – I went straight into it from school, being in the blood, sort of, with my grandad being in the trade, so to speak. You get good tips when these rich types come down from London for the drives, and it makes lots of extra work for everybody, so that's all good. Couldn't go on without the shooting.'

Kate was interested. 'So that's like an extra tourist season for you?'

'Fact,' said Kay. 'Make more money in the winter than the summer round here. And not just for the pubs and hotels and B&Bs and all that, but they always need beaters and pickers-up as well. That's what Darren come over from Watchet for, weekends, to make a bit of extra cash, and that's how we met. At the Blue Ball we give the beaters and pickers-up a meal at the end of the day, in the big barn at the back, and I was helping serve it one weekend, and there he was. Sort of love at first sight.'

'That's a lovely story,' Kate said.

'He's a lovely man,' said Kay. 'He knew I never wanted to move away from here, so after we got married we got this place and he drives to Watchet to work every day. Mind you, it means he can pop in on his mum, so that's all good.'

'And do you still work at the Blue Ball?'

'Me? I got two kids. They're at school, but it doesn't give you much time in the day for a job. But I do part-time in the shooting season, when they need extra help. Evenings, mostly, when Darren can watch the kids.'

'You don't look old enough to have two children at school,' Kate said.

'Oh, look at you! Aren't you nice?' Kay said, pleased. 'I wish you was my sister. 'Nother cuppa tea? Have a biscuit with it.'

'So tell me about the Blackmores,' Kate said, having selected a chocolate Hobnob. 'You say they owned my cottage?'

'Why, didn't you know who you bought it from?'

'I suppose it must have been on the contract, but I didn't particularly notice. The estate agent only talked about Mrs Brown.'

'Well, the Browns only rented it, o' course. I never thought the family'd sell, because after the war, they had to sell a lot of property to pay off the death duties, and Sir George, when he inherited, well, he swore he'd keep the rest of it together. *Not* selling was kind of like his big thing. Everybody knew that. I wonder if they're in some kind of trouble?' she mused, frowning.

Kate thought it was touching that she seemed to mind the idea. 'A lot of people are, these days.'

'Yes, but I thought they were all right now. I haven't heard anything. But o' course they wouldn't put it about if they was,' she concluded with a shrug. 'Wouldn't want people to know.'

'So Sir George Blackmore is the present owner?' Kate asked.

'No, he's dead now. There's Lady Blackmore, she's his second wife, and the two sons, Edward and Jack, they're the first wife's sons. Jack's a real laugh. You see him about the place. He's divorced, got a little boy. He's the biggest flirt you ever met. No harm to it, though, he's just a nice man who likes female company. You'd like him.'

Kate smiled. 'I don't suppose I shall ever meet him.'

'Oh, everybody meets everybody eventually in this place.'

'But I'm going to be busy doing my cottage – speaking of which, I should get back to work.'

'Yeah, and I've got to pick up the kids in a bit. Well, it's been real nice chatting to you.'

'Likewise. And thanks for the lunch.'

'No, my pleasure. Made a nice break in my day. And like I said, any time you get sick of the place and want to come over, you just come. You don't need an invitation. It can't be very nice having to live where you work, let alone the dust and everything.'

'You're very kind,' Kate said again, and in a spirit of reciprocation added, 'and any time you and Darren want to go out, I'll come and babysit for you.'

Kay's face lit up. 'You mean it? You're so nice! It'd be lovely to have a night out with Darren some time, even if it's only going down the Royal for an hour or two. We don't get out much.'

So with goodwill all round, Kate went back to her new home and started straight in, stripping wallpaper. By the end of the day the sitting room was down to the plaster and she had taken the hardboard off the doors – they were panelled underneath, and not in bad condition, which was a relief – but she had a big pile of the resulting rubbish in the middle of the floor, waiting for the skip.

It was supposed to come first thing the next morning, but it didn't appear. It was a lovely sunny day outside, and so in between ringing the skip company and getting either an engaged tone or an answering machine, she took her work outside and began rubbing down and making good the window frames. She eventually got through to the skip firm, who said they hadn't had one available but would bring it the first thing following morning.

But again it didn't arrive, and she had a repeat of the previous day, rubbing down in the sunshine, waiting for the skip, and having abortive telephone calls.

Which was the point when the Angry Man – surely a local nutter? – turned up, and she decided to walk down to the village and try out one of the pubs for lunch.

Not, she told herself, *that I shall be eating out as a regular thing*. She couldn't afford it, so she shouldn't get in the habit. And she shouldn't skive off, either. The sooner she got the boring basic work done, the sooner she could get on to the fun bit, making the place pretty; and also the sooner she could live in a place just a tad less filthy, which was definitely a priority.

She had a quick wash and changed into a less revolting T-shirt and jeans, and walked down School Lane with a healthy worker's appetite. If the skip came when she was down there, she told herself crossly, they could damn well come and find her. They had her telephone number. They needed to get it through their heads who was the customer around here. Of course, it was a hopeless attitude to take with skip firms, who were a law unto themselves, and only marginally less autocratic than scaffolding companies. But it felt good while she was thinking it, and it was all part of her new assertiveness, or so she told herself. The new Kate wasn't going to take crap from anyone – especially not a member of the male half of humankind.

Four

The two pubs, the Royal Oak and the Blue Ball, sat on opposite sides of the main village road, and could not have looked more different. The Blue Ball presented a long, elegant Georgian stone frontage to the road, three stories high, with the name in large gold letters along the facade. It had very posh hanging baskets, already in full flower, and a cobbled strip in front, divided from the road with white-painted staddle stones and some large wooden tubs containing smartly-clipped box bushes.

The Royal Oak was also three storeys, but there the resemblance ended. It was a tall, narrow, crooked building, evidently an ancient cottage on to which various additions had been tacked over the centuries, straggling up the slope behind it. It sat on the corner where the valley road crossed the main road. No hanging baskets; the pub sign, swinging in the breeze from a metal bracket between the first-floor windows, was a very amateurish-looking painting of a tree with a crown on top. The window frames, Kate noticed, were painted the same maroon as her own, signifying that it was, or had been, part of the same estate.

Given her general scruffiness, it was to the

Royal Oak that she took her custom that first time. Inside, it was all low beams, wooden floors, high-backed settles and mismatched wooden tables. There was the usual selection of old sepia photographs and dim pictures on the walls, and odd bits of china, ornaments and copper objects on shelves and across the mantelpiece of the brick fireplace. There seemed to be three bars, all on different levels. To her left as she entered was a slightly smarter area where two couples, obviously tourists, were sitting at tables, quietly conversing, while they waited for food. Straight ahead was the public bar, and three men in working clothes were seated on stools along it, pints before them. One had a dog lying at his feet, and that decided her. She went up to the bar, and the dog, a collie, heaved itself to its feet and looked up at her, swinging its tail politely.

'Lovely dog,' she said, bending to caress its head. None of the three looked at her, but she deduced that this was shyness rather than unfriendliness. 'What's his name?' she asked.

'Gyp,' said his owner, addressing the beer in front of him.

'Working dog, is he?'

The reply was a sort of strangled grunt. But the man behind the bar, who had been at the other end washing glasses, had spotted the danger and came hurrying down to the rescue.

'Help you?' he said. He looked about sixty, and was short and burly with a wide, flat red face under a shock of white hair. He gave her the sort of smile you give strangers who are also customers, the one that doesn't touch your eyes.

'I'd like a pint, please,' Kate said. 'Which is the local beer?'

'Well, there's the Cotleigh Tawny,' he said, tapping the pumps, 'or you've got your Hewish IPA, that's from Weston.'

'I'll try the Cotleigh, thanks. And can I get something to eat? I've been fancying a ploughman's.'

'Cheddar, Stilton or pâté?'

That was the tourist influence. Years ago the question wouldn't have been asked. 'Cheddar, please. Is it local?'

He seemed, just discernibly, to approve of the question. 'Just up the road. This side of Exton. Broad Farm Cheddar.'

'Sounds perfect.' Kate watched him put the food order through a hatch behind him and draw the pint. Her three companions had their heads down, contemplating their glasses so as not to have to look at her.

'Where'll you be sitting?' the landlord asked, placing her glass before her.

'Oh, I'll stay here,' she said. 'Got to make myself at home, now I've moved in to the place. This'll be my local.'

Now he looked at her properly. 'Moved in?'

'I've just bought Little's Cottage.'

The three heads came up and turned, like a line of cattle at a trough. The landlord, now examining her thoroughly, said, 'I heard it was sold. Thought it must be a mistake. So that was you, was it? You actually bought the place – not rented it?'

'Bought and paid for,' she said firmly. She

stuck out her hand. 'My name's Kate Jennings.'

He took it, though rather cringingly. 'Dave. Doing it up, are you?'

'That's right.'

'Then what? Selling it? Holiday cottage?'

She had enough sense to know this was a leading question. 'I haven't decided yet. I'm thinking of settling in the area. I used to come here as a kid. My dad's from Exford.'

'Is that right? Local girl, are you? Well, I hope we see a lot of you. Can do with some more young people settling round here. These three characters are Ollie, Wayne and Kev. You'll see a lot of *them* if you're in much.'

They gave her shy smiles, and she beamed back at them. 'So tell me,' she said to Dave, 'why were you surprised I'd bought Little's Cottage?'

'Never even heard it was for sale,' Dave said. 'No sign up or anything. Kept it quiet, didn't they? Then Terry from over the Blue Ball comes in and says did I hear Little's was sold. I said, "You must be mistaken, old son." But he says, fact.'

'Ed Blackmore, he swore they'd never sell any more of the estate,' Kev piped up from the end of the bar. 'Promised his dad he'd keep it together.'

'See, it's hard for local people to find somewhere to live,' Dave amplified. 'Cottages that used to be for rent, incomers buy 'em up for holiday places, and push the prices up so locals can't afford 'em any more.' He gave her a hard look as he said it, which she withstood as steadily as she could. 'And then, the Blackmores have owned the land round here time out of mind. Be a terrible shame if the estate was broken up and sold off and the family went. Piece of history gone, you see.'

'Yes, I see,' said Kate. 'Well, I can see why you were surprised. But it's all true – I bought it fair and square.'

''Course you did,' Dave said, exonerating her. A plate appeared in the hatch and he turned and retrieved it and placed it in front of her. 'Sure you're all right here?'

'Sure,' she said. 'It looks lovely.' It did – a big, crusty half of a French loaf, a slab of Cheddar, the smell of which was already making her mouth water, pickles, pickled onions, an individual dish of butter and a little mound of salad. Just what she had been fancying.

While she ate, she got her companions to talk, starting off with the dog, going on to local breweries, drawing them out on the village darts tournament, and ending up with whether Minehead would beat Bridgwater in the Somerset Premier League final.

And as they got over their shyness they asked her about her father's family and her local connections, and were interested and impressed that she was doing the work in the cottage herself. Ollie said she could get herself a lot of jobs as a handyman if she needed the money. Wayne was able to give her the phone number of a chimney sweep, and Ken knew a good plumber who, he said, could also put her on to an electrician. They seemed genuinely friendly, and altogether it was a very useful half hour: lunch, so to speak, had paid for itself.

She was just getting to the bottom of her pint, and thinking regretfully that she really shouldn't have another if she was going to do any work that afternoon, when the door opened and a man came in.

Kate, glancing over, thought it must be another tourist, because he was very smartly dressed in a good suit and tie. He was in his forties, she guessed, and with a firm, alert look about his face that suggested intelligence. His hair, prematurely silver, was very short, well cut and contrasted with his tan. The only point against him was an expensive camel coat over the suit, and leather gloves he was just taking off, but that was simply a personal prejudice: she didn't like camel coats and leather gloves – at least, not on men.

But that he was not a tourist was immediately proved when Dave looked across at him and said, 'Hello, Phil. Didn't expect to see you in here this time o' day.'

The man came forward, sparing Kate one hard, all-encompassing glance and then dismissing her, to stand between her and Ollie and say, 'Give me a G and T, Dave. Make it a double.' His mouth was set hard, as though he had something on his mind. He was heavyset and broad shouldered, and with his thick wool coat he took up a lot of room, forcing Kate to shrink back a little on her stool. As he changed balance to reach inside his coat for his wallet, he must have stepped on the dog, for there was a little yip and a scuffle of movement. The man looked down briefly, and

Ollie said, 'Come out of there, Gyp,' reaching down to take the dog's collar and pull him to the other side of his stool.

Putting the glass in front of him, Dave said, 'What's up, then, Phil? You don't look your usual cheery self.'

'Ach,' he said, a formless expression of disgust. 'I've been all the way to Taunton on a wild goose chase, that's all. People mucking me about. I'll get to the bottom of it, though, and when I do...' He threw back half the gin and tonic in one gulp, put the glass down, and said, 'You know you heard that rumour about Little's Cottage being sold?'

Dave gave him a warning glance and said, over-heartily, 'More than a rumour, my old son. We've got the new owner sitting right here. Came in to introduce herself, which I call very friendly and civil.'

The man's head swivelled round so sharply that Kate was afraid he must have ricked his neck, and the hard eyes were fixed on her in a penetrating stare that made her feel, for a moment, quite uncomfortable. She was aware that she was not presenting herself at her best, and simple pride made her think that if she'd met this man in London with her glad rags on he wouldn't have looked at her like a prefect looking at an inky new kid. She could have taken him on on his own terms.

'I'll do the honours, shall I?' Dave went on, evidently thinking the stare was not conducive to a happy bar atmosphere. 'Kate, this is Phil Kingdon. Phil, Kate Jennings, who bought Little's.

Phil's the land agent for the Blackmore Estate.'

'How do you do?' Kate said coolly, keeping her end up.

But suddenly everything changed. The man smiled, his eyes crinkling, the hard stare was history, and a hand was being offered. 'How do *you* do?' he said. 'Pleased to meet you. Sorry if I was a bit abrupt before – I've just had a long drive for nothing, so I was feeling a bit ratty. So, Little's new owner? Let me buy you a drink, introduce you to the village.'

Kate shook the hand (hard, well-manicured), and responded to the smile – why not? She was here to make friends – though she didn't quite feel it had a spontaneous warmth to it. 'I'm not a complete stranger here,' she said.

'Her dad was from Exford,' Dave amplified.

'So I'm half Exmoor,' Kate went on.

'I should have known from the name,' said Phil Kingdon. 'What'll you have?'

'Thanks, but I really have to get back to work,' Kate said, glancing at the clock over the fireplace. 'And I'm expecting a skip.'

'A what?' Phil said, startled.

'Kate's doing all her own work,' said Dave, with a sort of proprietorial pride that amused her.

'Hence my scruffy state,' Kate got in, with a gesture towards her clothes. 'I scrub up quite nicely, you know.'

Another crinkling smile. 'I'm sure you do,' Phil said. 'Perhaps I can buy you that drink another time? Tonight? Oh, no, wait, I can't tonight. What about tomorrow night?'

Woah, boy, Kate thought. *Fast worker*. And she

wasn't here to go out on dates, though it was flattering to get such an instant response. 'Thanks all the same, but I'm not really fit to go out, after a day working on the cottage,' she said.

He wasn't so easily put off. 'Oh, come on, just a drink. I bet you'll want to get out of that place for an hour or two. All work and no play, you know. One drink, all right?' He was giving her the full force of his charm, but she didn't know anything about him and, given his age and apparently comfortable income, she couldn't believe he wasn't married.

'I'm sure I'll see you around the place some time, now I'm living here, but I'm going to be very busy for a while. Thanks anyway. I'd better get back now.' She rose from the stool, noting out of the corner of her eye that the hard stare was back. *Didn't like being thwarted, did he? Bit of a control freak?* She was glad she'd refused the drink, now. He didn't seem like a man to get tangled up with.

Wayne spoke up, looking towards the door. 'I think I see a skip lorry just go past. Might be yours.'

'Oh God. They'll take it away again! I'd better run.' And she legged it.

It was hers, and she arrived at the top of School Lane, panting, just as the driver was getting back into his cab.

'Don't go! It's me! I mean, it's mine!'

He got down again. 'Gor, you don't half live in the back of beyond,' he informed her. 'Couldn't find the place. It's not on satnav.'

'So I was told recently,' Kate said. Didn't anyone look at a map any more? 'But you're here now.'

'Yeah. Where d'you want it? It's gonna block the road if I leave it here.'

'Can you swing it over the wall into the garden? There's nothing there it can spoil.'

'I see that, but I can't get the angle.'

'What about if you go up on to the track?'

He set his jaw. 'Mud track. Don't wanna get stuck.' He was punishing her for not being on satnav.

'It's not muddy. It's firm and dry. Have a look.' Under her insistent urging he walked up with her to inspect the track, and agreed reluctantly that it would take his rig. In a very short time the skip had been swung delicately over into her garden, and the lorry had gone away, chains swinging noisily, back down School Lane. He would have had to go on to the track anyway to turn round, she noted, so his objections were spurious. It puzzled and amused her that men were so inflexible: throw any kind of spanner in their works and they went to pieces.

'Never mind, I can get on with walloping walls now,' she told a tortoiseshell cat that was tiptoeing delicately along the top of her wall. It stuck its tail straight up in agreement, ducked a cheek briefly against her offered fingers, and jumped down into the jungle of her garden to stalk away through the weeds.

Wall-walloping was enormously therapeutic. Sometimes she imagined Mark's face, and sometimes Oliver's, and occasionally a composite of all the unsatisfactory men who had not even called back when they said they would. Over the next few days she knocked down the two-thirds of the dividing wall, finished stripping the paper from the staircase wall, and loaded all the debris into the skip. The latter was the most laborious part, because although she had a wheelbarrow – she had found a rusty one out the back under a riot of convolvulus – there was no way to wheel it up to the top of the skip and tip it, so everything had to be thrown up by hand. The work was so hard that at the end of each day she only just had the energy to bathe, cook a meal, and fall into bed. But at least she was tired enough to sleep right away, without worrying about the silence outside.

Kay came to the door one day and looked in. 'It's gone quiet,' she said by way of greeting. 'I wondered if you were all right.'

'I'm sorry – has the noise been a nuisance? The really bad bit's finished now.'

'Oh no – it's not a problem,' Kay said quickly. 'You're that far away, I can only just hear it. It don't bother me.' She looked round the stripped and devastated room. 'My Lord, you've really been working hard! Funny, it looks bigger this way. You keeping that old fireplace?'

'Yes, I'm going to put a log-burning stove in when I'm done. Those night storage heaters give a background warmth all right, but they're expensive, and they're not very cosy. You can't sit round one on a chilly evening.'

'Hmm,' said Kay, without enthusiasm. 'We

had our fireplace taken out and plastered over. Don't want the bother of fires, and cleaning out the ash and everything, these days. I like everything modern, me.'

Kate smiled. 'Ah well, I suppose I'm just an old-fashioned girl. It was the log-pile out the back that made me think of it.'

'Oh, that's been there ages,' said Kay. 'Margie and Wilf never had a real fire in donkey's. Margie had a 'lectric one for when it was cold. Those logs'll be years old,' she concluded doubtfully, apparently worrying that they might go off, like milk.

'Never mind,' Kate said, 'I'm sure there'll be lots of suppliers in a place like this. Did you want anything in particular?'

'Well,' Kay said, looking shy, 'I was thinking 'bout what you said, 'bout watching the kids. Did you mean it?'

'Of course I did,' Kate said quickly. 'When?'

'Well, Saturday night, if you're not doing anything else. 'Course, you might have a date...'

'I don't know anyone to have a date with,' Kate said.

'Only,' Kay went on, 'it's the darts final Saturday, down the Royal Oak, Withypool.' There were lots of Royal Oaks on Exmoor. 'They're having a pie-and-pea supper after, and I wouldn't half like to go. Darren's playing, and he says we ought to win this year.'

'Of course you should go. I'll be happy to babysit for you,' Kate said – though darts and a pie supper sounded so attractive, she'd have liked to go herself, had she known about it. But a promise was a promise.

Kay looked relieved. 'Oh, look at you, you're so nice! Are you sure? Listen, d'you want to come over tonight and have your tea with us? Then you can see the kids. You've not met 'em yet.' She grinned. 'Our Dommie can be a cheeky little monkey. You might change your mind.'

'I won't,' Kate promised. 'But yes, thanks, I'd love to come.'

'It's only shepherd's pie. We have it half past six when Darren gets home from work, then he can see the kids 'fore they go to bed, otherwise he only sees 'em weekends. How you managing for washing?'

'I'm not, at the moment.' The abrupt change of question caught Kate off guard. In fact, she had been wondering how to cope with clothes-washing, not having a machine. Bursford or any of the other local villages were not the sort of places to have a launderette, and having to go into somewhere like Taunton or Minehead for it was going to be a nuisance.

'Well, you give it to me, and I'll put it in with ours. No, go on, you're all right,' she continued against Kate's instant protest. 'I got so much your little bit more won't make any difference.'

'But my work clothes are filthy,' Kate said. 'I don't want to break your machine.'

'No, you won't. I'll do what I do with Darren's – his get filthy at work just the same. I soak 'em first in a big tub out the back. Listen, I'll swap a bit o' washing for babysitting any day of the week. D'you know how hard it is to find anyone round here? Feels like years since Darren and me got out. His mum used to come over sometimes, but she doesn't drive any more.'

At the end of the week Kate had a trip into Taunton in the car, to the B&Q in Heron Gate, to buy materials: plaster, wood filler, some lintel timber, quadrant and architrave, more sandpaper. Feeling optimistic about her progress, she also bought size, lining paper and paste, and wax for the doors. Then she did a Morrison's food shop, and drove home laden to the gunwales. The cottage looked more familiar as she drew up in front of it: not exactly a home yet, but at least definitely hers. The sun had come out, and the tortoiseshell cat was sitting neatly on the gatepost, squeezing its eyes in pleasure at the warmth. It stood up politely as she approached, four cinnamon feet bunched together on the small space, arched its back and gave her a cheek in greeting.

'You wait till I've got a wood-burning stove,' she informed it. 'You'll be knocking at my door to come in, then.'

The cat, offering an astonishingly loud purr, seemed to agree.

Five

When Kate arrived on Saturday evening, Kay said, 'They're fed and bathed, and Dommie can play for half an hour while you put Hayley to bed. Are you sure you're all right doing that?'

'Yes, I'm fine. As long as she doesn't mind,' Kate said. Four-year-old Hayley, playing with a Barbie doll at the kitchen table, was giving her another of the long, considering stares that had attended their first meeting. Six-year-old Dominic was drawing at the other side of the table and didn't even look up as Kate came in.

'No, she'll be all right. She's no trouble. I usually sing her a song when I put her down,' Kay added doubtfully.

'I can do that. What does she like?'

'I usually do "You Are My Sunshine". My mum used to sing that to me. But it don't matter – anything'll do.'

'I can do "You are my sunshine",' Kate said. 'What about Dommie?'

'He gets one story. You be strict about it, or he'll have you reading all night. You are a love to do this! I'm that excited about going out, you wouldn't believe.'

'Kay!' came Darren's voice from upstairs. 'Are you ready? I can't be late.'

'I'm all done but me shoes and coat,' she shouted back.

'You look very nice,' Kate said.

Kay smiled shyly, and touched her hair. 'I need to get these old roots done. I must make an appointment, only I've got to go all the way to Minehead, and what with the washing and shopping there never seems to be enough time between taking the kids to school and picking 'em up.'

'I could pick them up for you one day, if you like.'

'Oh, I can't keep imposing on you.'

'You're doing my washing. I don't call that imposing.'

'Well, if you're sure...'

Darren appeared in the doorway. 'Got your shoes on? Come on, girl, get a move on!'

In a flurry of movement and goodbyes they were gone. Kate heard the car start up and drive off down the road, and then the silence outside swirled to a halt, lapping round the house and settling. For a moment Kate felt daunted, very alone, and worryingly responsible for two little strangers. She caught Hayley staring at her again, and shook herself. Sixteen year olds babysat all over the country, so there couldn't be anything to it *she* couldn't handle, could there?

There was no difficulty about putting Hayley to bed, except for withstanding the continued silent stares. She sang 'You Are My Sunshine' to apparent approval, since Hayley demanded two en-cores, and was opening her mouth to request a third when Kate decided she was being made a monkey of, gave her a firm, 'Goodnight,' instead and beat a hasty retreat.

When she got back downstairs, she discovered that Dommie had decided to accept her, and while she helped him clear away his drawings and pencils, he chatted away about school and his friends and his plastic Power Rangers set and something he watched on the television that she'd never heard of. He even generously gave her one of his drawings, for which she expressed suitable gratitude without being able to tell what it was meant to be: caterpillar, spaceship, ray gun – possibly even a Power Ranger, for all she knew.

When it came to the story he asked for 'The Gingerbread Man', and she read it from the battered book on the shelf beside his bed, noting that the shelf was crooked and had been put up on too short a bracket, so it sagged forward as well. *I could fix that in a jiffy*, she thought, and banked the idea against further washing favours from Kay.

Once she had settled Dommie and looked in on Hayley, there was nothing to do but go downstairs and wait out the evening. She had brought a book with her, but yielded instead to the lure of the television. Without a fixed aerial, her own little portable only got two channels, and then only fuzzily, so it was nice to have a wider choice and a clear picture. She'd have to see about getting an aerial put in – but not until she'd repointed the chimney, she reminded herself. She ought to get on and do that while the weather was fine – and finish the outside windows. Put off the indoor work for a rainy day. There were bound to be plenty of those.

She was surprised when the front door bell rang, and glancing up, saw the time was ten past nine. She got up automatically, but had a moment of shivery worry as she went to answer it, thinking of the dark outside – she still found the countryside night-time vaguely threatening. But it was silly to be nervous, she told herself firmly, and opened the door to find Ollie standing there, with Gyp at his heels. Gyp surged forward in welcome, tail wagging and tongue at the ready, but Ollie looked startled.

'Oh – it's you.' He stared. 'Um – is Darren in, then?'

'They've gone to the darts final. I'm babysitting,' Kate explained.

'Oh, yeah. I forgot the darts.'

'Anything I can do?'

'No, you're all right. I just wanted a word.' He didn't seem inclined to go, or to come in. He leaned against the door jamb, looking at her with interest. He was in his mid-twenties, she guessed, lean but strong around the shoulders as a farm worker should be, clad now in his leisure wear of clean jeans, plain white T-shirt and leather jacket. His hair had been dressed into spikes with gel, and the smell of aftershave was competing with the smell of beer as he breathed through his mouth.

'Been to the Royal Oak?' she asked conversationally, to fill the silence.

'Yeah. Haven't seen much of you there lately.'

'I'm working hard – too tired at the end of the day to do anything but fall into bed.'

'Oh, yeah – you said that to Phil Kingdon when he asked you out.' A sudden grin. 'Didn't like you saying no, did he?' She assumed this was a rhetorical question. 'So how's it coming along, then?'

'The house? Oh, slowly. But I'm getting there.'

'Doing it all yourself,' he said. 'Funny thing that. Don't expect women to be any good at that sort of thing.'

'My father was a builder,' she said, wondering how she could get rid of him politely.

But her last comment had sparked something. His face was lighting up with a dawning realization. 'Not Jennings of Exford?' he asked excitedly. 'Dave down the Oak said your name was Jennings.'

'That was my grandfather's business. My dad set up on his own, but he worked for his dad for a bit when he was younger.'

'My Uncle Tim worked for Jennings,' Ollie said delightedly. Gyp, sensing the excitement, got to his feet again with an eager look, wagging and staring from face to face. 'He was a roofer. Tim Bentley, his name was. Did you know him?'

'My grandparents died when I was a kid,' she said, and then, hating to disappoint him, 'but I bet my father knew him. I'll ask him when I write to him next time.'

'I bet he did,' Ollie said happily. 'Everyone knew Uncle Tim. Well, fancy that! Makes you nearly family.'

Kate didn't know what to do with this sudden

kinship, but she smiled, and wondered if she ought to invite him in – though it was not her house, which made it a bit awkward. 'Look...' she began.

But at the same moment a thought seemed to cross Ollie's mind and he also said, 'Look...'

They both smiled, and she said, 'You first.'

'Well, I was going to say – about Phil Kingdon asking you out.' He chewed his lip awkwardly. 'None o' my business, but you did right to turn him down.'

'Did I? I must say, I wasn't really tempted. Not my type.'

'Well,' Ollie said hesitantly, 'he's kind of my boss, in a way, so I shouldn't say anything. Wouldn't want it to get back to him...'

'I won't say a thing. Promise. But why shouldn't I go out with him? Is he married?'

'Not that I know of.' Ollie seemed startled by the idea. 'Could've been before, I s'pose – before he come here. I wouldn't know. But he's not – well, not a very nice man, not for a girl to get mixed up with.' He seemed embarrassed by having to say this, and she put on an interested face and made helpful noises. 'See him in Taunton and Minehead, different girl all the time, and not nice girls like you, if you get my drift. And he's a hard case. Mixes with some dodgy characters. I shouldn't be saying this, but you'd do best to steer clear of him. I mean he's all right as a boss, if you don't get on the wrong side of him, but...'

'He's not the type of man a girl would take home to meet her mother?' she said lightly, to get him out of the pickle he seemed to be in.

His frown lightened. 'That's it. Just thought I'd mention.'

'I appreciate it. But like I said, he's not my type anyway.'

'Right. Nuff said, then. Well, I'd better be gettin' on.' He seemed eager to escape the embarrassing intimacy now.

'OK. See you around, I expect.'

'Yeah. C'mon, Gyp.' He turned away, dog at his heels, but turned again at the end of the path to said, 'You won't – like – say anything?'

'Not a word. Promise.'

'Only...'

'I understand. Thanks for the heads up.'

He didn't seem to understand the expression, looked quizzical for a moment, then worked it out, smiled, lifted his hand in an uncompleted gesture, and took himself off into the night.

Kate went back indoors, thinking, *well, what was all that about?* But just before she shut the door she stopped, opened it again, and looked cautiously out. She thought she had seen something, a dark shape – someone moving just beyond her garden wall, at the end where the road joined the track, where there was no street light. A darker shape among the shadows. But now shc looked again she saw no shape and no movement. Must have been mistaken. A trick of the light – or rather a trick of the dark. She went in, shutting the door, and telling herself that she wasn't yet used to living in the country. She'd have to stop getting jitters like that if she was to stay sane and balanced.

* * *

Kay and Darren came home in festival mood, the Bursford team having won the trophy. Company, supper and several drinks had added to Kay's simple delight in getting out of the house, and she was as flushed with pleasure as Darren was with triumph.

'Did you have any trouble with my two monkeys?' she asked.

'Not a bit,' Kate said. 'I think they were a bit overawed at having a stranger look after them. Dommie gave me one of his drawings.'

'Well, we're ever so grateful to you,' Kay began.

To cut short renewed effusions, Kate said, 'Oh, by the way, Ollie called, looking for Darren.'

'What, Ollie Fewings?' Darren asked, looking puzzled. 'What'd he want?'

'He just said he wanted a word.'

Darren continued to seem perplexed, but Kay, easing off her shoes, looked up sharply. 'What, come to the door, did he? The cheeky so-and-so. He didn't want no Darren. He wanted to have a crack at you. I bet that's what it was. He knew you was here alone, wanted to get chatting to you.'

Kate said, 'He seems a nice lad, but he's not my sort.'

''Course he's not. I'll give him what-for when I see him,' Kay threatened.

'But how would he know I was here?' Kate wanted to know.

'He's thick as thieves with that Denny Foss, that works at Wansbrough's, same as Darren.

Darren gives him a lift to and from work – pick him up and drop him off at the Royal Oak, don't you, love?'

Darren looked sheepish. 'Told him Friday you were babysitting for Kay. He must've gone straight in the Oak.'

''Course he did,' Kay confirmed. 'Well, I like that Ollie's cheek!'

'It's rather flattering, really,' Kate said with a laugh. 'Anyway, that solves the mystery.'

They saw her off with renewed thanks; but between the closing of their front door and the opening of her own was a piece of darkness in which only the strange, vague shapes of things could be seen, and the silence was invested with strange small rustlings and murmurs. She thought about the man she had thought she'd seen lurking, and quickly unthought it again. As she fumbled with her key and struggled with the door, which still stuck a bit, she suppressed the urgent desire to look over her shoulder to see that no-one was creeping up on her. Only when she got the door open and was ready to dart inside did she look round. Her heart gave a painful thump as she saw something on the track that ran past her house – a dark shape just visible against the slightly less dark sky. A man's shape, she thought. She strained her eyes, trying to work out if it was still or moving; and the next minute she had lost it. Someone walking home along the track, perhaps, passing out of sight behind the trees. Nothing to get antsy about.

She hurried inside, closed the door behind her, told herself not to be foolish – and made a mental note to leave a light on inside next time she went out in the evening.

On Sunday she decided to take a break from work, and went for a long walk over the moors. It was a fine, breezy day of sunshine and shadows, and she thought it would be absurd to move all the way to Exmoor and not sample its outdoor pleasures.

First she tried to discover exactly where her five acres were. She had seen it marked on a map, but it was not so easy to identify in reality. The fences had gone – or perhaps in some places had never existed – and the wild had crept – or rather rushed – back in. She could see a difference in vegetation in the part immediately across the track from her house, which presumably had been cultivated for longer than the rest, and she discovered a rusty iron water-trough hidden in the bracken which seemed to mark one corner of that field. But that was all. Standing back to get an overall impression of it, she saw that her five acres – if she was guessing right about how much an acre was – occupied the flat top of Lar Common, just about the only flat land in the immediate vicinity. But without any hope of planning permission, it was valueless – except to a member of the Irish diaspora suffering from land-hunger, of course. A vague thought wandered through her mind that, in deference to her people, she really ought not to waste it, she ought to clear the land and cultivate it...

At that point reality kicked in and she snorted. *Yeah, five acres of potatoes ought to do it! What are you, Scarlett O'Hara? 'As God is my witness, I'll never be hungry again!'*

Anyway, stupid girl, you're not staying here. This is a Cinderella project, that's all. You're doing up the cottage and selling it, and moving back to real life, in London.

But as she tramped away down the track, gazing across the wide moors, dappled with shadows of the fast-moving clouds, she felt a pang at the idea of leaving this place. It was so beautiful ... Yes, she told herself, but that's now, in May, with summer ahead. Think of winter here, cold and wet, shut indoors week after week with nothing to do. You'll do up the cottage and get out just in time. Enjoy it for what it is – a working holiday.

She had been walking for some time, enjoying the fresh air and the wonderful smells; she had spotted two groups of ponies at a distance, seen buzzards circling overhead, heard the trilling of skylarks, and underneath it the singing silence of the high lands. She had been following a sheep-trod, and the land under her feet began gradually to fall away from the flat top of the common, the drop growing steeper until she found herself at the edge of a coombe, on the other side of which there was a craggy rise to a green hillside, where a flock of sheep was peacefully grazing.

It was at that point that Kate heard the whimper. It came from somewhere below her, on the side of the coombe, which was thick with heather, bracken, whin and gorse. She turned her head out of the wind and listened. After a moment it came again, a whimper that turned into a long-drawn-out whine of distress. It sounded like a dog. She craned her neck, moved a little way along the valley edge in each direction, but she could see nothing. But she was a dog-lover, and if there was one in trouble, she had to go and see if she could help. Perhaps it had slipped and fallen, or got itself stuck in a rabbit hole, or – well, something. She had to find out.

She looked for a suitable way down, and found the faint mark of a trod through the vegetation which she began to follow. It was all very well for a sheep, but it was tricky going for a human, trying to find sound footing through the wiry heather-roots, loose stones and concealed hollows. And where was the dog? She tried calling, and heard a whimper of reply. She headed for where she thought the sound came from, but having to look down for her footing all the time meant she could not keep an eye on the direction her steps were taking her; and one bit of heather looked much like another. She called again, and thought she heard a sound from the vicinity of a large gorse bush – at least that gave her a landmark to aim for.

She laboured on. Calling elicited no more sounds. Her foot slipped and for a shocking, heart-in-mouth moment she was skidding down the coombe-side on her back, clutching at passing roots to try to stop herself. She took the skin from one set of fingers before something held and she arrested the skid. She lay for a moment, staring at the sky, while her heart-rate slowed. A cloud of tiny flies descended, interested in the sweat that had broken out on her brow.

She wondered what on earth she was doing. She'd heard no more cries of distress. If there had ever been a dog, it was probably long gone. Dogs didn't fall – they were as sure-footed as sheep. She was risking breaking a leg for nothing – and if she did break something, who would ever find her? She was far enough down the coombe now to be invisible from the top. She would lie here and die of hunger and thirst, and one day, years hence, some intrepid walker would find her bare bones sunk in the heather. It came home to her that Exmoor was a wild place, and very different from London. It was a place you could actually *get lost* in – lost as in *never being found again*.

Her heart was steady again, her breathing normal. She sat up and snorted at her own panicky fears and foolish fancies. She got over on to all fours and then carefully stood up, looked back up the way she had come, and saw that the gorse bush was only a few feet to her right, and above her. She had been going to give up on the phantom dog, but as she was so close, she might as well go and have a look. At least going up was easier – you faced the hillside and hung on with your hands, making yourself effectively four-footed instead of two. She called again, 'Where are you, boy? Hey, boy!' got no answer, but crabbed along and up anyway.

And here was the gorse bush, and here was the problem. Underneath it, on the downhill side, there was a big, earthy hollow, probably where some animal – a fox, perhaps – had dug out a scrape for shelter. There was also a wandering line of old, rusty barbed wire, presumably the remains of an old fence, and a big, black, hairy animal was caught in it. As she reached the place, it turned its head, and she saw it was a mongrel dog with a thick, bushy coat. She saw what must have happened. The dog had gone in to the hollow under the bush, perhaps to check out the scent or look for rabbits, creeping under the wire, which had got snagged in its coat. Then in turning round to get out, it had wound the wire deeper until it couldn't free itself. Subsequent struggles had only made things worse, and now it was hopelessly trapped, bound to the tough branches and roots of the gorse by iron teeth.

The dog looked at her with white-rimmed eyes, and she had a moment of misgiving: a trapped animal could be savage. But the eyes were fixed on her face, and she saw the ears go down and the tail beat the ground to show submission and supplication.

'All right, old boy,' she said soothingly, crawling closer. 'I'll help you. There, there, be still now.' The dog had tried again to struggle up to greet her. She put a cautious hand out, let it smell her fingers, and then stroked its head. It relaxed trustingly under her touch. Yes, trust was all very well, but how was she to release it? She didn't happen to have wire-cutters about her person. All she had was a rather feeble penknife in her pocket, attached to her keyring. She thought of going for help, but she had taken a long time to get here, without passing any other habitation, and even if she walked back to the main road and flagged down a car, what could a car driver do, except take her to a village where she might or might not find someone with wire-cutters? And she had little confidence she could find this exact bush again, once she had left it.

No, it was up to her. She used her fingers and felt around, tried working the animal free, but its coat was so thick and so well entangled that after ten laborious minutes she had only got two of the little barbed knots free. And as she sat back on her heels to rest for a moment, the dog began struggling again, tugging the barbs in deeper.

She soothed the animal again, and decided it was the penknife or nothing. It was one of those foldaway Swiss jobs, which in her case had nail scissors, nail file and a screwdriver as well as the blade; but the blade was only two inches long, and not super-sharp. The nail scissors, she thought, might be her best bet for cutting the dog free. She got them out and discovered that, if she took a few hairs at a time, and didn't try to cut the whole hank at once, the scissors would go through this animal's dense coat. But it was going to be a long job.

She had to attack it methodically, starting at the end of the strand, so that once it was free she could push it up out of the way and stop the dog reattaching itself. It was lying still now, and she wondered how long it had been here – long enough to be exhausted, weak from hunger and thirst? In a pause to rest her fingers – which were aching from the strain and sore from the pressure of the thin handles – she ran her hands over the dog's body, trying to feel through the coat whether it was thin. She could feel ribs, but came to no conclusion – some dogs' ribs you could always feel. The dog evidently saw this action as an endearment, for it moved its head and licked her nearest hand. 'Better get on and get you out,' she said, and it beat its tail in agreement.

She went on, sawing away at the caught bits of coat, carefully untangling the wire, rolling it up out of the way. Her fingers were bleeding now, and she had snagged her hands and wrists on the barbed wire, and scratched every exposed part on the gorse thorns. 'Next time,' she advised the dog, 'try getting snagged out in the open, preferably right beside a farm gate.' The dog, lying quietly now, only blinked in response.

And at last, at last, she cut through the last, and worst, knot – she had to go deep and take out quite a wide area of coat: it was going to have a bald spot on its back near the root of the tail – and lifted the hairy wire clear, rolling it with the rest of the coil and pushing it outside the bush, well away from the dog.

She sat back on her heels. Her neck and back ached from the constant bending. 'That's it,' she said. 'You're free now.'

The dog didn't move. It looked back at her without moving its head, as if it thought it would be caught for ever.

'Come on,' she said, and slapped her hand encouragingly against her knee. It lifted its head now and looked at her, wagging, but still did not move. She started to wonder if it had some other injury. But she wouldn't be able to tell unless it came out from the cave under the gorse. She reached for its neck, feeling for a collar. There was none, though there was a flattened ring of coat where it had worn one.

'So, you slipped it, did you? You're a runaway. Come out, out of there. Up, you lazy hound, up!'

She got hold of its ruff and tugged, still making encouraging noises, and suddenly the dog rolled, getting its feet under it, and started wriggling out backwards, belly to the ground, not daring to try to stand up. She moved out of the way, got a fresh hold on the ruff and pulled, encouraging it, and suddenly it was out, stood up, stared about it rather wildly, and then gave itself a great long shake from ears to tail.

Kate stood up, and grinned with pleasure at the sight. 'Well, well. How does that feel?' she ask-ed. 'Now, let's see if there's anything else wrong with you.' She bent over, putting her hands on the dog to check it over, but it gave a great leap out from under her, knocking her off balance so that she sat down again, hard, and without a backward glance it raced away up the coombe side and disappeared over the top.

'Well, I suppose that means you're OK,' she muttered. She had sat down on a stone, a sharp, pointy one, and it hurt. 'Think nothing of it!' she shouted after the dog. 'My pleasure!'

She got up stiffly, pushed the roll of barbed wire to where it could be seen clearly, examined her hands with a rueful expression, then put her penknife away and started up the coombe side for home. It was past lunchtime, and she was very hungry. And thirsty. She wondered if she had enough Elastoplast at home for all her injuries. She'd have to get some more when she did her next shopping. And she would definitely invest in a much more butch penknife. Carrying one in London could get you arrested, but out here in the wilds she reckoned it was only common sense. She could imagine a number of scenarios in which it would prove invaluable, even life-saving.

At the top of the slope she stopped to rest, and beguiled by a patch of sunshine, she sat in the warm grass and stared out over the landscape. The dog was long gone, and no other earthbound creature was in sight, but a buzzard was cruising, fingertips splayed, over the scarp opposite, and a lark hung invisible, high high above her, its song an agony of beauty.

How much her life had changed already, in the short time she had been on Exmoor! London seemed very far away, and improbably exotic, like an imaginary city. A fantasy land. Which in many ways, she reflected, it was.

Six

Dommie had decided, after that Saturday evening, that Kate was his special property, and every afternoon as soon as he got home from school, he came running from next door to see her. He followed her around, chatting about what he had done at school, and telling her his other little concerns – often incomprehensible to Kate.

She checked with Kay if it was all right, and Kay said blithely, 'Oh, Lor', you keep him! If he's round yours he's not under my feet. Send him back if he gets in the way.' So Kate gave him milk and biscuits, listened to him, and let him help her with a simple task here or there.

She had no idea how to talk to children, so she spoke to him as she would to anyone, which was probably the right thing to do. At any rate, Dommie seemed to like it. He blossomed under her adult interest. He brought her presents – a feather he had found, an interesting stone, an earwig in a matchbox – and gave her some of his drawings, which he bestowed with lordly beneficence, explaining them to her like Brian Sewell unbending to a well-meaning but dense patron of the Tate. Often the subject was the Power Rangers – she soon knew more about *them* than she had ever expected or wanted to.

'I'm a Red Power Ranger,' he announced. 'I got the helmet for Christmas.' He said she could be one, now he had adopted her. 'You can be Udonna,' he said, 'because you've got red hair, like her.'

'Udonna? What's she like?' Kate asked, mixing up Polyfilla.

'She's the White Mystic Ranger,' he said importantly. 'She's got a snow staff. She freezes stuff.'

'That must come in handy,' Kate said. 'Like, leftovers and so on?'

Dommie was patient with her. 'Like, evil, she can freeze evil.' He thought a moment. 'She lives in the Root Core.'

'Really? Oh well, it can't be more uncomfortable than this place.'

He watched her gravely as she Polyfilla-ed cracks in the plaster with a small trowel. 'Can I do some?' he asked, surprisingly humbly.

'All right,' she said. She found a crack at his level and a spatula and let him try. It was messy, but it kept him occupied. 'That's not bad,' she said after a bit. 'Keep it up.'

He blushed with pleasure at her praise. 'When I'm grown up, I'm going to marry you,' he announced.

'That'll be nice,' Kate said.

'I'm going to be an engine driver. You can come with me when I drive it and be in the cab and do the coal.'

'Coal? Oh, you mean a steam train?'

He nodded. 'Like Dad takes me on, at Watchet. He helps look after them.'

'Yes, I remember the steam trains,' Kate said. 'I went on them when I was a kid, visiting my grandparents.'

He was talking about the West Somerset Railway, which ran along the coast from Bishop's Lydeard, through Watchet and all the way to Minehead. It was mostly run by volunteers and used restored steam locomotives and old carriages, but it was not just a plaything for hobbyists and train fanatics: it ran a regular service which was a valuable resource to people along the route wanting to get in to Minehead for a bit of shopping. It linked at Bishop's Lydeard with the ordinary, boring railway, so they could run specials all the way from London to bring in extra funds to help keep it going.

'So your dad's one of the volunteers?' Kate asked. She could see it, somehow – Darren was just the sort.

'He's an engineer, my dad. He makes the engines go, and then they let him ride in the cab and he took me once and it was awesome!' His face shone with pleasure. 'You can come too, when we go.'

'I'd love that,' Kate said. 'I haven't been on a steam train for years and years.'

'But you might not be allowed in the cab,' he said, anxious she should not get too excited. 'Cos it's only special people they let. But when I'm the driver you can all the time.'

'Gor,' said Kay when Kate relayed the conversation, 'not choo-choos again! You another of 'em? I been once or twice but that's my lot. Leave me cold, steam engines. Darren's like a big kid with a train set, loves getting his hands dirty, and o' course Dommie's the same. Yeah, of course Darren'll take you one day, if you want. He'd be thrilled, show you everything. He can talk about his old locos till the cows come home – getting him to stop, now that's the trick. Fancy a cuppa?'

'Thanks.'

'You sure he's no trouble to you, Dommie?'

'None at all. I like having him around.'

'Sooner you than me. But I s'pose it doesn't matter too much if he makes a mess in there, does it?'

'Exactly. And I think I ought to teach him some handyman skills, given that we're going to be married when he grows up.'

Kay grinned. 'He said that, did he? Little monkey! Got a crush on you.'

'It's more than a crush,' Kate said gravely. 'It's serious. I count myself an engaged woman. Only one thing bothers me.'

'What's that?'

'How I'm going to feel about having you as my mother-in-law.'

On Wednesday at lunchtime she discovered that she had completely run out of food. She had been up early and done a good bit of work, and given that her stomach was completely hollow, she thought she would treat herself to lunch in the village before driving to the supermarket to stock up. *I deserve a decent meal*, she thought as she went upstairs to the bathroom to clean herself up.

She was feeling in need of company, too. This life was rather solitary. In London she had worked in a busy office and shared a flat with two others, but here if she didn't go seeking company, she was alone all the time. Not counting her superhero Dommie, of course – but much as she enjoyed his visits, she craved some grown-up conversation for a change.

She hadn't yet tried out the Blue Ball, so she thought she'd give them a whirl, and since they appeared from the outside to be rather a different proposition from the Royal Oak, she gave herself an extra good scrubbing, and fetched out some slightly better clothes than her usual grotty garb. A nice mid-calf-length floral skirt in dark blue and green shades, and a sage-green top that went really well with her hair. Redheads were always told to wear green, but the wrong shade could be unforgiving and make you look gingery. At school her hair had been bright copper, tending to be frizzy, and she had hated all the remarks and the automatic name calling. But in adulthood it had darkened a bit, and she had learned to tame it – though it still didn't do for her to stand out in the rain – so she didn't mind it so much now. At least she had inherited her father's dark eyes and sallow skin, so she didn't have to endure the pale, freckled face and tendency to bright pink sunburn that was the lot of so many redheads.

Having gone so far, she whacked on a bit of lippy and mascara – might as well go the whole hog – then shoved her feet into a pair of sandals and set off. The rain of Monday and Tuesday seemed to be pushing off: there were still a lot of clouds around, but it was warm and felt more settled. If it was dry tomorrow, she thought she would take the opportunity to do the chimney. Unless there were any nasty surprises up there, she could get it done in a day, and then she could see about getting an aerial. She was tired of just two fuzzy channels.

As she stepped inside the Blue Ball she could see the difference at once. As in the Royal Oak, there was a lot of wood around, but there the resemblance ended. The Oak was all low and crooked, dark and bumpy; the Blue Ball had high ceilings, straight walls, large windows and symmetrical rooms. The entrance hall was panelled, with a stone-flagged floor, and contained an original staircase of breathtaking Georgian elegance. Through the door to the left she could see a dining room, the tables laid with white damask cloths, sparkling silver and glassware, and real flowers in small silver vases. The walls were painted dark blue and were hung with dim old portraits in gilt frames, and at the far end was a magnificent marble fireplace.

To the right was a bar, also panelled and stone-floored, though the flooring was perfectly even and obviously new. The furniture was either original or good reproduction, with seat-cushions matching the curtains, tasteful chintz in muted shades; high-backed settles along one wall; a handsome, varnished bar with brass fittings and high stools in front of it. She could hear a murmur of conversation from inside, but from her position could not see anyone, and for a moment she felt absurdly shy about going in.

This was obviously a place for the moneyed and the county set. She glanced down at the dirt under her fingernails that she hadn't managed to get out, and the grubby plasters over the remaining cuts on her hands, and felt the Oak calling her back. Here she'd be a nylon anorak on a wax jacket peg.

While she still hesitated she heard a wuff behind her, and turned to see beyond the open street door a big black dog with a dense, rough coat. Glad of the excuse she took a step or two towards it. 'Is it you?' she said. It stared a moment, ears cocked, and then ran to her, tail swinging, eyes bright, tongue at the ready. Yes, it was the same dog. She could see the near-bald spot by the tail where she had sawn off inches of coat. 'So, you've remembered your manners at last, have you?' she said as she caressed it, fending off the worst excesses of the tongue, rubbing its ruff, scratching behind its ears until it was in a slobber of ecstasy.

As she bent over the dog, something blocked the light from the door, and she looked up to see a man standing there, observing. 'Seems you've made a new friend,' he said.

She straightened, one hand still on the dog's head. It was a man in his mid-thirties, she guessed, with sexy blue, slightly bloodshot eyes and a killer smile. He had rough-cut, toffee-coloured hair with blond highlights – both, she guessed, expensively wrought by a skilled barber to look natural; he was wearing chinos, expensive loafers, and a dark blue shirt that perfectly set off his eyes; and he was swinging a set of car keys on a worn leather fob as he looked at her with the intense interest of a man who likes women – all women.

'Oh, he's not a new friend. We've already met,' she said.

'He never mentioned you,' he replied, playing along.

'Probably ashamed. He didn't cover himself with glory on that occasion.'

The blue eyes examined her with increased interest. 'You wouldn't happen to know anything about his sudden acquisition of several bald spots, would you?'

She shrugged ruefully. 'Sorry about that. He was tangled up in some barbed wire and it was the only way I could get him out. He's got a very dense coat.'

'Don't I know it!' The man smiled – boy, was that devastating! – and came towards her, holding out his hand. She took it, and immediately he covered it with his other hand as well, drawing her slightly towards him. She smelled his subtle, expensive aftershave and, this close, realized that he was not particularly handsome, but that he had so much charm you would never notice or care. 'So you save old Chewy, did you? I owe you a huge debt. My kid would have been heartbroken if anything had happened to him.'

Kate swallowed a ridiculous disappointment at the news that he had a child, which meant he must be married. Ridiculous, because she wasn't on the hunt. Never again. She was done with all that nonsense.

She had to say something, and she said,

'Chewy, is that his name?'

'Theo named him. That's my little boy. After Chewbacca, because he's big and hairy. But he also does have a propensity for chewing things – shoes, mostly.' The dog licked their joined hands, and he released hers at last. 'So, are you just arriving or just leaving? Arriving, I hope. Come on in and let me buy you a drink.'

'Oh, no, I—' Kate began an automatic denial.

'Please,' he interrupted. 'It's the least I can do to say thanks. I promise you, we were out of our minds when we found he'd slipped his collar and run off, and then when he didn't come back ... Please, come and have a drink and tell me how you found him.'

She hesitated one more moment, on account of his being a married man, though it was broad daylight and a public place.

He looked at her quizzically and then said, 'Lord, where are my manners? I haven't introduced myself, and you don't know me from Adam. But I promise you everyone knows me around here, and the guv'nor here, Terry, will vouch for me. My name's Jack Blackmore.'

He put out his hand again, and as she retook it (it was warm and dry and strong, just the sort of hand a man ought to have) he grinned and said, 'Stupid name, I know, but I did the best I could with it – I managed to persuade most of the kids at school to call me Blackjack, which was way cooler than Jack Black, don't you think? Anyway,' he went on, using her captive hand to turn her towards the bar, 'I live just around the corner, at The Hall, and I promise I'm not a mad axe-murderer.'

She yielded, laughing. 'I'm quite sure you're not. And even though I'm new around here, I've heard of the Blackmores, and I know where The Hall is, so I'm sure I'm quite safe.' And hadn't Kay said that the younger Blackmore, Jack, was divorced? So hopefully she wouldn't be treading on anyone's toes.

They were in the bar now. There were a few people sitting around the room at the tables, chatting quietly, and one man on a stool at the far end, with a brown-and-white spaniel at his feet. Chewy ran to greet the spaniel, but he was evidently well known as the owner did not display any misgivings, though Chewy was large enough to engulf it.

The barman came up to the near end, eyebrows raised in greeting. 'Hullo, Jack. What'll it be?' He spared a glance for Kate, checking her over and obviously wondering about her.

Jack led her up to the bar, and turned to smile down at her. 'D'you know what we ought to have? A bottle of champagne to celebrate your saving Chewy, and my meeting you at last to thank you.'

'Oh, no,' Kate demurred. 'That's too much. Anyway, I—'

'No, really,' he said seriously, 'it's the perfect drink for this time of day. I prefer it at lunchtime anyway, because it's so much lighter, especially if you've got to go back to work.' He had guessed the last part of her objection. 'Unless,' he added, 'you don't actually *like* champagne?'

'I love it,' Kate confessed, 'but—'

'Well, then!' The devastating smile was back. To the barman he said, 'Bottle of Ayala, please, Ken. Ken here will confirm that I generally drink Ayala at lunchtime, I'm not just putting it on to try and impress you. Isn't that right, Ken?'

'S'right,' said Ken, his face determinedly neutral as he turned to the glass-fronted chiller cabinets behind him. Had he witnessed this sort of scene before?

'And beside,' Jack went on, still addressing Ken, 'this young lady is a genuine, gold-plated hero. She saved Chewy from an awful death, and me from having to explain it to Theo.' He looked down at Kate. 'You haven't told me your name. I can't keep calling you "this young lady".'

'Especially not for the length of a bottle of champagne.' Kate laughed. 'And it does sound rather evil-uncley. "Young lady" seems to have all sorts of connotations these days, doesn't it?'

He laughed too. 'Quite right, and there's the whole feminist thing as well – don't they object to "lady" as opposed to "woman"? It's a minefield.'

'I feel rather sorry for men these days. You must often think it's safer just not to speak at all.'

'I'm afraid there's no way you'd make me stop talking, unless you had me freeze-dried,' he said, grinning. 'So what is it, anyway?'

'What is what?'

'Your name. You still haven't told me.'

'Oh, sorry! Kate Jennings.'

He took the excuse for another handshake. 'Jennings – that's an Exmoor name,' he said enquiringly.

'My dad was from around here.'

'But you're new here, you said. Not just passing through, I hope?'

'No, I'm living here now,' she said.

At that moment Ken popped the bottle and they watched him pour, then lifted their glasses, and Jack said, 'To Chewy's brave rescuer.'

'There was nothing brave about it,' Kate objected.

'All right – to new friendships. How's that?'

Kate smiled. He was an operator, and yet he did it so nicely it was hard to object. 'I'll drink to that,' she said, and did so.

'So where exactly are you living?' he asked when they had put their glasses back on the bar top. 'Do you want to go to a table, by the way, or are you all right here at the bar?'

'Oh, I like sitting at bars,' she said, and hitched herself on to a stool. He remained standing – or leaning, rather – which put their faces comfortably on a level. 'I've just bought Little's Cottage, in School Lane,' she answered his question.

An extraordinary series of expressions flitted across his face. For a moment he looked almost disconcerted; but then it settled into friendly interest.

'So that's it!' he said. 'I heard someone had, of course. And now I come to think of it, I'd even heard your name mentioned. I *thought* it was familiar for some reason.' Chewy, having done the round of the patrons in the bar, came back to them at that moment, and jabbed a wet nose into their spare hands in greeting. Jack looked down, and then said, 'But tell me about how you found

Chewy. All the details, please.'

It seemed to Kate almost like a change of subject, but she was happy to oblige. He was a good listener, and interpolated the right questions at the right moment to allow her to make the most of the narrative. She finished with Chewy running away without thanking her, and vowing to buy herself a big penknife when she was next in Taunton.

Jack looked in concern at her Elastoplasts. 'Looks as though you cut yourself up a bit, rescuing this ungrateful hound.'

'The barbed wire and the gorse between them were a bit scratchy,' she said, making light of it. 'But *this* one, and *this* one, are not Chewy-related. This one was a bolster slipping, and this one was a nail in the skirting-board I didn't spot in time.'

'How can you cut yourself on a bolster?' he asked, looking puzzled.

'Not a pillow bolster, I mean a builder's bolster.' He looked blank. 'It's like a big, thick chisel.'

'Oh, I know what you mean. You are full of surprises! What were you doing with a bolster?'

'I'm renovating Little's myself,' she said.

'Really! Tell me – no, wait a minute, instinct tells me this story is going to be too long for this bottle. Let's take the rest of it through into the dining room and have lunch – they do decent grub here.'

'Oh, well, I—'

'My treat. Come on, don't tell me you don't *eat*?'

'Of course I eat. I actually came here for lunch. Well, it was a choice between here and the Royal Oak, and—'

'There *is* no choice. You did well to step this way. And look how it's turned out! Chewy had the chance to say thank you, and you and I met. Gotta be Fate, wouldn't you say?' He had stuffed the bottle under his arm and picked up both their glasses, bent on giving her no chance to object.

And, truth to tell, she didn't want to. She was enjoying his company so much, not just as another human being – and she was starved of adult conversation – but as a man, a warm, funny, sexy, charming man who looked at her with interest and wanted to spend time with her. As long as she kept her head, how could that be bad?

'Gotta be,' she replied lightly, and let herself be led. After all, she told herself as she followed him across the hall into the dining room, it wasn't as if she was in any danger from him. His wiles were unexceptionably obvious – he was like a genial magician revealing the secret of his tricks to the audience even as he performed them. And his warmth seemed genuine. She liked him enormously, but was not in the least danger of falling in love with him, even had she been in falling-in-love mode, which she was not. She was here on a sabbatical. She was post-Mark impregnable.

Anyway, Blackjack, just from the quality of his clothes and the thickness of the wad in his wallet, which had been revealed as he paid for the champagne, was way out of her price-range, and his interest in her could not be more than a passing, pleasant whim.

Seven

The difference between the Royal Oak and the Blue Ball could not have been more obvious than when, seated by the window at the far end near the fireplace (which was filled with a beautiful arrangement of fresh flowers) they were presented by the uniformed waitress with the menu. The Royal Oak served good, solid pub food – ploughman's, shepherd's pie, fish and chips, steak and ale pie, ham, egg and chips. The Blue Ball's was restaurant food. It was one of those places that identified the farm that the meat came from; it specified that the fish was 'fresh Cornish' or 'line caught'; the vegetables were 'local' and 'seasonal'.

Kate tried not to look at the prices.

'God, it all sounds so good, I don't know how to choose,' she said.

'When I'm in trouble that way,' Jack said, 'I go by the colour of the wine I want to drink.'

She looked at him sternly across the table. 'I can't drink any more. I shall be completely pie-eyed. And I have to work this afternoon.'

'But you're your own boss,' he said beguilingly. 'You can take time off whenever you want.'

'And what about you? Don't you have to

work?'

'Nothing I can't put off. Listen, it's a great mistake to allow work to interfere with the business of eating. Lunch is the most important meal of the day.'

'I thought that was breakfast,' she objected.

'Now abideth breakfast, lunch and dinner,' he intoned. 'And the greatest of these is lunch.'

'That's a very naughty blasphemy. You'll be struck down,' she warned.

'On the contrary, I seem to be blessed. Here I am lunching in the best restaurant on Exmoor, with the prettiest, wittiest woman I've met in a long time. Life is good.' He sat back in his chair with such a contented look she could only laugh. 'Now, what will you have?'

In the end she chose smoked salmon with poached pheasant egg and wood sorrel hollandaise for a starter, followed by roast breast of duckling with cabbage charlotte and truffled potato purée. Jack chose devilled rabbit kidneys and mushrooms on toast, and the roast rack of Broad Farm lamb with lentil and rosemary juices.

'Rather than risk breaking our luck, shall we just go on drinking champagne?' he asked when the waitress hovered for the wine order.

'You can,' she said genially. 'I'm about at my limit.'

He ordered a bottle anyway, and lunch went on for such a long time, and he was such fun, and she was enjoying herself so much, that she ended up drinking quite a bit of the second bottle – not exactly her share, but enough to make her very relaxed. Jack seemed to have hollow legs, and put it away with ease, but it didn't seem to have a bad effect on him. She remembered Gaga saying that when drink was taken, a man only became more of himself – which was a grand way of telling what his real nature was, she had added as a warning. Jack, after more than a bottle of Ayala, was relaxed, smiling, charming, voluble. Was it possible he was just a genuinely nice man?

She told about her family connections with Exmoor, and then asked him about his family. 'Your son, Theo – short for Theodore?'

'Oh, I know,' he groaned. 'What a thing to burden him with, poor little beggar! But have pity on me – his mother wanted to call him Titus.'

'No!'

'It's true. I said to her, "Do you want all those Titus A. Newt jokes thrown at him?" Then it was Tiberius. She actually wanted to name our son after the most corrupt and sexually depraved emperor in Roman history!'

'Wasn't Caligula—?' Kate hazarded.

'He was mad. Tiberius knew what he was doing – that made it worse. Hey, you're an educated woman!'

Kate shrugged. 'I read a book once.'

'That's more than I can say for Felicity. She thought Tiberius had a nice sound to it. Distinguished, she called it. In the end, we had to compromise on Theodore. It quickly got shortened to Theo, which isn't too bad.'

'I quite like it.'

'But I'm working towards "Ted", or "the Tedder".'

'So you and Felicity are divorced?'

'Oh yes – it's all legit.' He gave her a canny look. 'No need to be nervous.'

She smiled at the joke, but asked, 'What went wrong?'

He shrugged. 'We should never have married, really. But I'd known her all my life. Her family and my family have always been connected. Our fathers knew each other, our mothers were on the same committees, we played together as children, went to the same dances when she came out – all that sort of thing. We looked good together, and it was always sort of expected that we'd get married eventually, so when the time came I just – went along with it. It seemed easier than the alternative.'

'I'm guessing that going along with things is rather your weakness,' she said.

He grinned. 'How well you know me already! I like to avoid trouble whenever possible.'

'So you've been married a long time?' Kate said, puzzled.

'We got married when I was twenty-three.'

'Oh – then, how old is Theo? I was picturing a little boy.'

'He's five. Felicity didn't want kids straight away, and then when she was ready, it didn't happen.'

'I'm sorry – not my business,' Kate said.

'It's all right. I don't mind. The sad thing is that when eventually Theo did come along, it seemed to be the last straw for our marriage. We both adored him, but we couldn't stand each other any more. We'd been on rocky ground for a long time, but somehow it all became unbearable once he was there, and we fought like cat and dog, which obviously wasn't the right atmosphere to be bringing up a kid. So I left, went back to The Hall – the family home, you know? Flick and I had a trial separation, and it became permanent. Theo's only five, but we've been divorced two years.'

He sounded genuinely sad, and there was a moment of silence.

'But you obviously get to see him,' Kate said encouragingly after a bit.

'Not as often as I'd like, especially now he's at school. But they live in Dunster, so it's not too far away, and I get to see him weekends and holidays. Felicity travels a lot, so when she does, it makes sense for Theo to come to me, especially since it means he can see his grandmother and the rest of the family.'

'Back living with your mum at – what is it – thirty-five?' Kate said with a teasing grin. 'The tale of our times.'

'Thirty-six next month,' he admitted. 'But she's only my stepmother – I don't know if that makes it more or less pitiful.'

'I've driven past The Hall more than once. I don't think "pitiful" is the right adjective.'

'More about you, now,' he said, surreptitiously topping up her glass.

'Don't think I don't see what you're doing,' she warned.

'You can always leave it,' he said blandly. 'Is

your mother from round here too?'

So she told about the Irish connection, how Dad had gone to Dublin to do a job, fallen in love with Mammy and, since she was unwilling to leave Ireland, married her and stayed there, setting up his own business in a city that was just bursting into prosperity, with all the renovation and conversion prospects that opened up.

'So you were brought up in Dublin? You don't have an accent,' he commented.

'I dropped it when I moved to London. It wasn't difficult – I'm a fair mimic.'

'Are you going back there?'

'Only to visit. I like it over here. More opportunities.' She didn't mention the dating scene, but the thought of it shut her up, and there was another silence. She thought he would ask her about how she came to buy Little's – everyone else seemed interested in that. But perhaps it was a sensitive subject to a Blackmore, because of the breaking-up-the-estate thing. Instead he asked her about the job she had given up, and the conversation rolled on.

By the time the second bottle was empty, they both had their elbows on the table, and were talking like old friends. The waitress, who Kate had seen hovering about in the background, finally came near enough for Jack to notice her, and he sighed and straightened and said, 'I suppose we'd better let the staff clear up. What about coffee and brandy in the bar?'

Kate shook her head at him. 'You're incorrigible. I told you I had to work this afternoon. In fact, I was going to drive into Taunton to shop first, but I don't think I'd better, after all that champagne.'

'I'll drive you,' he offered at once.

'You've had more than me,' she said, though she was rather thrilled by the offer. He really did want to spend time with her. 'Aren't you worried about being stopped?'

'Stopped? Who by? This is the countryside. There aren't any police. Come and have some coffee, anyway.'

She thought the coffee would be a good idea, but of course when the moment came she found herself persuaded into a brandy, and they talked on for another hour, by which time Kate knew she was neither going to Taunton nor doing any work. All she wanted was to get her head down and have a snooze.

'I'm going home,' she answered firmly to all his beguilements and offers of alternative entertainments. 'This has been a wonderful lunch, but I really am going home.'

'I'll drive you.'

'It's only up the road, and I need the walk.'

'I'll walk with you.'

'No you won't. Really, thank you for everything, but no. You ought to take that poor dog for a walk. He's been lying about all afternoon waiting for you.'

'He's all right. Sleeping is his best thing. All right, if you're really sure this is it–' he gave in to her slightly squiffy firmness – 'I'll let you go.'

'*Let* me?' she queried, but he didn't seem to hear her.

'But I will see you again? Let me take you out

to dinner. What about Friday? Oh, no, wait, I can't do Friday. Saturday – what are you doing Saturday evening?'

She wished for dignity's sake she could say she was busy, but she hesitated just too long to lie convincingly. 'Well...'

'Good. Saturday evening, dinner. Do you like dancing? There's a dinner dance at the Country Club in Liscombe.'

'A dinner dance? I didn't think they still had such things!'

'You're in the countryside now,' he said, pretending to be offended. 'We may be a little behind the times but that's no reason to mock.'

'I don't have anything remotely suitable for a dinner dance,' she said.

'It's not as posh as it sounds. You don't need a long dress. Didn't you bring your London clothes with you?'

'Look, let's save time – are you going to take no for an answer on this one?'

'No. I'll wear you down with argument.'

'All right, rather than being worn down, I'll say yes – if you promise it isn't posh.'

'Not a bit posh. I'll pick you up at seven thirty.'

'I haven't told you my address,' she said, for just the fact of having a date again had thrown her back into a London mindset.

One eyebrow went up. 'Little's Cottage,' he reminded her.

'Oh, yes. I suppose you would know where that was,' she said.

'Considering my stepmother used to own it,' he said, and for a moment there was something unexpectedly grim about his expression as he said it.

When she got home, she sat on her bed to take off her sandals, and then it looked so inviting that she lay down, just for an instant, just while she sorted out her whirling thoughts, and the next thing she knew she was waking up and the sky was streaked with red outside. She struggled up, feeling as if all her senses were smothered in a blanket – and her tongue was made of one. She looked at her watch. It was well after seven. Too late to go to Morrison's now, not that she really needed a meal tonight, after that lunch. Oddly, though, her first thought was that she was hungry. What was it about food, that the more you ate, the more you wanted? Drink, though – she was never going to drink again. Ever in her life. That brandy was a mistake. Not that she'd been drunk, she excused herself hastily. Only pleasantly relaxed.

Omigod, Jack Blackmore! Had she made a fool of herself ? She'd been very relaxed with him – too relaxed? He was obviously well-off, from a prominent County family, and charming to boot. Why had he been interested in her? Not that she hadn't had dates with high-powered men before, in London, but she wasn't exactly showing herself to London standards here, in a cotton skirt, T-shirt and sandals and minimal make-up. Was it just that she was new? Did he have a crack at all fresh blood when it appeared? She could believe that of him. Divorced and sexy man on the loose, naturally he'd try out any eligible female who crossed his path.

But it hadn't felt like that. That was the trouble. They had got on so well. And he had asked her out again. Had been quite determined about it. He seemed really to like her...

She shook her head to clear it. First, a very large mug of tea. And second, a long soak in a bath. Sleeping in your clothes made you feel so grubby. Maybe she'd take the tea into the bath with her. And the telephone. It was a while since she'd phoned the girls. And she definitely needed to run Blackjack past another female of dating age.

'You sly boots!' Jess exclaimed. 'I thought you weren't going on the pull while you were down there!'

'Well, I'm not actually dead, you know,' Kate observed. 'And when it's thrown into your lap like that...'

'Yes, why was it?' came Lauren's dry voice. She was on the other handset so they could all hear each other.

'Why not?' retorted loyal Jess. 'It's our Kate we're talking about. She's gorgeous.'

'I wasn't *looking* particularly gorgeous,' she admitted. 'Dirty nails, grubby, curling plasters, and my hair dragged back in a scrunchie.'

'Well, maybe he likes the natural look,' Jess said. 'A sophisticated man might get tired of always having women in full warpaint and all the trimmings.'

'A lunch of bread and cheese as a rest from all that caviar and lobster, you mean?' Kate said solemnly. 'What on earth will I wear to the dinner dance – a sack?'

Lauren cut through this. '*Is* he sophisticated?'

'He's the son of Sir George Blackmore, who owned most of Bursford and the surrounding countryside.'

'Owned?'

'Well, Sir George is dead now.'

'And who owns it now?'

'I don't know,' Kate admitted. 'I believe Jack's the younger son. Not absolutely sure, but I think the brother, Edward, is the elder.'

'So presumably he inherited, and it doesn't follow that Jack is rich at all,' said logical Lauren.

'He *looks* rich,' Kate said feebly. Some nice clothes and cash in the wallet didn't really mean anything; nor did buying an expensive lunch and champagne. He looked the sort who would always do himself well, whatever his circumstances. And – she had a sudden horrid thought – what about the divorce? Surely he'd be in for massive alimony and maintenance? But perhaps living back at home meant he had few other expenses. 'Anyway,' she said, pulling herself together, 'you didn't ask if he was rich, you asked if he was sophisticated.'

'And is he?'

'Coming from that sort of family he's bound to be,' Jess said. 'Private school, country club, moving in the best circles.'

'But he seemed very down-to-earth and nice,' Kate said. 'Not at all "County", just – nice.' It sounded inadequate, and it was. 'He was really worried about his little boy's dog. And the dog – it's a big hairy mongrel, not some pampered Crufts' winner.'

'Oh, Kate,' Lauren sighed, 'be careful. The way you're defending him, it sounds as if you're smitten.'

'I am not!' Kate objected. 'I enjoyed his company, that's all.'

'Well, he sounds like trouble to me,' Lauren said. 'Divorced with a child, just for starters. Where would you fit in to that scenario?'

Kate laughed. 'I'm not planning to marry him, just go out to dinner with him.'

'He's already moved you in one encounter from lunch to dinner. Where else is it going to lead? You say he's good-looking, charming, flashes his money around, drinks a lot, gets you to drink a lot. What's he after, Kathleen Marie Jennings? You have to ask yourself that.'

'Maybe he just likes my company too,' she said, and this time it didn't sound feeble. 'And I appreciate your concern, but don't worry about me. I can handle it. I'm not falling for him, or anyone. I'm not going there, not after Mark. Not for a very long time. If ever.'

'Oh, don't say "if ever",' Jess objected with concern. 'You're lovely. You can't be wasted. That mustn't happen.'

'All right,' Kate agreed, 'but if I fall for anyone it's going to be a town man with London smarts. The County set doesn't appeal to me. And Mr Right'll have a hot job and a gorgeous flat. Jack Blackmore lives with his mum, for goodness' sake! And now,' she went on, reaching forward to add some more hot water to the bath, 'given that we all agree I'm not in any danger, let's talk about you two. What's on your horizons? Any new men? How is it working out with Marta?'

Kate went to bed early and woke early, to a fine sunny day with a near-cloudless sky. Just perfect for getting up on the roof and repointing the chimney, she told herself, leaping out of bed. She felt fine, not a hint of hangover – thanks, she felt, to the fine quality of the champagne – but she was ravenously hungry. She dragged on her clothes and hurtled downstairs to the kitchen, only to realize, as she opened the fridge, that she hadn't been shopping yesterday so there was nothing to eat. The bread was down to the last crust, she'd had the last of the milk the night before, and all there was otherwise was half a packet of water biscuits and a tin of tomato soup.

As she stared in dismay, feeling like Mother Hubbard, her stomach growled noisily, and as if summoned by the incantation, Kay appeared at the back door with an enquiring look on her face.

'Hello! You all right?'

'Yes, I'm fine. Why shouldn't I be?'

'Well, Dommie and me came over when he got back from school and you was spark out on your bed. He wanted to wake you but since you didn't wake when I called up the stairs, I reckoned you were out for the count, so I shut him up and took him away.' She grinned. 'Had a bit of a heavy lunch, did you? *Two* bottles of champagne?'

Kate gave up on ever having any privacy in a village. 'How on earth do you know?'

'Ken over the Blue Ball told Dave at the Oak, he told Denny Foss and Denny told Darren. You can't have secrets in a place like this. Jack Blackmore – you're doing well for yourself!'

'He's nice,' Kate said defensively.

'I told you so, didn't I? Told you he was a laugh. Told you he was a shocking flirt, too, as I remember.'

'You did. Forewarned is forearmed,' said Kate.

'Ken said something about a dog?' said Kay, her face wide open with curiosity.

'Oh, it was nothing. I rescued his dog, or his son's dog, that's all.'

'No! When was this? You never told me! Oh–' she distracted herself – 'I got to get their breakfasts, or I'd get you to tell me the whole story.' She examined Kate's expression, the one that been summoned by the word 'breakfast'. 'You all right. Got a hangover?'

'No, I'm fine, just ravenously hungry.'

Kay smiled. 'Come on over ours and have breakfast with us, then you can tell me all about it. Bacon and eggs?' she added temptingly.

Kate groaned. 'I'd love bacon and eggs. But you're not to do it just for me.'

'Kidding me? Got to give my Darren a good breakfast before he goes off to work, haven't I? A man can't do a full day's work on a bit o' toast or a bowl o' cereal. And come to think of it, you're doing a man's work, aren't you? So you need it too.'

Kate needed no more persuasion. Soon she was at the table in the Tonkins' kitchen, telling the whole story over a plate of eggs, bacon, chipolatas and baked beans, accompanied by copious tea and toast. Darren asked questions about exactly where the gorse bush was, until he had pinpointed the site of the adventure to his satisfaction. Kay was far more interested in Kate and Jack and how well they had got on and whether Jack was enough over his divorce to be looking for another wife.

Dommie listened for as long as he could, but he had far more important things to talk to Kate about, and eventually the dam broke and his flood of conversation overwhelmed everything else until Darren rose from the table and said he'd better be gettin' on, and Kay began to fret about getting the children off to school. Kate made herself useful by washing the children's hands and faces and keeping them chatting while Kay got their things ready, and then the two households parted, and Kate went home to keep her appointment with the roof and the chimney.

Eight

It was a lovely day to be up on the roof, warm, and dry underfoot and with no wind. Her first task was to clean out the gutters with a trowel and inspect them. They were not in the first flush of youth, but they would do for another year or two, so they were not her problem. Then she walked about the roof and examined it thoroughly. It was slate, and she guessed it was about thirty or forty years old, but a slate roof would last fifty years or more, and this one was in pretty good shape, so again it would not be her problem when the time came. There was one slipped slate, but it was an easy job to push that back into position and put another nail in.

The chimney obviously had to face a lot of weather, and the pointing on two sides needed redoing. Also the flaunching was breaking down and needed replacing, and one or two ridge tiles needed re-bedding. Altogether a nice, manageable job for a fine day. And pointing was a satisfying task, a bit like icing a cake, with something to show for it at the end. She went back down to mix herself up some three-to-one mortar, threw off her jumper, which she was not going to need, retied her hair more firmly out of the way, and went back up to work.

She worked steadily, looking up now and then to admire the view. From up here she could see a lot further over the moors. She could also see down over the village. She saw the stone cross sticking up from the gable of the old school; the Royal Oak's jumble of roofs and chimneys, and the top floor and roof of the Blue Ball opposite, giving rise to a few pleasant thoughts about Jack Blackmore, and some speculations, too, to keep her going. She could see the top of the old mill down the Stindsford road, and beyond it some high trees and the hint of chimneys just showing through them which she thought were probably those of The Hall.

When she had visited Bursford as a child she had had The Hall pointed out to her in passing as the 'big house' of the village – the place where 'the squire' lived. Of course, they didn't use those terms any more in this modern world, but she was glad at least that she had heard of it and knew where it was when Jack had mentioned it. Her memory from childhood was only of an old house of a largeness out of her experience, tall trees and many windows, and gateposts, which had seemed to her the apogee of grandness. No-one in her parents' or grandparents' circle had gateposts. The people who lived in The Hall were from another planet, as far as the child Kate had been concerned.

Well, now the adult Kate had had lunch with an inhabitant of Gatepostworld, and had a date with him into the bargain. She wouldn't, of course, be overwhelmed by the consideration, now she was grown up and sophisticated and had lived and worked in fast-paced London; but she couldn't help a little smirk of satisfaction and a wink towards the wide-eyed child she had been. She thought of Gaga, and how pleased she would be that her money was giving rise to new experiences for her granddaughter. *I must write to her tonight, and tell her about the lunch*, she thought. It would probably give her more pleasure than talk of flaunching and mortar and re-bedding tiles.

It really was a fine day, and it was beginning to get very hot up there on the slates. Kate wondered about sunburn – a fine thing to think of in England in May! She hoped she was going to be able to get the job done today. It was a nuisance that she had to remember she had no food in the house and mustn't leave it too late to go and do a shopping run. She had borrowed a bit of milk from Kay who, enquiring about the state of her commissariat, had also put her up a cheese sandwich for her lunch when she did the children's, so she was covered for lunchtime, at any rate. She began to feel very hungry, and looking at her watch, found it was half past twelve. Past time for a break.

She eased herself down the slope to the ladder, descended briskly, and went to wash her mortary hands in the bathroom. Glancing at her reflection in the mirror over the basin, she saw that she had caught the sun. She needed to be careful – it wouldn't do to go to the Country Club looking like a tomato. She rummaged about in one of the boxes until she found the remains of the suntan cream from her last holiday, and took it downstairs with her to put on after lunch.

She put the kettle on and made herself a big mug of tea, and then went outside and sat in the shade of the house on an upturned milk crate she had discovered in the tangle of the garden. The cheese sandwich was large and delicious – man-sized, just what she wanted – and blessed Kay had put in a couple of chocolate biscuits and a lump of cake as well. She'd save the cake for teatime, when she was bound to be peckish again. What it must be like to have a wife! she thought. Men didn't know how lucky they were. If *she* ever got married, all she'd get was a husband.

Lunch finished, she continued to sit, enjoying the wonderful smells of open air and green things, and listening to the birds. The tortoise-shell cat appeared, dissolved itself under the front gate and came mincing down the path towards her. It wiped its nose elegantly on her outstretched fingers, then settled down companionably a few feet away, just beyond the house-shadow, tail firmly tucked around its feet, squeezing its eyes blissfully in the sunshine.

It was all so peaceful; Kate felt extremely relaxed, and was in no hurry to call an end to lunchtime. Indeed must have nodded off for a minute, because she started awake as her head lolled forward, to find the cat had disappeared, and became aware of the sound of horse's hooves. It was the unmistakable thub-dub of un-shod hooves on the packed dirt of the track behind the house, and she stood up cautiously, expecting to see some of the wild ponies that used the track to take them from one grazing to another. She could only hear one set of hooves, but the others might be walking on the grass.

When the animal came into sight, it was indeed an Exmoor pony, with a dark bay coat, thick black mane and tail, and the typical mealy muzzle and eye patches; but it was no wild mare. It was beautifully groomed and glossy, was wearing a saddle and bridle, and was being ridden by a girl in a blue shirt, jodhpurs, and well-polished jodhpur boots. She looked about twelve or thirteen and had fair hair in a thick plait down her back, and a pretty, cheerful, freckled face.

Kate stood watching with pleasure, remembering the joy she had had riding at that age. Dad had been very horse minded, and had paid for riding lessons at O'Rourke's at Castleknock for Aileen and Kate – the others hadn't been interested. Aileen had given it up after a while, when she started to be interested in boys instead, but Kate had always loved it. When she visited Granny and Grandpa they arranged for her to go out riding from Langtrey's on Almsworthy Common. Sometimes Dad had gone with her – they were the most special times of all, when he shared with her his knowledge of Exmoor's history, flora and fauna. On ponyback you could get closer to all sorts of creatures than you could on foot, and could go so much further, and to places otherwise inaccessible.

She expected the girl to carry on past down the track towards the open moors, but instead she turned her mount firmly into School Lane and halted in front of Kate's garden gate as if that had been her destination all along.

'Hullo,' she said, fixing Kate with a solemn and perhaps slightly cautious eye. 'Can Daphne have a drink? Mrs Brown always used to give him a bucket of water if he needed it.'

Kate roused herself. 'Yes, of course. I'll have to wash the bucket out first – it's had mortar in it.' She got up, and tilted the bucket towards the girl to show her the remains.

The girl smiled, evidently relieved that Kate was disposed to be friendly, and said, 'Can I come and in and see what you're doing? They say you're doing up the cottage yourself. That must be fun.'

'It is. Hard work though.'

'I'd like to see how you've changed it. I used to come here a lot when Mrs Brown lived here. She was nice. She always used to invite me in.'

'You can come in and welcome, but there's not much to see yet. It's pretty bare.'

'What was the mortar for?'

'I was working on the roof this morning. Have to take advantage of a dry day.'

'You've caught the sun,' the girl observed, jumping down.

'Can you tie him up?' Kate wondered. The pony wasn't wearing a headcollar and she didn't think she had a piece of rope anywhere.

'I'll bring him in the garden and shut the gate,' said the girl. She looked round. 'There's nothing here he can hurt, really, is there?' she added with breezy self-confidence.

True, if slightly tactless, Kate thought. The girl led the pony through into the garden and shut the gate, and Kate went over to help by running up the stirrups. 'If you slip the end of the reins under one of them, they won't slip down where he can tread on them.'

'I know,' the girl said, but she looked at Kate with interest. 'You know about horses.'

'I used to ride,' Kate admitted. 'I thought you said his name was Daphne,' she admitted, patting the thick neck. The pony was already investigating what there was to eat in the tangle of the ground-cover. He shook himself as if shaking off her caress, and stamped a forefoot, but it was probably only a fly.

'I did – it is,' the girl said. 'You see, Ed bought him for me – my brother – because Chloe's a bit small for me now, and she doesn't like to jump, and *he* called him Daphnis, but Mummy said there was no such name and he must have meant Daphne, so that's what he got called after that.'

'Oh, Daphnis and Chloe – I get it!' Kate said.

'Do you?'

'The Greek story – the lovers, Daphnis and Chloe. Weren't they a shepherd and shepherdess?'

'That's what Ed told me. Mummy didn't get it. She said what was the point in knowing silly old stories like that if you couldn't even give a pony a proper name? Anyway, it was too late by then – the name stuck, and he's called Daphne. Except at shows, then we put him down as Daphnis because otherwise there's confusion over whether he's a mare or a gelding and it's a nuisance.'

'You show him, do you?'

'He's won loads of cups,' she said proudly. 'He's by Shilstone Zulu, the champion stallion, out of Sell Valley Doris – she was a champion too. And he jumps. We came third in the Junior Open at Little Buscombe last year.'

'Gosh,' said Kate, leading the way into the cottage. 'I didn't know I was in the presence of equine royalty.'

Inside, the girl stopped dead, and said, 'Oh, it looks so different with all the furniture gone! A bit sad, really. Mrs Brown lived here for years and years, and now there's nothing left.' Kate had nothing to say to this. The girl, staring around, went on cheerily, 'You've knocked the wall down. I like that. I can't believe how much lighter it looks.'

'Just getting rid of all that dark wallpaper made a difference,' Kate said.

'What else are you going to do?'

Kate told her a bit about her plans.

'It'll be so nice,' the girl said at last. 'Mummy will be ever so pleased.'

'Will she?' Kate said, passing with the bucket into the kitchen. 'Why is that?'

The girl stopped, and turned and looked at her. 'Oh. Don't you know who I am?'

'Well, I'm sort of guessing, but you haven't said yet.'

'Oh, sorry! Jolly rude of me. I'm Jocasta Blackmore. Mummy's Lady Blackmore – it was her you bought the cottage from.'

She stuck out her hand in a practised manner, and Kate shook it and said, 'I'm Kate Jennings.'

She scraped the last bit of mortar out of the

bucket – fortunately it was almost empty, and stuck it under the running tap to clean it. Jocasta watched, and said wistfully, 'Mrs Brown always used to give *me* a drink, too.'

'I'd be happy to oblige, but I'm afraid the only thing I can offer you is tea. I don't have anything else in the house.'

'I like tea,' Jocasta said happily. 'I didn't use to, but I started drinking it for breakfast instead of milk. Mummy says too much milk makes you fat.'

'You don't have to worry about that,' said Kate with a glance at the girl's slim, athlete's figure. 'Did Mrs Brown give you something to eat as well?'

'Well, usually. Cake or biscuits or something. But if you don't have anything...'

'I just happen to have a large piece of cake left over from lunch, that you're welcome to,' Kate said.

They took the bucket of water out to the pony while the kettle was boiling. He was head down, nosing among the weeds and eagerly tearing up mouthfuls, and seemed entirely indifferent to the water. Kate wondered if it had just been a ruse to get talking – not that she minded. When the tea was made she put the cake on a plate and they went out together to the front garden, Jocasta carrying one of the kitchen chairs, and they sat where Kate had been sitting, and watched the pony grazing as they drank their tea.

'He likes it because it's something new,' Jocasta said. 'I suppose it's a different taste.'

'The grass is always greener on the other side

of the fence,' Kate said.

'Is it?'

'It's a saying,' Kate explained. Amazing how these old bits of lore didn't get passed on any more.

'It's true,' Jocasta discovered. 'You always see cows with their silly heads stuck under the wire trying to get a bit of grass in the next field when there's perfectly good stuff on their own side. This is fab cake.'

'My next door neighbour made it. I was all out of food today, so she made me a sandwich for lunch, and put the cake in with it.'

'Oh, Kay, you mean. I know her. She's ever so nice. So why did you buy Little's?'

Kate explained she'd been left some money and had fancied a change – she left out the dating disasters from the story.

'I can't imagine ever being tired of London,' Jocasta said. 'There must be so much to do. I know Mummy would rather live there. She's always going up for the day, and she moans like anything when she comes back that she wishes she could have stayed.'

'Would you like to live there?'

'Well, maybe. Not all the time, because I do like riding and dogs and things. But I wouldn't mind some of the time.' She took another bite of the cake. 'There's been an awful fuss at home about Mummy selling Little's. Ed was mad as fire. Do you have any brothers?'

'No. I've got four sisters.'

'Five of you? That must be brilliant! I've always wanted a sister, but Daddy died when I was a baby so that was a washout. All I've got is two brothers, and they're really old,' she concluded gloomily.

'Aren't they nice?'

'Oh, I suppose they're all right, in a way, but it's not the same. Ed is so strict about everything, and he's always worrying about money, and he gets cross, and he and Mummy have terrible rows. Jack's all-right-ish. I mean, he's not strict like Ed, and he doesn't tell me off, but he's really embarrassing sometimes. He's so old, but he pretends to be young, which makes me squirm. He keeps going out with different girls, and some of them are my friends' sisters – God, it's embarrassing! I mean, why can't he just do old-people things instead of trying to be cool, which he *so* isn't? You should see him dancing! Honestly – gag!' She rolled her eyes.

Kate thought it was not the moment to reveal she was going to a dance with him on Saturday. Instead she asked what was more interesting to her. 'Why didn't Ed want your mother to sell Little's?'

'Because she's not supposed to sell any part of the estate. Daddy wanted it all kept together, because Grandpa had to sell so much of it because of death duties, and Ed feels the same. He hates the idea of letting anything go. When Daddy died, Ed thought it would all be left to him because he's the eldest, but instead Daddy left everything to Mummy for her lifetime. Ed says she's only supposed to spend the income from the estate, and not be able to sell anything, but apparently the way it was drawn up, the will and everything, there's a loophole or something. Anyway, it wasn't written down properly by the lawyers, so when Mummy needs more money, she sells something. She sold some paintings last year, and Ed made such a fuss, so she said this time she'd sell something no-one liked or wanted, which was Little's, because it wasn't a pretty cottage and no-one wanted to live in it. But Ed made even more fuss and said that selling real estate was even worse than selling chattels and if Mummy couldn't see that she was an imbecile and not fit to be in charge of a piggy bank.'

Kate saw the unhappy look on the girl's face, and thought she understood why she had paid this sudden visit, and why she was so eager to chat. She came from a divided household; and she was lonely. *I've always wanted a sister*.

'He didn't really say that?' she said.

Jocasta nodded. 'He was pretty mad,' she added in exculpation. 'And he apologized the minute he'd said it. But every time he comes down there seems to be a row. It's terribly boring.' She looked away as she said it. Not boring, Kate thought, but upsetting.

'What do you mean, when he comes down? Doesn't he live at The Hall?'

'Oh, yes, but he works in London. He's got his own company, and he's usually there in the week, three or four days, but he comes home for weekends because he's supposed to be running the estate for Mummy, and Jack runs the factory.'

'You have a factory?'

'Don't you know?' she exclaimed, opening her

eyes wide. 'Haven't you heard of Blackmore Tweed? It's famous all over the West Country, and it's sold in London and everything. We make all sorts of woollen cloth, lots of it from our own wool, but especially the tweed – even Mummy says it's beautiful, and she buys all her clothes in London.'

'I see. And Jack runs the factory,' she said thoughtfully.

'He's supposed to,' Jocasta said casually, 'but I think it probably runs itself, because he doesn't seem to go there very often. He's always messing around and having fun. *That* makes Ed mad, too.' She sighed. 'Everything seems to make Ed mad these days.'

'Poor Ed,' Kate said absently.

'Poor Jocasta,' the girl retorted vigorously. 'Stuck in the middle of it.'

'Yes, that must be tiring,' Kate said.

Jocasta warmed with the sympathy. 'I say, you could come riding with me! I don't mind having Chloe if you want Daphne. Though you're so small and thin you could probably ride Chloe if you wanted. She's only eleven-two, but Exmoor ponies are very strong. They can carry big heavy men, and keep going all day.'

'Shouldn't you be at school?' Kate remembered belatedly.

'Half term,' she said promptly. 'We finished yesterday, and we get all next week and go back the day after Bank Holiday. Wouldn't you like a ride?'

'I'd love it, but you'd better ask your mother first. She might not like you lending a pony to a complete stranger.'

'Well, you've bought her house, so you're not really a stranger. You're practically family. That was really good cake,' she added wistfully, wiping up the last crumbs with a forefinger.

'I'm afraid that's it. I only had the one piece,' said Kate.

'Oh well, I better be going. Daphne doesn't like stopping for long.' The pony was contentedly grazing, but Kate had an idea that Jocasta was belatedly feeling some social embarrassment, though whether for having revealed family secrets or for having eaten all the cake herself, she couldn't tell.

They stood up, and Jocasta caught the pony, pulled down the stirrups, and led it out of the gate, which Kate held open for her and closed behind her. She leaned on the gate while Jocasta checked the girth and mounted. The pony chewed its bit and flirted its ears back and forth, swishing the luxuriant black tail against early flies.

'Thanks for the water,' the girl said when she was settled. 'And the tea and everything.'

'You're welcome. Drop in any time.'

A heartfelt look of gratitude. 'Would you like to go riding next week?' Jocasta asked: her *quid pro quo* of hospitality, the one thing she had to offer.

'If your mother says it's all right,' said Kate.

'Oh, she will. She doesn't care what I do,' the child said scornfully.

Poor kid, Kate thought. 'Well, I'd love to,' she said.

Her reward was a brilliant smile. Jocasta gathered the reins and turned the pony. 'Great. I'll see you, then.'

'By the way,' Kate said on a last thought, 'your name – quite unusual. Did your mother choose it?'

Jocasta nodded. 'She just thought it sounded nice,' she said indifferently. With a wave of the hand she trotted away, turned on to the dirt track, put the eager pony into a canter, and was soon out of sight.

Jocasta: the queen of Thebes who notoriously married her own son, Oedipus, after he had killed her husband, his father. Quite some personality to be named after. But it sounded nice.

Yes, thought Kate, another thing Lady Blackmore 'didn't get'.

Nine

Kate gave quite some thought to what to wear on Saturday night. It was all very well for Jack to say not to worry, it wouldn't be very smart, but the words 'country club' and 'dinner dance' had never been thrown at her wardrobe before, and they were finding no resonance there. It didn't help that all her clothes bar the working ones were still in boxes.

It also didn't help that Kay was in a ferment of excitement about it. 'Ooh, it's ever so glamorous! All the nobs belong to the country club. I've waitressed there once or twice when they had big do's and needed extra staff. You'll have a lovely time, but sooner you than me. It's so posh I'd be so nervous I'd be knocking my glass over and dropping my fork every two minutes! What're you going to wear?'

Ah yes, what? Her little clubbing numbers wouldn't strike the right note, she felt. Jack had said you didn't have to wear a long dress, but she doubted that meant you could wear skirts so short that they were a mere pelmet to your thighs. She had longer things, but they weren't very special.

'I'm sure anything that's good enough for London will be good enough for sleepy old Liscombe,' Kay said loyally, with an abrupt reversal that did not fill Kate with confidence.

Eventually she chose her 'little black dress', as Lauren had always jokingly called it, reasoning that you could never go far wrong with black. At least, you couldn't be criticized for it – could you? It was short, but not ultra-short, the skirt ending just above the knees. It was of a clingy, shiny material that looked like satin but wasn't, and it was a good thing that a couple of weeks of hard work on the house had worked off any spare fat she had, because there wasn't room in there for anything but her basic body and a skintight pair of pants. It was sleeveless and low-plunging at the back, so she couldn't wear a bra with it, making it one of the few occasions she was glad of her lack of boobs. She paired it with glossy sheer black tights and strappy black heels, and relied on having her hair down to provide relief from all that monochrome.

'What do you think?' she asked Kay, who had come over – again – specifically to inspect her outfit.

'You'll catch the eye in that lot,' Kay said, which was not entirely reassuring. 'You got any jewellery? It's a bit plain, maybe.'

'I've got these earrings.' She got them out. They were shiny, faceted black drops, only plastic, but they looked like jet if you didn't get too close. And she explained about having her hair down.

'You'll look *lovely*!' Kay said with the sort of emphasis with which you tell a child going to the dentist won't hurt. 'And I tell you what, why don't you come over ours to dress? You can use our bathroom, and I've got this posh bath essence Darren bought me for Christmas. And I can help you with your hair. I've got these 'lectric curlers that'll take the frizz out lovely.'

A bit of comfort, a decent mirror and a bathroom that didn't have bare floorboards were more temptation than Kate could resist. It took a long soaking and some vigorous work with a scrubbing brush to get rid of all the building dirt, and Kay produced some Norwegian hand cream that Darren used when he worked outside in the winter to induce something like smoothness in the poor abused appendages. She washed her hair and used a special de-frizzing serum afterwards, and Kay proved very adept with the curling iron, and produced smooth, shiny curling tresses that Kate adored. Sitting in front of Kay's dressing-table mirror she said, 'Thank God it's been dry all day. One breath of damp air and it's back to coconut matting.'

'It's dry tonight,' Kay reassured her. 'You're lucky having such lovely-coloured hair. It looks great with the black. You hardly need anything else.'

'That was my hope,' Kate said. 'Because diamonds have I none.'

It was strange after all this time getting out her make-up bag and putting on her London war-paint. Kay watched in admiration until Kate stabbed herself in the eye with the mascara brush and said she was making her nervous. 'Can't have that,' said Kay, and disappeared.

Kate finished the job, hooked the hair back

from her face with two sparkly clips, and added the final touch – a black sequin neck band in place of the diamond choker she also didn't have. She stood up and looked at herself in the wardrobe full-length mirror. She looked taller, slim (*won't be able to eat much tonight*, she thought, sucking in her stomach) and dramatic, with her hair, like flames around her shoulders, the only contrast to all the black. She looked – dangerous.

Very well, she thought. *Let the games commence*.

Kay came back in with something in her hand, and stopped on the threshold. 'Well!' she said. And then, *'Well!'*

Kate gave her an uncertain smirk in the mirror. 'God, I hope so! What do you think – really?'

'You'll knock their eyes out. Here, I brought you this. Can't have you being nervous.' It was a tumbler of clear liquid. Kate looked the question. 'Vodka,' Kay explained. 'Doesn't smell. It's left over from Christmas,' she added warningly, as if it might have gone off. 'I like a vodka and lime at a party. Darren only drinks beer.'

Kate sipped cautiously. It was pure spirit, unsullied by tonic, ice, lemon or any other contaminant. She coughed. 'It's strong,' she said. 'I can't drink all this.'

'Have a swig, anyway,' Kay urged. 'Put you in the mood.'

Obediently Kate took the smallest swig she thought would satisfy her kind hostess, and passed the glass back. 'I'll have the rest,' Kay said. 'I'm that nervous, I need it more than you.'

She knocked it back, and went into a paroxysm of coughing, and had to sit on the bed and blow her nose to recover herself.

'Right,' she croaked when she was herself again. 'I've done my bit. The rest is up to you.'

'Off you go to the ball, Cinderella,' Kate said with a grin.

'But remember to be back by midnight, or your coach will turn into a pumpkin,' Kay said, entering into the spirit.

'Or in my case,' said Kate, 'be back before it rains, or my hair will turn into a giant orange Brillo pad.'

Jack was ten minutes late, which was plenty of time for Kate – in her own house and not daring to sit down in case she dirtied her dress or laddered her tights – to become nervous all over again. She heard the car pull up outside, the garden gate squeak (useful noise that – she must remind herself not to oil it) and then came the rap on the door. She opened it to find Jack outside in a navy overcoat with what looked suspiciously like a black bow-tie peeping out at the neck, his hair artfully tousled, and saw over his shoulder an entirely beautiful dark-blue Jaguar XJ parked in front of her garden wall, which took her mind off everything for an instant.

Jack looked at her and whistled. 'My God, you look *stunning*!' he said, gratifyingly. Kate tried not to smirk like a ten-year-old. 'I want to eat you *up*!' He leaned in towards her and instead of attempting the kiss she was expecting he nibbled her ear and said into it, breathily, 'I want a Kate sandwich. Kate caviar. God, you're entirely edible.' He straightened up. 'Do we have to go to this damned thing? Let's stay here and enjoy our own company.'

Kate laughed. 'In the first place, do you really think I spent all those agonizing hours getting myself to look like this, not to be seen by anyone?'

'You'll be seen by me. Anyway, how could it take hours – you're naturally beautiful.'

'Gallant,' Kate acknowledged, 'but I've spent the last two days up on the roof and the last two weeks knocking down walls and stripping wallpaper. From that to this, without use of a magic wand, takes hard work.'

'I'm too much of a gentleman to allow any effort was involved. What was your second point?'

'Second point? Oh, yes – stay here? Have you looked around you? The state of it? It's impossible to enjoy yourself in this house.'

'I'm sure I'd think of a way,' he said suggestively.

Kate felt a quick stab in her stomach at the thought, but did not allow it to show. 'No,' she said imperiously. 'Country Club. Now. Once my warpaint's on, it doesn't come off again until I've killed a paleface. Out!'

Jack grinned. 'I love this dominatrix bit. I'm putty in your hands.'

'I should hope so,' she said, picking up the black pashmina that had to do service as overcoat – it was that or a padded anorak. They went out into the evening, and, closing the door behind her, she dropped the act for a moment and said nervously, 'Jack, really, do I look all right? I've never been to this sort of thing before.'

'You'll cause a sensation,' Jack said sincerely. He went before her to open gate and car door, which he held open with a bow. 'Your carriage awaits, madam.'

He seemed in a merry mood all the way to Liscombe. She wondered if he'd had a few before picking her up, because he kept smiling to himself, and humming when they were not talking – which was most of the time, because having asked her how the building work was going, he seemed to have no more questions or observations once she'd finished the subject. The drive was through dark country lanes so there wasn't anything to look at, except the section of road thrown up by the headlights, and the occasional rabbit dashing out of the way (which kept her in a state of nerves, dreading to feel the soft jolt under the wheels if one of them didn't make it). Now the only thing she could think of to say was, 'Are we nearly there yet?' She looked at his hands on the wheel – he drove well, a bit fast for her taste, but country people always did on lanes they knew – and glanced at his profile, and had a little shiver. He was very attractive, and definitely all man.

She wasn't sure, all of a sudden, what she was getting herself into. A man like him – full grown and full of confidence – would surely expect more than a peck on the cheek at the end of the evening, and she wasn't sure how she felt about that. Certainly she fancied him, but she had not come to Exmoor to get herself involved in anything – the very opposite! Further, she thought of her chaotic living arrangements and her desperately spartan, unerotic bedroom. Perhaps that, and the fact that he lived with his mum, would keep her safe. Avoiding the occasion of sin, the Church called it: in her case, avoiding any suitable venue for sin.

As against which, he *was* very attractive...

Finally he slowed and said, 'Here we are,' and turned in at a gateway (*more gateposts – oh, Kate, we are going up in the world!*). He drove up a steep, curving drive, and suddenly a brightly-lit building appeared from behind the high-banked foliage. The Country Club was housed in a building called The Grange, a large, long, three-storey building that must once have been a country house: nineteenth century, white-painted, with a classical porch, a creeper growing over the face, and many lighted windows. On the wide gravelled area in front of it cars were parked and parking, and people were getting out and walking towards the open, lighted doorway. Kate felt her heart sink. The house looked grand, but what was grander was that all the women she could see were wearing fur coats. Not a pashmina amongst them.

She turned to Jack, who was concentrating on backing into a parking space. 'What have you got me into?' she asked.

'You'll be fine,' he said. 'Why the fuss?'

'Fur coats,' she said in a choked voice.

'They won't be wearing them indoors,' he pointed out. 'What's a fur coat, anyway? You're not going to go all Animal Lib on me, are you? Mink are thoroughly nasty creatures, and these ones have been dead for decades anyway. Most of those people inherited their furs from their mothers and grandmothers.'

Kate had to laugh. 'And that's what you consider reassurance, is it? Lead on, Macduff. I'm ready for the fray.'

'It's "lay on, Macduff", actually,' Jack corrected her politely.

'But I want you to lead, not lay.'

'Well, one step at a time, I suppose,' he murmured with a wicked smile.

Fortunately they hit the entrance hall at a moment of lull, and there were no other guests there as they shed their outer layers at the cloakroom counter, presided over by an elderly woman in a black maid's uniform, who looked as though she'd been doing it all her life.

Jack was in dinner suit and black tie. Kate was staring at him, silenced by exasperation, when he said politely, 'Do you need to use the ladies' room?'

'What's the point?' she said. 'Let's get it over with.'

He looked hurt. 'Get it over with? That's not exactly enthusiastic.'

'You said it wouldn't be posh. And here you are in black tie.'

'I said it wasn't as posh as it sounded. And you can't dance in a lounge suit. It looks silly.'

'Well, the only thing posher than black tie that I can think of is white tie!'

He laughed. 'Black tie's not posh any more.

You've only got to think of cruises. Come on, Cinderella. You look staggeringly beautiful, and I'm looking forward to making an entrance with you on my arm. Everyone will be staring at us in envy.'

She was touched by his words, straightened herself, put her hand through his offered elbow, and walked with him towards the door of the main room, from which the sound of muted music and conversation were issuing.

Well, he was half right. Everyone did stare (at least, it felt like everyone to Kate). The room was full of dinner-suited men, most of them middle-aged or older, with well-fed figures, greying or missing hair, and necks that bulged a little over their collars, and women of the same age in long dresses and mid-length cocktail frocks, permed hair, and suspiciously glittery jewellery. Jack squeezed her hand against his ribs (she wondered afterwards if he'd been afraid she'd run away and was keeping a grip on her) and started leading her up to groups – who greeted him by name, obviously knowing him very well – and introducing her. Kate fielded so many long stares, she felt as though she were naked. On the plus side, she noted a great many male stomachs being abruptly sucked in; on the minus, this was so obviously not her milieu that she really passionately wished she had an apron and a tray – she'd have felt happier that way.

But everyone greeted her kindly, and at one point, between tables as they worked their way down the room, Jack said, 'Don't worry about all the wrinkles and mothballs. We won't be the only under sixties. The younger set always arrives a bit late.'

'I was beginning to wonder,' Kate said.

'Our table's down the other end – the young end,' he said. And it was true, the average age did seem to be coming down as they got further from the door: they seemed to be among the thirties and forties now. 'The older set likes to stay up that end,' Jack explained. 'Nearer the loos.'

He really did seem to know everyone – and to be liked by everyone. People said hello to her kindly, but at once began chatting to Jack on people and topics she knew nothing about, so could add nothing to. Their table was the last but one before the stage, on which the band was playing quiet background music to establish the mood. It was round, and set for eight, but there was only one couple sitting there, late-thirties, very smart, the man lean-faced and prosperous-looking, busy talking into a mobile phone, the woman with enamelled make-up, perfect short blonde hair, wearing layered eau-de-nil chiffon and texting with rapid double-thumb movements.

'Steph, Gil, put those horrible things away,' Jack said cheerily. 'Nobody does business on a Saturday night.'

The man only waved a distracted hand and kept talking, but the woman paused and looked up with hard eyes and said, 'Rubbish, darling. The world never sleeps. Gil's talking to Dubai.'

'It's midnight there,' Jack said, with – to Kate – frightening knowledge. 'The markets are closed.'

'But the office isn't. Hello, Jack, darling. Lovely to see you. Kiss kiss.' He leaned over her and they air-kissed twice. 'And who is *this*?'

Kate felt herself raked up and down by the all-seeing eyes and bristled inwardly.

'This is Kate Jennings. She ate up London and spat it out, and now she's recharging her batteries in Bursford before going back into the fray,' Jack said. 'Kate, this is Stephanie Holland, and the boor on the telephone is her husband Gil. We went to school together. He never had any manners, even then.'

Gil smiled and waved a hand – the insults were obviously a part of their usual badinage – and carried on talking, but Stephanie stood up to shake Kate's hand and said, unexpectedly kindly, 'Call me Steph, I hate Stephanie. God, I wish I could wear something that tight! You look terrific. Come and sit by me and tell me how Jack met you. I must say you're wasted on him. Sorry about my husband. He'll be human again once he's tied up the sale. Dubai's talking to New York, you see, and if he doesn't do the deal, someone else will.'

Kate nodded as if this made perfect sense to her, told Steph briefly what she was doing on Exmoor, and heard in return how Steph had two children and bred Manchester terriers. 'I used to have a high-powered job too,' she explained. 'In fact, that's how I met Gil – we worked for the same company. So if I didn't have something to do I'd go nuts. Hence the doggies. They use up my slack. What did you do in London?'

'PR,' Kate said, and since Steph seemed

interested, she told her best stories and made PR sound like the most interesting job in the world – which she had sometimes found it to be. Gradually the table filled up, and the noise level rose. The other couples were reruns of Gil and Steph, though unlike them they weren't married and didn't have children; but they were extremely smart, obviously well-heeled, and all knew each other and everyone else. It was the County Set at play.

Kate had the same conversation over and over, answering the same questions about who she was, where she came from, and how she knew Jack. Jack had disappeared, was still working the room: she caught sight of him from time to time, always the centre of a loud, laughing group. He came back to refill her glass with a seemingly unlimited stream of champagne, pressed a hand on her shoulder or patted her cheek, and was gone again. The younger set had turned up and filled this end of the room, and wherever the noise was greatest and the fun liveliest, there would be a glimpse of Jack's unruly, toffee-coloured hair and his laughing face.

Only when the waiting staff started to appear with food did he come back to the table, slid into the seat beside Kate, and simultaneously slid a hand over her leg just above the knee. 'God, I love the feeling of sheer stockings!' he said into her ear. 'Having a nice time, my darling?'

Kate smiled. 'Yes, except that the person I came with seems to have disappeared, which makes it a bit awkward.'

'Ungrateful bastard!' Jack exclaimed. 'How

could he be such a mug as to abandon the loveliest girl in the room? Never mind, I'll grab my chance and his seat and entertain you instead.'

'Oh, yes, and who are you again?' Kate said. She wasn't quite ready to forgive him.

'I am Jack and I am contrite,' he said, laying his hand over hers and squeezing it. 'I'm sorry, I shouldn't have thrown you in the deep end like that, and I wouldn't have done it if I hadn't known you were more than capable of swimming, and if I hadn't *really* had to talk to all those people. It was work, you understand.'

'It didn't look like work,' Kate observed.

'That's what I do – you should understand, having been in PR. I have to make everyone like me, for the sake of the family business. But it's all done now. I promise I shan't leave you again.' He leaned closer and murmured in her ear. 'I must say I'm looking forward to the dancing. I'm longing to put my arms round you, you gorgeous creature.'

The man on her other side addressed her at that moment and she turned to him to answer his question. He was a nice, polite, but rather bland man who was an analyst in the bond market. She asked him what exactly that entailed and he explained it to her in some detail. Afterwards she still hadn't any idea what he did. By the time she turned back to Jack, he was deep in conversation with his other neighbour, a sparky and rather plump young woman in a dress so décolleté, it left little to the imagination. Kate wondered what it must be like to have the sort of bosoms that men looked down on, and addressed herself to her starter of pâté and toasted brioche.

Between courses there were lengthy hiatuses, during which the band played and people got up to dance. It also gave the opportunity for people to change seats so as to be able to talk to someone different, which Kate thought a good idea, making for variety. When the band struck up after the starter, Jack leaned over and said, 'Inter-course break. Shall we dance, oh blessed houri?'

He half rose and began to pull back her chair for her; but before the action was complete, Gil was at her side, had taken her hand and was bowing over it, lifting her to her feet and smiling in a way that quite transformed his dark, rather grim face. 'May I?' he said. 'You don't want to dance with Jack – he has two left feet.'

She let him lead her away, giving a smiling backward glance at her thwarted escort and thinking *serves you jolly well right*. He gave her an agreeably miffed look, and hurried to claim Steph's hand before anyone else did.

'If you're serious about that,' she said to Gil, 'it's rather ungallant of you to abandon your wife to him.'

'Just this once,' Gil assured her. 'Steph will be all right. She breeds terriers. She's used to handling unruly animals.'

Kate laughed, and said, 'You two insult each other so much, you must be really good friends.'

'Oh, Jack and I go way back. He's a really good sort. Heart of solid gold. Unfortunately he hasn't got the head to match.'

'Really?'

'Brain like honeycomb. Or, wait, what's that stuff – polystyrene packing? You know how when you try to grab hold of it, it breaks up and crumbles into little beads?'

'Not a good businessman?' Kate hazarded.

'The very worst. He hasn't his equal. Luckily, it doesn't really matter. He has an office and a secretary at the factory where he can go and play at being the big executive, but it's Phil Kingdon who does the work, and Phil's got a mind like a steel trap. What Jack does best is talking to people – as you've probably noticed.'

'I have,' Kate said drily.

'Don't underestimate it,' Gil said seriously. 'It's an important part of the business. He gets the brand known, builds up affection and loyalty for it, schmoozes the customers, brings light and warmth to the darkness.'

'Smooths down ruffled feathers when there are complaints?' Kate hazarded.

'There aren't too many of those,' said Gil. 'It's a pretty tight operation. But, yes, he does that. And I'll tell you another thing – part of the reason they can charge such a high price is down to Jack making people *want* to buy from Blackmore's, simply because they like him.'

'Well, thank you for the commercial,' Kate said, with a smile to show it was pleasantly meant.

Gil smiled too. 'I don't know what I'm doing, wasting my time with you talking about another man. Let's talk about *us*.'

'Is there an us?'

'I wish! Tell me how you get into that dress. Do you actually have to melt yourself down and pour yourself in, or is there some kind of devilish machine? I'm imagining something like a giant power-driven shoehorn.'

Kate began to enjoy herself.

It was pleasant to discover that she was very much in demand, both to dance with, and to be sat next too. Every time she was taken back to the table, someone else was waiting to whisk her away. Sometimes she didn't get as far as the table. As a result, she didn't see much of Jack. They saluted each other in passing when they happened to dance near each other, but it was not until after the sweet course that he hurried up, grabbed her hand, and said, '*My* turn! I don't care what promises you've made, I'm dancing with you now.'

'What a cave man you are. Are you going to drag me away by my hair?'

'Do I need to?'

'No, I'll come quietly. It took me hours to get it to look like this, I don't want the risk of it coming off in your hand.'

On the dance floor he put his arm round her waist and said, 'I warn you, I'm the world's worst dancer.'

'So I've heard.'

'Who told you?' He pretended indignation.

'I have my sources. And actually, I've been watching you.'

'Ah. Well, do you mind if we just walk?'

'Sounds good to me.'

Luckily it was a slowish number, so they just rocked from foot to foot, not moving very far. He hummed the tune, and sang a phrase into her ear.

'You have a nice voice,' she said.

'Church choir since the age of eight.' Kate was pleasantly surprised. It didn't seem to accord with the bad-boy image he seemed eager to establish. 'Are you having a nice time yet?' he asked.

'Actually, I am,' Kate said. 'It's flattering to have so many men want to dance with me.'

'It's that dress,' said Jack. 'Word's gone out that you can feel *everything* through it.' She punched him on the arm. 'Hey, that hurt. I was joking.'

'You weren't.'

'I didn't mean it in an unflattering way. And anyway, the dress would be nothing if you weren't interesting to talk to. Everyone keeps telling me how fascinating you are.'

'Fascinating?' she said derisively. 'What is this, nineteen-twenty?'

'I mean it. There are a lot of good-looking people in this room, a lot of smart ones, a lot of rich ones, a lot with high-powered jobs, big houses and bodies that owe everything to the gym and private instructor. But you can count the ones who are interesting to talk to on the fingers of one hand.'

'Well, thank you,' she said, and bestowed a kiss on his cheek.

He pulled back his head to look gaugingly into her eyes, and then kissed her back, on the lips. It was not a mere peck. Maybe it had been meant to be, but it lingered, and Kate felt various bits of her melting. He was a *seriously* good kisser. She broke off at last, and said, 'Hey! A person has to breathe now and then.'

'What a pity,' he said with a sinuous smile. 'Maybe you could learn a way to breathe and kiss simultaneously. It's a shame to waste a talent like that.'

Ten

Kate woke with the sun on her face, reminding her that she had not pulled the curtains last night. Reaching for her watch she discovered it was only just after six, and she turned over and snuggled back down, with a sense of luxury, to enjoy her thoughts.

She went over everything from last night, and had a few uncomfortable moments wondering if she had made a fool of herself. She remembered the fur coats and the Looks, the fact that even when the younger set had finally arrived, nobody there was dressed as she was. Yes, she had been besieged by men wanting to dance with her, but – oh my God, had that been because they saw her as some kind of tart? She went cold all over as the thought occurred to her. Jack had said it was because she was interesting to talk to, but he might just have been being kind. Would the County be talking in years to come of that woman from London who showed herself up, had everyone staring at her, and nearly ruined the evening for everyone else? Perhaps next time she went down to the village there would be covert glances and sniggers behind the hand. Perhaps she'd never be able to leave the house again without a sack over her head. Perhaps she'd better become a nun in one of those closed orders...

She turned over, looked out of the window at the pale morning sky, and better sense prevailed. What did she care if she wasn't dressed like everybody else? She'd been perfectly respectable. And the men she had danced with hadn't tried to take advantage or proposition her. No, either Jack was right, or it was just the novelty of a new face that had been attractive. Probably the latter. She got the impression all those people knew each other terribly well. Anyway, it wasn't as if she was staying here for ever: in a few months she would be gone, and it wouldn't matter what anyone thought of her.

And then she thought about Jack. He had driven her home, and when he pulled up outside the cottage he had turned off the engine. She had been wondering whether he expected to be invited in, and was remembering she only had instant coffee and nothing alcoholic to offer, when he said her name, and she turned to find him looking earnestly at her. And then somehow she was in his arms and they were kissing. It started gently, though warmly, but soon they were 'chewing the face off each other', as they said back home, and the temperature in the car was rising rapidly.

This time it was he who broke off, drawing back from her just enough to look at her, though his hands were still holding her. He began, a little uncertainly, 'Shall we—?' and she was sure the sentence was going to end, *go back to my place*? She remembered that he was living at home and wondered how awkward that would make things. She started to say, 'I think it's maybe a bit soon to be taking things further,' and only got as far as *I think* when he resumed with, 'I'm sorry.'

'Don't be,' she said quickly. 'I was enjoying it.'

But he looked for a moment confused and almost miserable. 'I was – I don't want you to think ... Things are a bit complicated.'

She cooled. 'You're seeing someone else,' she suggested with a hint of *froideur*.

'No, no,' he protested hastily, and it sounded genuine. 'It isn't that. It's – I can't really explain.' He coughed and started again, sliding his hands down her arms to take hold of her hands and press them. 'I really like you. I'd like to see you again. Would that be all right?'

She smiled. 'I'd like that. I had a lovely time tonight.'

'I'm glad. And perhaps we could—?'

'Take things slowly?' she supplied, since he seemed to be making hard work of the conversation.

He looked relieved. 'Yes! Get to know each other a bit, before—'

'Of course,' she said.

His trademark wicked grin made a return. 'Though I don't promise to be able to keep my hands off you for that long. The delicious and entirely edible Miss Jennings.'

'Oh, I have my gristly bits, like anyone else,' she said, and they parted on laughter.

This morning, lying in bed, she thought, *now what* was *that*? While they were kissing she knew he'd wanted to, just as she had, but then he'd suddenly stopped himself. Was it the difficulties of location? Something to do with the ex-wife and kid? Was there, in spite of his protest, someone else? Or had he a dark secret – something embarrassing perhaps, like a third nipple, or the inability to achieve sexual congress unless wearing parachute harness and a World War Two flying helmet?

She smiled to herself. *Maybe he just likes you, and doesn't want to rush things*, she suggested. Which made her ask herself what *she* wanted from *him*. He was attractive and amusing and she liked him, and she'd be glad to date him, have a fling with him: it would certainly enliven her time here in Bursford. Whether it would lead any further – whether she would *want* it to lead any further – were questions she couldn't answer. And there was no reason why she should. Just enjoy it as it comes, she told herself; and on this sage advice, she realized that she was too wide awake to doze any more, jumped out of bed and decided to go for a walk before breakfast.

Kay was out in the front, shaking out her doormat, when Kate reached home again, and called to her. 'Hello! You're out early. I'd a thought you'd be having a lie-in after last night.'

'I wasn't *that* late home,' Kate said. 'It wasn't much after one.'

'I hear you were a roaring success – everyone wanted to dance with you,' Kay said.

'How on *earth* could you have heard that already?'

'My friend Tanya was one of the waitresses. She rung me up when she'd finished clearing up and said you were dancing every dance and poor old Blackjack wasn't getting a look-in.'

'He had plenty of other people to dance with.'

'Oh, I know. I bet he asked every girl in the room. He's a card, isn't he? I told you! And I told you you looked gorgeous. Liscombe has never seen anything like you. Want to come over and have breakfast? I'm just putting eggs on.'

'Oh, no, thanks,' said Kate. It wasn't that she felt fragile, but she didn't want a post-mortem, which would in any case have to compete with Dommie's insistent chatter. 'You're so kind, but I just want a quiet cup of tea and my own thoughts this morning.'

'Bet they're good ones,' said Kay, and went indoors.

In the quiet of her own shabby kitchen, Kate had two cups of tea, and toast and lime marmalade, and when she had cleared it up she thought about what work in the house she ought to do. It was then she discovered that her taste of the high life last night had made her restless. She didn't want to put on her working clothes and get dirty, and spend the day alone scraping wallpaper. *Get used to it, girl*, she told herself. *You didn't come down here to hobnob with the nobs*. Jack said he wanted to see her again but he hadn't made any specific date, and apart from him she only knew Kay and the Royal Oak crowd, and it was too early to be going for a pint.

Suddenly she remembered her childhood visits to Granny and Grandpa Jennings, and how they had always all gone to church on Sunday morning, the whole family clean and shiny in their best, walking off together to the dear little stone church of St Salvyn (at least, old folk like Granny and Grandpa called it that, although it had been renamed St Mary Magdalene's, because the Church wasn't even sure St Salvyn was really a saint). Somehow, she always remembered St Salvyn's with daffodils blowing in front of it, their yellow brilliant against the grey stone.

That's what I'll do this morning, she thought. I'll go to church.

She repeated it out loud and it still sounded like a good idea, so she went off to bath and dress.

There were lots of churches in Somerset dedicated to All Saints, which presumably saved having to make a choice and risk offending anyone in Heaven; but the good folk of Bursford must have been even less decisive than the norm, because the parish church was called St Mary and All Saints. It didn't get more inclusive than that. It was bigger than St Salvyn's, mostly fifteenth century, and its square stone tower was much taller, perhaps because, being built in the valley, it needed a higher tower to be seen from a distance and over the trees.

Kate had made an effort, put on her smartest pair of trousers and a decent top, even polished her shoes – or buffed them, at least, with a cloth, since she couldn't find any shoe polish among her boxes, wasn't even sure she owned any. Her hair, amazingly, was still unfrizzy from last night, and she tied it neatly in a tail behind, and put on the minimum of make-up for self-respect.

It was such a nice day that she decided to walk, which was almost her undoing as it was further than she had realized, down the hill, through the village and up the Withypool arm of the cross-roads. She heard the five-minute bell start and had to hurry, and got in just as the procession was entering up by the altar. A rather severe-looking sidesman gave her a prayer book and hymn book and directed her to a penitential pew at the back and to the side. The church wasn't full, of course, but there was a fair turnout, and a good number of hats, always an indication of a wealthy parish.

At the end of the service the vicar stood at the door and shook hands with everyone as they passed out, which caused something of a traffic jam as many of the parishioners wanted a leisurely chat. When her turn came Kate said a quick, embarrassed, 'Good morning,' and got a clerical smile and an interested inspection from the vicar. Most people were still hanging around the churchyard, having a natter – the parish church in rural places like this was often an important part of the social life of the area. Kate planned to slip away quietly, but as soon as she stepped out into the sunshine, her name was called with loud enthusiasm, and Jocasta came bounding up and flung her arms round her waist in greeting.

'How *nice* you came!' Jocasta cried. 'When did you think of it? You didn't say anything, or I'd have saved you a place by me. What did you do to your hair? It looks fab! Mummy's still inside talking to Mr Braithwaite. She always talks longer than everyone else so she'll be ages yet. Did you have a nice time last night? I have not seen Jack this morning, but Mrs B – our housekeeper – says she heard you were a wow, and everyone wanted to dance with you. I wish I'd seen what you wore. She said you were all got up like the Witch of Endor. It must have been epic!'

'You're looking very smart,' Kate said, blinking at the Witch of Endor remark, and deciding the questions really weren't designed to have answers. Jocasta was wearing tight pink pedal-pushers with a matching pink cotton jacket and ballet flats, and her hair was loose and held back by a pink Alice band.

'I like pink,' Jocasta said. 'You could wear it too.' She took hold of a length of Kate's hair and held her arm up against it. 'Look, it goes with your hair. Oh, here's Mummy. Gosh, that was quick. She's usually in there for half an hour once she gets started.'

'I'd better go,' Kate said. She wasn't sure whether she was up to meeting Jack's step-mother yet.

'Oh, don't go,' Jocasta said with evident disappointment. 'You should say hello to Mummy. You said she mightn't want to let you ride with me if you were a stranger, and you won't be a stranger if you meet her now, will you? Anyway, it's too late, she's seen you,' she concluded with satisfaction.

Kate turned, and couldn't work out who she was supposed to be looking at. Unless – no, surely it couldn't be? – was it this slim young-looking woman coming rapidly towards them? There was nothing in the least like a Lady Blackmore or a mother about her. But of course, Jocasta being only twelve-ish, her mother might easily be no more than thirty-five – could even be younger.

'Mummy!' Jocasta cried, putting it out of question. 'This is Kate!'

The woman who halted beside Kate was fashionably slim – almost thin – with perfect, enamelled make-up and golden hair expensively cropped into the modern version of the 1920s shingle. She was dressed in a short-skirted daffodil yellow suit so beautifully tailored, it would make you faint – surely a designer label? Kate thought. Her handbag Kate was able, thanks to Jess, to identify as Prada; her shoes were nude platform court heels which looked very similar to the Yves Saint Laurent pair Jess had been admiring on the Internet (and which, Kate remembered, with shock that such things could be, had cost £683).

The whole outfit looked gorgeous, wickedly smart, and effortlessly superior. Looking as she did she could have walked in through any door, into the most elite and expensive establishment in the world, and been admired for her appearance.

And she could have passed for twenty-eight, Kate added in her mind, in envy.

She was looking Kate over with a very sharp and noticing eye, and Kate almost withered, feeling a lumpy and ill-kempt mess beside this bird-thin paragon. Only her pride kept her from visibly shrivelling up and dropping to the floor like a discarded snakeskin.

But apparently something about her was right, because Lady Blackmore suddenly smiled (perfect teeth) and thrust out her hand (exquisitely manicured) and said, ‘This child of mine has done nothing but talk about you for days. And Jack’s no better. You saved that wretched dog from starving to death. I can’t tell you how grateful we all are. Jack must have told you how Theo dotes on it – we’d never have heard the last of it if anything had happened to it. There’d have been floods and tantrums and no doubt blame cast about for not making sure it was tied up properly. So, really, you are a complete saviour.’

Jocasta was giving her a ‘there, told you it’d be all right’ look.

Kate said, ‘Really, it was nothing. Anyone would have done the same.’

‘I wouldn’t have approached a strange dog in those circumstance,’ Lady Blackmore said. ‘You certainly have courage. Anyway, the fact is, whether or not anyone else *would* have done it, *you* did, so please accept our grateful thanks.’

Kate smirked and muttered something. She had worked in PR where she was known for her ability to talk to anyone and deal with any situation, but for some reason this elegant woman was making her feel like a fumbling gnome. She was sure her feet were growing as she spoke.

Fortunately Jocasta was not lost for words. ‘So now, Mummy, it’s all right if we go riding, isn’t it, Kate and me?’

Lady Blackmore raised her eyebrows at Kate. 'Do you really want to? You mustn't let her be a nuisance.'

'I'd like to very much. And she couldn't be a nuisance. I enjoy her company,' Kate said. Out of the corner of her eye she could see how pleased Jocasta was by the words. In front of her, the eyebrows went even further up.

'Well, if you're sure ... We'd all be grateful to have her occupied. School holidays are so long.'

Kate smiled. 'I only remember them being much too short.'

Lady Blackmore shuddered. 'But then you're not a mother.' Something occurred to her. 'Where are you off to now?'

'Just home,' Kate said.

'Well, then, come back with us to The Hall for lunch.'

'Oh, Mummy, yes!' Jocasta cried, jumping up and down. 'Brill!'

'Oh, well, really, I—' Kate began.

'You haven't anything else planned?'

'No, not at all,' Kate had to admit. And, though she didn't say it, she would like to see the inside of The Hall, see where Jack lived.

'So, then, do come. Please, we should like it very much.'

'Well, if it's no trouble – you're very kind, Lady Blackmore.'

'Oh, Camilla, please. Call me Camilla. "Lady Blackmore" makes me feel like Sybil Thorndike, or who ever it was. You know, Lady Bracknell.'

'Edith Evans,' Kate supplied.

Camilla looked as though she didn't enjoy

being corrected.

'The car's just over there.' They started walking down to the road, with Jocasta still frisking like a lamb. 'You can meet the other dogs,' she told Kate, 'and I can show you Chloe, and after lunch we could try them out, if you like.'

'She won't want to ride after lunch,' Camilla said, indifferent to her daughter's excitement. 'She's a grown-up, not a child. And do walk properly, Jocasta. A piece of gravel just hit my shoe. If you've scratched it ... What's the point of sending you to ballet and fencing and deportment lessons if all you can do is lumber about like a cow?'

Kate had just been admiring the way Camilla managed to walk downhill, over an uneven surface, and on gravel, on five-inch heels, even with an inch of platform to help out. She felt less well-disposed, though, when she noted Jocasta's crestfallen look. No-one likes to be told off, especially in front of a third party.

To take the attention away from her, Kate said, 'I hope I won't be putting anyone out.'

'Of course not,' Camilla said. 'It's practically open house on Sunday. We never know how many are going to turn up at table. Everyone invites someone. Besides, Ed, my stepson, is here, so really, the more the merrier. Anything to distract him. He won't be able to go on nagging me and being a complete bore in front of a stranger. I'm glad you're coming.'

So Kate was able to stop feeling oppressively grateful, and to wonder instead what sort of ménage she was about to be plunged into.

* * *

There were the remembered gateposts (a bit shabby now, some of the rendering chipping off and one of the balls that topped them missing) and beyond was a wide gravel sweep with most of the gravel missing, on which several cars were parked. The house proved to be Victorian Gothic: tall, red brick, all angles, very steep gables with ornately carved bargeboards and finials, and even taller chimneys.

The first thing that struck her – literally – as they stepped into the entrance hall was a wave of dogs. They came charging out of the room to the right and flung themselves, tongues and tails waving, on Kate and Jocasta – Camilla avoiding them with a very nifty sidestep that spoke of years of practice. There was a black Labrador, an English setter with a sad, freckled face, a Jack Russell, an Italian greyhound, and a large black hairy thing like a small bear that Kate recognized, and who shouldered his way effortlessly through the crowd to claim her as his new best friend. Bringing up the rear was an enormous ginger tabby, which sat down at a safe distance to wait for recognition.

Jocasta embraced and saluted them all, and told Kate their names. 'The Lab is Milly, the setter is Ralph – isn't he adorable? He looks so sad, but he's not really. They're supposed to be Ed's. The Jack Russell is Jacob – he's a terrible thief. Never leave anything edible at Jacob-level. He's supposed to be Jack's. And the greyhound is Esmé. She's Mummy's. She always gets left out because she's so shy – don't you, darling?

Yes, you do, you do my little poppet,' she interpolated in a cooing voice while dragging the dog close for an embrace. 'So you have to make a point of petting her, or you'll hurt her feelings.'

'Supposed to be?' Kate queried.

'Well, they're all everyone's, really. They sort of belong to the house. And you know Chewy.'

'He seems to know me,' Kate said, trying to push him off her legs, where he was leaning so hard that it was difficult for her to stand upright. 'And who's the cat?'

'He's Sylvester. He's—'

'Kate doesn't need the whole menagerie,' Camilla interrupted in a bored voice. 'If you're going to let the dogs slobber on you, go upstairs and change before you ruin that jacket. Kate, don't let the dogs be a nuisance. Everyone in this house seems to be mad about animals, and lets them run wild. Shove them off, or kick them if they won't leave you alone. That's what I do.'

Kate noted that the pack seemed to have a healthy respect for the area around Camilla's feet.

'Come and have a drink,' Camilla continued, turning away, 'and see who's here.'

Kate followed, pausing when her hostess couldn't see to caress the cat, who stood on tiptoe and erected his tail like a flag pole to receive her, and purred so loudly, Kate was afraid Camilla would hear.

They went through the door to the right into an enormous room, a Victorian's idea of a baronial hall, oak panelled, with an elaborately moulded ceiling, a vast inglenook fireplace, and tall narrow windows. There were old, much worn Turkish rugs on the oak floorboards, heavy red velvet curtains that had seen better days at the windows, bookcases full of books and in a far corner a grand piano on which Kate could see the undisturbed dust even from this distance. A number of old sagging sofas and armchairs were dotted about, with footstools and pouffes, and a variety of tables of varying size and height were loaded with newspapers, magazines, and empty cups and glasses. The remains of a log fire were grey in the fireplace, and on the hearth stood a vase full of dead flowers, an apple core, some screwed-up balls of paper and more empty glasses.

'We spend most of the time in here,' said Camilla, unnecessarily. For such an immaculately-turned-out person she didn't seem to mind or even heed the mess.

Sprawled about the room in various attitudes of relaxation was a number of people who all looked up as they came in, though only one stood up. Jack was sitting on a sofa with Phil Kingdon, drinking Guinness: he smiled at Kate, rather nervously, she thought, while Kingdon gave her a narrow-eyed stare of calculation which she did not at all understand.

Also present were Steph and Gil Holland, and another, older couple who looked vaguely familiar from last night. Camilla introduced them. 'Don and Annie Culverhouse. And this is Hilary.' Their daughter was a girl of about Jocasta's age, rather pale, meek-looking and plain, with dark frizzy hair and glasses. She was perching on the edge of the sofa beside her parents looking awkward and uncomfortable, and showed a flash of steel braces when she managed a shy smile at Kate. 'Jocasta's upstairs getting changed,' Camilla said to her briskly. 'Why don't you go up and see her, or she'll be there all day.'

Hilary ducked her head in assent and hurried gratefully out.

A smart, trousered woman in her early thirties was introduced as 'Susie Orde. And where's Eric?'

'Gone out to the stables with Ed,' Susie replied, and smiled at Kate. 'Eric's my husband, in case you didn't guess.'

And finally Camilla came to the man who had stood up: a tall, soldierly-looking man, with a firm, brown face, keen blue eyes and neatly-cropped grey hair. He looked to be in his fifties, with the vigour of the prime of life and the sun-lines and wrinkles of experience in his face. 'And this is Brigadier Mainwaring. Harry.'

He alone shook Kate's hand, a firm, cordial grip, and looked down from his height with a twinkling sort of smile. 'You can imagine what I went through when I was a captain,' he said. 'It's a shame there's no way to skip a rank in the army.'

'You could always have not joined,' Don said, overhearing him. 'You've a perfectly good brain – could have done anything with it.'

The brigadier swallowed this near-insult like a man. 'Given that my father and grandfather were both generals,' he said genially, 'it would have taken more courage than I have *not* to go into the army.'

'Oh, Harry,' said Annie languidly from her sofa, 'surely a soldier has to have loads of courage?'

'Excuse my wife, she's terribly literal,' Don said.

'I'd sooner face the Taliban than my father in a rage any day,' said Harry, and then, to Kate: 'Can I get you a drink, since no-one else seems to be stirring. And you, Camilla, my dear?'

'I'll get them,' Jack said, heaving himself out of the sofa, which seemed reluctant to let him go. 'Anyone else need a top-up while I'm at it?'

There was a period of movement and rearrangement, at the end of which Kate found herself on a sofa with a gin-and-tonic large enough to wash in, Jack beside her, several dogs at her feet, and Sylvester the cat planted in her lap as if he was stuffed with lead. Other conversations had broken out all round the room – everyone seemed to know everyone else very well – which meant Jack could talk to her without being overheard.

'It was quite a surprise to see you come through that door,' he said.

'I thought you looked disconcerted,' Kate said.

'Not disconcerted – just surprised. How did it come about?'

'I went to church, bumped into Camilla and Jocasta, and was invited back for lunch. Well, not so much invited as ordered,' she added. She didn't want him to think she was stalking him and had angled for the invitation.

He looked awkward. 'I'd have asked you

myself, but I didn't think you'd want to get bogged down with my family.'

'Don't worry, I didn't expect it. It's early days for you to be inviting me home to meet your mother!' she teased.

He relaxed a bit. 'Well, it's nice to see you. Not tired after last night? No hangover?'

'I'm not made of glass, you know. Though with drinks this size–' she gestured with her glass – 'all that could change.'

'It's mostly tonic,' he reassured her. She had tasted it. She knew it wasn't.

'This is a nice room,' she said. 'Must be cosy when the fire's lit.'

'Oh, the house is a nightmare,' he said with easy affection. 'Much too big, cold as the tomb. We have to have a fire in here most nights of the year, even in the middle of a heatwave. And you'd need an army of servants to keep it clean. All we have is Mrs B.'

'Camilla mentioned her – your housekeeper?'

'She's been with us since the year dot. Mrs Bradshaw, but she only ever gets called Mrs B. Her husband helps with the horses and does chauffeuring and odd jobs. They have the cottage by the stables. She shops and cooks for us and does one or two other things – answers the phone and orders the logs and so on – but you couldn't expect her to clean as well. Every now and then we get a contract firm in to go through the place like a whirlwind, but it's expensive, so mostly we just do it ourselves.'

'Or don't do it?' Kate suggested, with a look around.

He grinned. 'I suppose nobody cares very much. We just cover the mess up with dogs.'

'So who are these people?' Kate asked next.

'Neighbours. That's who we always socialize with. Too much effort to go further afield.'

'Unlike London, where your friends move away and you all have to travel to the centre to see each other.' She looked across to where Kingdon was now talking to Camilla, he leaning forward with an air of urgency and she leaning back, her head slightly turned away as though he bored her. 'And Phil Kingdon? Is he a friend or a neighbour? I thought he was your agent, or manager, or something.'

Jack looked embarrassed. 'He's the estate's agent. Officially, he's supposed to run the whole thing, with me overseeing the factory and Ed overseeing the land.'

'And unofficially?' Kate prompted.

'Well, it's not like feudal times, you know,' he said. 'You don't keep people who work for you like that at arm's length. I suppose he's more of a family friend. Why do you ask, anyway?'

'Oh, no reason, really. Except that he keeps looking at me in a strange way.'

'He's a strange man,' Jack said lightly. 'What sort of way?'

'I'm not sure. Almost as if he's inspecting me. And doesn't approve.'

'Imagination. He's not much of a smiler, that's all.'

Kate accepted it. 'And who's the delicious Brigadier?'

'You think he's delicious?' He seemed worried

by the idea.

'Oh yes. Every girl's dream of a daddy.'

He seemed relieved. 'Oh, right. A father figure.' Kate hadn't meant that, but she let it pass. 'Well, he's another neighbour, of course, but he's sweet on Camilla. Wants to marry her, but he's twenty years older than her. Still, she keeps stringing him along and not saying yes or no. I suppose she likes the attention.'

'What girl wouldn't?' Kate said lightly, watching him laugh with Susie Orde.

'Well, he's not her only suitor,' Jack said. 'There's a pack of them.'

Before Kate could ask more about this intriguing suggestion, they were interrupted by a newcomer, a fair, slightly pudgy man coming in from the hall. 'The missing Eric,' Jack murmured to Kate. 'You wouldn't think it to look at him, but he's a demon in the saddle – a hard rider to hounds.'

Behind him came another man, with Jocasta clinging affectionately to one of his arms and bouncing a little as she chattered to him; the monochrome Hilary was trailing in the rear. The dogs all rose from their various positions of recumbency to run to him. Even the cat vacated her lap and stalked towards the obvious master of the house.

'My brother Ed,' Jack explained, unnecessarily.

He was much taller than Jack, lean and hard and powerful around the shoulders. His hair was black and springy, his face very tanned, his eyes a contrasting bright blue like a Siamese cat's. He was very handsome, but grave-looking, as though he didn't smile very often; a dark, severe, strong, perhaps difficult man.

He was also – and of course, now she thought of it, which was why the greyhound had looked familiar – the Angry Man who had berated her for rubbing down her own window frames.

Jocasta was still chattering, and let him go to fling out an arm in Kate's direction. 'Oh, and here's Kate, who bought Little's. You haven't met her yet, but I have. She rescued Chewy, and she's terrific, she can do *everything*. We're going to go riding together.'

Jack groaned quietly. 'Oh no! Why did she have to mention Little's?'

Kate stood up – she felt she couldn't help it – and moved a couple of steps towards the man. He took the other couple, and they were standing close enough for her to feel – in her imagination, at least – the heat radiating from his body. She looked up into his unsmiling face.

He held out his hand, and she placed hers in it, aware at the outposts of her body how large and strong it was, warm and dry, a hand to put your trust in. The rest of her was focused on his face. Tense, dry-mouthed, she registered his eyes looking directly into hers like a fork of blue lightning that went all the way to the pit of her stomach. Her stomach and her knees felt warm and weak. *Oh no*, she thought, far away and faintly, *what are you doing? You can't lust after this man.*

She was, though. He was so solid and real, he made every other man in the room – including

Jack – look like a cardboard cut-out. Even the Brigadier was a mirage. He was – stunning!

'We've met,' he said.

Eleven

A great deal more was drunk before they were called, by some signal Kate missed, into the dining room, so everyone was extremely relaxed and the conversational volume had risen almost to party level. When everyone stood up and started trekking towards the door, she immediately found Jocasta attached to her arm. 'Oh *please* can I sit next to you? They'll make me sit with that boring old Hilary. She's so wet, I hate her, but they're always making me hang out with her because we're the same age. You don't like someone just because they're the same age, do you? I mean, she doesn't like *anything* interesting. She doesn't even ride.'

'Perhaps her parents can't afford to buy her a pony,' Kate hazarded, feeling sorry for any fellow-sufferer from frizzy hair.

Jocasta looked exasperated. 'She could ride Chloe if she wanted. I've told her a million times. But she won't. She's scared of horses.' This was said with withering contempt, obviously a sin past redemption. Kate was saved from answering by Camilla, coming up behind them, who said severely, 'Stop bothering Kate, Jocasta. You're to sit with Hilary in the middle, and help Mrs B with the dishes, and for goodness' sake don't spill anything.' Jocasta gave her a martyred look and mooched away. Camilla closed up with Kate and said, 'I'm seating you next to Ed. *That* should keep him occupied.'

Kate didn't know whether to be pleased or dismayed.

The dining room was as large as the drawing room, a vast oak-panelled chamber with another huge fireplace, and was dominated by a massive oak table and high-backed, carved oak chairs with tapestry seats. There were no fewer than three great solid sideboards, laden with tarnished silver accoutrements, and there were many dim old paintings on the wall – as well as two rather obvious clean patches where paintings had once hung and did no more. The only rug was in front of the fireplace, and was immediately colonized by the dogs in a panting, eager jostle. Elsewhere, the bare polished floorboards underfoot, coupled with the height of the ceiling, magnified every scrape of a chair or shift of a foot to a clashing noise like giants clog-dancing in a municipal swimming pool.

But the company only raised their voices to compensate. They were obviously used to it. Camilla was busying herself directing people in a piercing voice to the seats she wanted them to occupy, and they moved with good-natured languor, getting up when they were told they were in the wrong place and changing seats without ever breaking off what they were saying. All geared, Kate calculated, to seat her next to Ed, where she could distract him from Camilla; and also away from Jack, with whom she might otherwise converse too much to do her duty.

As she took her place Ed gave her an unsmiling, though not unfriendly look. 'I feel that I owe you an apology,' he said, and the tightness of his lips suggested that he didn't find those words easy to say. 'I'm afraid I didn't make a good impression when I saw you outside the cottage.'

'It was certainly an interesting first meeting,' Kate said lightly, to reassure him she held no malice.

But he wasn't to be deflected. 'I shouldn't have called you a squatter, or disbelieved you. It was rude of me. I'm sorry.'

'Quite understandable, when it was your stepmother who owned the place,' she said. He seemed to flinch slightly at that. 'If I'd known who you were, or that you didn't know she'd sold it—' She realized belatedly that she was talking voluntarily about the very subject Camilla had put her there to avoid. 'Anyway,' she said hastily, 'let's forget the whole thing and start again.' She held out her hand. 'How do you do, I'm Kate Jennings.'

She thought for a moment he would leave her hanging, but at last he gave a little quirk of the lips that might charitably be construed as a smile, and said, 'How do you do? I'm Edward Blackmore. But please call me Ed.'

Jocasta appeared between them and leaned over, breathing strenuously in Kate's ear with concentration, to place a bowl of soup in front of each of them. 'There,' she said triumphantly, 'and I *didn't* spill.'

'Smells good,' Kate said.

'Mrs B is a great believer in soup. It uses up the leftovers,' Ed explained. 'She says she remembers rationing – though I can't really believe she's that old. Her actual age is one of the great mysteries of life. I don't think even Ted – her husband – knows.'

'She's been with you a long time?' Kate said, glad to have found a safe topic.

'I was about four when she came, so I don't really remember a time without her. She came as a general maid, but not long after that my mother died, the cook left, and she took over. She's been cooking for us ever since.'

'How old were you when your mother died?' Kate asked.

'Six,' he said. 'Jack was only two, so he doesn't really remember her.'

'But you do,' she said, seeing that there was something there, still, all these years later – a sadness. He made a sound that might have been a yes, and ate some soup to cover up. 'How did she die? She must have been quite young.' She held her breath, in case being asked annoyed him; but he didn't seem to object.

'Peritonitis,' he said. 'It was a tragedy. Only about ten per cent of cases die from it. The important thing is to get treatment quickly enough. My father thought she just had indigestion and sent her to bed with a hot water bottle. By the time he realized it was serious, it was too late. We're quite a long way from the hospital, here.'

'Oh, I'm so sorry,' she said. 'It must have been terrible for him.'

'It was,' he said. 'He was always one for telling you to buck up and stop making a fuss. He didn't believe in being ill. But he adored my mother. It broke him when she died. He blamed himself, of course.'

'Did *you* blame him?'

He looked at her. 'Oh, for a couple of years, when I was a teenager, I did. But you always find something to blame your parents for at that age. I soon realized that he just did what he thought was right. Besides, he punished himself for it far more harshly than I ever would have.' She saw him shake himself mentally. 'But this is no topic for the lunch table. Tell me about yourself. What brings you to Somerset?'

So she told him an abbreviated version of her life in London and her desire for change, Gaga's legacy and – touching on it as briefly as possible – buying Little's, jumping from there quickly to remembering Bursford from childhood, and Granny and Grandpa living in Exford.

There was a gleam in his eyes, as though he knew what she was up to and was amused. 'PR,' he said. 'Now that must be an interesting job.'

'It probably sounds more interesting than it is,' she said. 'And you really don't want to know about it anyway,' she added with a smile. 'You're just being polite.'

'That's what society is all about,' he said solemnly. 'You ask me a question and I ask you one. It's tit for tat.'

'And is the honesty of the answer also tit for tat?'

'You,' he said, looking into her eyes with

devastating effect, 'are a dangerous young woman. Where would we be if everyone answered all questions honestly?'

They were interrupted at that moment by Jocasta collecting their soup plates, and Mrs B on the other side dumping an enormous roast rib of beef in front of him. 'Ah, I have to perform my carving duties,' he said, and introduced her to Mrs B, who turned out to be a tall, strong-looking woman with short, curly grey hair and the remains of great beauty in her face and her still dark eyes. She didn't smile at Kate, but gave her a slow, considering look that Kate didn't take amiss. If she'd been looking after everybody for all these years, she was entitled to make judgement on the people they brought home.

Ed carved, laying slices on plates that were passed down either side, and since Kate's other neighbour, the plump sportsman Eric, was busy talking to *his* other side, she occupied herself with studying the portraits around the room and finding no resemblance in the faces to either Jack or Ed. There were no very modern paintings, so none could be his mother, though there was one from the nineteen twenties or thirties, to judge by the clothes, which she supposed might be his grandmother.

Dishes of roast potatoes and vegetables had come in, and Yorkshire puddings, and gravy, and there was much handing up and down, while Jack got up and went round the table filling everyone's glasses with wine, after which he dumped several bottles at intervals along the table and said, 'You'll have to help yourselves from now on.' As he put a bottle down in front of Kate he gave her a searing look, part entreaty and part warning. She smiled gaily back, not having the slightest idea what he wanted her to do or not do. Perhaps he was just worried that Ed might be eating her up. They seemed to regard him as a bit of an ogre; but she felt she was well up to him. He hadn't bitten her head off yet. In fact, he was talking to her remarkably freely. Long may it last! She loved his voice – sheer black velvet.

When Ed was settled again, she said, 'You and Jack don't look much alike. If I didn't know, I wouldn't take you for brothers.'

'We get that a lot. There are similarities of feature, when you get to know us.' She was glad he had said 'when' and not 'if'. 'But I'm very like my father, and Jack's more like our mother. She was very fair and pretty, and everyone loved her. My father was tall and grim, and people were wary of him. He didn't have the knack of getting on with people. I'm afraid I take after him.'

'I don't think you're grim,' she said – rather daringly, all things considered. 'And you don't seem to be having any trouble getting on with me.'

He levelled a look at her. 'Are you flirting with me?'

She laughed. 'If you think that's flirting, you obviously don't have much experience of the thing. Why do you think you haven't the knack of getting on with people?'

'I don't suffer fools gladly,' he said. 'Or dishonesty. Or people who don't keep their word.'

She nodded sympathetically. 'And as so much of social interaction is based on dishonesty, I can see why you'd find it a burden.'

'Not a burden, exactly. It just – doesn't interest me.' He did that mental shake thing again – it was as if he realized he was getting too far in and needed to change direction – and said, 'Tell me about the Great Rescue.'

'What – Chewy? It was hardly that.'

'You were a fool to approach a strange dog in a situation like that. You could have been badly bitten.'

'I was careful. Anyway, he was so tangled up, he couldn't really have reached me.'

'He could have bitten you when he got free.'

She shrugged. 'Well, he didn't. And I couldn't just leave him, could I?'

He nodded. 'We're all very grateful to you.'

'And you're showing it,' she said. 'This splendid lunch! It'd be bread and cheese at home. And Jocasta's going to take me riding.'

Now the cautious look left his face for the first time. 'You like horses?'

'Love them. I used to ride as a child, here and in Dublin, but of course opportunities are limited in London.'

'That's why I come back every weekend – or part of the reason, anyway. I must show you the stables after lunch. When are you and Jocasta riding?'

'We haven't made a date yet,' she said, glad that he, at least, didn't tell her not to let Jocasta be a nuisance.

He nodded, but didn't follow up the question. He was looking at her with interest now, and she felt a pang of connection with him, accompanied with that quaky feeling in the stomach. He began to say, 'I wonder—' when his other neighbour, Steph Holland, sitting on his left and opposite Kate, finished what she was saying to the Brigadier, and turned to Ed to say:

'What have you heard about the War Memorial restoration, Ed? Surely something ought to be decided soon, if they're going to have any chance of getting the work done before November?'

Ed turned to her and they fell into a discussion of local affairs that meant nothing to Kate. Eric was still busy on his other side, so Kate concentrated on her dinner, which was delicious. Mrs B was evidently what was called a 'good plain cook', but the phrase did nothing to convey the pleasure good plain cooking could impart.

A movement further down the table made her look that way, and she saw Jack staring at her with raised eyebrows, mouthing some question at her. She had no idea what it was, so she just smiled at him, and he looked relieved, threw her a wink, and went back to his conversation.

After pudding – rhubarb crumble and custard, very traditional, but raised to new heights by the addition of a hint of ginger – they all went back into the drawing room for coffee. Large brandies, whiskies, and Cointreau on ice for Susie Orde were distributed. Everyone settled deeply into their seats for a long afternoon of drinking and gossip, except for Jocasta who, with Hilary trailing in her wake, disappeared with the dogs, evidently accepting for the moment that Kate was one of the grown-ups for the purposes of this afternoon, and was not to be annexed for her own pleasures.

Kate found herself on a sofa somewhat out of the main scrum with the Brigadier, whom she found fascinating, and who had plenty of stories to tell her, since he had served both in Iraq and Afghanistan, and didn't mind talking about it. From there it was an easy step to what he was doing with his retirement from the army.

'Well, I have a house and a few acres I inherited from my father, and the army pension, which is enough to live on in a small way, but not enough for what I want to do.'

'And what *do* you want to do?' Kate asked.

'Get married,' he said. Kate's mouth said a silent, 'Oh,' and she thought of Camilla, but she managed through great strength of mind not to look at her. The Brigadier hurried on. 'I couldn't support a wife on my pension alone. And besides, I can't sit about doing nothing. I'm not used to it. So I've set up a business which I'm in the process of expanding – a consultancy.'

'Consultancy in what?'

'A sort of specialized employment agency, placing people as bodyguards, either long-term, or for specific events.'

'Ex-army personnel?' Kate guessed.

'That's right. Trained men, many of them personally known to me, and plenty of contacts within the army for vetting those who aren't.

There's a supply of men coming out of uniform all the time, looking for a job. And it's a growing market, with so many celebrities and millionaires around.'

'You're right,' Kate said. 'In my business – PR – we're coming across more and more of them. You hardly used to see a bodyguard, but now everyone seems to have them. What a good idea!'

'Thank you. I'm hoping at least that it will make my fortune.' He gave an apologetic smile.

'And then she'll marry you?'

He gave her a quizzical look. 'Well, that's the hope. Bit of a hopeless hope, all things considered.'

'But why? I mean, *why* won't she marry you?' Kate asked on the burst. 'I'd marry you like a shot.'

He laughed. 'You do blurt out the first thing that comes into your head, don't you?'

'Oh, I know,' Kate said, blushing. 'It's a terrible habit of mine – comes of having five sisters who share absolutely *everything*. Conversation without the filter.'

'It's refreshing,' he said. 'Most people are so guarded, you never get near what they really think. You have to guess, and if you get it wrong – it's a minefield!'

'It's a minefield saying what's in your head, too.'

'That's true. Especially in a country community like this. But your secret's safe with me. You can say what you like to me, and be sure I won't pass it on.'

'Army discretion?' Kate hazarded. He nodded, smiling. 'What about Ed?' She felt a ridiculous thrill in getting his name into the conversation. 'He doesn't look like a man who'd pass things on.'

'No, he's no gossip – one of the things I like about him. But of course people pass things on *to* him.'

Kate wasn't sure if there was a warning for her in that, and if there was, what it might refer to.

Every now and then there was a sort of 'general post' and people changed seats for fresh conversation. In one of these Kate was corralled in a corner by the fireplace with a coffee cup in one hand, a brandy glass in the other, and Phil Kingdon blocking her escape. Close up, she saw that the skin of his face was strangely shiny as though he used moisturizer, and the smell of his after-shave was competing with another fragrance, perhaps deodorant or some kind of man-cologne. It made her want to sneeze. There was something trap-like about his mouth, and his eyes were grey and dead-looking, like boiled fish eyes. She didn't like him.

'So, having a good time?' he asked her.

'This afternoon, or in general?' she parried.

'Well, I can see you are this afternoon. It must be nice to get away from that slum of a cottage, even though it's only for a couple of hours. Must be uncomfortable and lonely for you there.'

'Oh, I don't notice it. I'm so busy, time just flies.' She didn't know where his line of conversation was tending, but just in case he was thinking of asking her out, she wanted to lay in an excuse beforehand. 'And I'm too tired at the end of the day to do anything but flop into bed.'

He took a sip of coffee. 'What are you going to do with it when you've finished?'

'I'm not sure yet,' she said warily. She had been here long enough to gather that selling houses as holiday cottages was not universally smiled upon.

He raised an eyebrow. 'Well, you can't be thinking of staying on and living there,' he said positively.

This was an unexpected line. 'Why not?' she asked.

'You'd miss London, the bright lights, and so on,' he said, waving a hand to express all that London meant. 'There's nothing to do here. You'd hate it.'

'It's a lovely place,' she objected.

'Oh, it's all right at the moment, when it's warm and summer's coming, but you'd never stand the winters here. They're long, and very cold. Endless rain, freezing winds, and when the snow comes down you're cut off. You'd be utterly miserable.'

Why all this care for my welfare? she wondered. 'A lot of people do live here,' she pointed out.

'People who've lived here all their lives,' he said. 'And Little's can never be made comfortable, not the sort of comfort you're used to. It's a farm-worker's cottage, and it'll never be more than that, whatever you do to it. You'd do better to sell it.'

'Well, it's one possibility,' she said cautiously. 'As I said, I haven't decided yet.'

He looked away across the room. It was a relief not to have his eyes on her, and she relaxed a smidgen. 'You may have difficulty in finding a buyer,' he said, without emphasis.

'The estate agent didn't seem to think so,' she said, matching his indifferent voice.

'Oh, they're bound to say that, to get you to buy it. I expect you paid too much for it, too.'

'I'd have thought *you'd* know exactly what I paid for it,' she said, with a hint of annoyance. No-one likes to be told they've been sold a pup.

Now he looked at her again, and smiled. It was not a pretty sight. 'I'm not trying to interfere in your business – just offering you helpful advice, from someone who lives here and knows about these sort of things. I'm just saying, Little's isn't a pretty cottage, the sort visitors like. And there's a bit of a glut on the market, so prices are low, even when you can shift them at all.' He seemed to think a moment. 'Look here, when you decide to sell, come to me. I'll help you.'

'You will?'

'I know everyone around these parts. I'll help you find a buyer.'

'That's very kind of you,' she said, wondering if they had irony in this part of the world.

'Not at all. My pleasure.' Apparently not. 'There's no point in paying an estate agent's bloated commission just for putting a couple of ads in the paper. These people don't know the lie of the land the way I do. I can find you a local working person looking for a home. And if I were you,' he added with a serious look, 'I'd sell sooner rather than later. Prices are still going down. Don't wait until the end of summer and the bad weather. Get out while you can, whether you've finished your renovations or not. Let the purchaser finish it off. Don't throw good money after bad – that's my advice.'

'Well, thank you. I'll take that on board,' Kate said, and managed this time to escape, though she had to almost duck under his arm to do it. Now what was all that about? she wondered. Had she misjudged him? Was he really trying to be helpful? Perhaps he couldn't help the way he looked – it would be galling to be misunderstood all the time when you were trying to be nice. Or was it in fact just basic old anti-Townie hatred raising its ugly head? Trying to get rid of her – Exmoor for Exmoorians, foreigners out?

He did make sense about the estate agent's commission, though. When the time came to sell – and she felt a small pang at the thought of that – she might do well to swallow her instinctive dislike of him and ask his help, see what he could do for her. If he found her a buyer, well and good; if not, she still had the estate agent to fall back on. She couldn't lose either way.

Some time later, when she had popped out to the loo, she was returning to the drawing room when a movement caught her eye, and she saw, down the side passage that led to the kitchen, Kingdon and Camilla standing talking. Kingdon had his arm resting against a door jamb above his head, which made him look rather threatening as he leaned over Camilla's slim form.

Camilla was protesting. 'But it was your idea in the first place!' She sounded quite indignant. 'You suggested it!'

'For God's sake, woman!' Phil said explosively, making a movement of impatience which brought his arm down from the door jamb and had him half turning from her and towards Kate. Kate hurried on so that they should not see her, feeling slightly shocked that he should talk to Camilla like that, when he was an employee of the estate, no matter how important.

She decided she really didn't like him, and wondered that Camilla should allow him such licence. But of course, she had not hung around to hear any more – maybe Camilla was tearing him off a strip for his rudeness at this very moment. She hoped so, anyway.

When people started to stir and go, Kate was sitting on a sofa with Jack. He had plonked himself down next to her some time ago, resting his arm along the back of it behind her in the classic first-date-at-the-cinema ploy, and sure enough by now it was hanging heavily over her shoulder. Fortunately, he wasn't making any further amorous moves on her: she'd have felt awkward about that, in front of all these friends, and his stepmother. And Ed. Most of all Ed, though she managed not to ask herself why.

Jack had been drinking a great deal, and though he was not drunk in any obvious way, he seemed to have become rather somnolent, sinking bonelessly into the sofa, talking in a low voice to Annie Culverhouse, who was sitting catty-corner to him in the next armchair, about local matters, and entirely forgetting to flirt, entertain or be outrageous. The wolf in sheep's clothing. It was rather a relief. It made Kate feel like one of the family, and she looked round this big, shabby, people-filled room with liking, remembering Sundays back home in Dublin in the past, before the first of them had left the nest.

Idly – as the conversation did not really include her – she thought what she would do with the room if it were hers. Clean it, for a start: wax and polish the panelling, mend the cracked and broken bits of the ceiling moulding – repaint the ceiling, for that matter. It was almost brown with generations of smoke: she couldn't imagine how long ago it was last painted. And then—

Ed appeared in front of her, and she realized that people were getting up to leave, saying their goodbyes and thanks.

'I'll run Kate home,' Ed said, addressing it mainly to Jack.

He struggled to extricate himself from the cushions. 'Nice try, bro, but no chance. I'm doing it,' he said.

'You've had too much to drink,' Ed told him firmly.

'Don and I can drop her off,' Annie said.

'You're the other way,' Ed said.

'It's quite all right, I can walk from here,' Kate said, feeling a bit like a parcel.

Ed looked at her. 'It isn't safe to walk about these lanes at night. There are no pavements, you know, and the way local people drive –

especially when they've had a few...' He gave Jack a quelling look. 'I'd feel happier if I drove you.'

Kate was about to protest again, and then shut her mouth. *What am I thinking? Trying to avoid being in a car alone with Ed, even if it's only for a few minutes?* 'Thank you,' she said meekly.

She went to thank Camilla, who was – she was glad to see – deep in conversation with the Brigadier. Camilla stood up and air-kissed her, and said, 'Drop in any time – we don't stand on ceremony here – do we, Harry?'

'Not very often,' he replied, with that twinkling smile at Kate.

'In fact,' Camilla went on, 'you do seem to have had a civilizing effect on Ed. I wish you didn't have to go – he'll probably attack as soon as we're alone.' She thought a moment. 'What are you doing next weekend?'

'Nothing that I know of,' Kate said, with a lift of the heart. Was she about to be invited to Sunday lunch again?

'Well, I'm getting a house-party together. Dinner Saturday night, the show at Cothelstone on Sunday, and Buscombe on the Bank Holiday Monday.'

'Buscombe – you mean the point-to-point meeting?' Kate said. She had sometimes been to it when she was a child – Buscombe was not far from Exford.

'Yes,' Camilla said. 'Ed's entered for something, and Jocasta will be in the junior open. Would you like to come?'

'To the point-to-point? Yes, very much.'

'No, I meant for the weekend,' Camilla said impatiently.

'You mean – to stay? But I live so close.'

'Well, you don't want to be driving back and forth. It breaks up the party, and it's so dreary to have to watch what you drink. It's much better if you stay over. There are plenty of bedrooms. So that's settled, then? Good. Come at teatime on Saturday and stay until Tuesday morning.'

Kate managed some thanks, though her mind was already busy wondering whether her wardrobe would stand the strain; and also what sort of tensions and social difficulties she would encounter, staying under the same roof not only of Camilla and Jack but Ed as well, and presumably a host of friends into the bargain.

And now Ed was waiting to drive her home, jiggling his car keys on his forefinger as if impatient to be off. She hurried to him. 'Sorry,' she said.

'What for?' He sounded surprised.

'Keeping you waiting.'

'Oh, not at all. Did you have a coat?'

'Just a jacket. Yes, that's it.' She let him help her into it, and followed him to the front door. 'Your stepmother just invited me for next weekend,' she said as he held the door for her. 'To stay,' she added, so there should be no misunderstanding.

'Yes, I thought she might,' Ed said. They stepped out into the dark. It was surprisingly cold, and she shivered in reaction. 'She seems to have taken a shine to you, inviting you to lunch the instant she met you.'

She wondered whether he could really think that, and looked back at him. He seemed grimly amused. She felt there was nothing to be gained by havering. 'She thought I might distract you from her.'

'Yes, I thought that was it,' he said. 'She made a point of seating us together at lunch.' He didn't sound upset about it. She wished she could keep looking at him to judge his feelings, but she was picking her way in almost complete dark over uneven ground towards the car and had to watch her step.

'Did it work?' she asked boldly.

'You *are* quite a distracting person,' he said. Now she absolutely had to look at him. She stopped and turned. He was closer behind her than she had expected, and she found herself looking up at him almost vertically, their bodies only inches apart. He looked down at her, and she felt vertigo – though that may simply have been the angle of her neck. The moment and the silence that went with it seemed to go on for a long time; then he put out a hand to steady her, touching her elbow. He said, quite neutrally, 'She may find it didn't work as well as she hoped.'

'Why?' she asked faintly.

He used the touch on her elbow to turn her. The car was only a step away. He reached past her to open the passenger side door.

'Because I'll have her to myself when I get home from dropping you off,' he answered.

She felt a jab of disappointment, and got into the car.

They drove in silence along the dark lane. She

racked her brain for something to say – can't waste this opportunity! – but found herself unusually tongue-tied. His presence, so close to her and in such a confined space, was robbing her of normal intelligence. She felt the heat and power of him next to her, looked at his big, strong hands on the wheel and shivered, imagining them – *no, no, no! Don't go there!*

When he halted at the crossroads, she took the opportunity, under the guise of scanning the road, to look at his face. His profile, she thought, was even better than his full face: profiles are designed by nature to be grave rather than smiling. She realized suddenly that she knew nothing about him. It seemed he wasn't married – there had been no wife at the house, nor any mention of one – but had he ever been? She couldn't imagine someone like him remaining single to this advanced age. She wished she could ask him, but she couldn't – she *really* couldn't, even with her famed blurting-it-all-outness. Difficult divorce, she thought: surely that must be it. The ex's fault – hence his grimness. Broken heart – no longer trusted women.

But if the whole County was all over Jack, why weren't they even more all over Ed, the elder, after all, and the better looking (in her opinion)? He had said he didn't have the knack of getting on with people: did he actively drive them away?

The car moved off, turning right, and he said, 'You and Jack – is it serious?'

Well, that was blunt all right, she thought. Did he want it to be serious or not? Even as she wondered what the right answer would be, she had come out with the truth. 'It hasn't had time to be serious. I've only had two meals with him – or three if you count lunch today.'

'Do you count it?'

'Well, it was a family meal, wasn't it, not a date.'

'But you like him?'

'He's very likeable,' she said, wondering if that sounded evasive. She felt evasive. She might well have taken things further with Jack, had she not met Ed. Now she was wondering how committed to the younger brother she would find herself to be.

Ed seemed to give vent to a small sigh. 'He is. Everyone likes him.'

There was nothing she could easily respond to in that. She racked her brain for something safe to say. Finally she managed, rather feebly, 'So you're competing in the point-to-point next weekend?'

'Yes,' he said. Then, 'Oh, we didn't get to go to the stables. I said I'd show you. You should have reminded me.'

'Everyone was talking too much,' she said.

'Yes, that's true. Well, another time.' He glanced sideways at her. 'Next weekend, for sure, if not before.'

'Before?' she queried with hope in her heart.

'You're going riding with Jocasta, aren't you? She can show you.'

'Oh. Yes. Of course,' she said, hope sinking again.

The following silence lasted all the way to her door. He stopped, and sat for a moment, staring at nothing, while she tried to make herself move, open the door, say, 'Thanks for the lift,' in a normal, casual voice. Then, still not looking at her, he said hesitantly, 'About Jack...'

'Yes?' she encouraged him cautiously.

'Everyone likes him. He's very easy to get on with. But he's something of a flirt.'

'I was warned about that before I ever met him.'

'Were you? Well, I just wanted to say – to tell you ... I don't mean this in a bad way – I don't know what goes on between you—'

'Just say it,' she suggested to get him out of trouble. 'Whatever it is.'

He looked at her. 'It's easy to read more into what he says than he really means. He's very open and full of fun, and sometimes people think – women think ... Well, he's broken a lot of hearts, without in the least meaning to. I just wanted to put you on your guard.' In the darkness inside the car she could not read his expression; there was just the warm black velvet of his voice. She wanted desperately to touch him; and as if in answer to her thought, he laid his hand over hers, and she almost started at the sudden warmth. 'I hope you aren't offended.'

'No,' she said. 'I'm not offended.'

He withdrew his hand. 'Good,' he said. 'Well, goodnight, then.'

And so there was nothing to do but say goodnight and get out. Her moment with Ed alone was over.

Twelve

She woke on Monday to a grey world, low cloud and fine, drifting rain – what her grandfather used to call an Exmoor Special. Kate moved her activities indoors, and spent the day filling in the cracks and gaps in the sitting room, to ready it for the lining-paper – the walls were not good enough to paint straight on to them. She worked in a languorous, almost listless rhythm, the radio on in the background, her thoughts far away, and not very coherent.

Her head was populated with a jumble of people who all seemed much more real and vibrant than she did to herself. Ed – that glimpse of his profile at the crossroads – was the most vivid of all; the touch of his hand on hers in the car kept replaying itself. Like the early warnings of an approaching cold, she had all the symptoms of falling for him. She ought to have roused herself and dismissed him firmly from her mind, taken a large dose of mental vitamin C by reminding herself that she was here to get away from all that hopeless, painful man-malarkey; but in the dreamy languor that prevailed she allowed herself to yield, and drifted with her thoughts like the misty rain drifting over the soaked heather.

Kay popped in at lunchtime with the intention of inviting her over for a sandwich, so that she could hear all about how she had spent her Sunday, but finding Kate so distracted she had gone away without issuing the invitation, and had further prevented Dommie from dashing over after school. She recognized a girl with things to think about when she saw one. She could see Kate wanted to be alone. She supposed it must be something to do with Jack. She hoped Kate was not falling for him, because Blackjack was a noted hound, and only safe to be let out because everyone knew he was. There *had* been girls in the past who had got hurt – younger, unsophisticated girls – but she had assumed Kate was savvy enough to avoid the trap. Anyway, she'd find out all about it at some point. Kate liked to talk, and who else was there for her to talk to?

In the evening, Jess and Lauren phoned, and Jess soon noticed her lack of liveliness.

'What's up? You're not brooding about Mark, are you?'

'Of course not.'

'No "of course" about it. Oh no, don't tell me it's *new* love problems. You said you weren't going to get into all that, but you did talk rather a lot about this Jack person last time.'

'No, it's nothing,' Kate said. 'I'm just a bit listless after all the jollification yesterday.'

'What jollification?' So Kate told them about church, Camilla, the invitation and the lunch. 'And did Blackjack make a move on you?' Jess asked.

'No, he didn't. It wasn't like that. It was a family occasion.'

'You aren't glum because he *didn't* make a move on you, I hope?' Lauren put in sternly.

'No! Anyway, I'm not glum – just a bit jaded. Too much to drink, probably.'

'Debauchery,' Lauren said wisely. 'I thought better of you. Haven't you seen those pictures, The Rake's Progress?'

Kate laughed. 'Roast beef and Yorkshire, and a bunch of County people talking about planning applications and school governors. I've hit rock bottom!'

'So you're not getting serious about this Jack bloke?' Lauren demanded.

'No,' Kate said. For some reason she didn't want to mention Ed, so she didn't pass on his warning about Jack.

'I'm glad to hear it.'

'Maybe I'm a bit homesick for you guys,' Kate added, to distract her.

'Funny you should say that,' Jess jumped in, 'because it's probably escaped you, cut off from civilization as you are, that next weekend is Bank Holiday weekend.'

'So we thought we might come down and see you,' Lauren finished.

There was a brief silence, during which Kate was shouting in her mind, *Oh no! No, no, no! What lousy timing*! She really wanted to see the guys, but there was no way on earth she was going to miss that house party.

'I'd really love that,' she said, 'but the thing is, I've been invited somewhere, to stay, for the weekend. What about the weekend after?'

But she didn't get away that easily. She had to explain, and it sounded nutty over the phone to be staying at a place so close to where she lived. There were suspicious questions about Jack, and some hurt feelings, and when she'd smoothed those down and made a tentative arrangement for the following weekend, and managed to turn the conversation to Jess's and Lauren's lives, and listened to their news, she said goodbye feeling exhausted. Her involvement with the Blackmore family was complicating her life, and it was her own silly fault for getting mixed up with them. She ought to end it. She ought to telephone Camilla and tell her that she wouldn't come.

But somehow, even as she thought it, she knew she wouldn't. Wouldn't Gaga have said it was a feeble soul that avoided adventure because it might interrupt routine? Live life to the full, that was her maxim, because you only passed this way once.

And anyway, she had to find out how this story would end.

On Tuesday the rain had passed, leaving behind a day of sunshine and sharp, fast-moving showers. Still too wet to work outside, though. She checked the filled places from the day before to see if they had hardened all right, rubbed down a few of them and, since she was over her cultural hangover, or whatever had ailed her the day before, she decided to start papering. It was a fiddly and time-consuming job, because the ceiling and the floor weren't parallel with each other and the walls weren't plumb – actually, there wasn't a straight line or right-angle in the whole blessed house! – so every piece, not just the bits round the doors, window and fireplace, had to be cut in. And each length had to butt perfectly against its neighbours so as to leave no visible seam when it was painted afterwards.

It was slow and painstaking work, but quite satisfying in its way. She worked happily without any sense of how much time was passing, until she was roused from her concentration by the sound of a car drawing up outside. She had left the front door open to get a through-draught to dry the paper once it was hung, and a moment later Jack darkened the doorway, rapped facetiously on the open door and carolled, 'Knock knock! 'Ello, missus, can Kate come out to play?'

She looked over her shoulder at him. He looked big and handsome and completely out of place in her shipwrecked cottage in his smart, dark business suit, even though the top button of his shirt was undone and his tie had been loosened. He started towards her, and she cried, 'No, no, no! Hang on, wait a sec until I've finished setting this piece, or it'll go all over the place.'

He stopped dutifully, and ostentatiously held his breath until she had butted it, smoothed it down and trimmed off a sliver along the skirting board. 'Wow!' he said as she straightened up and turned to him. ''It's incredibly sexy watching a woman do something skilled like that. Come here, you gorgeous little handyman, you!'

He opened his arms for a bear-hug, but she made a fending-off gesture. 'You'll ruin your suit,' she warned. 'I'm filthy.'

He groaned. 'Stop, stop! I can't take any more. I adore filthy women!'

'You ass,' she said kindly, and reached up to kiss him lightly on the lips while keeping her body arced back away from his natty tailoring. 'No Chewy?'

'She asks after the dog,' he observed to the invisible witness. 'No, no Chewy because I've been to the office. Can't you tell from the suit?'

'Why aren't you still there?'

'Cruel slave-driver! Because I was there before eight o'clock and it's now after two, and six and a half hours is a decent working day by any standards.' She laughed at that. 'Anyway, I'm hungry, I need lunch, and more than that, I haven't had a drink since Sunday night and I'm gagging for one.'

'Why no drink? Have you taken the pledge?'

'Ed's on the warpath,' he said succinctly. 'Hence the virtuous day at the office, showing him I'm pulling my weight. By the way, I'm sorry I couldn't drive you home on Sunday, but he's very anti drinking and driving, and once he gets into his pantomime Tyrant King role, there's no earthly use arguing with him.'

'That's all right. I could see you were almost asleep.'

'No such thing – I was just comfortable.'

'So where is he now?' Kate asked, trying not to sound wistful.

'Ed? Gone back to London by the earliest train.

That's why I got into the office so early – set off at the same time as him so he could see I was really going.' He grinned suddenly. 'No sooner did she realize he was gone than Camilla decided *she* was going to London, too. Rang me up to tell me. He'd have had a fit if he knew, because he told her on Sunday night no more London trips this month. She took Jocasta – oh, by the way, before I forget, Jocasta's put in an urgent request for you to go riding with her tomorrow. She wanted to ride today but her mother had other ideas. If it's a "yes", she'll come over for you around nine o'clock.'

'If it's not raining?'

'Oh, it'll be fine tomorrow. These showers are the last of it,' he said with the easy confidence of one who knew. 'They'll blow out by this evening. Well, come on, woman, chop chop!' he added, clapping his hands. 'Run and wash your hands. I'm taking you to the Ship Inn for lunch. No need to change – you look amazingly hot in those dungarees. Woof woof !'

'Oh, Jack,' she said, 'I can't. If I go out to lunch with you that'll be the whole day gone—'

'My idea exactly,' he said with an evil grin.

'And I wanted to get this papering finished.'

'There's no rush, is there? You're your own boss.'

'But there's a certain rhythm to a job, and if you break it...' She saw this was not making any impression. 'And if I'm taking half tomorrow off to ride,' she went on.

'Oh, you'll play with Jocasta but you won't play with me,' he said, pretending petulance.

'Wait! I've got an idea! Don't go away.'

'Now where would I be going?' she began, but he had dashed out of the house. She heard the car door slam and the engine start, so she went back to work, measuring and cutting the next length of paper. She was wondering if she ought to start pasting it, when she heard the car again, and a moment later he reappeared, carrying a brown paper grocery sack.

'You have to eat, don't you?' he anticipated any protest on her part. 'You'll faint and fall off your ladder otherwise. So if you won't come to lunch, lunch will have to come to you. I assume you have plates and glasses and things in your 'umble abode? Or should I say 'ovel?'

He walked past her into the kitchen, and she shrugged and followed him, washed her hands at the sink, and watched him unpack the bag. 'Ta-da!' he fanfared. 'Come on, girl, plates!'

'Cornish pasties!' she exclaimed. They smelled wonderful.

'Just pasties,' he corrected. 'According to the EU, you're not allowed to call them Cornish pasties unless they're made in Cornwall, and these were made just up the road at Broad Farm. Freshly baked on the premises – they're still warm.'

'I've heard of Broad Farm cheese. They do pasties as well?'

'They do just about everything. You ought to visit the farm shop. Ice cream, sausages, cheese, cakes. It's the only way a small farm can keep going these days. And, to go with the pasties...' He drew a tall slim bottle from the bag.

'They sell wine as well?'

'No, but the Blue Ball does. Hock. I know it sounds weird, but you'll be amazed how good they taste together. Glasses? Now sit, sit, eat while it's still warm.'

They sat down opposite each other at the table, and Kate discovered she was famished. She'd had nothing since toast at breakfast and it was well past lunchtime. The pasty was delectable – 'The best I've ever tasted,' she said sincerely – with crisp, golden, melt-in the-mouth pastry and a rich meaty filling.

'There's just an intriguing hint of sweetness to it,' she said enquiringly.

'Maggie uses butternut squash instead of swede,' Jack informed her.

'And then that pepperiness to contrast,' Kate went on. 'And they both seem to go well with the wine.'

'Didn't I tell you? I don't know why people don't trust me,' Jack complained. 'And there's Maggie's famous strawberry-rhubarb pie for afterwards. With clotted cream.'

'Oh, you hedonist!' she teased.

He smiled at her across the rim of his glass, and said, 'Seriously, I really *was* impressed watching you hang that paper. You're doing a really nice job. I had no idea – I thought you were just going to give the place a lick of paint and then sell it.'

'Oh, well, I'm a bit of a perfectionist. I don't like to do a bad job.'

'But surely it can't be worth all that effort, if you're just getting rid of it anyway?'

She raised an eyebrow. Had he been talking to Phil Kingdon? 'I suppose it's a sort of project,' she said. 'You know, the Cinderella thing – the transformation. That's always irresistible.'

'Cinderella? This place is more of an ugly sister.'

'Don't insult my house, please.'

'But it'll never be worth what you put into it.'

'Well, it's worth it to me,' she said firmly. Why did everyone want her to go? She changed the subject. 'What's Camilla gone to London for, that Ed wouldn't approve of ?'

He shrugged. 'What she always goes for – shopping. And lunch. And the spa. Add in the train fare – and she likes to go first class – and she can drop a couple of thousand in one day. Of course, with Jocasta along, there won't be the spa. But still ... I tell you, if there was an Olympic event in getting through money, Camilla would be up there on the podium.'

'Oh dear. But isn't it her money to spend?'

'That depends on your point of view,' Jack said, not smiling now. 'You see, when Dad died, he left the estate to her for her lifetime, which means she can spend the income but not the capital – that's the theory, anyway. But with land, you can't really separate the two. If you want to keep the estate in good heart, you have to keep ploughing money back in, maintaining it, building it up. It should support the family, but it's not a cash cow to be endlessly milked. If you run it down beyond a certain point, the whole thing collapses – and it's not hers to collapse. Camilla doesn't understand that, though Ed tries to make her see it. She just spends, and runs up bills, and Ed won't let her be in debt so he has to find the money somewhere to pay them. Clothes, shoes, handbags, lunches – club memberships – a personal trainer ... it just goes on. She can spend two hundred quid just getting her highlights done.'

Kate cast a look at his own artfully tousled, skilfully highlighted locks. To his credit, he did manage a rueful smile. 'Oh, I know. But mine's fifty quid a touch, not two hundred.'

'I'm sure the European Monetary Fund will find that reassuring,' Kate said gravely.

'I know I'm not exactly a paragon of frugality – Ed's the one for that. But I do understand the limits. To an extent. From time to time. Or at least, I understand what the estate is for, and I wouldn't want to see it broken up and sold. Camilla wouldn't give a damn. She hasn't got land in her blood.'

'You sound as if you hate her,' Kate suggested cautiously.

He looked shocked. 'Not *hate* her, of course I don't! She annoys me sometimes. But it was hard when Dad first brought her home. I mean, she's only two years older than me. It's hard to take when your father marries someone your own age. I was twenty-one and Ed was twenty-five, and Camilla was twenty-three. You don't like to see your father make a fool of himself.'

'You don't remember your mother, I suppose?'

'No. I was only two when she died, so I don't remember her at all. I've seen photos, of course. She was beautiful – not glamorous like Camilla, but beautiful in her own way, a sort of timeless, classical beauty. Dad adored her. She was the daughter of the Earl of Bastwick, so she understood the land and the way of life, and local people looked up to her. She was a great lady.' He brooded a moment. 'And then Dad brings home someone Ed or I might have dated, for our stepmother!'

'Well, he didn't dash straight out and remarry,' Kate pointed out. 'He waited until you were grown up. Wasn't he entitled to a bit of pleasure after that?'

Jack shook off the frown. 'Oh, well, of course! All power to the old man. God, I hope I can still pull the birds like that when I'm his age. Poor guy didn't get his money's worth, though. They were only married three years before he died.'

'That must have been hard. Hard on Camilla, too,' she added. 'I'm surprised she hasn't married again, when she's so attractive.'

'She can't,' Jack said. 'Another result of that dopey will Dad made. She only gets the income from the estate if she doesn't remarry. Dad thought it wouldn't be fair on us to keep supporting her if she had a husband to do it. Fair enough, except that it means she can't marry anyone who isn't rich enough to replace what she gets from the estate – which, the way she goes about it, is a lot. To date, no-one's come up to scratch. She has a string of admirers, but none of them's rich enough.'

'Oh, hence the Brigadier,' Kate said, enlightened.

'Harry? He's a decent stick, but he'd never be able to support Camilla's shopping habit. I'm not sure she really favours him, anyway. He's a bit old for her.'

'She married one older man,' Kate pointed out. 'Maybe she has a taste for them.'

Jack sighed. 'Well, Ed would be glad if Harry took her off his hands. He works every hour God sends trying to put the estate on a firm footing, but it's a bit like pouring water into the sink without putting the plug in first.'

'What does he do in London? Jocasta said he had a company.'

'Yes, he has his own firm, a procurement consultancy.'

'Procurement? Don't tell me he runs a brothel?'

Jack roared at that. 'The last person! My God, imagine old straight-laced Ed...! No,' he said, settling down again, 'he advises companies on how to source the things they buy more efficiently and cheaply, and set up management systems and develop relationships with their suppliers and so on. It's a joke, really,' he concluded. 'He spends his time in London saving other companies money, then comes home and spends the money he makes that way paying Camilla's bills.'

'No wonder it makes him mad,' Kate said with sympathy. The sink with the plug out – what a potent image!

Jack smiled and shrugged. 'Ed's problem is that he's always felt responsible for everyone and everything, from the time our mother died and he thought he had to look after me – *and* Dad come to that, because Dad was a basket case for a long time afterwards. And he was only six years old. He needs to lighten up, realize he doesn't have to solve the problems of the whole world. That's my role in all this, in case you hadn't twigged.' He gave her a wicked look. 'To provide the comic relief, make him laugh, get him to relax once in a while and have a bit of fun. Generally loosen the corsets.'

'I can see you try really hard at it,' Kate said solemnly. 'Does it work?'

'Not too well.' Jack grinned. 'I do my best to set him a good example, but however much I loaf around and mess about, he insists on treading the straight-and-narrow and being generally reliable and conscientious.' He shook his head. 'I'm afraid he's a hopeless case.'

Kate thought of the brother with the chronic feeling of responsibility, and all he faced in a world that generally approved of self-indulgence, and was sorry for him. She was sad for the little boy all those years ago who, having just lost his mother, took up the burden of the whole family because he thought no-one else would. And he had grown up seeing himself as 'dark and grim' and without the knack of getting on with people, like his easy-going, happy-go-lucky younger brother. Life was so unfair.

'But why are we talking about my brother,' Jack went on, breaking the brief silence, 'when there are two much more fascinating people right here at this table? Camilla says she's asked you next weekend. I'm glad! I might even enter for one of the classes at Buscombe, if you'll be there to be impressed.'

'Can you still enter at this late stage?'

'Oh yes, right up to the day before. Of course,' he added less positively, 'it would mean I'd have to practise a couple of times before then, which sounds too much like hard work. Especially when I could be impressing you by taking you out to expensive restaurants instead.'

Kate mimicked wiping sweat from her brow. 'Phew! For a minute then I thought you'd abandoned your lifelong hedonism. Don't give me shocks like that.'

'You,' Jack said severely, 'are a very wicked woman.'

Thirteen

As promised, the showers marched through on Tuesday night, and Wednesday dawned sparkling bright, the sky so brilliantly clear that it looked as if it had been washed and polished. Kate looked at her half-finished papering with no regrets at leaving it for another morning. After all, she was in no hurry – as Jack said, she was her own boss.

As she was putting the kettle on, Kay popped in with two brown eggs: 'For your breakfast. New laid. Bill Crang give my Darren a box yesterday from his hens in his garden. I s'pose you wouldn't be able to babysit for a bit tonight, would you?' she concluded wistfully. 'Only there's that James Bond film I wanted to see and it's finishing this week and there's this friend of Darren's and his wife going, and we thought we could make a foursome if...'

'Of course I will,' Kate said. 'No problem.'

Kay looked as happy as if she'd just won a raffle. 'Oh, look at you, you're so nice! And we thought we'd go for a curry after, if that's all right? If we catch the early film, we'd still be back by half-ten-ish, if that's not too late?'

'Fine,' Kate said. 'You enjoy yourselves, take as long as you want.'

So she had a breakfast of two delicious boiled eggs and toast under her belt when the sound of hooves brought her to her door at ten to nine, and she saw Jocasta coming round the side of the house on Daphne, and leading a smaller, darker-coated pony by the headcollar it was wearing over its bridle.

'Isn't it a lovely day!' she called out in greeting, kicking her feet free of the stirrups and jumping down. 'This is Chloe, she's a darling. Are you riding like that?'

Kate looked down at her jeans. 'Is that a problem?'

'Oh, no, as long as you don't get sore knees. Jeans aren't very comfortable.'

'Well, jeans will have to do. I don't have any riding clothes.'

'So,' Jocasta said, 'which do you want to ride? Chloe's very quiet, and you're so slim she'll carry you easily, but if you want Daphne I don't mind swapping.'

Kate could tell from the tone of voice what the right answer was. 'I'll try Chloe, shall I, and see how we get on?'

She fetched the halved apple she had put ready and shut her front door behind her. The ponies' soft muzzles wrinkled at the smell of the apple and they took the pieces eagerly from her palm, though Daphne gave her a gleaming sidelong look and allowed her to feel just a touch of teeth against her skin, to let her know who was boss around here. *See, I could bite you if I wanted, but I won't.*

'Do you want me to check your girth and do

your stirrups?' Jocasta offered as Kate tied the rope loosely around Chloe's neck.

'No, I'm fine,' Kate said. Chloe stood patiently for her; and one good thing about her size – she was easy to mount. Kate could almost have stepped on. Daphne swung round, impatient to be off, and Jocasta swung him back with easy, accustomed skill, saying, 'Oh, this is so nice! It's lovely to have someone to ride with. Ed's always so busy these days, and Jack hasn't got on a horse for ages. He's supposed to exercise the horses when Ed's in London but he's too lazy, he just turns them out. I wish I had a sister. You don't know how lousy it is only having brothers, like mine.'

'Well, only one of my sisters rode, and she soon gave it up,' Kate said, adjusting herself to Chloe's short stride as they rode off down the track. It was a long time since she had ridden a pony, and she had forgotten how the short neck made you feel as if you were going to come off over the front all the time.

'Why?' Jocasta asked in astonishment.

'Why did she give it up? Because she got interested in boys instead.'

'Oh, *boys*!' Jocasta said witheringly. 'I'm *never* going to get mixed up with boys. Horses are much nicer.'

'I have to agree with you, on the whole,' Kate said. 'Much nicer, but not nearly so easy to marry.'

'I'm never getting married,' Jocasta said definitely.

'Really? Are you sure?'

'What good does it do you? My mother was only married a little while and then my father died and now she's stuck here when she'd much rather live in London. And stuck with Ed, when he'd much rather be without her.'

'Oh, I'm sure that's not—' Kate began.

But Jocasta went on in a very matter-of-fact way, as if it didn't upset her in the least, 'No, it's true. There was a terrible row on Sunday night when he got back from taking you home. You were lucky to miss it. All about Mummy selling Little's – *again*. And Mummy said he was irrational because he's always telling her he won't pay her bills, and then when she finds a way to pay them herself he doesn't like that either.'

'I'm not sure you should be telling me all this,' Kate said uneasily.

'Oh, that's all right. You're one of the family now. And everyone knows all this stuff anyway. So Ed said the whole point was not to run up the bills in the first place, and he said *everyone* must try and spend less, and Mummy said *that* was rich, what about Jack, and Ed said Jack paid his way working at the factory, and Mummy gave such a honk – like this, *"Hah!"* – that she nearly choked herself and she said Jack hadn't done a day's work in years. So then I said if *everyone* had to save money, I'd leave St Hilda's and they could save my school fees. Because I hate it there,' she added as an aside. 'The other girls are so lame, and I'd much sooner go to day school so I could come home every day and go riding and stuff. So then Mummy said she'd be damned if I left St Hilda's, it was the best school and she was damn well going to make sure I got something out of the estate because it looked as though my school fees were all I ever *would* get, and then she burst into tears and ran upstairs.'

'Oh dear, that must have been awkward,' Kate said.

'Not really, she does that a lot. But it was horrible on Monday, with everyone humping around in a bad mood, and Mummy having to stay home because Ed was there and he'd have asked where she was going if she went out. And it was raining so much I couldn't go riding. And then on Tuesday, as soon as Mummy heard Ed had gone to London, she said we'd go up too and buy me some new clothes and have lunch at Harvey Nick's, which is my favourite place, and she bought some new clothes too, so that put her in a good mood again, and that's why I couldn't come and ride with you yesterday.'

'The weather's nicer today,' Kate said consolingly. 'I don't think I've ever seen a clearer day. It's gorgeous.'

'Yes, and this afternoon I'm going to see my friend India who lives at Porlock Weir – she's the only one at St Hilda's I really like. Mummy's going to drive me, because she's in a good mood because Ed's not coming back until tomorrow night. She's going to have tea with India's mother while India and I go to the beach. Mummy says the water will be far too cold for swimming but if we want to give ourselves heart attacks that's our lookout.' It was said quite serenely. Either Jocasta was a very good actor, or she had developed an indifference to the conflicting passions of her family that should stand her in good stead against the buffets of the wider world.

'It probably will be too cold,' Kate said, from experience.

'Well, we can paddle and mess about, anyway. Are you settled in now? Shall we have a canter?'

'I think I can manage that.'

'OK. Just shout if you want me to stop. Chloe's quite fast for her size, but she won't overtake Daphne.'

And she was off. Daphne had evidently been waiting for this moment, because in a few strides he was no longer cantering but galloping flat out. Chloe followed willingly, her little hooves slamming the earth in a rapid staccato like gunfire, but her first enthusiasm soon cooled and she dropped back to a more sustainable pace. Jocasta and Daphne drew ahead until they were only a dot on the horizon, but eventually she pulled up and walked the blowing pony back towards them. After that they left the track and turned on to the moors, and rode more quietly, while Jocasta, at Kate's request, pointed out landmarks and gave the names of hills and recounted some of the old stories about the places and the people.

The sun grew warm on their backs and the smell of the earth rose through the bracken as they disturbed it. The little becks sparkled down in the coombes, too far away to be heard, and the skylarks went up, laying their throbbing song against the blue heaven. Kate was in that rarest of human states, experiencing perfect happiness.

* * *

They came back a different way, describing a large circle, and when Kate found they were at the crossroads in Bursford, she said they might as well ride home to The Hall, and she would walk back from there.

'Are you sure?' Jocasta said. 'It's no trouble to ride up to your house – I don't mind leading Chloe back.'

'No, let's take them home. I'm sure Chloe's had enough of my great weight on her back.'

'Pooh! You're nothing. She can go all day.'

But Kate was feeling stiff, not having ridden for a long time, and thought the walk would do her good, loosen her up, so she insisted.

They didn't ride through the main entrance but through a five-barred gate, half hidden in the overgrown hedge, which led by a curved track through the trees to the stable yard. It was mostly red-brick Victorian, evidently coeval with the house, but with the addition of a modern range of loose-boxes and a big equipment shed.

Jocasta jumped down and led Daphne towards the old stable, and jumped in surprise when Ed came out. She scowled. 'You aren't supposed to be here. You're not supposed to be coming back until tomorrow.'

'I got what I wanted to do finished. And I want to have some practice rides before the weekend,' he said neutrally, and looked across at Kate. 'You terrible child, did you make Kate ride Chloe?' he said.

'She didn't mind,' Jocasta said.

'I didn't mind,' Kate confirmed, ever the

diplomat. 'She's nice – once I got used to the short stride. It's a long time since I rode a pony.'

He looked at her for a moment as if judging whether she meant it or not, then said briskly, 'I promised to show you the stables. What better time than now? Jocasta, take the ponies and turn them out. You'd better give them both a small feed – Chloe because she's old and Daphne because he's racing at the weekend.'

'How much?' Jocasta asked, coming back to take Chloe's reins from Kate, pulling Daphne behind her. She looked sulky.

'One scoop of oats and two of chaff for Daphne, half that for Chloe.' She turned away. 'Don't forget to brush out the saddle marks.'

'I know, I know.' She trailed off, leading the ponies towards the gap between the old and new buildings.

'And then take the dogs out for a walk,' he called after her. 'They don't look as though they've been out for two days.'

Jocasta muttered something under her breath that sounded like, 'You spoil everything,' and gave him a glower over her shoulder.

Ed watched them go. 'You can't imagine how it warms my heart to be welcomed back so enthusiastically,' he murmured.

I'm glad to see you, Kate thought, but didn't quite like to say it. He looked at her and gave one of his little quirk-of-the-lips smiles, as though he had heard the thought. He looked tired, Kate thought. Worries of the world on his shoulders, of course – who wouldn't be tired?

'You surprised her, that's all,' Kate said.

He looked at her. 'You don't need to defend her. It wasn't her fault her mother took her shopping in London as soon as I was out of the way.'

'Oh,' said Kate. 'How—?'

'I have my sources,' he said.

She remembered the Brigadier saying 'people tell him things'.

'It was one of the reasons I came back early,' he said. 'Damage limitation.' *What a life you lead*, Kate thought. 'Anyway,' he said, in a brighter tone, 'let's look at the stables.'

They had a quick peep into the old block, which had six stalls, with the typical high wooden divisions with bars at the top, wooden hay racks and a cobbled floor. 'It's a piece of history,' Kate said.

'I think so,' Ed said. 'Jack was for pulling it down and replacing it when we decided to have some loose-boxes, but I said it should be preserved. There aren't so many of them left around the country any more. So we added the new range on.'

'I've always wondered about the bars,' Kate said. 'Did Victorian horses bite?'

'Probably. I don't suppose they were treated with such kindness and affection as nowadays.'

'Why not?'

'There were more of them, for a start. And they were looked after by grooms, not their owners. I expect grooms had their favourites, but the rest were just a job.'

'How many horses do you keep?' Kate asked.

'Five, apart from the ponies. Two of the hunters are out already, and there's a general riding horse who lives out most of the time. We've just kept the two up for the point-to-pointing, Graceland and Henna, but I suppose I should turn Henna out if Jack's not riding her at the weekend.'

'He said he might,' Kate said.

'He won't,' Ed said with certainty. 'He's not in the mood at the moment. He tends to ride by fits and starts. For a few weeks he'll be out every day and taking it seriously, and then he'll suddenly drop it and lounge about doing nothing and saying he can't be bothered. He's in can't-be-bothered mode at the moment. Come and see the two in stables, anyway.'

As they crossed the yard, a head came out over the door of one of the boxes, and the horse nickered in greeting. It was a bay of about sixteen hands, big and handsome and fit-looking. It lowered its muzzle trustingly into Ed's hands, then ran its lips over his head, and finally rubbed the side of its face up and down his sleeve, solving the problem of an itchy eye in the way Kate always thought was probably the true root of the relationship between man and horse. At some point in history horses had discovered what humans were good for, and the bargain was made.

'This is Graceland – Gracie,' Ed said with so much affection in his voice, Kate was suddenly glad there was someone he could love unreservedly. 'He's mine.'

'He's a big fellow,' Kate said, stroking his neck.

'Sixteen-two,' Ed offered. 'Seven years old,

and jumps like a stag.'

'He's got a tremendous crest,' Kate said. 'I should think he takes some holding.'

'Mouth like a kitten,' Ed boasted. 'I just wish I could be here all the time so I could ride him more. It's one of the things I like least about going to London three or four days a week – leaving him behind.'

'And you're entering him at Buscombe? Are you going to win?'

'Not really. He's not experienced enough,' he said, stroking the other side of the neck. Graceland stopped rubbing his eye and investigated Kate with his prehensile, rubbery lips to see if any part of her was good to eat. 'I'd really love to have the time to three-day-event him. If I could be here all the time, running the estate, we could get into training. He's got it in him to be a champion – haven't you, Gracie? You could be a Badminton star, couldn't you, old boy?' His voice took on a note she had never yet heard in it. The horse regarded him with a kind and humorous eye.

'It's a shame to let your dream go by the board,' Kate said, quietly, so as not to break the mood. 'Do you really have to go to London?'

'My business needs me at the moment. We're expanding, and I have to keep a hand on the rein. And...' He sighed instead of finishing the sentence.

She thought she knew what the end was. 'It's a break for you, I suppose,' she suggested.

'It's nice sometimes to face problems you have the answers to,' he admitted. She almost held her breath at this admission: he was letting her further into his confidence than she had any right to expect. What might he tell her next?

But Gracie stuck his nose up between them and blew out sharply, giving each of them a blast in the ear, breaking the mood. And there was a peremptory banging from the box next door. The other horse had belatedly cottoned on that there were humans about, had stuck its head over and was rapping the door with a forefoot.

'Henna's getting jealous. We mustn't neglect her,' he said, and led Kate over.

'What a perfect name for her,' Kate said. The mare was about fifteen-two, and a wonderful dark red-chestnut in colour, with not a white hair on her. 'She's very Rita Hayworth. I'd better not stand too near her – we might clash. Is she bred?'

'Yes,' said Ed. 'She's fast, and she has tremendous stamina. It's a shame she's so wasted.'

Henna was tossing her head up and down and swinging from foot to foot, and her investigation of their hands and collars was much more urgent than Gracie's. She had all the classic signs of a bored horse.

'She needs more exercise,' Ed sighed. 'We bought her for Camilla, but she hardly ever rides, so Jack took her over, but he doesn't take her out regularly enough.'

'Well, now you're back...' Kate suggested. An idea had formed in her mind, but she didn't like to push it.

'But I really need to be riding Gracie,' he said. He stroked the mare's neck, and then looked down at Kate as if it had suddenly occurred to him. 'Would you like to go riding again tomorrow? But this time on a proper horse?'

'You'd let me ride Henna?'

'Don't you think you're up to it?'

'I'd love to try her – but remember today was the first time I've ridden in ages.'

'You obviously didn't have any trouble. It's like riding a bicycle.'

'Not entirely,' she said, laughing.

'You know what I mean. If you do it properly and for long enough when you're young, you don't forget. Will you? A long ride, to get the fidgets out of their feet.'

'I'd love to,' Kate said, feeling her insides swoon with how much she'd *really* love to.

'That's great,' he said, and then, 'I won't be taking you away from your work?'

'I'm my own boss,' she said. 'I can take time off when I want. Though I don't know if Jocasta will forgive me. I think she sees me as *her* friend and no-one else's.'

'Oh, she can come too,' he said easily, and Kate cursed herself for having mentioned it. 'She needs to get Daphne hardened up for Monday. We don't need to go fast, so he'll be able to keep up. We'll do a long ride and lots of hill work and get some muscle on their quarters.'

Jocasta came trailing back from the field, laden with saddles and bridles which she dumped unceremoniously on the ground. 'I don't really have to take the dogs out, do I? Can't they just run about in the field?'

'You know it's not the same thing,' Ed said. 'There's no mental exercise in it.' He picked up one saddle and started towards the tackle shed, so Kate picked up the other leaving Jocasta to gather the bridles. 'I'd take them myself,' Ed went on, with a hint of sympathy for the beleaguered child, 'but I have to go and see Jacobsen about his sheep, and then I have to go over the estate books, which will take all afternoon, at least. Be a good girl.'

'Oh all *right*,' Jocasta said moodily, and then brightened. 'Will you come?' she asked Kate.

'I have to go home and do some work,' she said.

Jocasta thought rapidly. 'Well, if you're walking home, I can walk with you with the dogs, can't I?'

Kate took pity. 'Of course,' she said. 'It'll be nice to have the company.'

And as well as Jocasta's instant joy, her reward was an approving look from Ed, who was obviously fonder of his half-sister than she appreciated, and was glad someone was being kind to her.

Fourteen

She went over to Kay's at a quarter to six so they could get away by six. Darren had just arrived, having left work a bit early; Kay was rushing about like a scalded hen.

'I'm all behind like the cow's tail,' she wailed. 'Darren's having a quick wash and changing his shirt, but I haven't even brushed my hair and I've still got to feed the kids.'

The children were in the kitchen, sitting at the table ready, and there was a smell of fish in the air.

'I'll do it,' Kate said. 'What are they having?'

'Would you? Oh, you are a love,' Kay cried. 'It's fish fingers, beans and mash. It's all ready, bar the serving up. I did you some too, seeing as you're coming over so early. I didn't think you'd've had time for tea. Fish fingers are in the oven, should be done now. And the kettle's boiled, if you want to make yourself a cuppa—'

'Come on, girl, get your skates on!' came a male bellow from up the stairs.

'Go,' said Kate, making a shooing motion. 'I'll see to it.'

She was starving, actually. She served the fish fingers, baked beans and mash on to three plates and sat down at the table with the children while upstairs various bumps and scrapes attested to hasty preparation. Darren came down, put his coat on and stood by the front door jingling his keys. Kay appeared at last, looking flushed, one side of her jacket collar caught under and one side of her hair sticking up more than the other. 'All right?' she asked breathlessly. 'Oh, you found the tomato sauce. Don't let Dommie have too much. He just swamps it. And—'

'Come *on*, Kay,' Darren called, halfway out of the front door now. 'We'll be late.'

'I can manage,' Kate said. 'Have a nice time and don't worry about anything.'

And they were gone. The children carried on eating serenely. Dommie picked up a piece of paper from beside his plate and pushed it across to Kate. 'I did you this at school yesterday, but it got squashed.'

It was a sheet of paper with some smears of paint on it, and two other odd shaped pieces of paper stuck on it for no apparent reason. One corner of the large sheet was torn off, and there was what appeared to be a muddy footprint across it.

Kate handled it gingerly. 'What is it?' She had noticed now that the word Mummy was written in wobbly letters at the bottom. The child was a chancer.

Dommie stared at her across a bulging mouthful of potato and beans as if she had asked a totally irrational question. Finally he swallowed massively and said, 'Jason trod on it. When he fell over. Miss Cornish says we're having a feel trip tomorrow. About weather.'

‘Whether what?’ Kate asked, distracted.

‘But only in the playground, cos of elfin safety. We have to be-tend.’

‘Pretend what?’

Dommie’s face became costive with effort. At last he started afresh. ‘Jason cut his chin. There was all blood.’

She realized she had lost the moment. ‘Don’t just eat potato and beans. Eat some fish finger, too,’ she said, noticing he had been concealing it under the mash and the sea of tomato sauce.

‘I *like* fish fingers,’ Hayley announced, a piece teetering on a fork towards her open mouth.

‘Good. I do too,’ said Kate.

‘Do fish have fingers?’ Dommie asked. His face brightened as the full glory of the thought expanded in his mind. ‘Kate, do fish have fingers? I bet they do. Do they have fingers and feet and noses and ears?’ He began to giggle.

Kate could see the situation deteriorating. ‘Eat your supper,’ she said, trying to be stern.

‘Fingers and toes and noses and heads and legs,’ Dommie chanted.

Hayley banged her fork down messily in her potato, splashing herself with dots of tomato sauce in a scarlet pattern that would send a forensic investigator into delirium. ‘Fingers!’ she shouted.

‘Eat properly, or there’ll be no pudding,’ Kate commanded. They were both banging forks now, shrieking with giggles at the splashes. She wondered for a moment why anyone had children.

To calm them down after their Mr Men yoghurts,

she took them both on the sofa to watch a Postman Pat DVD (*Pat – The Glory Years*). Hayley curled up in her lap and Dommie scooched up as close to her as he could get without actually ending up on the other side. Hayley only watched for a few minutes before her thumb went in her mouth, she turned her face into Kate's chest, and was soon slumbering deeply. Dommie watched with close attention what was obviously a favourite DVD, for every now and then he would tell her what was going to happen just before it did. Whenever the theme song came on – which seemed agonizingly often – he sang it with his own words: 'Postman Pat, Postman Pat, Postman Pat in his silly old hat.' And repeat. He was obviously delighted with himself for thinking of it, because he giggled inordinately each time.

Kate was afraid the stories were just too drama-packed and he'd never settle down.

But at the end of the DVD he went unexpectedly meekly to bed, doing his own teeth while she put the still sleeping Hayley down. She heard him singing quietly to himself in the bathroom. When she went in, she found he had spread toothpaste all over his face and was shaving himself with the handle of his toothbrush.

When he was in bed too, she went down and cleaned up the kitchen, then back to the sofa to watch an episode of *Grey's Anatomy* she discovered (oh, the glories of satellite!) on one of the many channels she didn't get. She didn't get to the end of it, however, for she woke with a start to a completely different programme as Kay and Darren came in, very cheerful and smelling sweetly of curry.

'You all right?' Kay asked.

'Fine,' Kate said, struggling upright and covertly wiping a bit of drool off her chin. 'Just watching TV.'

'Kids all right?'

'Yes, they were no trouble at all,' Kate said with mental crossed fingers. 'Did you have a nice time? Was the film good?'

'Ooh, that Daniel Craig,' Kay said. 'I'd have him between two bits of bread, any day of the week. Darren liked the Bond Girl an' all, didn't you?'

'Nice,' he said. He wasn't a chatty man.

'So,' Kay said, and looked at Kate speculatively, her head slightly on one side, as though she had something to impart.

'Yes?' Kate asked.

Kay opened her mouth to speak, but Darren said, 'Kate's tired, she wants to get off to bed. And I've gotter get in early tomorrow. Want me to walk you to the door?' he asked.

'No, I'm fine,' Kate said. She patted her pocket. 'I thought to bring a torch with me this time.'

So they said their goodnights. Outside it was black, and her eyes took time to adjust after the lit house. She shone the torch on the path in case of trip hazards. It was a feeble little blue light – the sort of torch you hang on your keyring to help you find the keyhole – but it was enough to show her her way. Her gate squeaked under her hand; she tramped carefully up her own overgrown path, and pulled out her key, and as she reached the door, shone the torch on it to locate the keyhole.

Someone had painted something on her door. She touched it cautiously, and her finger came away sticky. She opened the door and turned on the inside light to see better.

Large, rough letters, and the paint was red – of course! She hoped it was paint, anyway. Hastily, splashily painted, so that there were drips on the doorstep. She found herself thinking of the kids and tomato ketchup. Better think of that than the words someone had felt strongly enough to paint roughly on her front door.

GO HOME
YOUR NOT WANTED

She was out at first light with turps and a rag, but the paint had sunk deeply into the old, dry wood and was hard to remove. Darren came out of his house to go to work while she was still labouring, and came across to her gate to say, 'You're starting early.' Then he saw what she was doing. He came up the path and stood beside her silently a moment while she rubbed, then said, 'Probably some drunk kids having a laugh. Don't mean anything.'

'That's what I'm telling myself,' she said, though she was quite shaken inside.

Darren's big hand reached across her shoulder and he touched the paint and scraped at it with a fingernail. 'Try sandpaper,' he said. 'The paint's loose underneath.'

'I was going to sand this door down anyway,' she said, 'and repaint it properly. It wasn't the first job on my list, though.'

'Right.' He laid his hand an instant on her shoulder. 'Don't take it to heart. People don't think like that.' And then, 'Gotter go. Be late for work.'

Kate gave up with the turps, went and fetched a can of undercoat and quickly painted over the whole thing. You could see a ghostly outline of the words, but only if you looked. From the road it would look like part of her redecorating. She hoped the perpetrators wouldn't come back to admire their handiwork and feel obliged to restore it.

With a pub at the bottom of the street, she told herself, there was always the possibility of drunks wandering past late at night and making fools of themselves. It was a shame she had fallen asleep, or she might have heard them – heard the gate squeak, anyway.

She had the ride to look forward to today, and determinedly dismissed the incident from her mind. She wasn't going to let it spoil her day.

She was to drive over to The Hall for a ten o'clock start. At half past nine she was just thinking of getting ready when Kay appeared, back from taking the kids to school.

'You all right? Darren rung me, told me about your door. Rotten little scrotes. You didn't hear anything?'

'Not a thing,' Kate said. 'But I'm not letting it upset me. I'm not even going to think about it.'

'Quite right,' Kay said, and hesitated with that

same look of impending communication. 'Last night,' she began.

'Yes?' Kate said, mainly to hurry her along because she wanted to do something with her hair before the ride.

'Well, Darren didn't think I should tell you, but if it was me, I'd want to know.'

'Know what?'

'Well, last night, after the pictures, when we went for a curry, we went past Coco's – it's like a wine bar, but quite posh. And we saw Jack Blackmore in there. With a woman.'

'Oh yes?' Kate said neutrally.

Kay looked at her with sympathy. 'When I say "with a woman", I mean he was all over her. Young thing, she looked, blonde hair, miniskirt up to here and low-cut top – you wonder why some of 'em bother getting dressed at all. Anyway, they were smooching over the table and I don't know what his hand was doing under it. I'm sorry, Kate.'

'Don't be,' she said. There was no denying she felt a pang, but she was sure now she had never been serious about him. Her pride might have taken a dint, but nothing else. 'We went out a couple of times, had a bit of fun. That's all.'

'I did warn you about him,' Kay said, still anxiously, not taking Kate's assurance at face value. 'This one we saw him with, she's much more his usual sort. He likes 'em obvious. I was surprised he was making a play for you, you being a cut above, but then I thought maybe that was proof it was serious. So I was worried...'

'I'm fine,' Kate said, and smiled to prove it.

'He wasn't making a play for me. He only took me out really to thank me for rescuing the dog. There was nothing between us, just friendliness.'

'Oh,' said Kay, looking at her carefully, as if she still didn't believe.

'Look, thanks for telling me, but I'm really all right, no broken heart, listen.' She rapped her chest dramatically. 'See? Sound as a drum. And now I have to chuck you out, because I have to get ready to go out.'

'Going out?' Kay was instantly interested.

'Riding,' Kate said.

'Up The Hall? Jocasta again?'

'And Ed.'

'Oh,' said Kay, and it was quite different from the previous one. She gave a grin. 'Better let you get glammed up, then.'

'I'm just going riding!' Kate exclaimed, exasperated. And then, 'So you wouldn't mind if it was Ed instead of Jack – not that it is, but I'm interested in your thought processes.'

'Ed's a different kettle of fish,' Kay said mysteriously, and went away.

Jocasta was thrilled that the three of them were going out together. Ed seemed, Kate thought, perhaps just a shade less grave than on previous occasions, as though he was looking forward to the outing.

Henna looked enormous when she was led out, though that was just the contrast with Chloe, the last thing Kate had mounted. She also looked very fresh, and was skittering about, wanting to be off. Ed gave Kate a leg up, and held the mare while she adjusted her stirrups, and then told her to cock her leg forward while he tightened her girths. Jocasta was already up on Daphne. He went back and led out Graceland, checked the girth and was up in one graceful spring. Kate gave an inward sigh of pleasure. He looked simply perfect in the saddle. She didn't know why that was gratifying, but it was. She'd have hated for him to look at all ungainly.

They rode out the back way and straight on to the hills, climbing steeply through the woods for the first ten minutes before emerging on to the green hilltop and turning on to a wide mud track.

'All right?' Ed asked after a while, looking back at her.

Kate was not entirely comfortable. 'She keeps throwing her head up and down,' she said. She had narrowly missed a couple of painful – and probably bloody – bangs on the nose. 'And she won't let me take up her mouth at all.'

'It was a bad habit she had when we got her,' he said, halting Graceland so she could catch up with him. 'Hanging behind the bit, and letting her hocks trail. Probably ridden by someone heavy-handed, who hung on to her mouth. I thought we'd broken her of it, but I suppose she just isn't getting ridden enough, and she's reverting to her old habits.' When she was beside him, he moved Gracie on again so they were riding side by side, and looked her over critically. 'Your leg is slightly too far forward,' he said. 'Move your seat an inch further forward, and draw your lower leg back an inch. That's better. Now push your heels down, and use your seat to drive her on to the bit.' Kate obeyed. 'Any better?' he asked after a moment.

'A bit,' she said.

'It'll be easier at the trot,' he said. 'She's not paying attention. We'll trot for ten minutes or so and that'll steady her and bring her head down.'

He called to Jocasta, who had wandered ahead of them, and put Gracie into a trot. Henna jostled and flung her head around, wanting to race, but as Ed increased the pace to an extended trot, allowing Kate to drive her on, she found she couldn't overtake, and settled down to a lovely, long, ground-eating pace. They passed Daphne, who laid his ears back in annoyance and made a swiping pass of his teeth at Kate's leg, and she heard Jocasta cry, 'Woo-hoo!' as she put her pony into a canter to keep up.

And magically, after five minutes of fast trotting, Henna's head had come down, her hocks had come under her, and she was going as straight and steady as a line drawn with a ruler; Kate could feel her mouth, and felt in control again. Looking ahead between the pricked red-gold ears, she felt a great surge of happiness.

Another five minutes and the pace had become the long, easy, relaxed stride that covers miles and can be kept up for hours. Ahead of her, Ed posted in his saddle to Gracie's smooth pace; Jocasta and Daphne had dropped back but were still in sight. Finally Ed put his hand up, slowed to a collected trot, then a walk, and halted Gracie across the path, looking back with what was almost a smile.

'That looks better,' he said as Kate reached him

and halted.

'It is better,' she said, leaning forward to slap Henna's neck in approval. The mare blew out percussively through her nostrils, but stood quietly, though alert and ready. 'That awful head-tossing has stopped. And she's on the bit.'

'I can see. You two look very good together. How do you find her paces?'

'Lovely, now she's settled down.'

Jocasta came up to them at a canter, Daphne with his ears back and a very savage look on his face at the idea that any other equine could be at the head of the ride. 'You look brilliant together,' she called out to Kate. 'All that red hair! I didn't realize you rode so well.'

'Nor did I!' Kate laughed. 'It's been years since I was on a horse. But I suppose it comes back to you. I'll be stiff tomorrow, though.'

'Oh, that soon wears off,' Jocasta said, and to Ed: 'Are we going to do some jumping? There's that track down Badger Coombe with the tree trunks and the stream at the bottom, and the walls on the other side.'

'Yes, OK,' Ed said, 'as long as there's some serious hill work afterwards. We're not supposed to be enjoying ourselves.'

'Kate is,' Jocasta pointed out.

'Are you all right, jumping?' Ed asked.

'If it's not too high. I used to do cross-country, back in Dublin.'

'Ah! Well, this is just the same sort of thing – a woodland track, downhill, and a few natural hazards.'

'Lead me to it,' she said, with a happy grin.

Henna turned her head to look back at her, and the eye seemed good and kindly. 'I think she likes me,' she said.

'She likes being out,' Ed said, and then seemed to realize that was not very flattering. 'But she's going well for you, so she must like you, too.'

It was great fun, slithering and wiggling down the steepest part of the track, cantering where it was flatter, jumping the fallen tree trunks – which had obviously been trimmed and positioned specifically for riders – and a couple of laid hedges, then bursting out of the woods at the bottom, jumping the fast-running, stony little brook, and galloping uphill on the other side on open ground, over several drystone walls and a couple of jumps made of straw bales. They pulled up at the top to breathe the horses, and Kate said, 'That was terrific. She jumps like a stag.'

'Yes, she's got quite a pop in her,' Ed said.

'Daphne was brilliant too,' Jocasta said quickly.

'Yes, he was,' Kate said. 'He clears everything by miles.'

'You weren't watching,' Jocasta objected. 'How would you know?'

'I looked back several times, and when you were coming up the hill I thought you were going to overtake us.'

'That's what the ponies do best,' Jocasta said smugly. 'Running uphill. They're made for it. Close to the ground, not like those long-leggedy beasts.'

They were standing next to a low wall on the

other side of which was a tarmac road, and the sound of shod hooves on the hard surface heralded the arrival of another horse. Round the bend came a big, heavyweight grey, and Jocasta exclaimed, 'It's Neptune!' an instant before the rider was revealed to be the Brigadier.

'Hello, Harry,' Ed greeted him, as he halted beside them, on the other side of the wall, and, incorrigibly polite, lifted his cap to Kate.

'Lovely day for a ride. Hello, Jocasta. That pony of yours is going well.' His eyes came back to Kate. 'I was watching you as you came up the hill. You look as if you've been riding that mare for years.'

Kate patted her. 'I'm loving it. She feels wonderful.'

'She goes well for Kate,' Ed put in.

'So I see. You ought to ride her at Buscombe,' said Harry. 'Give the locals a run for their money.' He grinned. 'I get tired of seeing the same old names in the slot year after year.'

'Oh, thank you,' said Ed ironically.

'Not you, of course,' said Harry with a sidelong smile. 'But I wouldn't mind seeing Mrs Murray knocked off her pedestal. She was infernally rude to me out hunting last season, when she thought Neptune was in her way at a bullfinch.' He patted his mount. 'My old boy likes to take a good look at an obstacle, but he never refuses. How's Graceland going?'

They talked for a bit about the chances for various contestants, most of whom Kate didn't know, and then Henna sneezed, and Ed said, 'We'd better be moving along. Don't want the muscles to get cold.'

'See you at Buscombe, then,' Harry said in farewell, and, looking at Kate, 'and you with a number on your back!'

'I don't think there's any chance of that,' Kate said, laughing.

Back at the stables, Kate offered to rub down Henna, since Bradshaw was doing Graceland. 'I'm sorry, I have to dash,' Ed said. 'I have a meeting.'

'I'm happy to do it. I've had a wonderful time, thank you so much.'

He paused. 'Look, what Harry said – wouldn't you like to ride Henna in one of the classes on Monday?'

'I couldn't possibly,' Kate said, surprised. 'I'm sure he was only joking.'

'He wasn't. And I'm not. You ride quite well enough, and she goes well for you.'

'Out for a hack, yes, but not point-to-pointing.'

'You've done cross-country. That's harder. Pointing is faster, but the nice thing about Buscombe is that the course has got a bit of variety about it, a bit of up and down, so it's not just a slamming gallop round a course, like at Cothelstone, say. The pace won't be so fast. And you don't have to try and win.'

'Just as well!' Kate laughed.

'I'm serious,' Ed said, and he looked it. 'I'd like her to have the experience. And I think you'd find it fun. Look, we could put in a couple of days' practice, Friday and Saturday. You'd feel completely at home with her by then.'

Kate was running out of excuses. And she certainly liked the idea of competing: it gave her a bit of the old thrill she remembered from her teenage years. Plus, the thought of two days practising with Ed, one on one, monopolizing his attention, was very sweet.

'But I don't have any riding clothes,' she said, the last objection. 'I can't ride in jeans.'

'You said "can't", not "couldn't",' Ed said with his almost-smile. 'That means you want to.'

'All right, I want to. But the clothes *are* a problem.'

'Not at all. We can borrow some for you. Camilla's maybe. She's a bit taller than you, but you're about the same build. Or I think Susie Orde's about the same size as you. I promise you, finding clothes to fit you won't be a problem. There are hundreds of spare sets floating around. Will you do it?'

'Do what?' Jocasta asked, poking her head out from the stables. 'What are you two talking about?'

'Kate, riding at Buscombe on Monday.'

Jocasta's face lit up like a Christmas tree. 'Oh yes! *Epic*! You will, won't you, Kate? You and Henna – what a team!'

'It looks as though I'll have to,' Kate said.

'I'm glad,' said Ed, and looked it. Kate wondered why it mattered to him, but was happy anyway to have lightened his day by agreeing.

'I thought you were in a hurry,' Jocasta said to him, as he lingered, looking at Kate with satisfaction.

The mood broke. His face shut down again in seriousness and he said, 'God, yes, I am. Sorry, I must dash. Can you be here at ten tomorrow?'
'Yes,' said Kate, and he was gone.

Fifteen

She had entirely forgotten the painted words, until she parked her car in front of her house again, and saw the grey undercoat covering her front door. It made her heart sink a bit, and took some of the shine off the day.

She heaved herself out of the car – she had stiffened up in the short drive back – and hobbled up the path, aware also that she had some interesting chafes on her legs where the seams of her jeans had rubbed. There was a good reason that jodhpurs and breeches were made they way they were. It would be a relief to have some proper riding trousers for the practice tomorrow, if Ed was as good as his word.

She was in the bathroom anointing her wounds with Savlon when she heard someone knocking on the door below, and a moment later Jack's voice calling, 'Hello! Anyone at home?'

'Just a minute!' she called back. She pulled up her jeans and inspected herself in the mirror. Her hair was wild, and she grabbed the hairbrush and raked it through, even while telling herself she didn't have to look nice for Blackjack any more. Still, a girl had her pride.

When she came down the stairs, he was standing just inside the open door (she was getting to be a real local, not locking it when she came in). He was staring at it, but as soon as she appeared he stared at her instead and said, 'You *are* a sight for sore eyes! Please tell me you haven't had lunch yet. I'm starving, but even more than food, I'm starving for company. And I still haven't taken you to the Ship Inn yet.'

'I really ought to—' she began.

He slapped his brow. 'Oh, God! Please don't tell me you ought to do some work! After taking most of the day off to go riding with my brother and sister, the least you can do is give me a little bit of your time. Or do you want to be the cause of sibling rivalry?'

'Far from it,' she said.

'Right, then. Come with me. Come now. No arguments.'

'I ought to change. I'm all horsey.'

'Nonsense. You will illuminate any company just as you are. And I like the smell of horse.'

'Well, let me at least wash my hands,' she said with a laugh. She dashed upstairs, washed her hands and face, and at lightning speed changed her jeans and T-shirt for a clean pair and a nicer top.

When she got downstairs he was staring at the door again, and said, 'Is it my imagination or is there something written on this door?'

'I'll tell you about it over lunch,' she said.

The Ship Inn was genuine Tudor, all beams and thatch, but with discreetly done additions and a large car park out at the back attesting to its popularity.

'It's a long way from the sea to be called the Ship,' Kate observed as they parked.

'That's the old country way of pronouncing "sheep",' Jack said. 'All the old inland pubs called the Ship, or variations thereof, are really about sheep.'

'That explains a lot,' Kate said.

He was evidently well known there, for he was greeted in a friendly manner as they went in, and Kate was given a quick, interested scrutiny. The inside was beams and different levels, like the Oak, but much posher, with everything rubbed down and waxed, brass lamps with acid-embossed glass shades, and curtains and seat cushions in muted tones of oatmeal and faded rose.

They were shown to a table in an odd little alcove with a leaded window. The other people they passed, Kate noted, looked very well-to-do, and were conversing in quiet, cultured voices. Her jeans suddenly felt very wrong, but everyone was too polite to look up as they passed, so she hoped she had gone unnoticed.

The waiter gave them menus and left them to peruse. The food was a notch fancier even than the Blue Ball, which she had thought fancy enough, and she tried not to notice the prices for fear of a heart attack. There was obviously a lot of money around in this part of the world. Even as she thought that, she thought falteringly of Ed trying to make the books balance and the estate viable – and here was Blackjack, spending like a sailor, and her helping him! But she couldn't back out now, so she might as well enjoy herself, if she could.

But there was something to be said first. When they were alone she cleared her throat and said, 'Before we order, and just in case you change your mind about buying me lunch, there's something I have to tell you.'

'That sounds ominous,' he said, but with a grin that showed he wasn't worried.

'I'm afraid you were seen last night.'

The grin was wiped off. He tried to look puzzled, but it didn't work. 'Seen?' he said feebly.

'With a pneumatic blonde in Coco's wine bar. Someone was kind enough to pass on the information to me.'

'Oh,' he said, thinking furiously. 'Oh, that was just someone I was interviewing for a job.'

'I'm not sure what sort of job involves intimate body searches,' Kate said. He opened and shut his mouth without finding any words. She laid a hand on his. 'Look, it's all right. I'm not upset or anything. You're entitled to go out with anyone you want. I only thought I'd better tell you before you lashed out on an expensive lunch for me.'

'I don't know what to say,' he said, looking disconcerted.

'Nothing *to* say,' Kate said. 'You and I – there was never anything in it really, was there? We just had a couple of nice meals together, that's all.'

'But I really, really like you,' he protested.

'And I really like you.'

'You do?' He seemed surprised, which she found oddly touching.

'Yes, I do. So we could be friends, perhaps? If

you'd like that?'

'I'd like that.' He managed a smile. 'Though I can't promise not to try and take it further.'

'You don't need to. A friend is something I need at the moment. But are we still having lunch?'

'What kind of a cheapskate do you take me for? Choose what you like. And let's have some champagne, to show there are no hard feelings.'

She laughed. 'Being your friend obviously has its perks.'

So she chose warm salad of calves' sweetbreads with ceps, cauliflower, almonds and white truffle, followed by Parmesan breaded guinea fowl kiev with oyster mushrooms and tarragon linguine. Jack went for lasagne of Dorset crab with a cappuccino of shellfish and champagne foam, and thinly sliced loin of Mounsey Farm pork with baked quince, bacon-wrapped prunes and sherry.

The champagne came and they toasted each other silently and drank. There was a faintly awkward pause as they recalibrated their responses to each other. Then he said, 'Oh! Your front door – tell me what happened.'

So she told him the story, such as it was. 'Darren next door said it was probably just some drunk yoofs coming out of the pub,' she concluded.

'But—' he began, and then checked himself.

'I know,' she said. 'It occurred to me, too. If they were just passing, where were they passing to, given that mine is the last house in the street and there's nothing but open moor beyond me?

And how did they happen to have a can of paint and a brush with them? But I really don't want to think someone deliberately came up the road to play a prank on me. I'd sooner not consider that. So I'm going with the drunken yoof explanation, however implausible.'

Jack was looking upset. It touched her to think he cared that much. Perhaps she had been too hasty in redefining their relationship. 'It's horrible,' he muttered. He seemed to pull himself back from thought. 'I hate to think of anyone doing a thing like that. Making you feel unwelcome.' He frowned quite fiercely. 'I'll find out who did it,' he said. 'I'll get to the bottom of it.'

She touched his hand. 'You're very sweet to worry about me. Thank you.'

He folded his fingers quickly round hers. 'I'm not. And I don't deserve your thanks. But—' He managed a wavering smile. 'If I'm your friend, it's the least I can do.'

Their first course arrived, and with tasting and praising they seemed to arrive at a more comfortable place. They began to talk as friends do, not asking each other questions, but discussing neutral topics, remembering meals they had had in the past, good and bad, which led on to favourite pubs and favourite parts of the country, music they liked and books they'd read.

And quite naturally, it seemed, he began to talk to her about his wife again, remembering happy times *they*'d had together.

'You told me you should never have got married,' she reminded him.

'I say that sort of thing,' he admitted. 'I think

probably we shouldn't have got married *when we did*. You see, neither of us had had a chance to go out with other people. We'd known each other all our lives, played together as children. So after a couple of years of marriage there was nothing new to discover. If we'd had a break from each other early on...'

'You think you *were* suited after all?'

'No-one understands me better than Flick,' he said rather bleakly. 'We're from the same background. She knows what makes me tick.'

'So what about the blonde in the bar?' Kate asked. 'My sources tell me she's rather more your type.'

'My type? What's that supposed to mean?'

'That she's the sort of female you are frequently seen with.'

'People should mind their own businesses,' he said sharply. She raised an eyebrow. 'Oh, all right,' he climbed down with a rueful smile. 'I suppose I *have* been sewing wild oats for the last couple of years.'

'And oats have to be sewn where oats will grow,' Kate suggested.

'You have a wicked tongue on you, young lady,' he said severely.

'Do you miss her?' she asked quickly.

'Do I miss Flick? Yes, I suppose I do. You can't spend all that time with someone and not miss them. Someone who knows your past, shares all the same memories. But it's Theo I feel really bad about. I know what it's like to lose a parent. In my case it was my mother, but my father was never the same after she died, so I sort of lost him too.'

'And Ed tried to be a father to you, but was just too young.'

'Poor old Ed,' Jack said with a smile. 'Pudding? Coffee?'

'I couldn't possibly manage pudding, thank you. Coffee would be nice.'

He summoned the waiter with a flick of the eyebrow, ordered coffee, tried to press a brandy on her and failed, and settled down again with his elbows on the table.

It seemed to be Kate's chance of asking something she had wanted to know for a while, and since Ed had been the last topic of conversation, it wouldn't look too particular to ask now.

'What about Ed?' she opened. 'He's a good-looking bloke – why isn't he married? Wasn't he ever? No-one ever says anything about an ex-wife.'

'Yes, he was married, but it's not a subject that's ever brought up. Ed wouldn't allow it.'

'Oh. Bad divorce?' she hazarded.

He looked serious for once. 'Far from it. I'll tell you the story, but for God's sake never mention it in front of Ed, and don't tell anyone I told you. He'd skin me alive if he knew I'd talked to you about it. Ed got married the year after our father brought Camilla home. I think he minded about her even more than I did, I suppose because he could just about remember our mother. Or perhaps because he's more serious about everything. So maybe it meant that he was – I don't know—'

'Looking for love?'

'Perhaps. Or maybe just susceptible. Anyway, he met Flavia at a hunt ball, and they fell madly in love. He was totally nuts about her. I couldn't see the attraction – she was beautiful, OK, but she always struck me as cold. Still, you don't know how people are when they're alone together, do you?'

'No,' Kate said thoughtfully.

'Well, everyone said they were a perfect couple, anyway. She was in the stud book, went to the right school, knew everybody. Her father owned land in Dorset – she was only at the ball because she was staying with a friend in the Quantocks. He had to put in a lot of miles to court her. But they married after only six weeks, so he didn't have to travel long.'

'And were they happy?' she asked. Her voice came out a touch husky, and she sipped her coffee to cover herself.

He didn't seem to notice. 'Oh yes. It was like something from a film – the prince and princess in the fairy story, happy ever after. Like I say, they were madly in love. And then one night she was driving home from Taunton and met a car coming round the bend in one of those narrow lanes. It was going too fast to brake or even swerve, smashed into her head on. She was killed outright. Turned out the driver was drunk.'

'My God, how terrible! I suppose that's why he's—'

'So down on drink-driving, yes. Even worse, she was pregnant. Only three months – the baby didn't survive. They hadn't told anyone. She'd gone to Taunton for the first routine scan and they were going to announce it when she got back if all was well.'

Kate couldn't think of anything to say. It was so dreadful – to have lost his wife and his child at the same time, and in that needless way. No wonder he was so grave and unsmiling.

'And then, just six months later, Dad died, and all the troubles of the world came down on his shoulders, and that was that.'

Kate frowned, trying to remember dates. 'So how long ago was that?'

'Ten years.'

'But – that's a long time,' Kate said. 'Oughtn't he to be getting over it now? Surely there must have been other women since?'

'Oh, I should think every unmarried female in Somerset has thrown herself at him. A lot of the married ones, too. No-one seems to have stuck. Maybe they're all too much the same, too County-thoroughbred – remind him of Flavia. I don't know. I'm just guessing.' He sipped his coffee. 'Of course, it's possible he *has* got over it and his gloomy act is just a habit now – because lately there's been a rumour that there's someone in London, some high-powered businesswoman, works for a merchant bank or something. Well, he's up there three days a week, sometimes four, who knows what he gets up to? But it would make sense: whoever she was, she'd be as unlike Flavia as possible.'

Oh, Kate thought. And then she told herself that it would have been stupid to think a perfectly beautiful man like Ed wouldn't have a woman somewhere. Yes, a banker-woman in a power suit would look very good on his arm, and explain why he went to London when he said he'd sooner be at home. It must be like a tug of war for him: London, his firm and Wonder Woman on the one hand, his ancestral acres and his duty to his family on the other. Except – why didn't he bring Wonder Woman home and show her off, enjoy her and the acres at the same time?

'How long?' she asked, cleared her throat and began again. 'Has he been seeing her long?'

'Who knows?' Jack said lightly. 'Ed never tells anyone anything about himself. But the rumours have been around for months, so maybe it's serious. It'd be nice to see the poor old blighter married – as long as she makes him happy. He deserves a bit of fun. Not that one can exactly imagine him cutting loose. There are some people who seem to be born aged forty in a stiff collar and tie. But you never know.'

'You never do,' she agreed, somewhat glumly. But she could never have stood a chance with him anyway, so who was she kidding?

'And I don't know why we're wasting our precious time together talking about my brother. We should be talking about Us.' He reached across the table and gathered her hand, and gazed soulfully into her eyes.

'I thought we'd agreed there wasn't any Us.'

'There could be,' he insisted. 'One should never rule anything out. There's this whole weekend coming up, when you'll be under my roof and helpless to escape my evil wiles.'

'Perhaps I'd better lock my door.'

'None of the locks on any of the doors have

worked in my lifetime. I think all the keys were melted down for scrap during the war.'

'Then I shall just have to submit and think of England.'

He grinned. 'I'll try to live up to your patriotism. By the way, what's this I hear about you riding Henna in the races on Monday?'

'How did you hear about that? Weren't you in the office today?'

'I was, Miss Time-and-motion-inspector. And so was Ed – came in to look at the books, having just finished his ride with you. He told me about it. Asked if I was intending to ride.'

'And are you? I'll stand down in a second – she's your horse.'

'She's Camilla's officially, but don't let that worry you.'

'You told me you might ride,' she pointed out.

'But I didn't mean it. She's not really up to my weight. Put on a bit of padding since I last competed on her.' He slapped his stomach comfortably. 'And she never really went well for me – she's more of a lady's horse. No, you have her and welcome. Ed says he's going to help you do a bit of practice.'

'Yes. He's very kind to spend so much time on me.'

'Oh, not kind,' Jack said, and for a dizzy moment she thought he was going to say Ed liked her. But he went on, 'It's his famous sense of responsibility. He'd be afraid you'd fall and hurt yourself if you didn't practise, and then he'd feel guilty.'

'Well, I shouldn't like to add to his burden of

guilt,' Kate said. 'Perhaps I should pull out.'

'No, you do it. You'll be all right. No-one's hurt themselves seriously at Buscombe in years. And I don't think we've ever had a death.'

'How you comfort me!' she said drily.

All good things, even expensive lunches, come to an end, and the time came when they couldn't justify sitting there any longer.

'Anyway, I ought to head back to the office,' Jack said. 'Just in case Ed's been asking for me.'

'And I suppose I'd better get back and finish painting my door.'

His jolly mood deserted him in a rush. 'I'm so sorry that happened. It's the last thing I would have wanted.'

'It's all right,' she comforted him. 'It was probably just a one-off. And I have a very nice, tall and burly next-door-neighbour to call on if anything goes bump in the night.'

He shuddered. 'God, don't say that. Look, lock your door at night – front and back. Don't get all sloppy and leave it open, like it was today.'

'I will,' she said. Though she found herself thinking that none of the windows locked. Perhaps a trip to B&Q was indicated. And actually, it didn't help her peace of mind that he was taking the paint incident so seriously.

He went on, 'And if anything else happens – which God forbid – or if there's anything that worries you, anything odd or suspicious, call me. You've got my mobile number, haven't you? Ring me and I'll come right away. Will you promise?'

'I promise. You're too kind.'

'That's what friends are for, aren't they?' he said, taking her hand under his arm as they stepped out into the sunshine and the car park. 'And we *are* friends.'

'We are.'

'Although,' he paused, turning to face her and looking down with a wicked smile, 'that isn't necessarily set in stone.'

'Now, now, no backsliding. That's the champagne talking.'

'It is not,' he said indignantly. 'You are, need I remind you, an utterly gorgeous girl, and I'm a pretty fabulous guy myself, so it would make perfect sense for us to join forces. Are you sure you wouldn't like to date properly?'

He was nice – much nicer than he had first appeared, and nicer than his reputation. And they had fun together, and it would be easy – and very nice – to have a fling with him. But she was sure now it could never be more than a fling; and some secret, and really stupid, part of her didn't want Ed to see her as Jack's girlfriend. It could make no difference, she knew that, but she didn't want him to think of her that way.

She kept it light. 'What about Coco's?' she said.

'Forget Coco's. I already have.'

Kate laughed. 'That poor girl.'

'So, what do you say?' he insisted. 'What about Us?'

She pressed his hand and looked up at him with great seriousness. 'We'll always have Paris,' she said.

* * *

Jack dropped her off at her door, and she let herself in with no particular anxiety, but her scalp prickled when she saw a square white envelope lying on the floor by the front door. She picked it up with flinching fingers, as if it might bite. There was nothing written on the outside, and for a moment she thought about throwing it away unopened, but in the end curiosity got the better of her. *That was where Bluebeard's wife went wrong as well*, she told herself.

Inside was a single piece of paper, on which was written in large felt-tip letters:

YOUVE BEEN WARNED
GET OUT

Hands trembling, she went into the kitchen, found the matches, held it over the sink and burned it, watching the black flakes fall like sinister snow, and washing them away with a blast from the cold tap. Only when there was no more trace of the thing, did she let out her breath and draw in a fresh, deep one. She thought about ringing Jack, but she had monopolized enough of his day – she didn't want to get him into trouble. And the large amount of alcohol she had consumed was cushioning her a bit. In spite of that, she found a bottle of wine and poured herself a glass. *I will not be intimidated.*

And on the principle that the best thing for any emotional state is good solid work, she went out and gave the front door another undercoat, so that she could no longer see the words underneath. She knew she had drunk too much to hang paper successfully, so she made a start on sanding down internal window frames, which was boringly repetitive but somehow soothing.

At least she had something really good to look forward to tomorrow. She made herself think of that whenever other things intruded.

Sixteen

Camilla's bedroom was startlingly modern after the rest of the house, with a low six-foot bed built-in to a unit of shelves and cupboards all in pale oak. There were sunken halogen lights, fitted carpet, two big armchairs in the window angled for the view, and everything was in harmonious shades of sand, shell and cream. Kate was surprised that there was no wardrobe, until Camilla led her through into a huge dressing room fitted out in the most modern and luxurious style. She couldn't help exclaiming, 'It's like something out of Hollywood!'

Camilla looked pleased. 'There's no reason to live like a peasant even if one is in the country,' she said. 'Flick designed it for me.'

'Is that what she does?'

'Yes, she has her own interior design company, and a shop in Dunster.' She sighed. 'I miss her. I liked it when she lived here. It gets so dull around here with no-one to talk to.' She gave a little laugh. 'Believe it or not, I even miss Jocasta sometimes, when she's at school.'

Proudly she showed Kate round. There were drawers for everything: special tilt-down shoe-drawers, drawers lined in cedar solely for sweaters, silk-lined handbag drawers, a slide-out rack for storing long boots; and then the wardrobes, lining a whole wall, mirror-fronted, the mirrors hinged so they could be angled to give you a back or side view. There was a large comfy couch and two upright chairs, and a movable pole-rack on which you could hang your choice and see if it worked before going to all the fag of putting it on.

And every wardrobe section was filled with exquisite clothes, all carefully arranged – full length here, trousers there, suits in one place, dresses another – and then colour-sorted, and everything hanging clear and crease-free on its own padded hanger. Kate thought of her wardrobe back at the flat, stuffed higgledy-piggledy, often several items to a hanger, everything mixed up together so that finding anything involved dragging stuff out and chucking it on the bed. And when you did find what you wanted, it usually needed ironing. Camilla might not take much interest in housekeeping, as the tatty, chaotic drawing room attested, but she was evidently willing to take endless pains over something she cared about. The order in here was awesome. Kate knew she was in the presence of true genius.

She also began to have an idea of where all Camilla's money went.

Now Camilla was sitting on the couch, covertly looking at herself in several of the mirrors, and otherwise watching as Kate tried on the riding clothes. She had been wondering how she would feel about borrowing a stranger's gear, but it had obviously been put away freshly dry-cleaned, so it was practically like new. She was glad she had thought to put on her least tatty underwear, just in case. Even so, she felt like hunching up and crossing her arms over her chest when she got down to it.

Fortunately, Camilla's attention was taken by the red marks left by the seams of her jeans. 'Oh, goodness, look at your poor legs,' she said. 'You really do need some proper riding clothes. Do they hurt?'

'Only when something presses on them,' she said. 'I'm afraid your riding clothes are going to be too big.' She saw her hostess bristle a little, and added quickly, 'I mean, too long. You're taller than me.'

Camilla was mollified. 'I don't think that'll matter with the breeches – they're stretch. But you are very flat-chested,' she added with a complacent glance at herself in the mirror. 'My jacket will probably hang on you.'

Both these statements proved prophetic. The breeches were comfortable, and the length of the leg would be hidden inside the boot. The jacket looked as if it were wearing Kate rather than the other way round.

'Well, it doesn't matter,' said Camilla. 'You'll just have to go without. It's summer, no-one will mind.'

The boots Kate had anticipated would be a problem, but though Camilla was taller she had small feet, and with an extra-thick pair of socks they would just about do. 'It's not as if you'll be walking in them.'

'We hope not,' Kate said wryly, turning back

and forth to look at herself in the mirror. *Not bad*, she thought. There were occasions when not being busty worked to one's advantage. She looked slim, and sporty – athletic. 'You're very kind to lend me your things – and your horse. I understand Henna's yours really.'

'Well, she was bought for me, but I'm not as horse-mad as the rest of the family,' Camilla said. 'I hunted her quite a bit last winter, but it's mostly the meet I go for. I don't care to bash around the country for hours on end and come home frozen and covered in mud. I usually go home after the first run, or even after the first draw if the weather's really bad.'

'Have you competed with her?'

'Hunter trials once or twice, never pointing. I'm not that interested, to tell you the truth – I prefer to stay in the marquee and chat. But Ed says you manage her, and she never refuses. All you've got to do is stick on and get round. You'll be fine,' she pronounced, elegantly concealing a yawn. 'How are you getting on with your cottage?'

'Oh, pretty well,' Kate said.

'I can't think why you want to bother, but I'm glad you did. It's nice that someone's bought it that we can get on with, or Ed would have been even more down on me. I don't know what you see in the place.'

Kate picked the easiest answer. 'I enjoy DIY,' she said, even though she guessed that would damn her in Camilla's eyes.

Camilla raised an expressive eyebrow. 'Well, each to his own, I suppose. I don't know what it is about that ugly old shack that attracts so much interest. Finding one person who wanted it is surprising enough, but two...'

'Two?' Kate queried.

'Phil wanted it as well.'

'Phil Kingdon?' Kate said.

Camilla shrugged. 'It was his idea for me to sell it, when I needed money. He said no-one would miss it – unlike the paintings! Then when I did sell it, to you, he got mad and said he'd meant me to sell it to him.' She looked affronted. 'He should have made that clear, that's what I told him, not just suggest I sell it and say nothing. I'm not supposed to be a mind reader.'

'Why did he want it?' Kate couldn't help asking.

'No idea,' she said indifferently. 'I asked him the same thing and he wouldn't answer. He's got a house, though I suppose it *is* a bit of a drive away, over towards Bridgwater. Perhaps he wanted Little's as an overnight base or something. But it would never do for him to live in unless he extended it – a *lot* – and you'd never get planning permission for anything like that.'

Kate was remembering the exchange between Kingdon and Camilla that she had overheard in the passage. Especially the familiar way he had spoken to her. There was evidently more between them than was apparent. And he had known Camilla was in debt and advised her of a way of bypassing Ed, his boss in all but name. Odd behaviour.

She had to ask. 'How come he didn't know you'd sold it, when it was his idea?'

'Well, I didn't want Ed to know, because he'd have made *such* a fuss, so I didn't tell anyone. I told the estate agents to keep it quiet and not advertise it locally. I suppose it would have got out in the end, but fortunately you snapped it up quickly and they got the whole thing sewn up before anyone needed to know. So you can see you're in my good books,' she added with a bright smile, 'because things were getting *quite* sticky, and now I shall be all right for months.'

'Glad to be of service,' Kate said ironically. Kingdon had said to her that if she wanted to sell, she should come to him. He'd said he'd find her a buyer – perhaps he knew someone who'd wanted it all along. But then why the mystery? Kate suspected there was no unnamed third party, that Kingdon wanted it for himself. But that did not answer the question, only displaced it. Why did *he* want it? And why not just go to Ed and ask straight out to buy it?

Because he knew Ed was dead against selling any of the estate. Ed would say no. Camilla might be bamboozled into selling.

But why did he want it? If he really wanted a pied-à-terre, there must be other cottages around that weren't owned by the Blackmore Estate. Well, maybe it was the five acres he was after, maybe he was planning on setting up as a smallholder. It could be his retirement plan, for all she knew.

Her musings were interrupted by a knock on the door, and when Camilla called out, 'Come in, we're decent,' it opened to let in a surge of dogs with Ed behind them.

'Are you ready? Oh yes, that looks much better,' he went on, looking Kate swiftly up and down. 'Much more workmanlike. Everything fit all right?'

'Well enough for the job,' Camilla said. She picked up the greyhound and cuddled it, moving the other dogs away with a practised foot. 'Are you hacking over to Northcombe?'

'No, driving – hacking would take too long. Bradshaw's boxing them now.'

Camilla stood up with the greyhound looking blissfully happy in her arms. 'I'll probably be out when you get back. Some bits and pieces to get. Don't bother Mrs B about lunch, will you – she's already cooking for the weekend.'

'What's Northcombe?' Kate asked as they clattered downstairs, with the dogs racing after them.

'Northcombe Grange. The Ordes' place. They have a cross-country course set up in their fields, so you can get used to jumping Henna. These poor dogs,' he added in parenthesis as they went out, still pressed against by hopeful hounds. 'They really want a walk.'

'Where's Jocasta?' Kate asked.

'Gone to Weston to spend the day with a friend, so I suppose it will have to be me, later.' They walked round into the stable yard, where a horse trailer was hitched up to an old-fashioned khaki Landrover. Bradshaw was securing the doors at the back. From inside there was a sound of hooves shifting and dust being blown from horsey nostrils. 'All serene?' Ed asked.

'No trouble,' said Bradshaw. 'I put Gracie in first, and the mare followed like a lamb once she seen him.'

'You do have a predilection,' Kate remarked, going round to the passenger side of the Land-rover, 'for giving your boy horses girls' names.'

Northcombe Grange was in a very different sort of country. One of the things Kate loved about Exmoor was the way, in just a few miles, you could go from bleak open moorland, good for nothing but grazing sheep, to lush fertile valley with dairy cattle, orchards and arable fields. Northcombe was in what she thought of as 'soft' country. The Ordes had a large modern house, extensive stabling, an indoor school, an outdoor manège – and the cross-country course.

Susie met them as they pulled into the stable yard, calling to them cheerily before Ed had even turned off the engine, so Kate missed the first part of her greeting.

'—awfully good sport. I'm really looking forward to it. Hope you're not nervous?' Kate was in the process of climbing out of the car, and only managed a smile by way of a reply. Susie went on: 'No need to be. Buscombe's not one of those big, grand meetings. Everyone's friendly, and the course is fun. That's all it's meant to be – a bit of fun for hunt members and their friends. Let's get those horses down. Eric's out on our course, checking everything's in order.'

'Is he going to ride with us?' Ed asked, walking round to the back.

'We both are,' said Susie, following. She

smiled at Kate. 'We thought it would make it more fun for you, and better practice if, as well as letting you try Henna over the jumps, you got used to riding her in competition. Don't you think, Ed?'

'Sounds like a good idea,' he said. 'Who are you going to ride?'

'Magic,' she said, 'and Eric's taken Talley.' She grinned. 'So it'll be no holds barred. No point in racing if you don't try to win.'

They hacked up to where the course was laid out along a field, up the hillside, over the top and down into a coombe, across a stream then back, and up, over and down to the field again. Eric was there pounding flags into the ground, his horse, Talleyrand, a powerful-looking black, tied up to the fence.

'This'll be the flat at the end of the course,' he explained. 'You start down that end, jump all these fences, and when you come back, instead of jumping them again you race down the side of them, between the flags, to the finishing post. It's not quite three miles, which the point will be, but near enough.'

'And some of the jumps are higher than four-foot-three,' Susie added, 'but not much. You know that's the height of point jumps?'

'I do now,' Kate said.

'Also, at Buscombe you go round the whole course twice,' Eric said. 'But I expect Ed will tell you all about it before you get there. Now, let's have some fun!'

Kate had begun to feel nervous, but the Ordes

were so cheery that she soon began to think it *would* be fun, and it was. Despite his shape, Eric mounted nimbly and was obviously a diva in the saddle. Susie's grey was, she said 'elderly' and 'getting past it now, poor old boy' but he seemed as eager as any of the others to be off, and showed no sign of his age. First they all rode the course at an easy pace, jumping the fences in turn rather than together, and allowing Kate a couple of shots at anything she felt she hadn't quite mastered. Going over a jump uphill and going over one downhill required different techniques, and different again from jumping on the flat. Henna was eager, excited, and back into her bad habit of head-tossing, and Kate got one painful blow on the nose that made her eyes water, though fortunately it didn't bleed.

'You ought to put her in a martingale,' Susie said bluntly.

'Ed doesn't believe in them,' Eric snorted. 'Do you, old boy? Thinks they're bad manners.'

'I'd sooner correct the fault with schooling,' Ed said. 'Too often people just strap the horse down and leave the fault untouched.'

'Well, martingales have their place,' Susie said. 'And Kate's not going to be riding her long enough to school her.'

'She'll settle down,' Ed decreed, leaving Kate to wonder whether he was referring to her or the mare. 'Remember yesterday?' he said to her. 'Heels hard down, and keep riding her hard up to the bit.'

Eric shook his head. 'You'll exhaust the poor child! This is supposed to be a bit of fun.'

Ed rolled his eyes. 'If she's not settled down in ten minutes, Susie can ride back and fetch a martingale.'

'Gee, thanks,' said Susie.

By the time they had gone right round the course, Henna had settled, and Kate felt pleased with herself for having kept her on the bit, though her legs and buttocks were exhausted with working so hard. 'I'll never make it to the end of Monday,' she said to Susie as they dismounted to rest the horses for five minutes. 'My legs feel like string.'

Eric had lit a cigarette and was talking to Ed a little way off.

Susie looked across at him, and then back to Kate. 'Don't let him bully you,' she advised. 'Make him put her in a martingale. He's a big old party-pooper, is Ed. Everything always has to be done right. You wouldn't believe it to look at him,' she added with an affectionate glance, 'but he used to be a perfect fool when he was a kid. Such a joker! I remember a Christmas party when he smuggled a ferret in and slipped it into the rector's wife's handbag. There were such ructions! I had to lie down behind the sofa, I was laughing so much. And he used to do simply *evil* impressions of people. *So* accurate, they were scorchers!'

'Is this before or after his mother died?' Kate asked, intrigued.

'Well, after is what I mostly remember, though the ferret was before.'

'But I thought that was when he became so serious – when his mother died.'

'Well, he was always a solemn little boy, but with this great sense of humour underneath,' Susie said. 'You know, he'd do something funny with such a straight face, it just made it funnier. It gradually went more into hiding, but it was always there, really, until – well, something bad happened,' she concluded sotto voce.

'Jack told me about Flavia,' Kate whispered.

'Oh! Right. Well, I suppose a lot of things combined that year to make the sun go in for him, and it hasn't come out again. But we all love the old grumpy-boots, even so.'

'You love who?' Eric called, catching that bit. Ed looked too.

'We love Ed, even if he is an Olympic-class sour puss, killjoy and responsibility junkie.'

'I'll admit the last bit,' Ed said, looking a bit startled and – perhaps? – a bit hurt, 'but sour puss? Killjoy?'

'I must say, I can't see it,' Kate said. 'You've been nothing but kind to me.'

'Wait till he knows you better,' Susie said, but with the sort of smile that said she was teasing, 'and starts improving you. I used to smoke till he bullied me out of it.'

'You must admit that it *was* an improvement,' Ed said. 'Don't you feel better?'

'Not when I see Eric smoking away and I can't. It was my one little pleasure,' she said mournfully – and, Kate guessed, untruthfully.

Eric threw down his cigarette butt and ground it out. 'Enough of that. Any minute now he'll start on me,' he objected, 'and I've too much to lose! Are we going to have this race, or are we going to stand here gassing all day?'

They mounted up and checked their girths, and Kate threw Ed a covert look under her eyelashes. He seemed thoughtful – not that he wasn't always, but in a different way. She thought Susie really had hurt his feelings a bit. Who *would* like to be called a sour puss, even in fun?

'Right!' said Eric, and then there was no more time to think about anything, because the race was on.

'That was simply amazing,' Kate said to Ed as they drove back to The Hall. 'I can see why people go in for it – racing, I mean. Completely addictive! The speed, the adrenalin rush...'

He gave her an amused sideways look. 'I thought you were having a good time. You weren't nervous?'

'I thought I might be, but no. Though it may be different with more people, and strangers.'

'I don't think so. You know you can do it now. And you don't have to try and win. Just get her round, for the experience.'

Kate wondered if it would be possible to race and not try to win. 'The Ordes are fun, aren't they?'

'Yes, they're good sorts. I've known them all my life,' Ed said absently. Was he thinking again about what Susie said?

'So, they've always lived at Northcombe?' Kate asked, to keep him talking.

He roused himself. 'On the land,' he said. 'There was an old house, further up the valley towards Stockham – the family seat, if you like –

and Eric's family owned all the land round these parts. Sold most of it, of course, and the house got into disrepair and cost too much to keep up. Eric was working in the City, making his fortune, but he didn't make it quickly enough to save the old place. By the time he came back there was only five hundred acres left, and the house had fallen down. So he built the new place.'

'It must be sad for him, to lose his family home,' Kate suggested tentatively.

'I don't think he cares,' said Ed. 'A lot of people have decided trying to keep up the old ways is too much of a burden. Sell up and get out, make your money some easier way, live a more comfortable life. It makes sense.'

'Not to you,' she suggested.

'Not to me,' he agreed. 'But then according to Susie I'm a responsibility junkie.'

'I don't think being responsible is anything to apologize for,' she said.

He looked at her for a moment curiously, and she thought he might say something, reveal something about himself: the moment seemed poised on the brink of intimacy. But the gates of The Hall came into view, he had to concentrate on backing the trailer into the yard, and the moment passed.

Bradshaw came out. 'How did it go?' he called to Kate as she jumped out.

'Marvellous,' she said. 'She went beautifully. It was just like flying.'

'Ar, she's not a bad lass,' Bradshaw said. 'Needs more exercise, that's all. Crying shame letting a nice horse like that go to waste.' He went round to drop down the back of the box and lead the horses out. 'I'll take care of 'em,' he told Ed. 'You must want your lunch. Go on, I've had mine.' He included Kate in the glance.

Seeing he was determined, Kate let him take over. With nothing more to do, she hesitated, saying, 'I suppose I'd better be on my way.'

Ed had been in a brown study, and came out of it abruptly at her words. 'Um,' he said. She had never seen him hesitant before, and waited, trying to exude willingness for whatever he had in mind. 'I need to take those dogs for a walk. And Camilla said not to bother Mrs B about lunch. I suppose you wouldn't like to come with me, help me walk them, and get a sandwich or something in the pub?'

Kate could think of nothing she'd like better, but she tried not to show her joy for fear of frightening him off. 'I'd be happy to. Which pub? The Royal Oak?'

'I'm not keen on the Oak, and there's nowhere for the dogs. There's a pub up the valley towards Withypool, the Barley Mow. They're dog friendly and they have a garden we can sit out in. It's a nice walk, too, across The Barrow and along the brook on the edge of the wood.'

'That sounds nice,' said Kate – oh, understatement!

'You're not too tired?'

'No, a walk's just what I need to loosen me up. I just need to change into my own clothes.'

'Yes, I must change too,' he said. 'Can't walk in these boots. I'll meet you back down here in five minutes.'

Seventeen

If you're hoping to get to know someone, going for a walk with them is by far the best way. There's something about the gentle exercise – probably coupled with the slight anonymity of being side by side and not face to face – that gives rise to relaxation and confidences.

The dogs were having a whale of a time, running around them, racing away and coming back, sniffing deeply in the hedges and undergrowth, marking every tree until Kate wondered if they were carrying a secret spare tank. Everywhere she looked Kate saw waving tails and doggy grins of delight.

'They *need* to walk,' Ed said. 'It's a social occasion – a pack thing. Running round by themselves in the field at the back of the house is not the same.'

Kate threw a stick for Ralph, the setter, and he pretended to go after it to be polite, but stopped before he reached it, arrested by a compelling smell in a clump of grass. Chewy was bouncing puppy-like all over Esmé, but she was a different dog out of the house, kept her end up, and looked much less frail and cowed.

'They look happy,' Kate said. 'Mind you, it's such a lovely day, who wouldn't? And those woods – I love the colour of the new leaves. "The woods are lovely, dark and deep."'

'Robert Frost,' he said. 'But that was woods in the snow.'

'It applies all year round. There's something about them that just makes you want to plunge in and explore, don't you think?'

'This particular wood is not all that deep. If you plunged in, you'd have plunged out the other side before you knew it. But I know what you mean. There's always a sort of mystery about them.'

'Do they belong to you?' she asked.

'Not to me, but to the estate, yes,' he said; a shadow crossed his eyes and she was afraid she'd spoiled it. But it passed, and he said, 'We don't have much on this side of the valley any more, but The Barrow – that's this hill – and the wood, and the quarry over that way, they're still Blackmore. Everything up as far as that footpath over there – can you see the line? It runs back down to the road and comes out opposite the Barley Mow. That used to be an estate pub as well, once upon a time.'

'How big is it all together – the estate?' she asked.

'A bit less than thirteen thousand acres.'

She opened her eyes. 'That sounds enormous!'

'It's fair. But you have to remember that most of that is not premium land. It's high moor, rough grazing at best. The Blackmore fortune was originally based on wool – and there was a time when wool really did produce a fortune. Most of the churches were built on wool money, and the big houses, and the old schools. "White gold", they used to call it. But it's not a valuable commodity any more. Sometimes you can't give it away. Which was why my great-grandfather built the factory, to process and weave our own wool, and sell the cloth. Blackmore tweed is still pretty famous. Not as famous as Harris tweed – but not as scratchy, either.' She saw it was all right to laugh. He didn't laugh, but he looked pleased by her amusement. 'We make a certain amount of clothing as well, for a few exclusive markets, mostly in London and New York.'

'So, does it pay now?'

'The cloth makes a good contribution to the estate, and we're hoping to improve on that. Tweed is becoming fashionable again, and in particular the Chinese market for top-quality English cloth is opening up and promises to be huge. The clothing is probably marginal. It's labour-intensive and it needs a lot more expansion to get the overheads down. That's where I hoped Jack would make his mark – getting out and talking to people, finding new markets. People like him and he gets on with everybody. He has charm. He could sell ice cream to Eskimos if—' He stopped abruptly.

It was easy for Kate to guess the end of that sentence, and to understand Ed had stopped himself out of loyalty. Jack *could* do it, if he would put his mind to it, if he stopped lounging about and spending money and put in some solid hard work instead.

'He *is* charming,' she said, allowing the 'but' to show in her intonation.

Ed sighed. 'It's in his own interest to buckle down to it. The estate has to provide for all of us, and the better it does the better *we* do.'

'Surely he must know that?' she said tentatively. She didn't want anything to break this delicate thread of trust between them.

'Of course he knows it.' There seemed to be more coming, but instead there was silence. She looked sideways at him. He was frowning, obviously thinking something through. She waited with bated breath. At last he said – quite low, and almost as if not to her but to himself – 'The estate ought to be doing better than it is. I can't understand it. But I'm going to get to the bottom of it.'

'You mean – make it more efficient?' she asked carefully.

'That too,' he said. 'But there's something else going on.' A pause. 'I'll do whatever it takes. I'm not giving up on it. There have been Blackmores here for five hundred years. I'm damned if I'll let us be the last.'

They came out on to the footpath he had mentioned, which ran gently downhill to the road, and Kate could see the Barley Mow on the other side of it, snugged down under the lee of the steep wooded hill that rose up to Lar Common. It had a thatched roof and tall chimneys, small windows and deep eaves, so it looked like someone with a fancy hat pulled down very low over their eyes.

Ed called the dogs to him and leashed them, and with the leads held between them they crossed the road and went in. It was a small place, cosy and unpretentious, with a big fireplace, slightly battered comfortable furniture, a few pictures on the walls: it felt exactly like what a 'public house' originally was – someone's home into which the public were welcomed. The landlord, a chunky man in his fifties, came out to greet them – they were the only ones in there – and said, 'Hello, Ed. Long time no see.'

'I've been rather busy lately – too busy. All right with the dogs?'

'Of course. Good dogs always welcome.' He smiled enquiringly at Kate, and Ed introduced her, then exchanged a few comments with the landlord that proved they had a long and comfortable friendship. Kate, looking round, could see, without having thought about it before, how this would be Ed's natural milieu, just as the Blue Ball was Jack's. Strange that two brothers could be so different.

They ordered sandwiches and pints, and carried their glasses outside. There was a small, sheltered garden on the south-west side of the pub which was warm in the sunshine: an area of lawn; a flower bed, edged with forget-me-nots and lady's mantle, in which iris and achillea rose up from a riot of marigolds and multicoloured snapdragons; and a tangle of white jasmine hanging over the boundary hedge that was just coming into flower. Posh and manicured it wasn't; but it felt homelike and easy and safe. They unleashed the dogs, and sat down at one of those table-and-bench combinations with their backs to the warmed white wall of the cottage, and Kate felt completely, utterly happy.

As the level of the pint sank, Ed seemed to relax more. They talked, carefully at first, but gradually with increasing ease, like friends. The sandwiches came – crusty white-bread doorsteps of local cheese and ham – and he talked about the estate. He told her things out of its history, the people who were its stay and its purpose, great characters from the past when most estate workers never went more than a few miles from the place they were born. He recounted things about the area, folklore and festivals, recalled great celebrations and never-forgotten disasters, brush fires and storms and escaped bulls. He talked of dogs and horses he had loved; dug out funny incidents from his childhood, stories involving Jack and various friends who had grown up with them. She saw his tense dark face relax and grow animated, heard his voice lighten as the warmth and humour that was normally suppressed came into it. He didn't quite smile, but she could see what he would look like if he did.

She talked about her childhood, too. It seemed the safer place for them both to be – the past, before their separate hearts were broken.

'It must be wonderful to come from a big family,' he said. 'Five sisters, eh?'

'That's how I learned to dance,' she said. 'Waiting for the bathroom.'

And he laughed. He stopped immediately, but she had proved it was possible.

'It must be lonely for you here, stuck in that cottage all by yourself,' he said.

'I've hardly had time to be lonely,' she said. 'People here are so friendly, I have to be quite stern to get a moment to myself.'

'I'm glad you find it so,' he said. He hesitated. 'Jack is – a friendly fellow.'

'We've agreed he has great charm,' she said cautiously.

He frowned and chewed his lip. 'This is probably none of my business. I don't want to...' He looked at her, and then quickly away again – a flash of blue barely seen, like a kingfisher on a shadowy river.

'We're just friends,' she assured him, cutting through his difficulties. 'I had a very upsetting relationship in London with a man of great charm, so I know what to look out for. I'm not in any danger. I like Jack enormously, but in a purely friendly way.'

'I'm relieved,' he said, and for a moment her heart jumped, her fertile imagination racing on to how that sentence could end – *because that means I have a chance with you myself.*

But he continued, sounding more comfortable, 'It's not a popular view, least of all with Jack himself, but I'm convinced he's still in love with his ex-wife.'

Well, what had she expected? *Fool*, she berated herself.

'I think it's a large part of his trouble, why he can't settle to anything,' he went on.

'And how does she feel?' she asked in a remarkably steady voice.

'I'm not sure. You might have a chance to judge for yourself this weekend. It's Jack's weekend to have Theo, so she'll drop him off, and I dare say she'll stop for a chat and a cup of tea, so you might see her.'

'I'm looking forward to meeting Theo,' she said.

'He's a great kid,' said Ed with enthusiasm. 'You'll love him. It's nice that you get on so well with Jocasta, too.'

'I love her. She's a hoot,' Kate said.

'She needs someone like you – an older sister, if you like, someone she can look up to as well as confide in. Camilla's—' He stopped, probably loyalty kicking in again. 'I don't think girls ever confide in their mothers, do they?'

'You're asking the wrong person. I had all the sisters I needed. But I'd be happy to be hers. As to Theo – I've been putting in some good practice with my next-door-neighbour's six year old, so I'm about up to GCSE level with little boys. Does Theo like Power Rangers?'

'I think he's more of a Thomas the Tank Engine man.'

'I can do Thomas,' Kate assured him gravely. 'And I've majored in Postman Pat.'

The almost-smile was there again. It seemed to warm him, talking with her about his family. Perhaps there weren't many people he could. Except – *what about Banker Lady*? the thought came to her like a cold breeze down the back of the neck.

She had to know. Not that there was any chance for her, but she wanted to know if he was happy, or was in process of becoming happy. So after a pause she said, 'Tell me about your firm in London.'

He explained to her what a procurement

consultancy did, and it sounded complicated but, she could see, necessary to modern big business. 'We're small, but getting a good reputation. It's an area that's expanding rapidly.'

'And it helps support the estate?'

'Cash income,' he said. 'Sometimes you can't do without it.'

'But you must be sad that it takes you away from here,' she tried. 'I don't suppose you like London all that much – or is there something about it you enjoy?'

It didn't work. He shrugged. 'It's a necessary evil,' he said. 'And I'm pretty much my own boss – I can come home at short notice if I'm needed. What I'm hoping to do is build up the firm until it attracts a takeover offer from one of the big agencies, then I can bring the money back and stay here. Perhaps just do the odd consult when it suits me.'

'So you don't want to leave London completely. I mean, never go back?'

He gave her an odd look. 'Do you?' he asked. 'I thought when I first saw you that you were a complete cosmopolitanite, but you seem to have settled into this place like a native. Are you meaning to settle here, or are you going back?'

'I haven't decided,' she hedged, and felt a bit glum. She hadn't found out a thing about Banker Woman. If she existed, Ed-in-the-city was out of bounds. And if she didn't, he'd come and live permanently here, and Ed-in-the-country would be out of reach.

They both lapsed into silence after that, busy with their own thoughts, and though it was a friendly silence, the sort of silence that only people at ease with each other can have, it didn't satisfy Kate. He had reminded her that her time here was finite. Well, she had better get on and enjoy it as much as possible. She leaned back against the wall and half closed her eyes so she could look at him under her eyelashes. He was big and strong and dark, but more than that he was so *real*, as if he sucked some power or essence from this place which illuminated him more than anyone else. She saw vividly for the first time that it would be more than a shame if the estate failed and had to be sold – it would be a crime against nature. He and the land belonged to each other. She thought, when the time came, she would try to sell Little's back to him, even if it meant forgoing any profit. She didn't think she could ever now sell it to a stranger for a holiday cottage. It would just feel wrong.

It was quiet in the garden, with only the sound of the occasional passing car to disturb them. The dogs had stopped running about and were flopped on their sides in the sunshine, at peace with life, and bumblebees were working the snapdragons, slipping in and backing out industriously, humming like well-tuned engines. Ed was leaning back now too, and his hand was resting on the bench beside hers. It took all her will-power not to slide hers along a fraction so that they touched.

At last he stirred. 'God, I was almost asleep.'

'Me too,' she lied. 'It's very peaceful here.'

'It is. But though I hate to break up the party, I do have some work to do.'

'Me too,' she said again. She stretched luxuriously. 'Thanks for lunch.'

He gave a quirk of the lips. 'Not quite in the same league as the Blue Ball or the Ship,' he said.

She turned to face him, so that he would believe her. 'This is a different world, and much more real. I've enjoyed it so much.'

He looked at her gravely. 'Yes, I have, too.' But he seemed thoughtful. She was afraid she had sounded too eager and scared him. *Back off, girl.*

'Would you look at those dogs,' she said, standing up. 'Will we have to carry them home?'

They didn't talk much on the walk home, but it was not an uncomfortable silence. If she had alarmed him, he seemed to have got over it. When they did talk, it was like old friends – or old acquaintances, at least.

At the house, they unclipped the dogs, he took over the leads, and said, 'Thanks for helping me walk them.'

'It was a pleasure. Thanks for lunch.'

'Are you up for another practice tomorrow?'

'You bet. At the Ordes' again?'

'No, I think we should do some gallops and some hill work. Can you be here at ten? No, make it ten thirty, I've got some phone calls to make. You're taking the riding clothes back with you?'

'Yes, they're in my car.'

'Good. Well – tomorrow then? We'll just have a couple of hours – what time did Camilla invite you for?'

‘She said teatime. I suppose that’s four, four thirty-ish?’

He nodded. ‘So that’ll give you time to go home after the ride.’

‘And clean up and pack a bag,’ she agreed.

‘Right. Tomorrow, then.’ He had been looking directly into her eyes; now he broke the contact quite abruptly and walked off. She turned the other way, towards her car. He was no flirt, that was for sure. People like Jack – like Mark – all smiles and easy kisses – were much easier to get on with. That was why idiots like her fell for them, over and over again. But no more. Once you’d met the real thing, you couldn’t be fooled again.

And much good would it do her!

She was too restless to stay home for what was left of the afternoon, so she drove into Taunton to B&Q to buy things she was going to need next week, and window locks, and four heavy-duty bolts, one for the top and bottom of each of her doors. The front door was only on a Yale which a child could slip, and the back door had an old basic lock-plate which she felt could be shouldered in. It was not pleasant to be thinking of locks and bolts in a peaceful place like this; but even in Eden, once you had spotted the serpent’s trail, you couldn’t pretend it wasn’t there.

She got home and was unpacking her goodies when Dommie bounced in. ‘Where’ve you been? I got home from school but you weren’t here. I got a star for my English test. I can spell shark and aircraft and all the months except Janry and

Febry. I got a goal in football. Jason picked his scab off and it bled again.'

'It sounds like a full, rich day,' Kate said. 'I had a full, rich day, too.'

Dommie, the centre of his own universe, wasn't interested in that. He grabbed her hand. 'Come on,' he said, tugging her towards the door. 'I'll draw you a picture of a frog turning into a prince, but you have to do the horse cos I can't do horses.'

'Hold on, scout. Isn't it about your teatime?'

He stopped, scowled a moment, and then it cleared. 'Mummy says,' he chanted in the sing-song of the remembered message, 'would you like to come and eat with us? She sent me when she heard your car.'

'That's very kind,' Kate began, thinking of refusing.

'It's steak an' kiddly pie,' he added, 'so you've *got* to.'

'I quite see that,' she said gravely. 'Who can say no to a kiddly? Lead on, captain.' Suddenly she felt the last thing she wanted to do was to stay in alone. She was tired and a bit stiff and just slightly low, and an evening with Kay and Darren in front of the telly was all she asked of life. She took Dommie's appallingly sticky little paw in hers and let him tow her away.

When they got back from the ride the next day, they rode in through the main gates, and Kate said at once, 'Whoo, nice car!'

It was a silver Mercedes sports car with black leather interior. The smell of exhaust on the air proved it had just arrived.

'It's an SL five hundred,' Ed said automatically. He sounded distant, and she saw he was frowning. He slipped down from the saddle, so Kate followed suit, and was a little surprised when he thrust Gracie's reins into her hands and walked away.

'Whose is it?' she said, but he didn't seem to have heard her. She walked after him, leading the horses, who dragged a little. *This is the wrong way – stables are in that direction.*

Before Ed reached the car, the driver's door swung open and a three-inch heel and a long, long leg emerged, followed sinuously by a body that unfurled itself into a tall woman in a tight-skirted, pinstriped suit over a white silk blouse, a woman with a high-cheekboned face, perfectly made-up, and thick, glossy black hair done up in a chignon behind. Everything about her exuded wealth, power, and being at the peak of the social mountain.

'Edward, *darling*,' she said in an American accent, holding out both hands. 'Surprised to see me?'

'Very surprised,' he said woodenly. 'What are you doing here?'

He didn't move to take her hands, so she grabbed his instead, pulled him to her, and kissed him on both cheeks and then lightly on the lips. Foolishly, Kate felt herself bristle.

'I thought you were in New York,' he said, freeing himself.

'I was, but they had a particular job that needed doing in London so I took the opportunity of a little vacation. I knew it was your bank holiday this weekend, so I thought I'd find you down here.'

'You didn't think of telephoning first? We have a houseful.'

'Great, you know I love parties! I checked with your office and they said you'd taken most of the week off, so you're obviously taking a vacation too. So I thought I'd drive down and surprise you. What a place! It was really hard to find. Talk about back of beyond!'

'Well, I don't know where we'll put you,' Ed said, a little fretfully.

She gave him a reproachful smile. 'Sweetheart, I'll throw in with you, what did you think? I don't mind being a little cramped. God,' she added with a laugh, 'I'm used to it in England – except in my own apartment. As you know.'

Her eyes slid past him to Kate, and gave her a quick appraisal that was like being stripped and sanded down. It didn't seem as if Kate had impressed her much. She raised and pressed her plip key and the boot sprang open like a crocodile's mouth, revealing some very expensive-looking grey leather luggage packed inside. She gave Kate the sort of full but utterly professional smile you give a waiter or bellhop. 'Have my bags taken up to Mr Blackmore's room, when you've finished with the horses,' she said.

Ed's ears went a bit red. 'This is a friend, Addison. Allow me to introduce you. Kate, this is Addison Bruckmeyer; Addison, Kate Jennings.'

'Pleased to meet you,' Addison said. 'Edward's never mentioned you. He and I were very close in London. *Very* close.'

Kate mumbled something awkwardly about being 'new on the scene'. She was in a mild state of shock.

In a magnificent gesture, Addison reached behind her head, removed a single clip, gave one shake and released her hair to tumble in spectacular fashion about her shoulders. It was black as ink and as glossy as a shampoo ad, and made her eyes look as green as a cat's. It was a mesmerizing piece of theatre. Kate had never seen it done better – and she'd been in PR, hanging around models and actresses.

'Now, you will be a sweetie and take the horses away, won't you?' Addison continued. 'Edward and I have such a lot to catch up on.' She slipped her hand through his arm and drew him close. 'And find someone to take my bags up afterwards. You are a lamb!'

She turned towards the house, drawing Ed with her. He gave one glance back over his shoulder, but whether of entreaty or apology or whatever else, she couldn't tell, because it was too brief. Addison was as tall as him, and evidently very strong. Kate watched her lithe figure, with its mane of shiny Indian-black hair, and thought Ed didn't have much of a chance.

If he even wanted a chance.

She was pretty sure she had the answer to most of her questions about Banker Lady now.

Eighteen

She went home feeling low, in two minds whether to go back at all. She couldn't pit her shrimpy little flat-chested bod against Venus as sculpted by a Greek master, her current jobless status against Addison's obviously glittering career, her one pleasant pub lunch with Ed against months of being 'very close'. It wasn't a fair fight. In fact, she had no reason to believe it was a fight at all. When had Ed ever given her the idea he'd welcome the chance to get closer to her? It was all on her side. She'd do better to get out now, before she had her heart broken again – and this time by someone who wasn't meaning to, who was no ultimately forgettable Mr Shallow, like Mark.

She let herself in through her front door, and knew something was wrong even before her eyes registered it. Beyond her knocked-through arch she could see that the back door was open – perhaps it was the difference in the light and air pressure that had immediately alerted her senses. Closer to hand there was something black on the newly-papered bit of living room wall.

Her eyes shifted focus, and the hair stood up on her scalp as she realized it was a bird. A crow, to be precise. A big, dead crow, with something white on its chest. She moved reluctantly closer. The dead bird had been nailed by its outspread wings to the wall, and a note was fixed to its chest with a drawing-pin. It was written in capitals in black felt pen.

GET OUT NOW
WHILE YOU STILL CAN

The bird had been dead a long time. Its eyes were gone and it smelled terrible. Her stomach rose and she had to run outside. She didn't throw up, but it was a close call. When she had recovered control, she turned back and looked at the door. The old lock-plate was lying on the floor in the kitchen, along with the keeper, simply burst off the door and frame by sufficient pressure from the outside.

Saturday afternoon, she thought. Sport on the telly. Anyone who was in would have been glued to the footy or the motor racing with their accompanying background racket and howling, over-excited commentators. One well-judged thump on her back door could hardly compete with that. And whoever it was could have approached down the track and not have to pass anyone else's doors or windows, and be in and out in little more than a minute.

If they knew she wasn't in. But they could have knocked first, she supposed. And her car wasn't there. They might even have seen her leave. She felt cold and sick again at the thought that they might have been watching her, unseen, waiting for their moment.

Someone wanted her out. How badly did they want it? And why? What lengths would they be prepared to go to?

Mechanically she collected a bucket and a claw-hammer, put on rubber gloves, went back into the living room and, holding her breath, removed the crow from the wall. She took it outside, went across the track and threw it as far as she could into the heather. The natural operations of nature would dispose of it from there. Going back in, she got out her tool box and went to see what she could do about the back door. The lock plate and keeper were undamaged – the inadequate too-short screws and the old wood had simply given way. She positioned it in an undamaged place, chiselled out a new groove for the keeper, found some longer screws, and re-fixed it. Then she fixed the two bolts, one at the top and one at the bottom, and did the same for the front door.

And then she went upstairs and had a much-needed bath. She stared at the ceiling through the steam and thought. There was still time to pack a bag and get over to The Hall if she wanted to. But did she want to?

On the other hand, did she want to stay here? Her presence might protect her property. Both attacks had happened when she was out. On the other hand, if whoever it was came back when she was in, might they escalate the action and hurt her? At the very least, did she want to be here alone, waiting and wondering?

She needed time to think what to do. Someone wanted her out, and the simplest thing would be to go. But that was giving in to it, and something in her stiffened its jaw and said *that* wasn't going to happen. It was her place, she had the right to be here, no-one was going to drive her away. But what could she do? She had no idea.

She remembered Jack making her promise to tell him if anything else happened, saying he would get to the bottom of it. She didn't know what he could do either, but at least if she consulted him it would be two brains instead of one. And perhaps he had local knowledge that would help.

It was another good reason to go to The Hall. And it would be rude to Camilla to drop out at the last minute. Jocasta would be disappointed, especially if she didn't ride in the point-to-point after all the build-up. And being over there would give her two days and three nights in safety to think out what to do. About everything.

She decided she would go.

Jack met her in the hall as she arrived. 'My God, have you *seen* her?' he exploded. 'Built like a goddess. Hair like Superman's, so black it's blue. Can she even be real? I wanted to touch her to make sure, but I was afraid she'd break my arm. What a dame! I take my hat off to old Ed. He can't be such a dunce with women after all, if he landed a hot property like that.'

'I saw her,' Kate said. It was all she managed to get in.

Jack was off again. 'I told you I'd heard there was someone in London, didn't I? But even I didn't guess anywhere near the truth. She's a bigshot in Friedman Bauer, the hedge fund management firm, and they don't get any bigger than that. Makes Ed's firm look like a Corgi toy in a Formula One race! They were living together in London, did you know? She had this fabulous riverside flat near Tower Bridge. And I thought he was staying in B&Bs!'

Kate's heart sank a little further. If they'd been living together ... That was why she'd assumed she'd be sleeping with him, of course. And he didn't exactly struggle against it ... Well, who could blame him? If she was a hotshot hedge fund operator, or whatever you called them, she'd be loaded as well. Not that she'd ever accuse him of being mercenary, of course, but when you added everything together the package was irresistible. And a far cry from the languid, pastel, drawling County females she imagined had been playing for him, who resembled the lost Flavia too much.

Far cry too from Kate, who didn't even have that going for her.

'I met her earlier today,' she said, firmly enough to be heard. 'She took me for a stable-hand at first.'

Jack grinned at that. 'She does rather tend to steamroller,' he said. 'She trod on Mrs B's toes by calling her "the help" and demanding some kind of fat-free spread we'd never heard of, and then telling her no-one over fifteen ought to be eating butter. She had a lot to say, one way or another, on the English diet!' He took her bag from her and plunked it on the floor, drew her arm through his and said, 'We're having tea on the terrace. Come and have some before the vultures get the lot. You can see your room later. I want you to meet my kid.'

They passed through the dark house, and Kate heard Addison's voice long before they passed out into the sunlight. She hadn't seen the terrace before. Like everything else at The Hall it was a little the worse for wear, with the paving stones cracked, bits of coping missing from the balustrade, and the furniture worn and faded by the elements. Quite a large party was gathered there, sitting on benches or lounging in wicker armchairs and sofas. The dogs were there too, and got up and rushed at Kate as soon as she appeared.

Addison's voice broke off in the middle of her sentence and she said, 'Oh, those dogs! Don't get them all worked up again. They've only just settled down, and I don't want them slobbering all over me like they did before.'

Kate, fielding their paws and kisses, felt guilty, like a grubby kid. She could see that Addison wouldn't want mud or slobber on her clothes, but Kate didn't own anything that would mind it. She straightened up, pushing them down, and Addison said with a social smile, 'It's Kate, isn't it? We met before. I'm still trying to figure everyone out. Now, you're not a relative, are you?'

'Friend,' Kate said.

'Oh, right, I remember. You're a friend of Jocasta's.'

Jack pinched Kate's arm in amusement, and she swallowed any possible retort, pointless in any case as Jocasta had come over in the wake of the dogs and taken her other arm. *Well at least someone's glad I'm here.* Actually, with the dogs' rapture and two family members affectionately attached to her, she ought to be feeling quite secure. But Addison was sitting thigh-to-thigh with Ed on a sofa-for-two, and wearing a scarlet jersey dress that clung to every magnificent curve and contrasted stunningly with the blue-black hair and the long, brown legs ending in matching scarlet platform heels.

'Let me introduce you to everyone,' Jack said.

Kate was glad to see Eric and Susie Orde among the guests, because the other three couples were unknown to her: all in their early thirties, smartly dressed, obviously well-to-do. They were introduced as Charlie and Beth, Greg and Sasha and Dan and Matty. The Brigadier was there, and another lone man in his late thirties, introduced as Jeremy, who was obviously there on account of Camilla, to judge by the way he gazed at her and glared at the Brigadier.

Finally there was a woman with a rather thin face and large blue eyes that looked shadowed and tired. She had the sort of pale fair hair you can't do anything with, dead straight, flat and slippery, and as much trouble in its own way as Kate's frizz. Jack did not indicate her from across the terrace as he did the others, but took Kate all the way over to meet her. She was Felicity, his ex.

Kate was surprised by her, having expected someone much tougher-looking, made-up and competent, a multitasking, life-work-balancing, omni-capable single mum. Felicity looked fragile. She was also surprised by the warm smile she got in greeting, along with a cordial handshake and the words, 'I'm pleased to meet you. I've heard a lot about you from Jocasta.'

'And this,' Jack interrupted in a voice brimming with pride, 'is Theo.'

The boy was tall for his age, thin as a rail, and ravishingly beautiful, with his mother's large blue eyes and Jack's toffee-coloured hair, but straight and silky like Felicity's. He regarded Kate solemnly and carefully for a moment, and then decided she was all right, and said, 'Daddy says you rescued Chewy, and you were very brave.' His voice was light and crisp, his accent exquisite.

'I wouldn't say brave. More lucky, really.'

He nodded, and then, probably remembering instructions, said awkwardly, 'Thank you.'

Jocasta was dragging her away to another sofa to sit with her, and Theo came too, saying, 'I wish we could have him to live with us all the time, but he's too big. I like it when we come here and I can play with him.'

'You used to live here, didn't you?' Kate said.

'I think so. I don't really remember.' He sat on the other side of her and said confidentially, 'I'm being a Roman centurion in the school play, because I'm tall.'

'That'll be fun,' Kate said. 'Will you have a helmet?'

He nodded. 'Our mothers are supposed to make them. And bress plates, and swords out of cardboard. Mum says it's an imposition. Does imposition mean a cheek?'

'Pretty much. Like a grown-up cheek.'

He nodded. 'But Mum says the other mummies will do it anyway because they complete with each other on every occasion.' He looked to see if she understood and added helpfully, 'That means she'll have to do it, too.'

Jack called across from where he was still talking to Felicity, 'Kate hasn't had any tea yet!'

Jocasta grabbed her arm. 'Come and get some. There's a really good cake.'

The two children hustled her to the cloth-covered trestle table at the end of the terrace where the tea was laid out. There was still a reasonable amount left, though it had evidently been descended upon by the hordes. Kate poured herself a cup of tea and put some little sandwiches, a scone and piece of cake on a plate. Both children asked if they could have more cake, and while she didn't see why she should be the arbiter, she also didn't see any reason to deny them when no-one else was bothered, so she supervised the cutting of slices and the placing of them on plates, and the three of them went back to their sofa. No-one else was looking their way – everyone was deep in conversation – so she sat with the children, and the cloud of dogs that magically appeared, ate her tea, listened to their chatter, and accepted the apparent division of the company. She was only younger than Jack by a few years, but it seemed that she was counted in the children's section, not the adult's.

Still, after all the worrying she had gone

through about approaching thirty, it was at least a change to feel too young for something.

Jack hadn't completely forgotten her. When everyone got up to go and change for dinner, he came and fetched her and said he would show her to her room.

'Flick's settling Theo in upstairs,' he said. 'What did you think of her?'

'She's beautiful,' Kate said.

Jack looked pleased. 'Do you think so?'

'She's not what I expected. I was expecting someone more—' She hesitated, feeling around for the right word. 'Robust,' she said in the end. 'You know, the sort of woman who manages everything so well it looks effortless.'

'Well, she does,' he said, puzzled.

'But she doesn't *look* like that, that's all.'

They climbed the stairs. 'Ed said I ought to make her stay.' He gave her a standard evil look. 'I think he's trying to keep me away from you, protect the maiden from the moustachio-twirling villain. What do you think?'

'I think someone ought to find out if she *wants* to stay, rather than talking about making her.'

'Oh, don't, you sound so po-faced! Of course it would be her choice. Don't let's have any more of that boring equality guff. We've already had half an hour of Princess Pocahontas going on about glass ceilings and how they don't apply to her because she's so different ... yada-yada-yada.'

Kate couldn't help sniggering. 'Pocahontas?'

'She also gave us a talk on how she's descended from some famous Indian brave.' He gave her a solemn look. 'I'm expecting her to come down to dinner in fringed leather, beads and a headband. Feather optional. Don't you think she looks like a Red Indian, with the cheekbones and the hair?'

'Oh God, you're not allowed to call them that,' Kate said, trying not to laugh. 'They're Native Americans.'

'Well, I'm a Native English, and I don't boast about it.'

The magnificent oak staircase led to various oak-panelled corridors, and Jack led her along one, and opened a door into a smallish, rather dark room, also panelled, with a small fireplace, an enormous wardrobe taking up too much space, and a single iron bedstead.

'This is you,' he said, 'It's one of the bachelor rooms. Bit Spartan, but we had to put the couples in the bigger rooms. Bathroom at the end on the left.' He pointed down the corridor. 'One advantage is that I'm just two doors down – thrown out of my pit for Greg and Sasha – so if you wanted to visit, nothing could be easier.' He ran a hand over her bare forearm.

'And which room were you planning to put *your wife* in?' she asked him pleasantly.

'*Ex*-wife. She'd be upstairs in the nursery wing,' he said. 'She'd never know a thing.'

Kate laughed. 'Good job I know you don't mean any of this.'

'My dear girl, why else do you think I got Camilla to invite you? Now, we need a signal. You could look at me and tap the side of your nose like this during the evening if it's on for later. Or maybe that's too obvious. Just leave your shoes outside the door and I'll see them when I come up.'

'Doesn't everyone leave their shoes outside the door?'

He raised his eyebrows. 'Are you mistaking this for the bleedin' Ritz? You must have been confused by the dozens of liveried footmen and scurrying housemaids into thinking this is 1908. Shoes left outside, the idea!'

'Forgive me, it's my first country-house weekend,' she said humbly.

He carried her bag in and dumped it on the bed. 'There you are, waif. Now, is there anything else you need?'

She remembered. 'Yes,' she said. 'There's something I need to tell you. Have you got a minute?'

He saw she was serious. 'For you, as many as you like. Has something happened?'

So she told him. At some point they both sat down on the bed, and when she'd finished she found he was holding her hand. He looked shocked.

'This is getting nasty,' he said. 'It can't go on.'

'You don't think they'd – they'd hurt me, do you? I mean, it wouldn't go that far?'

'No!' he said immediately. Then, more slowly. 'No, I can't believe that. God, this is Bursford, not Baltimore. I can't believe it's happening at all.'

'You said you'd try to get to the bottom of it.'

He looked chagrined. 'I'm afraid I haven't

done anything yet. Well, it was just one incident. I thought it was just some stupid thing that wouldn't happen again.'

'Is there anything you *can* do?' she asked, rather despairingly.

'I can ask some questions around the place.' He thought a moment. 'You didn't ring the police?'

She shrugged. 'I didn't think of it. My first idea was to fix the door and get rid of – that thing. So of course I'd spoiled the evidence. And when I did think of it, I didn't think there'd be any point. I couldn't imagine they'd send a squad car out from whatever distant place they hang out in, just because someone had broken into an empty house. It's not as if you could call out the village bobby.'

'You're probably right,' Jack said. 'In any case, it might be better if I try to find something out without involving them. I'd be more likely to get answers than strangers. Leave it with me.'

'I already have, once,' she said.

'I'm sorry,' he said. 'I should have taken it more seriously. I'm glad you came here, anyway. You'll be safe with us for a day or two.'

'That's what I thought,' Kate said, and couldn't help a bit of a wobble in her voice.

He looked at her. 'You poor kid! You must have been scared stiff.'

'It wasn't very nice,' she said in a small voice.

He took her in his arms, and she leaned into his nice-smelling, all-male warmth and felt comforted. After a while, he put her back from him a little, looked earnestly into her face, and then somehow they were kissing.

It was nice; it was so good to be kissing a man again, and Jack was an expert at it, and she did like him *so* much. It went on, and grew deeper and more urgent. In the end it was she who broke off, aware that the door was open and anyone could pass by; and that she'd assured Ed, and Jack himself, that they were just friends.

On the other hand, she thought, aware of his hands, one on her back and the other stroking her hair, Ed was fully involved with Addison, and even if Jack's wife *was* upstairs she was an ex-wife, wasn't she, so all was perfectly fair. Why shouldn't she have some comfort and pleasure like anyone else?

Jack was breathing hard. 'We'd better not get carried away. We're supposed to be dressing for dinner.' He grinned. 'Whole weekend before us. Plenty of time for me to act like a photographer, get you in a dark room and see what develops. But for now, I'd better go.' He kissed the end of her nose, then her lips again, but lightly this time, and stood up. 'I'm glad you're here,' he said seriously.

'I am too,' she said.

During the cocktail hour there was a lot of serious drinking, as everyone was staying and could let their hair down for once, not having to worry about driving home. Jocasta and Theo were there, and made a beeline for Kate and, feeling a bit like the au pair, she entertained them and was entertained by them, chatting and playing word games while she drank a glass of wine and they had ginger ale, and all three of them worked through a variety of canapés and nibbles that Jocasta foraged very competently.

It gave Kate the chance to observe the company from her outpost, which meant, of course, observing Addison. She certainly dominated the room, taller, more beautiful and more magnetic than anyone else in it, looking splendid in a wine-coloured silk dress sewn all over with self-coloured crystal spars so that it glittered when she moved; her hair loose, held back by a matching bandeau.

She had most of the conversation, too. But although when Kate caught Jack's eye from time to time he winked and rolled his eyes about her, she was winning favour with everyone else. Camilla was already enslaved – here was someone who could talk designer labels with her from a position of equal if not greater strength. But she kept the other women engaged with talk not only of clothes but of diets and health fads – she knew all the latest American ones – and celebrity gossip. Her voice, though loud, was not grating, and she certainly had plenty to say that people wanted to hear.

To the men she talked finance and markets, and they were dazzled by her knowledge and authority. It was girl-in-a-City-suit syndrome: a man's topic coming out of a woman's mouth had them dribbling with lust. Men were such unreconstructed cavemen, the poppets! And when the conversation turned to country matters, she was able to contribute world cattle and wheat prices, and to reveal with a modest little laugh that she was a crack shot. Her father had taught her, and she had shot mule deer in New Hampshire and reindeer in Alaska. She talked about ranching adventures, camping out in Yellowstone, and a scary encounter with a bear. She even had an amusing tale about how she had shot a burglar in the leg one night, preventing him from escaping until the cops arrived.

The children left, groaning and dragging their feet, to go up to bed, and soon afterwards dinner was announced and everyone decamped into the dining room, but apart from that nothing much changed. The conversation broke up from time to time into smaller groups, but then would recoagulate into one general topic, always led by Addison. She was undoubtedly the queen of the evening, and a stranger poking his head in would have assumed she was the mistress of the house and everyone's hostess. But she dominated with confidence and style, and Kate, looking round the table, thought that everyone was having a good time and would remember the evening as a success.

The only person she couldn't read was Ed. He said very little, listening to Addison and giving her his attention, but with his face even more inscrutable than ever. He didn't smile – though of course he never did – even when she included him in some anecdote: 'You remember, darling, that funny little man? We couldn't get rid of him – I think he was just so smitten with me – in the end Edward was forced to fake an emergency call on his mobile – didn't you, darling? And we literally *ran* away. It was such a hoot!'

He nodded or assented to joint memories, but added nothing to them. Even when Addison appealed directly: 'You tell the story, Edward, you tell it so much better than me,' he only shook his head and held silent until, inevitably, she took the narrative back herself.

Kate wanted to see this as less than a wholehearted commitment to the relationship, but it was dangerous to read anything into his behaviour, because she was not an impartial observer. She couldn't even swear to herself that he was not thoroughly happy, because that was very likely the purest self-delusion.

The only time she got any evidence for her side was during a long dissertation by Addison on health and diet, which was evidently one of her hobby horses. Kate had noticed that she had eaten very little of the delicious dinner that had been put in front of her. At one point she had said loudly, 'No salad? Where's the salad?' and Ed had said, quite sharply, 'You know we don't have a salad course in England.'

'Well, I *know* that,' she had said, with something of a pout, 'but I thought you'd become more civilized, darling, and learned something of our ways.'

Then she had gone off on how terrible the general diet was in Yurrup, even in France, while in England it was 'beyond terrible'. Too much fat, too much meat. 'I mean, look at what we've been served this evening,' she said, as if they were in a restaurant, not someone's house. 'Look at your plates! Dripping with artery-clogging saturated fats and animal proteins.' She went on about free radicals, superoxides and open-shell configurations, gliadin and the difference between sprouted and unsprouted grains, while around the table jaws champed in perpetual motion and forks full of Mrs B's delicious cooking were raised rhythmically from plate to mouth as the guests listened.

Finally, Ed interrupted her flow, saying, 'I'm sorry you're not enjoying your dinner, but everyone else is, so perhaps we'd better drop the subject.'

She gave him a look. 'But when the food you serve is so *unhealthy*—'

He interrupted a second time, before she could get going again. 'On a point of fact, food can't be healthy or unhealthy. It can be health-*giving*, nutritional, even therapeutic, but it can't be healthy.'

'Resorting to pedantics is what people do when they're losing the argument,' she said, not angrily, but with the calm of the righteous; but she graciously allowed the subject to change. Kate had been watching Ed the whole time, and now his eyes met hers the length of the table. For a moment their gaze held, and though his expression didn't noticeably change, she felt there was a pulse of sympathy passing between them. Out of the corner of her eye she saw Addison look towards her, and the next moment she addressed a remark to Ed, and the contact was broken as he turned to reply.

But, she told herself, if you're reduced to snatching at crumbs like that, you must be desperate. It's pitiful to imagine disharmony between lovers just because it would suit you. And, she should remember, he had only interrupted Addison because she was tacitly criticizing his other guests. And he'd only looked at her, Kate, because she was staring at him.

She gave herself a good shake, banned herself from looking at Ed again the whole evening, and concentrated on enjoying her dinner companions, Jeremy on one side and Greg on the other. Jeremy only wanted to talk about Camilla and Greg only wanted to talk about futures, but she did her best.

Back in the drawing room, she got into a group including the Brigadier and Jack and Felicity, and everything became more jolly and entertaining. Across the other side of the room, Beth had got Ed cornered in such a way that Addison couldn't get to him, and although talking about the Milan fashion show to the adoring audience of Camilla and Matty must have been something of a compensation, she kept throwing him frowning glances.

Jack nudged Kate. 'Heap big trouble. Pocahontas not like other squaw hang around big chief,' he murmured wickedly. 'But Pocahontas just have to suck it up!'

'Jack, behave yourself,' Flick said sternly. 'I'm sure she's a very nice woman.'

'You aren't,' he retorted, and she struggled not to laugh.

'At least I'm not enjoying the sight of a fellow mortal who's fallen into a bear trap,' she said. '*Schadenfreude* is an unattractive trait.'

'Oh?' he enquired. 'And what about when that terrible Pat Withenshaw made an entire speech at the flower show with a blob of mayonnaise on her chin? As I remember, a certain person not a thousand miles from here sniggered in a most inelegant manner.'

'Well, she deserved it, awful woman.'

'That, my love, is the very essence of *Schadenfreude*. We're not celebrating the downfall of innocent baby lambs and little helpless kittens here.'

The exchange was redolent of a long and satisfying relationship, of shared memories and feelings, attitudes and vocabulary. Kate thought Ed was probably right, and that Jack was still stuck on Felicity – and perhaps she was on him. It would be nice for them, probably, if they could get back together.

It made her feel like an outsider again. But she refused to feel that it would be any loss for her. He was just a friend. And after all, she was not a permanent resident here. She'd soon be gone – sooner than she had planned for, if her mystery enemy made any more attacks.

The evening showed no signs of breaking up. Everyone was relaxing, drinking and talking as hard as ever when the clock went past twelve. Kate slipped out to the loo, and at the end of the corridor was mobbed by the dogs, who had been banned from the drawing room on Addison's orders: she didn't want them jumping up at her, she said, and had earlier complained that they were allowed on the furniture and left their hair everywhere. It did no good for Jocasta to say they weren't *allowed* on the furniture, they just did it. It just let them all in for a lecture on proper dog-training, and the various diseases humans could catch from contact with their pets.

She comforted the dogs now, and they rolled their eyes up at her mournfully when she told them she hadn't come with a reprieve. On her way back, she met Addison just outside the drawing room door, and had an odd feeling that she had been waiting for her.

'Ah, there you are,' Addison said. 'I thought you'd gone off to bed.'

'No, I'm just getting my second wind,' Kate said, looking up into that carved, beautiful face, whose perfection of make-up was unsmudged even this late in the evening.

'Are you having a nice time, sweetie?' Addison asked.

Kate thought it was an odd thing for her to ask, since she was a guest too: it was a question the hostess might ask. While she was pondering this, and wondering what to say, Addison went on. 'There's something I want to talk to you about.'

Annoyingly, Kate felt herself blush as her imagination jumped ahead and pictured Addison saying, *Edward is mine, kid, so back off. Don't even think about him*.

'This point-to-point race on Monday,' she went on. 'I know you were planning to ride the mare – what's her name?'

'Henna,' Kate said woodenly. She had a horrid premonition about this.

'Henna, that's right. But I'm much the more

experienced rider, and Edward would really like *me* to ride her instead.'

'Oh,' said Kate.

'I know you've been practising, but I'm sure you won't mind stepping aside and letting me take her over, when it's what Edward wants.'

'Well, no – I mean—'

'You're not too disappointed? That's good. Because, frankly, he doesn't really think you're up to it, and the mare deserves a chance, don't you think?'

Through wooden lips, Kate said, 'It's whatever Ed wants. He's the boss.'

'Yes, he is, isn't he?' Addison said with a complacent smile. 'Good girl. I'll tell him you agree. Now, do you know where the bathroom is?'

'Straight down there, left at the end, and it's on the left,' Kate said mechanically, and Addison swept away, leaving Kate to enjoy her humiliation in peace.

Nineteen

Camilla told everyone when they began to drift up to bed that, after such late night carousals, breakfast would be at ten, and if anyone wanted to go to church, morning service was at eleven.

Kate could not be said to sleep well. The mattress was old, and so lumpy it was a question of avoiding the worst peaks and fitting herself into the valleys, which meant there were only one or at best two positions she could lie in without damaging herself. And of course, if you feel you can't move, that becomes the one thing you desperately want to do.

She dropped off at last into an uneasy sleep full of dreams that were not exactly nightmares but still very hard work. She mustn't have latched her door securely, for early in the morning it was pushed open by Ralph, who jumped up on the bed, closely followed by Toby. Both curled up on her feet with sighs of satisfaction. She was at that point of half-waking when you can't make yourself wake enough to do anything, and she dozed fitfully after that, much too hot with an extra covering of two dogs, until early in the morning they both suddenly deserted her, presumably having heard someone stirring below.

There was not a full complement of guests at

breakfast when she got down. The Brigadier had gone for a long walk with Eric Orde, Jocasta was out riding, and Greg and Sasha weren't down yet. Theo was at the table, brightly tackling a boiled egg, with Flick on one side of him and Jack on the other, a little cameo of family content that made Kate smile inwardly.

And Addison and Ed were missing. She thought of them curled up in Ed's bed, sleeping after a night of passion – she bet Addison was a real athlete in the pit and knew lots of new positions – but dragged her thoughts away from that determinedly. She helped herself from the sideboard and went to sit down by Susie. They chatted about this and that, but finally Kate couldn't contain it any longer and asked if Ed and Addison had stirred yet.

'Oh yes,' said Susie. 'Eric told me before he went on his walk that they were up really early – well, neither of them drank much last night, did they? – and they've taken Gracie and Henna out for a long ride so Addison can get used to her.' She looked at Kate curiously. 'I must say, I was surprised that you volunteered to give her up, when you'd put in so much hard work. And you seemed so keen to ride in the point.'

'I was,' Kate said. 'But I didn't exactly volunteer, did I? Addison said that Ed wanted me to give her up, because he wanted *her* to ride on Monday. So what could I do?'

Susie frowned. 'Wait, wait, Addison said it was *Ed's* idea?'

'She said he wanted Henna to have a chance, because Addison's a better rider than me, more experienced.'

'Well, not having seen her ride, I can't say if either of those things is true. But I do know it wasn't Ed's idea. I was there when the subject came up. It was after you went up to bed, and Addison came over and said you were worried about riding on Monday and you'd asked her to ride Henna instead, as long as Ed didn't mind. She said you'd said you didn't want to offend him when he'd taken so much trouble, so would she sound him out? So of course he said he didn't mind, and if Addison was going to ride they ought to have a practice this morning.'

Kate didn't know what to say. Her mind felt numb. She stared at Susie helplessly. 'I didn't say that. That wasn't what happened.'

Susie was less paralysed. 'I believe you,' she said vigorously. 'It's all of a piece with her domination of the conversation last night. I don't say she hasn't plenty to say, but she obviously has to be queen bee in everything, never mind anyone else's feelings. But this...! What a manipulative bitch! She couldn't just ask straight out.'

'She might just as well have. Ed would have said yes, I'm sure,' said Kate glumly.

'He might not have. He's very loyal, and if he'd given his word to you he'd want to keep it.'

Kate shook her head. 'He's in love with her. He'll give her anything she wants.'

'He might not be so in love with her when you tell him how she's behaved,' Susie said grimly.

'No,' Kate said. 'I can't do that.' Susie began to protest, and she went on, 'Think how that would make me look – petty and spiteful, a troublemaker. And I don't want to be the one to come between them. That wouldn't be right. I'm just a guest here. She's going to be family.'

'You are terribly forgiving,' Susie said. 'I wouldn't be.'

'Not forgiving, but – well–' she shrugged – 'no sense banging your head against a brick wall. Leave well alone, that's the best thing. You won't say anything, will you? Please, Susie.'

'If you say so,' Susie said with a sigh. And then she brightened. '*I* tell you what! I'll lend you Magic.'

'Magic?' Kate was puzzled for an instant.

'Magicman, my dear old horse. He's not so old he wouldn't like a little dash round the jumps, and you're very light in the saddle.'

'You mean – ride Magic in the point-to-point?'

'You're very slow, dear! That's exactly what I mean. I've seen you ride; you've got nice light hands and a good seat. And Magic's a much easier ride than Henna. All you've got to do is sit there and he'll do the rest.' She was beaming now. 'Do say yes! I'd so like to scotch that cow's triumph. You *ought* to have a ride, after working so hard. It's only a matter of changing the entry. You're already registered, and Magic's well qualified – I hunted him all last season. Say yes! Say yes!'

Kate began to laugh. 'Yes. I can't resist you when you're so determined.'

'No backbone, that's your trouble,' Susie said wisely. 'You give in too easily.'

'"Yes" to what?' Jack asked, looking across the table. 'What are you two hatching up?'

'Kate's going to ride Magic for me at Buscombe,' Susie said.

Jack looked puzzled. 'But I thought she was riding Henna?'

Kate saw Susie draw breath and kicked her warningly under the table. 'No, Addison wanted a ride, so she's having Henna,' Susie said neutrally.

'Oh,' said Jack, 'I heard her talking last night about what a good rider she is – does eventing in America, apparently. Won loads of prizes. I suppose she was building up her credentials ahead of asking.'

'Don't you like her?' Flick asked, giving him a curious look.

Jack seemed to embrace caution at the last minute. 'She's – rather a powerful character,' he said finally. 'Put it this way, I find a little of her goes a long way.'

'Well, be careful,' Flick said. 'It's whether Ed likes her or not that matters. And if he does – which seems to be the case – you don't want to make him choose between you and her. Because that's one you can't win.'

'I think she's marvellous,' Camilla said, catching on to the end of the conversation. 'It's so funny to think that if she and Ed get married, she'll be my step-daughter. Won't that be weird? Of course, it's already ludicrous that Ed and Jack are my stepsons!'

'You said it,' Jack muttered, and Flick reached across and rapped the back of his hand with her butter-knife.

* * *

There was just time for a quick dash across to Northcombe after breakfast by Kate and Susie so that Kate could try out Magic and put him over a few jumps. He was a very comfortable ride, quite different from Henna, and she soon found that he knew exactly what he was doing, looked carefully at each jump on approach and picked his own take-off.

'Just keep your leg on him and keep contact with his mouth all the time, so he knows you're awake,' Susie said, 'and he'll do the rest. You'll be fine.'

'He's wonderful,' Kate said. 'I hope Ed doesn't mind.'

'Why on earth should he?' Susie asked robustly.

Kate couldn't think of an answer – she didn't know why he might, she just had an uneasy feeling about it.

But when they got back to The Hall, he only replied to Susie's explanation, 'Yes, Jack told me.' And to Kate, 'I'm glad you'll be getting a ride. Magic's an old hand. I'm sure you'll be safe on him.'

But he looked, Kate thought, disappointed in her; and no wonder, if Addison had said she was scared. She blushed with annoyance and humiliation – and with hurt when Ed turned away, dismissing her and the subject. She had let him down; she wasn't the person he had thought her; and she would have to live with that judgement, however much it burned her.

The afternoon's entertainment had been arranged: they all went off, in various cars, to the country fair in the Quantocks, near Cothelstone, taking with them a picnic put up by Mrs B (and the girl who had come to help in the kitchen for the weekend) and a case of champagne. The fair had stock classes, and marquees housing a flower show, a dog show, and various crafts.

There was a field set aside for picnicking, which was obviously a large part of the ritual. Rather like Glyndebourne, Kate thought: people seemed to be competing to display the most sumptuous picnic, and to be seen to be having the best time. Some of them had gone overboard with picnic furniture and accessories of extraordinary elaboration, and one or two had even brought servants with them to set up and hand round.

The Blackmore picnic was not quite in that league: there were thick tartan rugs to sit on, but no table and only two folding chairs, seized at once by Camilla and Addison. But the cold collation was excellent, and they drank champagne out of proper glasses.

There was much to-ing and fro-ing as people visited and were visited from other groups, friends catching up with friends – which was obviously an important part of the occasion. The field echoed with the bird-cries of greeting and exclamation, and hummed with happy conversation.

When the major part of the eating was over, no-one seemed eager to go and see the show, preferring to sit and smoke and chat and pour more champagne. Eric and Dan did eventually walk off to look at some cattle classes, and the children, who'd been growing increasingly restless, finally begged Kate to go with them and look at the marquees. Kate, resigned now to her role as childminder, got up and went.

By an extraordinary coincidence the route Jocasta picked led right by an ice-cream van, so to offer to buy them one seemed, in all decency, the only thing she could do. It was while they were standing in the queue that she spotted Phil Kingdon standing a little way off, deep in conversation with a tall, smartly-dressed man who seemed somehow out of place in this setting. It was, she decided, because he looked such a product of the urban scene: an expensive business suit, shiny town shoes, immaculate haircut, a lean, hard face you'd expect to see across a table in the boardroom of a multinational, rather than in a field surrounded by the smell of bruised grass and cattle dung.

They were talking hard, heads close together. It pleased her slightly that, from their body language, the stranger seemed the top dog of the two. There was something she just didn't like about Kingdon.

Jocasta said something and she turned to her to reply. When she looked again, the two men had gone.

The displays in the marquees were very good, of a professional standard. The children were most interested in the tent where the dogs were waiting in their cages for the dog show judging; that, and the WI tent where there were displays of cakes among the jam and pickles. Kate was trying to answer Theo's wistful query about what happened to the cakes after the competition, when Jack joined them, much to Theo's delight. It was nice, Kate thought, though a bit sad, that he adored his daddy so much. The four of them went off to see the rest of the show, Theo holding Jack's hand and Jocasta with her arm linked through Kate's. A stranger, Kate thought, would have taken them for a family.

When they returned to the picnic field, the rest of the party were back there – or perhaps had never moved – and tea and coffee were being poured from flasks. Camilla, Kate noted, had given up her chair to an older woman who was deep in conversation with Addison, and for once Addison seemed to be getting the worst of it, listening while the other woman talked fast and determinedly, her tight jaw going up and down and a finger jabbing points in the air like a political debater.

Jack nudged Kate. 'The biter bit,' he sniggered. 'That's the ineffable Mrs Murray, head of every committee known to man, organizer supreme and hard rider to hounds. She's tamed Princess Pocahontas all right. What a hoot!'

'Maybe Princess P is just having a rest,' Kate suggested. 'Any minute she'll leap back into the fray refreshed.'

Jack shuddered. 'The thought of her with even more energy...'

Kate was looking at Camilla, who was holding court. As well as the Brigadier and Jeremy, she had two other men standing in a little group round her, and she seemed to be managing to charm all of them, and was giving four glad-eyes at once with effortless skill. 'Your stepmother's having a good time,' she said.

'Good luck to her,' Jack said tolerantly. 'I'm all for flirting. Flirting is good for people.'

'So you've taught me. I never thought—' She broke off. 'Oh, there's Phil Kingdon.'

He had approached the group, and having said something to Camilla, drew her a little out of the circle, talking to her with his head close to her ear.

'Don't tell me he's one of her admirers,' Kate said.

'He'd better not be,' said Jack. Kate glanced at him. He was frowning as if the sight of Camilla and Phil together was something he disapproved of. When she looked back, she saw, beyond them, the man she had seen him talking to earlier.

'Do you know who that is?' she asked.

Jack looked. 'He looks familiar somehow – I don't know why. Why do you ask?'

'I saw him and Phil Kingdon having a discussion earlier. It looked important. I just wondered who he was.'

'Dunno,' Jack said. 'I've got a feeling I've seen him somewhere, but I don't know where.'

'I've got the same feeling, but I know I don't know him,' Kate said. Suddenly she realized that the stranger was staring at her. She gripped Jack's arm, turning him away. 'He's looking at me,' she hissed. She edged away, taking him with her, until there was a group of standing people masking them.

'Probably because you were looking at him,' Jack said reasonably. And then, 'What's the matter? You've gone quite pale.'

She had tracked the memory down. It was not that she recognized the man. It was the shape of him, of his head and bulky shoulders, that seemed familiar. They reminded her of the shadow she had seen briefly standing outside her cottage, that night she had come home from babysitting. She peeped again through a gap between the shoulders of the protective group. Kingdon and the other man were walking away together, the smart man, it seemed, doing the talking. They disappeared into the crowds.

'What's the matter?' Jack asked again.

It was hard to explain. She had felt safe at The Hall, and it was as if the trouble had followed her, had breached the defences and exposed her again. 'He was staring at me, that's all,' she said at last. 'This business – with the house – it's got me all on edge. It's stupid.'

'No,' he said thoughtfully, 'you've got every right to be upset. But you're safe with us. And I'm going to make some enquiries, like I promised you. In fact, I'm going to start right now.' And he pressed her arm, and walked away, heading towards the marquees.

Back at The Hall, there were baths and dressing and then cocktails, a buffet supper, and a settling in for the evening. A card table was set up at one end of the room, and Camilla, Jeremy, the Brigadier and Felicity sat down to bridge.

'Camilla's mad about bridge,' Jack told Kate.

'She's got into this high-playing group – it's like the County set's version of a poker school. You know, the tense, smoke-filled room, the hard faces, the narrowed eyes, big sums of money changing hands. It's one of the reasons she gets into debt. Mind you,' he concluded, 'if she weren't playing bridge she'd be out shopping and she can drop just as much money that way, if not more.' He gave a short smile. 'At least Flick will get some of it back for the family. She's a demon at bridge.'

The rest of them gathered at the other end and played charades. Charlie had them in fits with his obscene rendering of *Grand Prix*. Addison got annoyed because nobody got her mime for *The Unbearable Lightness of Being*. Ed did *Casablanca* as 'cash a blank her' which Kate thought ingenious. He did it straight-faced, but with a gleam that hinted at suppressed laughter. She was glad to see him enjoying himself – he had seemed to get more grim as the weekend progressed. Jack was completely defeated by *Unforgiven* and demanded a re-draw, saying it was impossible, upon which Addison jumped up and said *she*'d show him how to do it, and proceeded to perform what looked like exactly the same mime as for *Unbearable Lightness*.

They went from charades to paper games, which got sillier and sillier as the drink went down, until the bridge players complained they could not hear themselves shuffle. Then Greg offered to play the piano and Jack and Charlie rolled up the tatty old Turkish rugs and there was dancing. Kate watched Ed and Addison revolving in each other's arms, not talking, but looking so good together, physically perfectly matched, that she felt heartsick.

Despite her good intentions, she had fallen for him. She was in no doubt about it now. All she could comfort herself with was being in his presence. It was painful, but it was better than nothing; otherwise she might have packed her bag and slipped out into the night, never to return. The time would come when she would have to leave Bursford, never to see him again, but it was not yet. While she could be near him and look at him, she would take those meagre crumbs. Ahead, she knew, was starvation.

She had been sitting one out, or rather standing it out next to the piano, allowing her dreamy gaze to follow Ed around the room. Now he had gone out of the room for a moment, so she chatted instead in a desultory manner to Greg as he obligingly tinkled away at old dance tunes.

Suddenly Addison was by her side. She was in black sequins tonight, her hair up in a high chignon decorated with two small black feathers – Kate had thought briefly of Jack's prediction about beads and feathers, but there was nothing laughable about her. She looked glittering, dangerous and beautiful.

'Can I talk to you?' she said. A hard hand gripped Kate's upper arm and turned her away from Greg into the privacy of the space between the piano and the dusty-smelling velvet curtains. Addison's face was smiling, but her eyes were hard. Kate looked into them, noting that they really were green, but with patches of blue and flecks of gold-brown – really rather remarkable.

'It's about your behaviour,' Addison said in a low voice.

Kate was startled. 'My what?' You might hear those words from your mum when you were fifteen, but from one adult to another, in a third party's house...? She couldn't believe she'd heard right.

Addison sighed. 'I don't like to be the one to say anything, but someone has to, and as I'm Edward's – well, *practically* his fiancée, I think it's down to me. Because you're making people uncomfortable.'

'What are you talking about?' Kate said in amazement.

The stare was *de haut en bas*. 'It was bad enough your coming here at all, on some flimsy excuse, when you *really* don't fit it.' A quick, searing look up and down Kate said it all: clothes, hair, make-up – she just was out of her league here. 'But you've developed a – well, a sort of *girly crush* on Edward. I can understand it – he's very handsome, and I dare say someone like you hasn't often come across a man like him. But I have to warn you that you're being too obvious. Everyone's noticed it. *Edward*'s noticed it, and it's making him very uncomfortable. I'm sure that's not what you want. And of course everyone else feels terribly sorry for you, but the fact is that you really ought to have more pride than to show your feelings so obviously when they aren't reciprocated.'

Kate felt her face going scarlet, never a good

colour with her hair. She was speechless. 'Well, of all the—!' was about all she could manage.

Addison patted her forearm kindly, with a smile that could have etched glass. 'Now, now, don't take offence. I mean it in the nicest way. You're a sweet girl, and I'm sure one day you'll find someone at your own level and be very happy. And believe me, you won't want to look back on this weekend and remember that you've made a fool of yourself in public. So *do* try not to stare at him all the time like a lovesick calf. I'm just telling you as a friend.'

In such a situation, the only resource was irony. 'Thank you so much,' Kate said. 'I really appreciate what you're doing for me. I can't think why you'd bother.'

Sadly, they didn't have irony in Addisonland. 'Atta girl,' she said encouragingly. 'You'll be fine. I just had to give you a hint. We girls have to stick together, don't we?'

'We certainly do,' Kate gushed, and gave Addison an adoring, hero-worshipping gaze upwards. She thought she might have gone too far, but Addison was so used to that sort of thing, it just rolled off her like requests for autographs off a film star. She gave Kate another pat and went away. Kate turned back to the piano, wishing she could play, because she'd certainly have liked to thump seven bells out of something just then.

Twenty

The Buscombe ground was packed, under grey bank-holiday skies. But it was warm, and the cloud was high, and everyone hoped it wouldn't rain. There was a flat area on the top of Buscombe Common where there was the car park, the horsebox park, the collecting ring, and the public area, hosting various tents, including refreshments, and an arena where there was going to be a dog agility competition and hound-racing. It was gay with flags and crowds, children and dogs, happy chatter, bookies calling odds, and the mingling smells of horses, bruised grass, fried onions and popcorn.

The course for the races started and finished on the common, which made a natural grandstand from which you could see most of the action. From there it went down a shallow descent, across some gently undulating ground and over a narrow stream, which had been made into a water jump, before turning back up the hillside to the common.

Kate stood with Susie looking down from the far side of the collecting ring. 'Do I need to walk the course?' she asked.

'Some do, but I wouldn't bother,' Susie said. 'You'll see where everybody else is going.'

'Suppose I'm in front?' Kate said with a grin.

'In that unlikely case, just keep looking for the flags. You won't mistake the jumps for anything else – they're obviously built, not natural.' She looked at Kate. 'We can walk it if you like, but I'd save my energy if I were you.'

'Addison's walking it,' Kate mentioned.

'That's only so that she can be alone with Ed,' Susie said robustly. 'And show off her technical knowledge to anyone who's listening.'

Kate smiled, as there had already been a bit of that this morning, over breakfast: talk of take-offs, ground lines, optimum approaches and so on.

'It's a nice course and you'll enjoy it,' Susie went on. 'The only place you need to be careful is down there.' She pointed. 'Where you take the turn to come back up the hill. A lot of people – the ones who are really competing – will try to cut the turn really sharply to get an advantage. They'll be jumping as far to the left as they can and there might be a scrum. You don't want to get mixed up with that. Just make sure you stay on the right.'

'Keep right at the turn. Got it.' Kate said.

'I feel sick,' Jocasta wailed. 'Absolutely chukkers.'

The pony races were first on the schedule: one open, and one Exmoor ponies only.

'It's supposed to be fun,' Kate reminded her.

'I know, and it is, but you can't help feeling sick when you see the opposition. Some of those ponies in the open are as big as elephants.'

'Never mind, Daphne's good and he's fast. And it doesn't matter anyway if you don't win.'

'Might not matter to you, but it matters to Daphne,' Jocasta said darkly. 'And there's no point in going in for it if you don't try to win. Have you got any money on you?'

'A bit – why?'

'There's an ice-cream van over there.'

'I thought you felt sick.'

'Ice cream's the best thing for stopping it. I'll pay you back.'

'No need. Here.'

'Oh, thanks! You're the best. Shall I bring you one?'

'I'm not nauseous,' Kate said.

'You will be later,' Jocasta assured her, and dashed off.

In fact, Kate did feel the onset of butterflies when she saw Jocasta line up at the start. A lot of the other riders looked like professionals despite being juveniles, and there was a certain amount of jostling and some hard glares. Once they were off, there was just excitement and a lot of shouting. Kate hadn't thought of herself as one for shouting, but in about two seconds she was yelling her head off like everyone else. Daphne came in fourth, which Ed said was pretty good, given the competition; and since in the pony classes there was a highly-commended as well as first, second and third, he ended up with a rosette after all, a white one, which Jocasta was very pleased with.

They watched the dog agility, which was great fun. The local foxhounds made an appearance, with the master and two whips mounted and pink-coated. They did a circuit of the ring, with hounds escaping at every juncture to mug the crowds for crisps, biscuits and bits of bun, and a couple of helpers went round with a collecting tin. Then the ring was cleared, the brush hurdles put up, and the hound steeplechase was run.

And after that it was time for Ed's first class. He was riding Gracie in the restricted and the men's open, which he said were far enough apart to rest him between them.

'This'll give you a chance to see the course properly,' Susie said. They watched together, with Jocasta on Kate's other side gripping her arm so tightly she left fingermarks. She had thought the pony race fast, but this was faster, the horses making a thunder you could almost feel come up through your feet. She fixed her eyes on Ed's figure, trying to keep him in sight all the way round, but at the farthest part of the course she lost him in the melee. He came fifth, and rejoined them at last saying he was well pleased with that, Gracie being a young horse and inexperienced. Addison descended on him with gracious words, and they led Gracie off to box him for his rest.

'I see now why everyone kept saying I wasn't expected to win, only get round,' Kate said, watching them go. 'If *Ed* can only make fifth...'

'He mightn't even make that in the open,' Susie said. 'The competition will be stiffer. But Gracie's young, I think he's really going to be something in a year or two. I'm starving,' she added. 'It must be time for lunch.'

'I couldn't eat a thing,' Kate said.

'Feeling sick?' Jocasta said with interest. 'You need an ice cream.'

They lunched on hot dogs from one of the tents – chunks of crusty French bread stuffed with fat, sizzling local farm sausages – followed by apple pie topped with a slice of Wookey Hole Cheddar from another, all washed down with plastic cups of real ale or cider or, in the case of the children, apple juice. They ate sitting on the grass looking over the course and chatting relaxedly. Kate sat with Eric and Charlie who talked cattle breeding and kept her mind off the race, but did not quite stop her from noticing that Ed and Addison were sitting together a little way off and talking – or at least Addison was talking and Ed was listening – as if no-one else existed.

Kate was glad to see Jack, Flick and Theo sitting together, with Jocasta, who seemed to be behaving like a big sister to him. She was wearing her rosette behind her ear like a flower and seemed to be delighted with herself and everything else.

She was also glad to see Camilla and the Brigadier sitting side by side with their heads together, talking contentedly and sharing cider from the same cup. Now and then Camilla looked up at him in a way that Kate would have sworn was admiring. Evidently Jeremy thought so, because he sat a little way off staring at them moodily, not talking to anyone else, and savaging his lunch as though he wanted to make something suffer.

* * *

Magic surprised her when he was led down from the trailer by letting out a huge, long whinny that made his sides vibrate. His head was up and his ears were so pricked, they were almost crossed.

'He's just excited,' Susie said affectionately. 'He loves all this stuff, dear old boy. Maybe I've been premature in retiring him. He's fourteen, but he's still got plenty of go in him.'

He looked around him at everything with such a tangible equine delight that despite the butterflies, Kate was really pleased she would be riding him. It was nice to give a fellow-creature pleasure. For the first time she stopped minding about Henna. Susie had plaited his mane and put a shine on his coat – not easy to do with a grey. Eric, who had gone to fetch Kate's number, came back to pat him admiringly and say, 'He really looks the business. I'm actually envying you, having this ride. I wish I'd entered now, but it's late in the season and I thought my boy had had enough.'

'I've been envying her all morning,' Susie said. 'Have you seen the opposition?'

'The ineffable Mrs Murray's riding Fly Direct, and Celia Carnforth's brought Surprise Me. Obvious first and second. Then there's Brightwell, though he's not on form, and I spotted Tudor King being walked about. I don't know who's riding him. They ought to be placed.' He looked at Kate. 'You could easily make fifth. But anything could happen. That's the joy of pointing. I'm just praying for Mrs Murray to fall off.'

Kate smiled. 'That's mean.'

'You haven't met her.'

'Anyway, I'm not expecting to be placed. I'm just here to have fun. As long as I don't let him down,' she added, patting the firm grey neck.

'Just remember what I said, keep your legs on and keep contact with his mouth,' Susie told her, 'and you'll be fine.'

'There's your real competition,' Eric added, gesturing with his head. 'If I read the runes right.'

Kate glanced to where Henna had been led out, and was dancing about on the end of her rope like a sprat on a griddle. 'Competition?' she said vaguely, puzzled.

'And Ed is the prize,' Eric said with a wicked grin.

Kate blushed, and Susie berated him. 'Now stop that, Chubby. Behave yourself.'

'Chubby?' Kate queried, feeling better.

'It's not what you think,' the round-faced Eric said with dignity. 'I happen to be a champion coarse fisherman. I got my nickname for a prize-winning catch of chub. One of them was a real monster – a nine pounder!'

'Eight pounds thirteen,' Susie countered.

As they rode down to the start, Kate's butterflies were completely routed by her concern over Henna. The mare was wildly excited, was tittup-ing about, making as much progress sideways as forwards, and was back to her bad old head-tossing habit. Addison, she noted, looked magnificent in the saddle, but her expression as she tried to control her mount was grim. Kate thought she was hanging on to the mare's mouth too hard, and longed to call out some advice – but to say that would not have been well received was an understatement. Ed would have told her what was what during the practice yesterday, anyway. And Addison, as an experienced rider, ought to understand.

At the start, Kate found herself more or less in the middle, and Henna was several horses to her right. She looked about quickly at the others, and thought they all looked like hardened professionals, with steely eyes and grimly determined mouths, and their horses were all gorgeous, gleaming beauties packed with muscle under their shining coats. *The hell with them*, Kate thought, patting Magic's neck. *I've got the nicest horse in the world and I'm going to have fun.* Magic's ears were going back and forth, and he was fidgeting on his toes and mouthing his bit eagerly.

There was some surging about as horses tried to go and were reined back, and Kate, busy looking around her, missed the actual 'Go'. But Magic knew the drill, and as the other horses leapt forward, so did he, almost unseating her. She lost a stirrup, and spent the gallop to the first jump desperately fishing for it. Magic rose like a bird and she grabbed a handful of mane to make sure she went with him. On the other side she found the stirrup, regained her balance, and settled herself down, all nerves gone.

It was amazingly exhilarating, the hard pounding of hooves, the solid, muscular bodies to either side, black and brown and bay and chestnut, the snorting breaths, the flash of legs below and the narrow focus of the green and brown course between the pricked grey ears. In a pack they galloped, gradually spreading out after the first hurdle. There were horses ahead of her now – but plenty behind her, too. Jump after jump appeared before them, Magic thrust down with his mighty hind quarters and they flew and landed and galloped on. It was heaven, it was glorious! She never wanted it to end.

She caught a glimpse of Henna off to her right. The mare was sweating and trying to poke her nose, but Addison, crouched forward, seemed to have an iron grip on her. She seemed to be controlling the head tossing by sheer force. Kate had a moment to think *poor Henna*, but another jump was coming. There were five horses ahead of her, she thought, startled – only five! And Magic was going strongly, his muscular shoulders working under her hands, feeling as though he could do this for hours yet. A light contact with his mouth told her he had more to give. She would have to decide when to let him out. But they were well placed for now. Another jump. As he rose, she saw two horses going up at the same moment on her left, and Henna just a beat behind, rising on her right.

She began to cherish the idea that they might come in somewhere – not first second or third, but fourth or fifth did not seem out of the question, and she *so* wanted to do him justice, the darling horse! A loose horse galloped past on her left, stirrups flapping. Someone would be walking home. Without its rider it was keeping up easily, almost cantering, and at the next jump it went round the end rather than over, giving it several lengths' lead.

Another jump coming. She glanced up and saw the leaders, some way ahead now, veer left after it, and realized it was the turn Susie had warned her about. The horses to her left were moving over, taking the line, but she was more or less in the middle and a touch on the rein kept Magic going straight. A glance right showed Henna pounding along, level with her, matching stride for stride. Addison, crouched and grim, returned the glance; then Kate saw her drive Henna on faster.

Not time to race yet, Kate thought. Henna pulled ahead, white foam flying from her mouth now, spattering back over Addison's boots. *Concentrate on the turn after landing – don't want to lose too much ground.*

It happened in an instant. Afterwards, Kate only had a broken memory, a jumble of fragmented impressions, but she knew what must have happened. In the last paces before the jump, Henna, perhaps seeing the line of the lead horses, or perhaps at Addison's instigation, veered suddenly left, across Magic's path. He swerved left to avoid her, unbalancing Kate; he stumbled slightly, and made a heroic effort to clear the jump. She remembered the touch of the brush on her legs as he went through the top of it. He stumbled on landing, took another stride and fell, on his knees and over on to his side. Kate lost him at the stumble, hurling off sideways and forwards. Her left foot caught a moment in the stirrup and there was a violent, wrenching pain, so fierce it made her feel sick. Then the ground came up and hit her, and there was a momentary trembling, thundering, wind-shaking feeling as the rest of the field went past her.

Somehow, Ed was there. She was still feeling sick and confused, but had managed to get to her knees, seeing Magic a little way off – the darling horse had stopped for her. She saw a spectator run forward and catch his rein to lead him off the course, glad to see he was moving smoothly, didn't seem to be hurt. She tried to stand up but the savage pain in her ankle and foot made her cry out – *broken it*! she thought dismally – and she collapsed again, her head spinning. And it was then that Ed reached her. She wondered how he had got there so soon. He was kneeling beside her, his hands on her.

'Don't move,' he said. 'Where does it hurt?'

'My foot. Left. Think it's—' she began, trying to sit up, but the black whirlies got her and she slumped back down.

'I said, don't move,' he said grimly. She looked up vaguely into his face and thought how good it was to be in his hands, even if he did look angry.

'I love you,' she said, or thought she did. He didn't seem to hear her. He was feeling his way down her leg.

'Can you move your toes?' he asked.

'You just told me not to move,' she protested mumblingly, closing her eyes. But she moved them.

'Thank God. Not broken then. I'm going to carry you up to the first-aid tent. Quicker than waiting for them to bring a stretcher.'

'Don't need a stretcher,' she muttered. *Just you.* She didn't think she said that out loud.

His arm was under her shoulders, his other under her knees, and he lifted her and stood up as though she weighed nothing at all. 'Good job you're so small and light,' he said with a grunt.

Nice compliment, shame about the grunt, she thought, and then wondered what was wrong with her. As well as sick, she felt rather drunk, and her thoughts didn't seem to be entirely under her control.

Being carried up a slope, even by a tall strong man, was not the most comfortable thing, especially with a foot and ankle waking from shock into throbbing pain. But her hand was on the back of Ed's neck, and her head was against his shoulder, and the subtle, wonderful smell of him was around and inside her, so on the whole she didn't mind. It was better when they were on the level. She opened her eyes and said, 'Magic?'

Susie was beside them – where did she appear from? She said, 'He's fine. Eric's boxing him, but he seems fine.'

'Not his fault,' she mumbled, closing them.

'You were doing so well,' Susie said. 'It's a shame. But it wasn't your fault. Just an accident.'

Tactful, Kate thought. *Not going to blame Addison with Ed there.* She opened her eyes again and saw the first-aid tent ahead, with the first-aiders hovering outside, looking excited and pleased at having a real casualty coming in. One of them was holding the stretcher. *Sorry, not this time, guys*, she thought. And then she saw, beside the tent opening, looking at them, the smart man from Cothelstone, still in his ritzy suit, hair immaculate. *Where he is, there shall ye find Phil Kingdon also*. Why was he staring at her? 'It's him,' she said, gripping Ed's neck to convey the urgency. 'That man. Saw him at Cothelstone with Phil.'

'Don't worry about it now,' Ed said, but she knew he had looked, had seen and registered the man, so she relaxed. And when she looked again, he'd gone. *Scared off by my hero*, she thought contentedly.

Except he wasn't *her* hero, was he? And she'd let Magic down, let them all down. Now he'd think she couldn't ride for nuts and would be extra glad he hadn't let her out on Henna, and he'd despise her. She'd made trouble for everyone and she wished she was dead.

There was an actual, real doctor who showed up at the tent, so it wasn't just the first-aiders, and because of that, on Kate's pleading, she was allowed to go home when her ankle had been strapped up. Or back to The Hall, at any rate.

'You can't look after yourself when you can't walk,' Ed had said tersely. 'You'll stay at The Hall for as long as is needed. I still think you should go to the hospital for a check-up.'

'The doctor said I was all right,' Kate asserted. She didn't want to make any more trouble than she already had. Nothing broken, just a sprain;

nothing to be done for it but support and rest, and alternate hot and cold compresses; paracetamol for the pain. Ed was worried about concussion but the doctor had looked into her pupils with his little pen light and said he didn't think she had it.

Camilla, unexpectedly, backed Kate. 'Don't fuss, Ed,' she said. 'People fall off horses all the time. I bet Kate's fallen off plenty of times in her life. All she needs is rest and quiet.'

Ed carried her to the Brigadier's car and put her in, settling her fussily, frowning to himself. He had to drive the box back so had to leave her to Harry and Camilla. Kate now had a pounding headache and wanted nothing but to sleep, so she didn't care who drove her. But at the last minute, when Ed had withdrawn and was about to shut the car door, Susie took his place, leaned over her to reassure her that Magic was really all right, and added in a whisper, 'Don't you want to know how Addison did?'

Kate didn't care, but knew she would want to know later, so she opened her eyes again. Susie was grinning. 'She came in third.' A momentary pang of jealousy. 'But she missed out half the jumps. She fought Henna all the way round and Henna won, went round the end instead of over. She was eliminated.'

Kate wished she could join in Susie's glee, but she could only feel sad. For Henna most of all, but for Ed too, and even Addison. You had to be feeling top-notch, she discovered, to get any pleasure out of *Schadenfreude*.

Twenty-One

Jocasta was the first one in to see her the next morning, tiptoeing in, breathing heavily, carefully carrying a mug.

'Are you awake?' she hissed penetratingly. 'I brought you up some tea.' Kate struggled to consciousness. 'How are you feeling?'

Kate considered. Her ankle was throbbing, and she felt the sort of bone-weariness you feel after shock, but her headache had mostly gone. She started to sit up and discovered some additional pains, a bruised elbow and some torn muscles around her ribs. 'Not too bad,' she said. Jocasta put the mug down and came to help her sit up. Kate discovered Chewy was sprawled across the end of her bed, and Sylvester was resting against her waist, a big warm marmalade lump. He didn't shift as she sat up, but purred loudly and placatingly. 'What's the time?'

'Half past seven. Mummy said not to wake you but I wanted to see you before I went. And you were awake, weren't you?'

'Yes,' Kate said obligingly. She'd been asleep for sixteen hours. She discovered she had a raging thirst. 'Thanks for the tea,' she said, and sipped gratefully.

'Everyone's gone,' Jocasta said discontentedly.

‘Mostly last night, but Addison went this morning. She’s gone to London for two days, back tomorrow night. And I’ve got to go back to horrible school. I’ve got to leave in a minute, and I won’t be able to see you until next weekend, if I can get an exeat. I *hate* school!’

‘But you’ll see your friends,’ Kate offered. ‘You do have friends there?’

‘Oh, some, but they all live so far away, right on the other side of Taunton, so I only see them at school, and you can’t really be proper friends like that. If only I went to day school, the other girls would be living nearby, and I could see them after school and weekends and everything.’

Kate saw the point. ‘*Is* there a day school you could go to?’

‘Course there is,’ said Jocasta eagerly. ‘That’s why it’s so stupid making me go to St Hilda’s. There’s Comyns at Withypool, which everybody says is a brilliant school. If I went there, Mummy could drive me, or I could even go by bus. I’d *love* to go to school on the bus. And then I’d be able to ride Daphne every day instead of once in a blue moon. And walk the dogs and everything. It would be awesome.’ She sighed. ‘But Mummy won’t listen.’ She caressed Chewy’s head, and he beat his tail, but without opening his eyes. ‘I’m glad you like animals. That horrible Addison hates them. She made such a fuss last night about the dogs. She made Ed shut them out in the welly lobby. And then she found Sylvester’s hair all over her suit that she wanted to wear today, and you should have heard her! I told her he’s part Persian and they shed all the time but it didn’t make any difference. She looked at him as if she'd like to kill him. And shedding's the only pleasure he's got left in life, poor darling, since he's been fixed – isn't it, poor Wester?' she crooned, stroking him. Sylvester purred even harder in agreement.

Jack put his head round the door. 'Oh, there you are. You'd better get your stuff together. I'm leaving in five minutes.'

'Jack's driving me to school,' Jocasta explained, 'because Mummy's having a lie in.' She got up from the bed. 'I say, you *will* still be here next weekend, if I can get an exeat?'

Kate hesitated, not knowing what to say, but Jack intervened. 'She will,' he said firmly. 'Now go and get your stuff. Be downstairs in five minutes or you can walk to school.'

'I would, too,' she said, exiting. 'It'd mean less time there.'

'How are you feeling?' Jack asked when she had gone.

'Not too bad.'

'No headache?'

'No, just a stiff neck.'

'No headache is good – that means no concussion. Ed was terrified you had a secret one and would wake up dead this morning, and it'd be his fault for not making you go to A&E. That man is seriously short of things to worry about. Look, I've got to go – I'll see you tonight. Don't even think about leaving – you're to stay here until you're a hundred per cent.'

She nodded, feeling exhausted. All this enthusiasm was wearing her out. 'Did you have a nice weekend?' she managed to ask. 'You seemed to be, with Theo and Flick.'

'He's a fabulous kid, isn't he? And it was surprisingly nice to catch up with Flick, too. She didn't harangue me, for once. She's good company when she's not reminding me of my various sins – which I know all too well in any case.'

'I'm starting to think there's more talk of sin than actual sinning,' Kate said sagely.

He grinned. 'How little you know me!' And went.

About half an hour later, Mrs B came up with a tray of breakfast, chased the animals off her bed, plumped up her pillows and placed the tray across her knees. Ed followed her into the room, and she answered the same questions again.

'If you feel the slightest bit sick, headachy, faint, spots before the eyes, anything like, you're to tell me at once,' he ordained.

'I haven't got concussion. I just feel tired. And my foot hurts.'

'I've brought you paracetamol,' he said, placing two on the tray. 'Have a sleep when you've finished breakfast. That's the best thing for you.'

He was looking more than usually grim this morning, and she felt it was her fault. 'I'm sorry,' she said as he was going.

He turned back. 'What for?'

'For falling off Magic. Giving you all so much trouble. Letting you down.'

'Letting *me* down?' He raised his eyebrows.

'Look, I can see you're cross with me,' she said, 'and I don't blame you at all. I loused up your day. Dragged you away before you had a chance to ride in the open.'

'I'm not cross,' he said, and sounded genuinely surprised, though there was no hint of a smile anywhere. 'It wasn't your fault. And I don't care about the open. I was worried about you, that's all.'

She bit her lip. 'About Henna,' she began hesitantly. She wasn't entirely sure what she was going to say. She wanted to tell him she hadn't pulled out of riding Henna because she was scared, but she couldn't do that without exposing Addison.

He interrupted her. 'Let's not talk about it. No post-mortems. Eat your breakfast and have a sleep. I'll look in on you later.' She liked the sound of that. 'Is there anything you need?' She shook her head. He looked at her a moment as if he was about to say something, and abruptly left her.

She had not long finished breakfast and was sipping the last of her second cup of tea when Camilla came in, in a negligee of fabulous luxury, all chiffon billows and foamy lace. Her face was shiny with moisturizer, and without make-up she looked younger and, somehow, prettier. She had Esmé in her arms, and plonked the dog down on the bed before sitting herself. 'Well, you look better,' she said. 'I *told* Ed you didn't have concussion. He was fretting himself to an ulcer last night. It was all Addison and I could do to make him sit down properly to dinner and not keep dashing upstairs to check you were still breathing.'

'He has a strong sense of responsibility,' Kate said, suppressing any pleasure this evidence of concern might give her.

'I know, but there are limits. Addison got quite short with him in the end, told him to stop spoiling everyone's dinner. She's gone up to town this morning, won't be back until tomorrow.'

'I know. Jocasta told me.'

Camilla sighed. 'I shall miss her. I hate it when everyone goes away after a weekend, and I'm left all alone here. This place is so dreary without company. I even miss Jocasta – though she made such a fuss about going this morning I almost smacked her,' she added with an abrupt change of expression.

'Wouldn't you like to have her around all the time?' Kate asked, thinking of the day school.

'Well, yes and no. It would be better than being here all alone. But it's not the same as adult company. Especially male company.'

'You have Ed and Jack.'

'But they're my stepsons. You don't count them.' She sighed again, staring off into space. 'There are times when I almost think it would be worth...' She trailed off.

'Yes?' Kate encouraged.

'Oh. Nothing.' She shifted restlessly. 'There's just nothing to do here. And you can't spend every minute of every day shopping.'

Kate swallowed this near-heresy with silent surprise. If Camilla was tired of shopping, she was tired of life.

'I almost envy Addison, having her job. Not

that I'd like *her* job, but it's something to do. Don't you think she looked fabulous on Henna?' she asked abruptly. Kate nodded. 'It was such a shame she got eliminated. She ought to have had more practice on her before the race. But she looked so good in the saddle, I'm thinking of maybe riding more myself. There aren't many points left, but there are the shows in the summer, and she jumps really well. Harry was saying that head-tossing can be cured with schooling. He said he'd help me if I wanted.'

'That would be good,' Kate said. 'He's a kind man.'

'Yes,' Camilla said. 'One feels such confidence when he's around. You should have seen how he organized everything yesterday after you came off, talked to the doctor, got the horses boxed, calmed Ed down, told him to take Addison and Henna home while he and I drove you.'

'I should think he must be a capable man,' Kate said. 'Used to command, after all.'

'Mmm,' said Camilla, deep in her own train of thought. 'He's a good dancer, too,' she said at the end of it. 'It's such a shame he's not better off. Well, I suppose I'd better go and get dressed. I think I'll drive over to the country club, see if anyone's around for lunch and a few rubbers of bridge.' She stood up. 'One has to do something.' She reached the door, and said, as a throwaway line, 'Harry's a good bridge player. I couldn't respect a man who couldn't play bridge.'

She was gone. Sylvester, with the air of having been waiting just outside, walked in, tail aloft,

purring like a dynamo, and sprang lightly up on to the bed, squinting his eyes at her beguilingly.
'All right,' she said. She moved the tray to the bedside cabinet. Sylvester walked up the bed, flirted his nostrils delicately at the tray and decided there was nothing there worth investigating, turned round three times and settled himself in the hollow of Kate's waist.

Kate fell asleep.

When she woke, the sun was shining outside her small window, and Ed was there, sitting in the armchair, working on a laptop. He looked across as she stirred, and said, 'I decided I'd have to appoint myself gatekeeper or you wouldn't get any rest.'

Kate counted ostentatiously on her fingers. 'I think I've seen everyone. Oh, except Mr Bradshaw.'

'Nothing to stop people coming in twice.' He wasn't looking so grim, and that was almost a joke. She tried, carefully, to smile. It didn't seem to annoy him. He said. 'How do you feel now? Would you like some lunch?'

'Mm. Maybe something light. I would like a bath, though, or a shower. I feel slummy.'

'Better give that a miss today. That strapping ought to stay on at least for today and you need to keep it dry. If I help you to the bathroom, though, you could have a wash at the basin.'

'Thanks. I need to go to the bathroom anyway,' she added, feeling rather embarrassed at mentioning it.

'Of course. I should have thought. I'm sorry.'

He helped her to sit up and she swung her legs out of bed. She was wearing pyjamas, and she wondered in a searing moment who took off her clothes and put her in them. She stood up on her good leg, put the bad one to the floor for a second, and lifted it again sharply.

'Don't try to walk on it yet. The doctor said it's a bad sprain. Complete rest for a couple of days at least. I'll carry you.'

He did, and she rested her head against his shoulder and tried not to think that this was as close to him as she would ever get. He deposited her carefully in the bathroom, warned her to hop and hold on to something, and left her. 'I'll be outside. Call when you're ready to go back.'

She went to the loo, washed as much of herself as she could reach, cleaned her teeth, did something about her hair, and was carried back to bed feeling a lot more human. She discovered he had made her bed while she was out, and now he helped her into it, drew up the covers and arranged her pillows with a competent hand.

'What makes you such a good nurse?' she asked.

'Anyone would do the same,' he said.

'Not anyone. Some people get annoyed by helplessness, others respond kindly to it.'

'I suppose it's being brought up with animals,' he said. 'My father used to take me round the farms, especially at lambing time. If there was a lamb or calf that had to be bottle-reared, I always wanted to do it.' He paused, remembering. 'He had a pointer bitch that we helped to whelp. He gave me a pup. That was my first dog – Hazy. I had her fifteen years. She was a good bitch.' His face had softened. 'And then there was Jack, of course – the most helpless creature of all, growing up without a mother. I always had to look after him.'

She didn't point out that he had grown up without a mother, too. She could see that he automatically discounted himself from the ranks of those who needed comforting and looking after. She longed to show him it could be a two-way street. She somehow couldn't visualize Addison mothering him.

But of course, as a wise person had said, you never know how people are when they're alone together.

She said tentatively, 'I hear Addison's coming back tomorrow.'

'Tomorrow night,' he said tersely.

She had spoilt it. The slight softening had gone. The grim expression was back. But he looked – she studied him covertly for a moment – troubled, rather than angry in any degree. Unhappy. Something about Addison coming back made him unhappy. Well, perhaps it was *her* presence in the house. Addison had made it clear she didn't want trespassers on her patch, and Kate had seen how she was perfectly willing to make her feelings known. Probably poor Ed was anticipating a storm from the beloved about Kate not having been sent away.

'I could go home, you know,' she offered in a small voice.

'Home?' He came back from his thoughts abruptly.

'To Little's. I don't want to be a nuisance.'

'Don't be silly,' he said firmly. 'You stay here. Now I'm going to get you some lunch.'

She got up the next morning, dressed, and Ed carried her downstairs to the drawing room where he arranged her on a sofa near a window so she could see out. 'You can't think what a difference it makes, just to have a change of scene,' she said. 'I feel an awful fraud, being treated like an invalid when I feel fine.' But she didn't, quite. She still felt very tired, and strangely languid.

Chewy generously offered to sit on her lap, and when she declined, he agreed to express his devotion to her from the floor at her side. Ed was in and out all morning, with 'stuff to do', but she had her first visitor from outside the house. The Brigadier came in mid-morning, looking handsome and smart in dark green tweed with a buff waistcoat, his hair, unusually, slightly ruffled, which made him look younger.

She was reading an old leather-bound copy of *Pride and Prejudice* she had found in one of the bookcases. 'Very suitable reading for the sofa,' he said cheerfully. 'Jane Austen ladies seem to have a lot of sofas in their lives.'

'Have you read it?' Kate asked.

'I'm waiting for the movie,' he said, straight-faced. From behind his back he produced a bunch of flowers, already in a vase. 'For you. It's very dull in here, I thought you'd need some colour. Mrs B gave me a vase on the way in.'

Kate was enchanted, and thanked him heartily.

'The place does need a bit of TLC,' she agreed. 'I'm surprised, really, that Camilla hasn't done anything to it, given how posh her bedroom is.'

He sat down catty-corner to her, the sunlight coming in at the window lighting his face, and the fine lines of experience which gave it its character. He'd make a wonderful father, she thought – and husband.

'I don't think she cares about the house. Doesn't consider it her home, which is odd given how long she's lived here. But then, it doesn't belong to her. That must make a difference.'

'I imagine so,' said Kate.

'And of course, it would take a lot of hard work. I think she'd be happier with a smaller place where she could make an impact and see the results more easily.'

'Are we talking about your house, by any chance?' she asked slyly.

He almost blushed. 'No chance,' he said. 'But it *is* smaller, as it happens, and really rather a lovely house – the best period of Queen Anne. The drawing room is particularly handsome – beautiful proportions and a very fine fireplace. Needs a woman's touch, though. You must come and see it when you're back on your feet. When is that going to be?'

'I'll be limping about in a few days. But apparently it takes a couple of weeks to heal completely. But I don't want you changing the subject.'

'What subject?'

'We're talking about you and Camilla.'

'There *is* no "me and Camilla",' he said sadly.

'She'd never have me.'

'But have you actually *asked* her?' Kate urged.

'No point,' he said. 'I know what she thinks.'

'Excuse me, but no-one ever knows what another person thinks. I saw you together on Monday; you looked so comfortable. And I saw the way she was looking at you.'

Now he did blush. 'Please. You mustn't say such things. I couldn't afford to keep her in the style she's accustomed to.'

'I've been talking to her, and I think she's bored and lonely and would be willing to give up a house she doesn't like living in anyway in exchange for a husband. You're not actually stony broke, are you?'

'Not at all, but my income is modest compared with all this.' He waved a hand. 'But I do have some good news, which is partly what I came to share. You know I talked about the firm I've set up?'

'I remember. Bouncers R Us,' Kate said.

He laughed. 'That's a good name for it. I wish I'd thought of that. Well, I just heard this morning that I've landed a contract I've been angling after – a big contract to supply security personnel to Balkan House – that big new skyscraper in the city, on Threadneedle Street. The HR director's an old army buddy of mine, so of course he understands the value of what I'm offering, the reliable, personally-vetted ex-army bods.'

'Congratulations,' Kate said. 'That sounds like good news.'

'It is, very – it's a lucrative contract, and it ought to open the door to more like it. My friend can put me in touch with useful people in that area. As long as I don't muff it—'

'Which you won't.'

'It should guarantee the success of my firm, and make all the difference to my income.'

Kate sat up straighter. 'That's brilliant! Then there's nothing to hold you back!'

He shook his head. 'The impetuousness of youth! You jump straight from my new contract to Camilla as if there's nothing in the way.'

'Well, isn't there? Oh–' she suddenly thought – 'unless you won't want to be a stepfather to Jocasta.'

'I love Jocasta,' he said, 'and I think she likes me. We do at least have horses and dogs in common. But I've no reason to think Camilla favours me over any of her other suitors.'

'I think she does.'

'Or that she wants to get married.'

'I think she does – listen, she said to me yesterday that she's *tired of shopping*.'

There was a brief silence. 'She said that?' he breathed. Kate nodded. He said, thoughtfully, 'When we were talking on Monday, she said something about being sorry she'd never had the chance to have more children. It made my sad old heart dance a hornpipe, I can tell you – until I told myself she couldn't possibly have been thinking about me when she said it.'

'Well, I tell you one thing,' Kate said sagely, 'you'll never know if you don't ask her. It seems to me she's been giving you hints, but you can't expect her to do all the work. *She*'s not going to propose to *you*.'

'I wouldn't expect her to,' he said with dignity. And then, 'But suppose she refuses me?'

'Then you won't be any worse off than you are now. But suppose she doesn't?' His face took on a dreamy cast as he imagined it. 'Look here,' she said briskly, 'I think she deserves the chance to say yes or no, don't you? And she can't do that unless you ask the question. You're disenfranchising her.'

'You're right,' he said, though still a little uncertainly.

'I expect a bit more decisiveness than that from an army chap,' she said sternly. 'Where's your backbone, Brigadier?'

He grinned. 'It seems you've got it. Hand it over, will you?' She held out her hand, smiling, and he shook it heartily. 'You're right, I've been behaving like an ass. I shall cease and desist forthwith from being a...'

'Blancmange?' she supplied helpfully.

'Blancmange it is. I shall ask her. I'll do it properly, take her out to dinner, put the facts before her, and pop the question.'

'Good for you. She's at the Country Club again this morning. If you rang her there, you could make a date right away.'

He stood up. 'I'll do it.' He bent over and kissed her cheek. 'Thank you,' he said. 'I'm glad you came to Bursford.'

He went away with a spring in his step, and she went back to Jane Austen, thinking that she might prove good at solving other people's problems, but it didn't get her any nearer to solving her own.

Twenty-Two

Jack came back from the factory at lunchtime, and between them he and Ed helped her hop to the table so she could eat more comfortably. It was only soup and a sandwich, but it was nice to be civilized again.

The brothers talked about business and local affairs, and Kate was happy just to eat and listen, and bask in the comfort of their company.

When they were drinking coffee, Jack said to Ed, 'Oh, I brought those figures you asked me for. But I can't see what they've got to do with Kate's problem.' He looked at her. 'I told him I promised you I'd investigate. I'm getting nowhere and I thought two heads would be better than one – especially his. He's got all the brains in this family.'

'You don't need to apologize,' Kate said. 'I'd be glad of anyone's help.'

'I spoke to your neighbours,' Jack went on, 'and I used your key to have a look inside, but there doesn't seem to have been anything else done to it.'

'Which is interesting,' Ed remarked.

'Is it?' Jack looked blank.

'It suggests they know Kate is away. They don't want to attack when she's not there.'

'But I thought we agreed that they attacked when they knew she was out,' Jack said, puzzled.

'Yes, out,' Ed said patiently, 'not away.'

Kate got it. 'You mean, I'd have to be going back there so I could see what they'd done?'

'Of course. No point otherwise.'

'So they know she's not just out shopping or something, but staying away?' said Jack. 'So who does that give us? Her neighbours?'

'They'd never do anything like that,' Kate said firmly.

'No, I don't think they would. They sent their love, by the way. But who else knows?'

'Anyone they've told,' said Ed, 'and anyone who knows us.'

Jack looked disappointed. 'That's just about everybody. I asked Phil who that man was he was talking to at Cothelstone, by the way, but he didn't know who I meant. He said he spoke to a lot of people at Cothelstone. I tried describing him, but it didn't ring any bells. Maybe I'm not very good at describing.'

'That reminds me,' Ed said, getting up. 'Wait here a minute.' He returned with his laptop, tapped something up, and then swung it round to show Kate.

There on the screen was a lean-faced, professional-looking man in a dark overcoat with a tall building behind him; he had evidently just quit the building and was walking away in company with another overcoated man, his mouth open in conversation, his eyes narrowed at the camera as if he had just seen he was being snapped.

'Yes,' said Kate. 'It looks like him. The man I

saw at Cothelstone.'

'Jack?' He showed the screen to Jack.

'The one on the left? Looks like the same bloke.'

'And you saw him again at Buscombe,' Ed said to Kate.

'Did I?'

'When I was carrying you into the first-aid tent, you said you saw him.'

'I'm a bit muddled about that time.'

'Doesn't matter. I saw him too. I thought I recognized him but I couldn't place him.'

'Yes, I thought he looked familiar,' Jack put in.

'I've been trawling around Google trying to find him. It's not easy finding a face without a name. But then it suddenly came to me where *I'd* seen him before – at a fund-raiser in London – so I was able to access the guest list.'

'So who is he?' Kate asked.

'Tony Rylance. He's a developer mainly, backs some start-ups, does a bit on the market. Beginning to make a name for himself, and thought to have political ambitions. Addison's met him.'

'That's right! I've seen his picture in the paper. He's a bit of a player,' Jack said. 'So what was he doing down here over the Bank Holiday weekend? Has he got a place down here?'

'I don't know that yet. I've only just got his name,' Ed said.

'Well, a big wheel like that can't have any interest in me,' Kate said, feeling at once slightly relieved and slightly concerned. 'He can't have been staring at me. It must have been just coincidence.'

'Some coincidence!' Jack protested.

'No, really – he looked at me at Cothelstone because I was staring in his direction. And at Buscombe – well, anyone would look at someone being carried into the first-aid tent.'

'You're probably right,' said Ed. 'But I'll look into it anyway. Meanwhile, you put it from your mind. Jack, those figures?'

Jack produced the sheaf of papers, and lunch was over. Ed went off with the papers and his laptop, Jack helped Kate back to the sofa, and with an apology went back to work. As the house grew quiet, Sylvester found her lap, and with her living hot-water-bottle on her stomach, Kate fell asleep.

Camilla came back from another session of bridge at the country club, and breezed in on Kate with a smile so wide, it was a wonder her face didn't fall in half. 'I shan't be in to dinner tonight,' she announced. 'I'll tell Mrs B. You'll be eating down, won't you? So it'll just be the four of you, assuming Addison arrives in time for dinner.'

'I believe she intends to,' Kate said. That would be a fine meal, she thought, with no-one to keep Pocahontas occupied with talk of shopping and designer labels. She wondered if she might stage a judicious relapse and have a tray in her bedroom. Then she caught up with Camilla's news. 'Are you going somewhere nice?' she asked casually.

'Harry's taking me out to dinner,' Camilla said. Kate studied her, and could not for the life of her tell how pleased she was. Pleased, yes – but *intensely* so, or just glad for the variety? 'He said something about Armandine's in Dunster. Said he had some news to tell me. It must be pretty good news – Armandine's is *ridiculously* expensive. I've only ever been there once. I hope he's not going to ruin himself in the hope of impressing me, because I'd be happy enough with the Ship or the Blue Ball.'

It seemed to Kate rather a good sign that she was concerned about Harry's welfare. She didn't seem to consider the expense of anything else she did.

'I don't think he'd take you somewhere he couldn't afford,' she said. 'He's too sensible. What are you going to wear?'

That set Camilla off on a long debate about various outfits, none of which Kate knew so she couldn't offer any opinions. After a bit, Camilla said she had better go and have her bath and start getting poshed up, and apologized that she didn't have time to take tea with Kate. 'But he's picking me up at seven thirty.'

Kate nodded understandingly. A mere three hours to get ready? Camilla was cutting it fine.

Camilla was only just ready when the Brigadier arrived, punctual to the dot, and Kate was upstairs in her room so she didn't get to see the result of all that labour, or to judge how nervous or confident the Brigadier was feeling. She silently wished him luck, and looked through her own meagre collection of clothes, wondering what to wear down to dinner.

'Not that it matters,' she said to Chewy, who was watching her from her bed. 'All eyes will be on Pocahontas. Still, one has one's pride.'

Chewy wagged his tail in agreement, giving her a wide smile. *I'd love you in anything*, he said.

'That's very nice,' she told him, 'but you are not noted for your sartorial taste.' Jack had told her he had once chewed up one of Ed's riding boots, and it was not just a cheap rubber one, but an expensive leather Ottoviano. Or was that, *au contraire*, a sign that he only liked the best? 'In which case, thanks,' she told him.

The sound of the Brigadier's car had hardly died away before Addison arrived. Kate heard the arrival from upstairs – first the sports car roaring in and screeching to a halt on the last of the gravel, then voices, then the unmistakable sound of Addison's voice dominating everything, then noises on the stairs. They went the other way at the landing, to the family side, and grew fainter, though the underlying rhythm of her talking never quite ceased. After a time, there was a tap on Kate's door, and Mrs B was there to tell her dinner was being put back half an hour: 'So Miss Bruckmeyer can have time to change.'

She looked glum, and Kate said, 'Is everything all right?'

'No, it is not,' she said. 'I can't be expected to change the way I cook after all these years. I've never had anything but compliments on my food, and suddenly it's nothing but carping and fiddle-faddle and "can't eat this" and "can't eat that". If it goes on I shall give my notice.'

'Oh no! Surely you wouldn't do that?'

Mrs B stuck her lip out, but her eyes were moist. 'I never thought I'd leave Ed and Jack. They're like my own boys. And we'd hate to have to find somewhere else to live, Bradshaw and me. But tofu and mung beans and I don't know what else? Stuff I've never heard of, nothing but parrot-food. And no cream or butter or anything good and wholesome to eat? It's not to be borne. If Ed's not satisfied with my cooking, I shall go.'

'I'm sure he's perfectly satisfied,' Kate said.

'Maybe, but it's not his opinion that matters any more, is it?' And she stomped away downstairs.

Kate heard the others go downstairs, Addison still talking, and after a bit realized she had been forgotten. She could hop all right on the level, as long as she had something to grab on to, but stairs were beyond her. About five minutes later, however, Jack came galloping up to fetch her. 'Sorry,' he said. 'We were wondering where you were when I suddenly realized you couldn't make it alone.'

He had wondered, she thought. Not Ed. Ed's attention, of course, was now fully occupied.

'Was the wait worth it?' she asked. 'Is she gorgeous?'

'Surprisingly muted,' Jack said, arm round her as she hopped through the door. 'Almost virginal.' After a pace or two he said, 'Look, this'll take all night. Why don't you let me carry you?'

'If you think you can manage,' she said with

relief. Hopping was exhausting.

'You're just a feather,' he assured her. 'Now if it was Pocahontas...'

'She's very slim,' Kate pointed out.

'She's also very tall. And she gives the impression of being enormous. Not fat, I don't mean, but unignorable, like an elephant. Don't you think?'

Being in Jack's arms was not like being in Ed's, but it was very nice. 'You smell nice,' she told him.

'So do you,' he said promptly, and kissed her lightly on the lips.

'Mrs B thinks Ed's going to marry Addison and install her as mistress of the house, and then she'll have to leave. Mrs B will.'

'Over my dead body,' Jack said.

'You don't think Ed will marry Addison?'

That made him think. 'Dunno. I think *she* might marry *him*,' he said at last. 'If she sets up here, I'll have to set up somewhere else with Mrs B.'

'She's already married,' Kate told him.

'You must be feeling better – you're getting cheeky.'

In the drawing room, Addison was standing before the fireplace with a glass of champagne in her hand, looking magnificent in a clinging, draped white dress that ended just above the knee and was slit up the side to show her toned, brown thigh. Her super-shiny hair was in a great, loose chignon, and something sparkled in her ears – could they be real diamonds? Kate somehow couldn't imagine her wearing fakes. She seemed to suck all the light in the room into herself, like a black hole, so that you didn't see anything else – or if you did, it was only to notice how dull it was by contrast.

She was talking when they came in, but stopped abruptly to look at Kate with a smile that didn't reach her eyes.

'Ah, there you are,' she said. 'I thought you'd be eating upstairs.' *In the servants' quarters*, Kate translated for herself. 'How are you feeling?'

It was not a tender enquiry. It sounded almost brusque. 'Fine, except for the foot, and a few bruises and sore muscles,' she said.

'You were very lucky, you know,' Addison said severely. 'Someone could have been badly hurt. And what if one of the horses had broken a leg? You really shouldn't have ridden at all if you weren't up to it.'

'I was all right until you swerved across me,' Kate said, managing at the last moment to control the tone of her voice, though the words slipped out.

Addison's nostrils flared. 'I beg your pardon,' she said icily. 'It was you who impeded me. I was taking the correct line. You rode too far to the right and cut up my horse.'

Ed intervened hastily. 'No post-mortems,' he said firmly. 'It was an accident, it's over and done with, and that's the end of it.'

Kate didn't feel it was the end of it by any means, but Jack, who was in the process of putting her carefully down, pinched her hard in warning and she swallowed what she had been about to say. She wouldn't embarrass Ed by quarrelling with his guest in his drawing room.

'Have some champagne,' Jack said, sealing her silence.

She accepted the glass and sipped. 'Are we celebrating?' she asked, to restart the conversation.

Addison gave her a pitying smile. 'You don't have to wait for a celebration to drink champagne. What a curious idea. We had it because we fancied it, didn't we, darling?' she said to Ed.

'Well, I'm all for it,' Jack said. 'Cheers. Did you find out any more about that man, Ed?'

Before he could answer, Addison intervened. 'Oh, no parochial business tonight. Let's just enjoy ourselves. Where is Camilla, by the way?'

'Out on a date,' Jack said.

Addison looked pleased. 'It's about time she started looking around for another husband. Your father's been gone a long time. She has to think about her future now. She needs a home of her own.'

'This is her home,' Ed said, rather woodenly.

'Well, perhaps it is just now,' Addison said, throwing him a fascinating smile, 'but who knows what the future will bring?'

Ed didn't bite, but Kate knew exactly what Addison meant.

They were called into the dining room, taking their glasses with them. Mrs B served them with a martyred air. The food didn't seem very different to Kate, except that there was a salad course, American-style; and with the lamb chops, instead of Mrs B's crisp sauté potatoes

Addison had a dish of some kind of messy cereal stuff that looked a bit like the linseed mash you give horses after hunting.

Addison only picked at the food, but her jaw got plenty of exercise all the same. She talked. She talked about what she'd done in London, the deal she had had to go up to supervise, its global importance and how no-one else could have secured it. She talked about finance and politics, the new governor of the Bank of England and who she would have chosen instead, and the important financial post in the EU she had been offered and turned down. She talked about cars and the Maserati Grancabrio she was thinking of buying. She talked about property prices and property taxes, and finally, looking around disparagingly at the dining room, she talked about The Hall.

'I don't know how you could have lived like this all these years,' she said. 'The place is practically a ruin.'

'I don't really notice it,' Ed said.

'No, I suppose men don't,' she said with a brittle laugh, 'but you'll see the difference it makes to everything in your life when your surroundings match your lifestyle and your aspirations.'

'I'm not sure I have aspirations,' Ed said.

'Darling, of course you do. And I've looked around this place with a critical eye and, frankly, I can't see it.'

'Can't see what?' Jack asked through a mouthful of claret. He seemed to be enjoying his brother's apparent discomfort. Kate ate quietly and watched, feeling uneasily that a storm was approaching, though she wasn't sure from which direction.

'Can't see how this house can be made viable,' Addison answered. 'I do see, darling,' she added to Ed, 'how you'd want a country place – and it can be a valuable tool. People love to be invited on country weekends, and it's a good way to get important people together in the one place – and put them in a good mood. But Bursford's too far from London. And from the airport. The journey takes far too long, the trains are impossible, and if you're driving you can't work. Global business moves fast these days, my sweet. People need to feel *in touch*, more *accessible*.'

'Who are all these people?' Jack asked in a slightly ribald fashion.

'Our contacts. Our circle,' Addison said impatiently.

'What about friends?' Ed said quietly.

'Of course, once we're set up, we can afford to have friends as well,' she said graciously, 'but they'll have the same concerns. And we'll see much more of them in London anyway. Now, I've been thinking, and I'm not sure at this stage it makes sense to buy a country place, not until we know where we're going to be based. It would make more sense to rent one as we need it.'

'I already have a country place,' Ed said.

'But I've explained to you, it would take too much investment to make it even tolerable.'

'I like it as it is,' Ed said stubbornly.

'Darling, I know you have a sentimental

attachment to the house, but even you must see it's a horrible mess, a dump. And, frankly, I don't envisage spending all that much time down here. Now, there are some nice places along the M40 corridor, with good transport links. We should be looking there. Have you any idea what this place would go for?'

'What about me?' Jack put in, pouting, but with a covert wink at Kate. 'What about Camilla and Jocasta? Are we all going to live with you?'

Addison's nostrils flared again. 'If necessary, a small house can be found for you. *We* shall be spending most of our time in London.'

'I'm not selling this house,' Ed said quietly. 'You don't seem to understand, Addison, that it's my responsibility to keep the estate together.'

She waved a hand. 'Oh, I know you have a *thing* about that, darling, but you have a manager, or whatever he's called, that horrid little man I see about the place. It's his job to run the estate, not yours. Any executive decisions that have to be referred to you can be done remotely. That's what email is for.'

'I've put the coffee in the drawing room.' Mrs B spoke from the doorway. Kate wondered how long she had been standing there.

Addison got up at once, and so the men had to stand too, and they all followed her into the other room. She looked round it with distaste. Sylvester was comfortably ensconced in an armchair, paws tucked under and eyes half-closed, but as soon as Addison appeared he was wide awake, jumped from the chair and scooted out of the door as if scalded. Ralph was lying on the sofa chewing something, and was too busy to notice in time that he had been spotted. 'Those damned animals are on the furniture again,' Addison said angrily, turning to Ed. 'I've asked you to keep them off. The way you let them run riot around this house is simply disgusting. It's insanitary to allow animals into your living space.'

'Ralph, off,' Ed said. Ralph looked at him to judge how serious he was, and climbed down in leisurely fashion, depositing the rag he was chewing at Ed's feet.

'What *is* that thing?' Jack asked.

Ed picked it up and unravelled it. It was a bright red pair of skimpy lacy knickers, now irrevocably soaked in dog saliva and the worse for teeth.

Addison was suddenly almost as scarlet as the underwear. 'That's mine!' she cried. 'Who gave my panties to that filthy dog? Is this your idea of a joke?' she demanded of Jack.

He held up his hands. 'Not guilty.' He was laughing.

She whirled on Kate. 'Then it's you! I know how you feel about me. You're eaten up with jealousy – and you're mad about these flea-ridden dogs.'

'Kate's been tied to the bed and the sofa since Monday,' Ed said. 'She can hardly walk.'

'She could walk enough for that if she wanted,' Addison said venomously.

That was true. 'But I didn't,' Kate said. 'Maybe he's been in your room.'

'I always leave the door shut. *Someone* must have deliberately opened it.' Her panties were still dangling from Ed's fingers. 'Oh, *give* me that!' she cried, exasperated, and snatched them away. Ralph grinned, seeing a game starting up, and jumped up at them, his teeth snapping closed several inches from Addison's hand.

She shrieked. 'He tried to bite me!' She backed away, holding the panties high over her head, and Ralph danced after her, jumping up in glee. 'Get him off!'

'He thinks you're playing,' Ed said. 'Stop waving those things about and he'll stop.'

But she was too agitated to heed him. 'Get him off me! Get him off!' she kept shrieking. Jack, laughing fit to bust, grabbed hold of Ralph's collar and pulled him away.

Addison, breathing hard, glared at Ed. 'Will you have the kindness to shut that animal out of this room?' she hissed. 'You ought to have it put down. It's dangerous. It tried to bite me.'

'I'll take him,' Jack said, towing Ralph towards the door. But as he reached it, Chewy pranced in, with what was only too obviously an expensive high-heeled shoe in his mouth. It was black patent, with a six inch heel, and a shiny red sole.

Addison goggled. 'My Laboutins!' she cried in a voice of genuine bereavement.

Ed stepped forward, efficiently removed the shoe from Chewy's mouth, and examined it. 'Hole right through it, I'm afraid,' he said. 'I'm sorry.'

'*Sorry*?' Addison took it from him, and recovered her breath. 'Do you know what they cost?' she moaned.

'I'll buy you a new pair,' Ed promised.

Addison was not placated. 'This is beyond enduring! Someone has deliberately let those foul dogs into my room to root about in my things. It's a deliberate ploy to humiliate me.'

'Oh, come on,' Ed said, 'it's nothing of the sort. You probably didn't pull the door closed hard enough. Those latches are old, and they sometimes don't catch.'

'That's true,' Kate said. 'You have to really tug my door before it will sneck. It's always coming open.'

Addison whirled on her. 'Don't you dare speak to me! I know what's going on here. Ever since you arrived with your mealy-mouthed, butter-wouldn't-melt, country-girl act, it's been one thing after another. You're trying to get your claws into Edward, but it won't work, I promise you that! With your stupid freckles and your horrible hair – do you think any man would look twice at a pathetic slob like you? You don't seem to realize he just feels sorry for you. Where's your pride? For God's sake, buy yourself a hair-brush and do something about your face!'

'Addison,' Ed said warningly.

She turned on him. 'Don't you dare take her side! You're an idiot, you don't seem to realize what she's doing, trying to drive a wedge between us. Look at her! What rational man would want – *that* – instead of me? There isn't even a choice!'

'Then you've nothing to worry about, have you?' he said quietly.

She glared at him, trying to read his face, trying to work out what his words meant. Kate knew that, because she was doing the same thing. The wounded Laboutin was still in Addison's hand, and, growing bored with the talk, Chewy stood up and put his nose up to sniff it, wondering if he could have another go. Addison pulled her hand sharply back, and kicked Chewy hard in the ribs.

He yipped and backed away, ears down and soulful eyes rolling in hurt. There was a sense of the room holding its breath.

'Do not,' Ed said in a quiet voice that was menacing, 'kick my dog. Do not ever kick a dog in my house.'

'*Your* house?' Addison cried. She sounded angry, but her eyes looked close to tears. 'I start to wonder who really *is* in charge here! Shut those dogs up, and get *her* out of here, or—'

'Or what?' Ed asked, exquisitely polite.

Addison's eyes narrowed. 'Or I leave. Right now.' Ed said nothing. 'I mean it. Which is it to be?'

Kate held her breath. Jack held his breath. The world seemed not to dare to breathe for the moment.

Then Ed said, 'I can't ask Kate to leave in her present condition. And I won't. As for the dogs—'

'I see.' Addison's breath came out in a long hiss. 'I'm not going to stand around and be insulted. You'll be sorry for this tomorrow. But it will be too late. Don't think I'll take you back, because I won't. I won't have to do with a man who doesn't know how to treat the best thing that's ever come into his life. I don't know what

I ever saw in you! There are men out there *fighting* over me, you know!' She whirled on her heel and stormed out.

Ed stood where he was, his head a little bowed, staring down, it seemed, at Ralph, who stared up at him hopefully and swished his tail against the carpet to indicate he was ready for anything that might be required of him. Then he said, without addressing anyone in particular, 'I'm sorry you had to witness that,' and left the room, with Ralph and Chewy at his heels.

In the silence that followed, Kate did not want to meet Jack's eyes. She was afraid he would say something flippant, and she was too upset, both because of the row, and because of what it must have done to Ed, to bear that.

But in the end he said quietly, 'Poor bugger. He does choose badly. First Flavia, then ten years of nothing, then Addison. Why can't he fall for a nice, normal girl?'

'Will he be all right?' Kate asked in a small voice.

Jack shrugged. 'As all right as he ever is. Look, if she's going now, we don't want to run into her on her way out. I'll carry you up to your room by the backstairs. Unless,' he said thoughtfully, 'you want to stay for another drink?'

'I don't think I want to talk any more,' she said. 'I'd like to go to bed.'

'Very wise,' said Jack. 'There's probably been enough talk tonight.'

Twenty-Three

Kate slept heavily, and woke to the sound of rain, pattering on leaves and gurgling in the gutter that ran above her window. The patch of sky outside looked grey and chilly, and the trees were bending in a brisk breeze. She was warm, however, with Chewy, Ralph and Jacob all curled up on her bed; Sylvester, she saw, was neatly couched down on top of the clothes she had discarded last night and thrown on to the chair. His paws were folded under like the bluff bows on a barge, and from this angle his mouth looked as if it was smiling.

The rain suited her mood. After the emotions of yesterday, she felt worn out, and there was a curious stillness inside her, as if she had no capacity to feel anything more. Her time here was coming to an end, she knew that. As soon as she could put weight on her foot, she would have to leave – back to Little's, yes, but more than that: back to London. She had been involved for a little space with an upheaval in this family she had come to care for, but she didn't belong with them. She wouldn't hang around until they were forced, ever so politely, to point that out. She would keep her dignity and take her leave.

She drifted back into a doze, until Mrs B

knocked and came in with a tray. 'I thought you'd prefer to have breakfast in bed and take your time about getting up,' she said. She set the tray down, straightened up, and said with some triumph, 'She's gone.'

'She has?' Kate queried.

'Miss Bruckmeyer. Went last night apparently. Ed didn't say much, but I gather she's not expected back.' She looked at Kate to see how she felt about that, but Kate didn't feel it was right for her to express anything either way. Mrs B sniffed and supplied her own epitaph. 'She didn't fit in with our ways,' she pronounced. 'Too much of a town person, to my mind. I'm not sorry to see her go.'

'I expect Ed is, though.'

Mrs B looked sceptical. 'I don't believe he was that fond of her. Anyway, she wasn't good enough for him, that I *do* know.'

Kate's eyes slowly widened as revelation came to her. 'It was *you*!' she said.

Mrs B stiffened. 'I beg your pardon?'

'*You* let the dogs into her room.'

'What an idea! As if I would. I expect she didn't shut her door properly.'

But there was a gleam of satisfaction in her eye. Kate found herself wondering about the lost ten years and all the women Jack said had thrown themselves at Ed. Had Mrs B had a hand in seeing them all off – setting brisk, judicious action in the scales against Ed's diffidence?

But perhaps she hadn't needed to. Anyone who married Ed would be marrying the Blackmore Estate, the farms, the family, and the animals as well. They would have to love him very much to take all that on. It would be enough to daunt the casual enquirer.

Mrs B was taking her departure, but paused to look back at Kate with what seemed, to Kate's startled glance, like approval. 'You take your time getting up,' she said kindly. 'Nothing to hurry for. And I'll tell you something else – Madam didn't come home last night.'

And having bestowed this nugget, she took her leave.

Someone had thoughtfully left a walking-stick propped against her wardrobe, and with its aid, she could get about all right, even managed the stairs. She could just dot her foot down this morning, though she still couldn't take any weight on it. Realistically, she couldn't go back to Little's yet – would have to stay here at least another day. She was torn two ways about that. She longed just to be near Ed; but the sooner she got away and started the healing process, the better it would be for her. She knew that's what Lauren would say. Jess, being an incurable romantic and having little grasp of reality at the best of times, would tell her to stay as long as she could in the hope of being suddenly noticed *à la* Barbara Cartland: 'My God, but – you're *beautiful*!' Some hope!

All was quiet downstairs. She got back on the sofa with Lizzie and Jane. She realized that this probably was not the best book for someone in her frame of mind; but she spent as much time staring at the rain running down the window panes as reading, in any case. The dogs surged in, suggesting she'd feel much better if she went out for a nice long walk, and that rain was *lovely*, really it was; but when she didn't take the bait, they folded up philosophically in various spots around the room, just glad of the company.

The sound of a car outside broke into the somnolence, everyone perked up and looked at the door, and a moment later Camilla came in, wearing – Kate would never have thought to see the day – a pair of tracksuit bottoms and a sweater too big for her. She had her dress from last night over her arm, her face was innocent of make-up, and she looked about twenty-five and wonderfully excited.

'Well!' Kate said.

Camilla tried to look stern, but her mouth wanted to smile and wouldn't cooperate. 'You knew,' she accused.

'I knew what?' Kate hedged.

'You knew Harry was going to propose.'

'Advice to the lovelorn is the prerogative of the bedridden,' Kate said. Camilla blinked at that, long words not being her forte. 'You're going too fast. Tell me everything. Was Armandine's nice?'

'It's lovely, very romantic, but that's not the point. It was Harry – he was so different! I've always liked him, always thought he was a lovely man, but nothing more than that. He never behaved as though he wanted to be anything but a friend.'

'Diffidence,' Kate said. 'He didn't think he had a chance with you.'

'Well, I call that silly,' said Camilla. 'How could I know whether I liked him, when I didn't know he liked me?'

'That's what I said. And you did? My God,' she said, suddenly realizing, 'you haven't said yet if you accepted him. I'm assuming – oh, please say you didn't turn him down. Please say you said yes.'

'Of course I said yes,' Camilla exclaimed, and Kate felt a ridiculous surge of relief and satisfaction. 'Would I have stayed the night if I'd said no?'

'I hadn't thought of that,' said Kate. Camilla blushed slightly, which made Kate blush. They'd hit a very personal point in the conversation, and Kate was suddenly afraid Camilla might tell her how it was, while Camilla feared Kate might ask. 'I'm so happy for you,' Kate went on quickly, to steer away from the rock. 'I think he'll make a wonderful husband and you'll be very happy.'

'I think so too,' said Camilla. 'He was so different last night – at the restaurant, I mean,' she added hastily, though it was clear she was meaning afterwards as well. 'So strong and masculine and determined and – well, you could just imagine him in the army, leading his men, and them all adoring him. The sort of man you'd follow into battle. That you'd trust with your life.'

'Yes,' said Kate. 'I can see that.'

'So when he asked, and he said he didn't expect me to answer right away, that I'd need time to think about it, I didn't even stop to think. I just said yes, and as soon as I said it I knew it was right.' She sighed, looking around the room but probably not seeing it. 'It'll be strange to be going away from here after all these years. Harry has a lovely house – I remember when I was a child his mother used to open it to the public on Queen Alexandra day. Of course, it needs redecorating. Harry says I can have a free hand – it'll be such fun! Re-doing a house that will really be my own, not like this place. I shall get Flick to help me – might as well keep it in the family. Oh, and he wants to buy me a new horse as a wedding present. He says Henna's not really right for me, and I think he's probably right.' She smiled as another thought occurred to her. 'It'll be nice to have a permanent bridge partner, too. We can have bridge parties at home. The morning room would be perfect for that – you could easily get six tables in there.'

In all this joy and expansiveness, Kate gave a thought for Jocasta. 'I wonder what Jocasta will think. I know she likes him, but how will she feel about leaving The Hall?'

'Oh, as long as she can take the ponies, she won't mind. Though Harry says we ought to start thinking about a proper horse for her. She's old enough. There's a lovely room at the back that will be just right for her bedroom, with a linen cupboard next door we can convert into an en-suite shower room. In any case, she'll be away at school a lot of the time, so it won't be such a big adjustment for her.'

It seemed as good a time as any to put in a word. Kate said, 'She really hates being at boarding school. She was talking to me about it. She'd love to go to day school instead. She mentioned a place called Comyns?'

'Oh, a child her age doesn't know her own mind. She talks about hating school, but everyone does. *I* did, when I was her age.'

Kate left it. It wasn't for her to interfere. She had planted the seed – anything more might be counterproductive.

'So, when's the happy day going to be?' she asked.

'We're talking about the beginning of September,' Camilla said happily. 'I'll need time to have my dress made and arrange the wedding. I've been thinking of venues...'

She went off into a happy burble of wedding plans, and Kate allowed herself to drift on the stream of warm air, only half listening, until Camilla came back down to earth and said briskly, 'I must go up and change. I look an absolute fright. And I've a million phone calls to make.'

And she was gone, the dogs following her in the happy delusion that brisk movement meant a walk for them. She was so happy, Kate realized, she hadn't asked about Addison.

Kate was alone for lunch. Camilla had drifted back down in a smart jersey two-piece and a cloud of perfume to say she was going out to lunch with Harry and some friends – presumably to make the announcement. Jack was seeing some potential customers, taking them to lunch at the Blue Ball; and Ed simply didn't appear. Mrs B brought her soup on a tray and the news that one of the gutters was leaking. 'Always something to be done with an old house like this,' she sighed, 'and Bradshaw shouldn't be going up ladders at his age.' Evidently Camilla hadn't told her the news, so Kate didn't mention it. It wasn't her place.

After lunch she was restless for fresh air, and as the rain seemed to be easing a little, she struggled into a wax jacket and elderly hat she found in the welly lobby, and with the aid of her trusty walking-stick managed to hobble round the dank and dripping garden for a quarter of an hour. The dogs watched her from the scullery door – so much for their fine words! Only Jacob ventured out to join her, but he dashed in as soon as she did, and seemed to take great pleasure in standing on his hind legs and making an interesting pattern on her jeans with his muddy front ones.

She found Ed in the drawing room, working on his laptop, with papers and notebooks all around it on the coffee table.

'Hello,' she said awkwardly.

He looked up, unsmiling. 'You found the walking-stick, I see.'

'Yes, thank you. Was that you?'

'I thought it would make things easier for you,' he said.

Easier for me to get out of here and out of your life, Kate translated for herself.

She hobbled towards the sofa. 'I think I could probably go home tomorrow,' she said hesitantly.

'I don't think that's wise. Jack says you have to live mostly upstairs at Little's. And you'd have no-one around if anything happened. I think you should stay here until you're steadier on your feet – at least a couple more days. There's no hurry, is there?'

'No – except that I'm running out of clothes.'

'Someone can take you over to fetch anything you need. And Mrs B can put things in the washing machine, you know.'

'Well – thanks,' Kate said. 'I will stay a bit longer, if it's no trouble.'

'No trouble,' he affirmed, and remained looking at her, as if he wanted a conversation. She couldn't think of a neutral topic.

'I'm sorry about Addison,' she said at last.

It was the wrong thing to say. The atmosphere seemed to chill slightly. But he said, 'Don't be. It was an awkward situation.' A pause, and then, almost to himself, 'I seemed to have raised expectations in her that I hadn't intended to.'

This was more of a revelation than she had ever had from him, so she ventured, 'I thought – in London ... Jack said ... Weren't you close at one time?'

He seemed to hesitate over whether to answer her or not. Then he said, 'At one time. But her firm moved her to New York, and I thought that was the end of it. That was definitely the impression she gave. I was – surprised when she turned up here, obviously thinking we were still...'

He didn't finish, and Kate thought: *you were too much of a gentleman to tell her she was wrong so bog off*. But, for goodness' sake, how far was he prepared to take it? Would he have ended up marrying her because he didn't want to hurt her feelings? That was too much chivalry by a very long streak!

Perhaps he read something in her eye, because he said, faintly rueful, 'I suppose I should have grasped the nettle. I didn't handle it very well. But I was – feeling confused at the time. Unsettled.'

She waited, but that seemed to be the end of that revelation. *Confused and unsettled about what?* Oh well – since there seemed to be confession in the air, she felt she might as well clear something up. 'Look, I don't want to speak ill of the – the departed,' she began, 'but I just want to say, about Henna, that I didn't tell Addison I was scared of riding her.'

'I know,' he said. She wasn't sure what she had expected him to say, but it wasn't that.

'You know?'

'Susie told me, when you were being seen by the doctor. She said Addison had told you *I* wanted you not to ride. I expect,' he concluded, 'it was a misunderstanding.'

Too much of a gentleman to slag her off, even now. Kate liked that. She'd let it remain officially a misunderstanding. Still, she had her reputation to save. 'And I didn't foul her at that jump.'

'I know,' he said again.

'You know?'

'Henna veered in front of you. It wasn't your fault. I was there, by the jump. I saw.'

'I wondered how you got there so quickly,' Kate said gratefully.

'I was afraid she'd have trouble. Henna doesn't like having her mouth hung on to.'

'I know,' Kate said in her turn.

'Can we drop the subject now?' he said. 'Inquest over.'

'Of course,' Kate said, a little mortified to have upset him. He returned to his laptop, and she picked up Jane Austen again, since he didn't seem to mind her being there. She still didn't get much read. It was easier, and more pleasurable in a probing-the-mouth-ulcer kind of way, to spend the time looking at him across the room, his thick, healthy hair, his beautiful face (what would he look like if he really smiled?) his lean, strong body, the flash of his hands over the keys, the little frown of concentration between his brows. She had to look at him as much as possible, to store up fat against the winter to come.

And suddenly he looked up and caught her at it. 'Was there something?' he asked politely.

She knew what she had to say. It was rather blurty just to come out with it at a moment like this, but when else was she going to have his undivided attention?

'I'm going to sell Little's,' she said. 'I'm going back to London.'

'Oh,' he said. He didn't like that. His eyes cooled a fraction. 'I see,' he said. Then, 'I thought you liked it here.' He sounded hurt.

It was the last thing she wanted. 'I do!' she said quickly. 'I love it! I always thought the Bursford area was the most beautiful place on earth. And I've been so happy here – at The Hall, I mean. You've all been so kind to me.'

'But?'

'I can't trespass on your hospitality for ever,' she said wretchedly. 'I have to – well, get on with my life, I suppose. Go back to my job, all that sort of thing.'

'Of course,' he said, blankly. 'I should have realized. This has just been a holiday from reality for you.'

She didn't know how to answer that. She wanted to say this place was more real than any other to her, and that it was also the promised land and therefore, since she could not have him, since the promise would never be fulfilled, the ultimate in fantasy. *Way* too much information. You simply can't tell a man who has shown no interest in you that you have fallen in love with him. She appreciated all of a sudden Harry's courage in speaking up to Camilla.

Miserably, she pushed all those things down, and went on to the next point. 'What I wanted to say was that when I go, I want to sell Little's back to you – to the estate.'

His attention sharpened. He surveyed her with interest and, it seemed, some kind of caution, as you would look at a snake that might or might not be poisonous. 'Why?' he asked abruptly.

'Because it should never have been sold to me. You are trying so hard to keep the estate intact, and I know it upset you to have part of it sold away. So I want you to have it back. I'd *give* it to you if I could, but I'm afraid I really need the money.'

'I wouldn't let you give it to me,' he said.

Too proud to accept a gift from the likes of me?

Kate wondered. She ploughed on, 'I don't want to make a profit. I would like to sell it back to you for what I paid for it, plus what I've spent on it so far. I think that would be fair.'

'Extremely fair,' he said. Still there was nothing coming back from him.

'I wouldn't like to sell it to a stranger,' she tried.

He lifted his hand slightly, as if to stop her saying any more. He frowned in thought. 'Things are in a state of flux at the moment,' he said. 'You know about Camilla's news?'

'She told you?'

'Harry rang me.'

'It's wonderful,' Kate said cautiously. Surely he must be glad about *that* if nothing else.

'I'm very happy for her. I think he'll make her very happy. But it will mean an upheaval in the household, and of course there are legal implications. And I'm in the middle of a – a financial review. Will you hold off for a day or two? Shelve your offer to sell me Little's? And not make that offer to anyone else?'

'If you wish,' she said. 'In any case, I wouldn't think of offering it to anyone else until you'd decided.'

'Please,' he said, 'promise me.'

'I promise,' she said, a little hurt. Didn't he trust her? She went back, rather ostentatiously, to her book, and heard him rattling the keys again. After a little while he stood up, closed the laptop, collected up his papers, and went out.

Kate felt things had not gone well, and that his opinion of her had suffered. She had disappointed him in some way, though she didn't know how. She turned pages, but didn't read a thing.

Mrs B stuck her head round the door and asked if she wanted some tea, and she said yes, gratefully, and hoped that when it came she could get a spot of conversation with it. She was pining for some friendly human contact.

Before the tea arrived, however, her attention was drawn to the sound of raised voices outside, on the gravel area in front of the house. She got her stick and hobbled over to the window, to see Phil Kingdon's large shiny Range Rover parked in the entrance, blocking the drive, and Phil himself standing beside it, apparently involved in a row with Ed. There was fast talking going on, though she couldn't hear the actual words. Phil was making gestures, and jabbing his finger at Ed. Ed was standing straight, at his stiffest and coldest. Phil was getting red in the face. He walked away a few steps, and rapidly back, into the fray again, waving his hands.

Now Ed said something that gave him pause. He stared, and when he began talking again, he seemed to be blustering. He was on the wrong foot – now Ed had the upper hand. Kate wanted to cheer. Now Ed was talking, his face thrust towards Phil menacingly, and Phil was listening in silence, as if he very much didn't like what he was hearing. Then he stalked away, jumped into his Range Rover, did a violent three-point turn, and roared away, pulling out into the road without even looking.

Even as he disappeared, Jack's dark blue

Jaguar pulled in, parked, and Jack got out, staring back over his shoulder, then put the question to Ed that Kate had no difficulty in guessing. 'What's wrong with Phil?'

There was long, low and urgent talk from Ed, which seemed to fill Jack with surprise and consternation. At one point he looked over towards the house and Kate instinctively flinched back, though there was no reason she shouldn't be looking out. And after some more talk, questions from Jack and answers from Ed, Jack got back in his car and drove away, in the other direction from the one Phil had taken.

Ed turned and walked back towards the house. He looked across and Kate thought he had seen her. She hobbled back to the sofa, and in a moment he came in.

'Did you hear?' he asked her abruptly.

'I heard raised voices so I looked out to see what was happening, but I couldn't hear what anyone was saying,' she explained, a little nervously. She didn't want him to think she was a congenital eavesdropper.

He seemed to sigh, and his shoulders looked heavy, as though the world was pressing down on them.

'It concerns you,' he said. 'Some of it, at least.' He thought for a moment, his brows drawn in a frown. 'I think I'd better tell you everything, but I must ask you to keep it to yourself for now. Absolute discretion. Can I trust you?'

'Yes,' she said, and meant so much more than he had asked.

He sat down opposite her, gathered his

thoughts, and said, 'You may remember I said to you once that the estate ought to be doing better than it was.'

'I remember,' she said.

'I've been looking into the books of the estate and the factory. I really should have been much more hands-on than I have been lately, but with my firm in London taking up my time – and then, of course, I trusted Phil Kingdon. Jack's nominally in charge of the factory, but I've always been realistic about how much he really knows, or notices, about the day-to-day running.'

'You've found something wrong?' she asked, to help him along.

'Yes,' he said. 'I've found serious anomalies. Money going missing. Profits mis-stated, expenses double entered. I think – this is why I have to ask you to keep it to yourself – that there may be criminal action taken.'

'Against—?'

He met her eyes, and saw she had guessed. 'Yes, against Phil Kingdon. Did you know something?'

She shook her head. 'Sheerest woman's instinct – I just didn't like him.'

'Camilla did,' he said tiredly.

'No, she didn't,' Kate said quickly. 'She just found him useful.'

'Very useful,' Ed said. 'You may have heard she sold several pictures out of the house to give herself more pocket money. In fact, she sold them to Phil, or through him. He told her he'd find a buyer, but of course a large part of the funds went into his pocket. One of the things I've been doing on the computer is tracing them so I could match what was paid for them and what she ended up with. There is a large discrepancy.'

'Oh dear,' Kate said. 'But I'm sure she didn't know – I mean, she's not in league with him or anything. She *really* doesn't like him.'

'I believe you,' Ed said. 'I might not have yesterday, but today – the woman who values Harry Mainwaring properly can't be all bad.'

'I'm glad you think so,' Kate said. 'But you said it concerned me?'

'It was Phil who suggested to Camilla she sell Little's to get hold of some more cash.'

'Yes, she told me,' Kate said. 'She said he was annoyed that she sold it on the market, that he'd meant her to sell it to him.'

'Yes,' he said. 'But this went a little further than him taking a slice of the price. Which is why, once he found you'd bought it, he was so anxious to get you out.'

'So it was him at the bottom of those incidents!' Kate exclaimed. 'But why did he want to get hold of Little's? It's not much of a cottage. Unless it was the five acres? But I can't think what use those would be.'

Ed looked grim. 'You come very neatly to the point. Those five acres are right in the middle of Lar Common, and the only flat part of it.'

'I did notice that.'

'Ideal for the erection of wind turbines,' Ed concluded.

Kate looked aghast. 'Wind turbines?' She

stared, visualizing it. 'But that would be a monstrous eyesore! In a place like that? It would simply ruin the place.'

'Quite, and Phil knew I would never agree to it. Hence the urgency of getting Camilla to sell it to him. He'd met up with Tony Rylance – who, I've discovered from my Google searches, is very much involved in developing wind farms – and talked with him about viable sites. The money involved would have come in quite handy. You could get five turbines on that piece of land, which would mean an income for the landowner of around two hundred thousand pounds a year.'

'Two h—?' Kate was flabbergasted.

'Index-linked.' Ed shrugged. 'The developer would be making one point two, one point three million a year.'

'I had no idea,' Kate said slowly. 'No wonder people are willing to have them on their land. But surely,' she thought suddenly, 'you would never get planning permission, in the middle of a National Park?'

He shook his head, and she saw the greyness of betrayal in his face. 'You can always get permission for wind farms. The government is committed to them. Part of their green policy, cutting carbon emissions and so on. They simply override any local objections, and any other legislation or protections.'

'It's monstrous!' she exclaimed hotly.

He shrugged. 'It's a political commitment, and politics trumps people every time.'

There was a silence while she thought angry thoughts. He said after a pause, 'The one good thing is that you were never in any personal danger.'

'How come?'

'I mean he couldn't kill you, or the property would have gone to your next of kin and he'd have lost his chance. The only way was to scare you into selling privately to him.'

'Yes, I see.'

'To which end, he persuaded Jack to befriend you. I'm sorry.'

'Oh,' said Kate.

Ed watched her face. 'In his defence, I'm sure he liked you anyway. Especially as you'd saved Chewy. I mean, knowing Jack, it probably would have happened anyway.'

'He'd have a crack at any new female in the area,' she said wryly.

'I didn't say that.'

'But that's what you meant.'

'But look here, it wouldn't have worked if you hadn't been who you are, and if we hadn't all liked you so much. You've become so much a part of the household these last couple of weeks – in an ironic sort of way, you've been doing Phil's work for him.'

'Very ironic,' she said. 'But it didn't work, did it, because in the end I offered to sell it to you, not him.'

'Yes,' said Ed, and his face became very still. 'Which was why I didn't accept your offer when you made it. Why I asked you to hold on. I already had an idea about where this was leading, but I wanted to get the whole story first.'

'Why?' Kate asked bluntly.

‘Because, don’t you see, *you* could now do the deal with Rylance. He won’t care that you’re not Phil. You could go ahead with the turbines and collect the income.’

‘But—’ She was shocked into silence. It was an immense sum of money. As an income, it would mean she would never have to work again. She could buy herself another place, anywhere she wanted. Live the high life. My God, that was a return on Gaga’s investment all right!

Ed was watching her face, as if he could read all the thoughts passing through her head in a fevered rush. She stared, realizing what he had done. He could have taken the chance she offered, bought back the land leaving her in ignorance, but he had not. He had told her the whole story, placed himself and everything he valued in her hands.

It would break his heart if they built turbines on the Blackmore Estate, despoiled this area of such great natural beauty, ruined what his father had left to him and what he had struggled so valiantly to preserve. She knew, without having to ask, that if she had sold it to him, he would not do the deal with Rylance. Two hundred thousand a year – index linked – would make all the difference to the estate. It would take the struggle out of all their lives. He could do all the things he had long wanted to do. But he would never do it. She knew that as surely as she knew her own name.

‘You told me,’ said she at last. ‘You hardly know me, but you trusted me.’

‘I know you,’ he said. He added in a low voice,

'I know you better than I've known anyone in ten years – maybe ever.'

'But,' she protested wildly, 'it's a huge amount of money! How could you be sure I wouldn't take it? Anyone would be mad not to take it! God, I don't know even now if I can really turn my back on it – I mean, *really*?'

'If you'd wanted to take it, we wouldn't be having this conversation,' he said; and she saw that, somehow, something she had said had reassured him. He looked happy, happier than she had ever seen him. 'It's an appalling thing to ask, and if I *had* to ask, I couldn't do it. The only thing that beats money is love, and you love this place. I know that now.'

'I do,' she said, low and painfully. Because she'd just remembered that she was not going to be staying here. She would be selling up and going away. It made it all the more imperative that she sold to Ed and no-one else. 'I'm glad I'll be able to trust you to do the right thing,' she said, and the words were pulled out of her with pain. 'You will buy Little's, won't you? I want it to be safe.'

'If you want to sell. But do you really want to go back to London?'

'No,' she said. 'Not really. Not at all. I want to stay here. But–' she gave a snort of ironic laughter – 'if I give up an income of two hundred thousand a year, how can I?'

'I know what a fortune like that could mean to you,' he said. 'I could never make it up to you, not in money terms. But love *does* beat money – don't you think?'

'Love?' she said falteringly. The expression on his face suggested he wasn't talking about love of the land any more.

He slipped off the chair he was sitting in, and sat down on the sofa next to her. She could feel the heat of his big body as though he were a radiator. His adored face was close; she could smell the scent of his skin, which seemed to be something she had always known. She looked at his mouth, and felt faint.

'I can't offer you a fortune,' he said, 'but I could offer you this: a share in a great estate. Now the parasite's been removed, I mean to make it great again.' He took her hands. She felt how cold hers were as his strong warm ones engulfed them. 'I have that to offer you, if you could think it was enough. We could work together – it could be our life, building up the estate for the next generation. And all the generations.'

'That's a life's work,' she said faintly. 'And it's quite a fortune to offer. But – but you haven't said...'

She looked anxiously into his eyes, and he understood her. 'I was afraid you might not feel the same. But I've been in love with you since the first moment I saw you.'

'When you thought I was a boy,' she reminded him, humour returning with the hot blood that was suddenly coursing through her.

'All right, the second moment I saw you,' he corrected, getting his humour back too. 'But first there was Jack, then there was Addison, and everything was muddled up, and—'

'A comedy of errors, in fact,' she concluded.

'And now *you* haven't said it,' he pointed out urgently.

'Oh yes,' she said. 'I've been in love with you, too, all along. But first there was Jack, and then there was Addison...'

He pressed her hands. 'I know it's rather sudden, but – *will* you marry me?'

She didn't need to think. 'Oh, yes,' she said. 'I love you. And I can't think of anything more wonderful than to share the estate with you and bring it back to glory.'

And then the impossibly wonderful thing was happening, and she was kissing him; and it was just as blissful as she had never allowed herself to imagine. It went on for a gloriously long time, not even interrupted by the dogs rushing into the room and shoving their noses between them to find out what was happening.

When she hobbled down to dinner that evening, she was walking on air and a winged walking-stick. Apart from her own euphoria, it was good to know she was going to give so much pleasure to so many people. Gaga, who would simply love the whole thing – what a return on her investment! Jess and Lauren – to go from scraping the crud off a tatty old cottage to being lady of the manor would seem like real progress to them. She'd be able to have them to stay! Kay and Darren – Kay would be ecstatic, though Dommie might not approve – he might throw her out of the Power Rangers. Jocasta – she was pretty sure Jocasta would be thrilled, and she'd be in a good position to lobby for her for Comyns. Mrs B – no more fear of mung beans, spelt flour and low-fat spread...

Thinking happy thoughts, she reached ground level and found Jack alone in the drawing room, looking like a dog with his ears down.

'I understand Ed's told you about my ignominious part in this,' he said.

'That you pursued me on Phil Kingdon's instruction?' she said sternly.

'I'm sorry. I'm really sorry. But, you know, it wasn't anything I wouldn't have done anyway. I meant everything I ever said to you. You are a gorgeous girl, and I really, really like you.'

'I like you, too. And I forgive you.'

'This whole scam – Phil Kingdon – everything,' he went on, determined to get all the scourging out of the way at once, 'Ed's told you? It was him all along. Ed said we shouldn't talk about it until we know if it's a police case, but I want you to know I didn't know anything about it.'

'I believe you,' Kate said. 'Let's drop the subject. There's some happier news now, isn't there? We should be celebrating.'

'You mean about Camilla? Or about me?'

'I meant Camilla and Harry. I think it's wonderful.'

'So do I. He'll take up her slack all right. She'll be much happier married again, especially to him.'

'But what's this about you? What's happened?'

'Flick and I – she's agreed to give me another chance.'

'Oh, that's wonderful!' Kate cried. 'You looked so happy together at Buscombe. Like a family.'

'It'll be great for Theo if we can make a go of it. Of course, we'll probably quarrel like stink, but it'll be worth it. We're going to take it very slowly at first. She wants me to court her – take her on proper dates.'

'Every woman deserves that.'

'I must say, I'm quite looking forward to it. It'll be – kind of sexy, pretending I don't know her,' he said, grinning. 'Trying to get into a strange woman's pants – it's what I do best.'

'Yes, but you do know there's to be no more of that: strange women's pants? Not if you want it to work?'

'Of course I do – what do you take me for?' he said indignantly. 'Actually, I'd already got tired of all the totty – the empty bits of fluff. I have you to thank for that, partly.'

'Me?'

'You reminded me what an intelligent companion was like – someone you feel at ease with, someone you can talk about anything to.' He laid a hand on her forearm. 'I'm sorry it didn't work out for us. But I'm really glad about getting back with Flick.'

'I'm glad too,' Kate said. 'So, is that all?'

'All what?'

'No other happy news?'

'Isn't it enough?' Jack said, puzzled.

'You mean, Ed hasn't told you?'

'Ed hasn't told me what?' Jack asked patiently.

Ed came into the room at that moment, carrying

a bottle of champagne and glasses on a tray. Jack turned to him. 'What haven't you told me, big bro?'

'I was waiting until we were all together,' Ed said. He looked across the room and met Kate's eyes, and her knees went weak; because now, at last, she saw what he looked like when he really smiled, and it was *sensational*!